The Grey Cells of Mr. Poirot

23 Hercule Poirot Short Stories

Introduction

As Figs. I.1 and I.2 show, even small changes in the approach Mach number, M_∞,[1] cause considerable changes in the shock wave positions. Accordingly, the pressure distribution over the body surface and, thus, the location of the resultant wind force attack change dramatically. Consequently, the stability of the flight is greatly affected. This problem becomes even more obvious in practical cases of cambered wings and bodies under an angle of attack. Then, as seen in Fig. I.2, the shock waves on the lower surface of the body move in quite a different way from that on the upper surface (i.e., they are no longer opposite each other and their relative positions change markedly). Obviously, this leads to even less predictable changes in the flight stability.

A most devastating additional effect of shock waves is their tendency to cause flow separation. Behind the shock the flow over the body surface reverses its direction and may become highly turbulent. This may be seen from Fig. I.2. Consequently, the pressure over the separated region is higher than it would be if the flow remained attached. Such high pressure over a large portion of the upper surface usually reduces the lift of the body to the point where the air can no longer support the weight of the body. This so-called stalling of the flight article occurs at subsonic speeds as well if the angle of attack is increased beyond a certain value. In this case the flow separates from the tail section of the body even without a shock wave. On the other hand, in the transonic range separation may occur even at zero angle of attack because of the ever-present shock waves. For this reason transonic flight articles must be designed so that the shock separation length is very short. It is especially crucial that, at given Mach numbers and angles of attack, this type of separation does not merge with the separation from the tail region that occurs under conditions similar to those causing subsonic separation.

Transonic theory is not a comprehensive, firmly established system, but an effort will be made to point out the connections between seemingly unrelated approaches to the theoretical treatment of transonic problems. Since it is impossible to cover in an introduction to transonic flow even a small portion of the work that has been published so far, this book will be limited to discussions of the most important basic approaches to the solution of transonic problems and explanations of pitfalls that must be avoided. An effort has been made to derive the most important equations of inviscid and viscous transonic flow in sufficient detail to give even the novice a feeling of confidence in his ability to make accurate judgments as to the problems that can be solved with a given equation or set of equations.

Although emphasis is placed on the theory in the physical plane, in which the flow coordinates are the independent variables and the velocity components the dependent ones, a brief chapter is included on the treatment of transonic flow in the hodograph plane, where the roles of the variables are reversed. This chapter is needed both for historical reasons and because a modified hodograph plane has recently been found again to offer certain advantages in the treatment of transonic flow

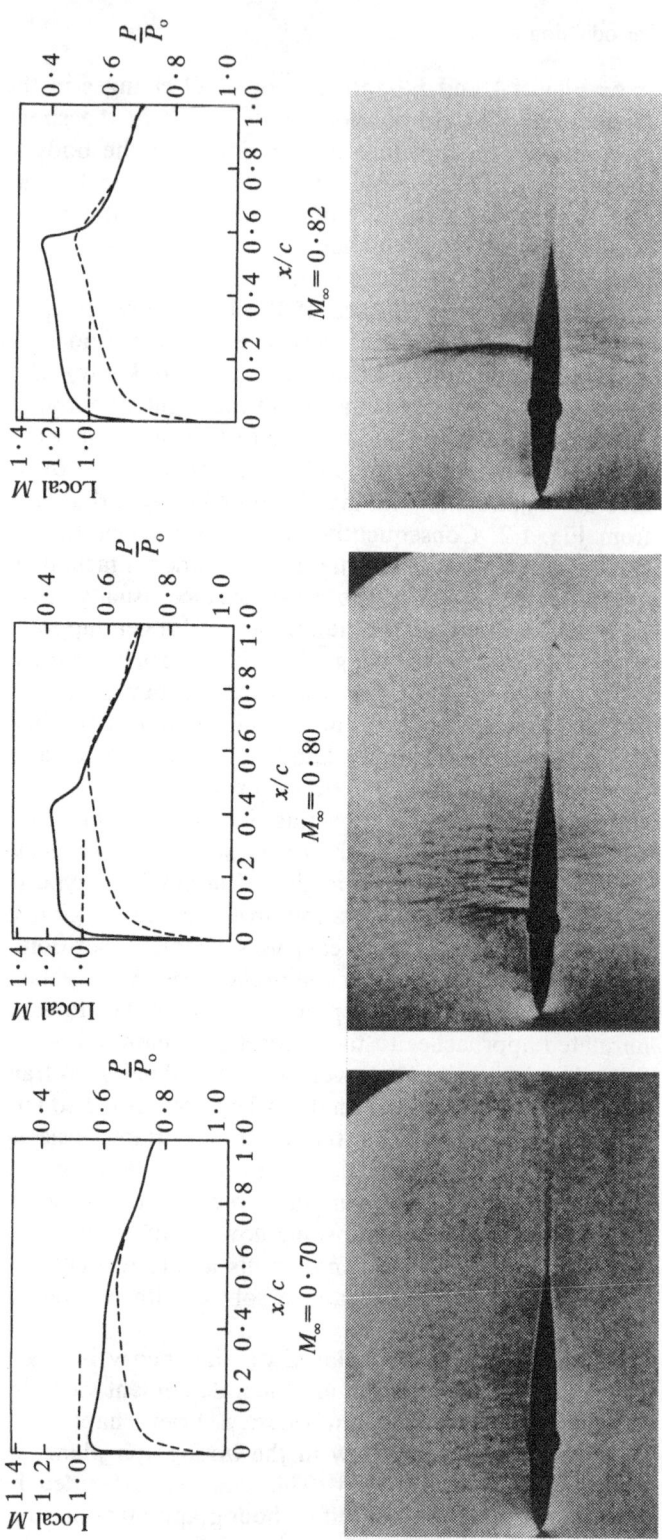

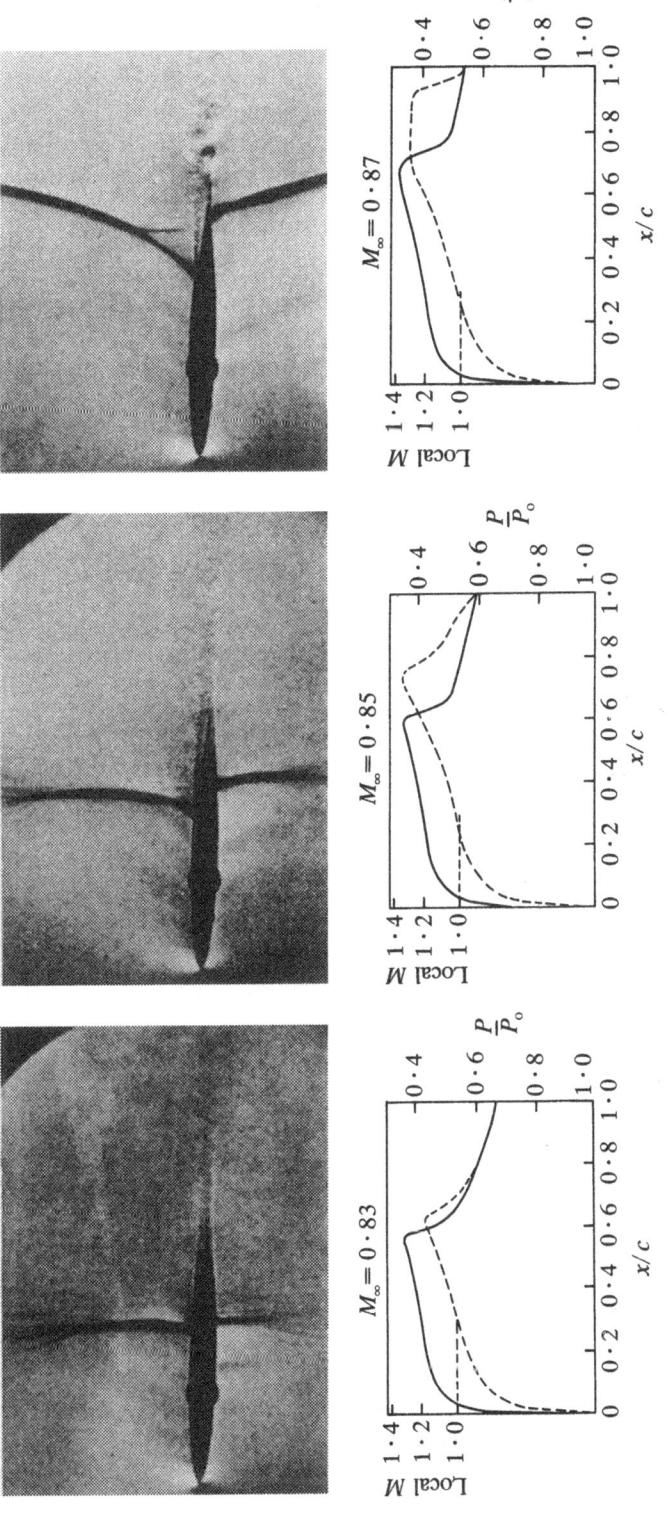

Fig. I.2. Transonic flow about a wing at fixed angle of attack. Pressure distributions on upper (———) and lower (– – –) surfaces. Flow separation at $M_\infty = 0.85$ and 0.87 causes pressure behind upper shock wave to remain almost constant, whereas it decreases steadily to the free-stream value when no separation occurs ($M_\infty = 0.87$–0.83). (From W. S. Farren, Aerodynamic flow. *J. Roy. Aeron. Soc.*, Vol. 60, July 1956).

problems. With the rapid change in mathematical procedures caused by the evolution of electronic computers, a comeback of hodograph solutions is quite possible. Historically, the hodograph method has played a decisive role in the development of an understanding of the peculiarities of transonic flow. The reason for the great value of the hodograph approach for a general exploration of transonic flow lies in the fact that the transonic equations in the hodograph plane are linear and, therefore, allow superposition of solutions for the creation of new solutions. This tremendous advantage over the nonlinear equations of the physical plane outweigh, in many basic studies, the disadvantage of the limitation of hodograph solutions to two-dimensional problems. That the hodograph method is not practical for the solution of specific problems is obvious from the fact that the independent variables in the hodograph plane are the velocity components. Therefore, boundary conditions for a specific geometry cannot be established. Only through an iteration process can a desired geometry be approximated. However, for a general understanding of transonic problems, specific geometries are not required and the advantage of the linear relationships can be fully exploited.

In the physical plane, the independent variables are the space coordinates, so that the geometric boundary conditions of the problem may be given directly. The decisive advantage of working in the physical plane is diminished by the nonlinearity of the flow equations. Thus, the analytical methods developed for the solution of specific transonic problems in the physical plane are limited to:

1. Certain linearization techniques
2. Asymptotic procedures
3. Similarity transformations of partial differential equations into ordinary differential equations that are more easily solved,
4. Applications of similarity laws, through which one solution can be applied directly to other problems with the same similarity parameter

An entirely new tool for the handling of many transonic problems became available with the advent of the electronic computer. Now the nonlinear equations can be solved numerically, creating a flood of methods giving highly accurate results within acceptable computer times. Unfortunately, the computer cannot eliminate the basic problems of nonlinearity: the impossibility of superimposing solutions or predicting the effect of a parameter on the solution. Because the computer methods are strictly mathematical exercises (i.e., having nothing to do with transonic aerodynamics as such), no attempt can be made within the framework of this book to acquaint the reader with this discipline in any great detail, and he is referred to the extensive literature of the past two decades or so. An excellent introduction to computer methods in aerodynamics is given by Roache [1].

To dispel misconceptions, it must be emphasized that all computer

Introduction

solutions are obtained by first converting equations identical to, or slightly modified from, those given in the following chapters into finite difference equations. Already in this process, errors are introduced into the computation whose magnitude must be assessed each time; if they are found to be excessive, a different scheme must be sought. From this fact alone, it becomes obvious that any attempt to solve a problem by starting out from the most general equations will lead to disaster because the checking procedure of the individual computer steps becomes too complex for a meaningful result. That is the main reason for the necessity of analytical studies that lead to the simplest possible differential equations for a certain problem. Then, by applying one of the four methods cited earlier, approximate solutions should be sought. These approximate solutions provide an indispensable framework for computer results. Comparisons with experimental results are always very helpful, though there is a great danger that good agreement with a few data points will be taken as a proof for the correctness of the computer program for an extended range of data. But only through very thorough checking procedures may the validity range of the computer program be established. Unfortunately, the magic of the computer and the absolute belief in its superiority over human capability has led quite a number of researchers into extrapolations that led to serious errors.

The difficulties in solving transonic problems are caused by both inviscid and viscous flow peculiarities. Because transonic aerodynamics is by definition the aerodynamics of mixed flow (i.e., of supersonic regions embedded in a subsonic flow field); two fundamentally different differential equations with fundamentally different boundary conditions must be matched at the interfaces of the two regions. The mathematical difference between the two regions is that the subsonic flow is described by elliptic differential equations, while the supersonic regions obey hyperbolic equations. Physically, this means that small disturbances created by the flying object propagate over the whole subsonic flow field, whereas disturbances are confined to the so-called Mach cone in the supersonic field. They are created at the apex and propagate throughout this cone. That matching these two kinds of flow at their mutual boundaries poses formidable problems can readily be appreciated.

In addition to these inviscid flow problems, transonic flow poses unique viscous flow problems, in particular through shock wave-induced boundary layer separation. However, for a detailed insight into the transonic flow problems, inviscid theory must first be thoroughly understood, because the decision as to the kind of viscous corrections that must be made depends on the results of the inviscid analysis.

A word must be said about the conditions under which transonic flow can be expected. There is no fixed range of Mach numbers for which transonic effects appear, because the Mach distributions on a body depends on both the approach Mach number and the body geometry. The same subsonic approach flow may produce a supersonic flow region on one body and none on the other. When the approach Mach number is increased from zero, transonic flow is produced at different values of this Mach number on bodies of different geometry. The approach Mach number at which transonic flow just sets in (i.e., at which a supersonic region just begins to form), is called the *critical Mach number*. Thus, the critical Mach number may have almost any value. For instance, a sharp corner in a flow whose viscosity is low enough to exclude flow separation would produce local transonic flow even at a very low (incompressible) approach Mach number. But in those cases, the supersonic region is too small for a noticeable overall change of the aerodynamics from pure subsonic conditions. Therefore, the critical Mach number is better defined as the Mach number that noticeably affects the flow pattern and, consequently, the trend of the aerodynamic coefficients. For a sufficiently thin body $M_{cr} \approx 1$, but such a body would be structurally impossible. The critical Mach number of practical vehicles lies between $M_{cr} \approx 0.6$ and 0.9.

Note

1. $M = W/a$ is the flight velocity W made dimensionless by the speed of sound a.

1
BRIEF REVIEW OF THE BASIC LAWS OF AERODYNAMICS

Since transonic flow covers a small portion of the realm of compressible flow, superficially it would not seem to require a special treatment. As the name implies, however, transonic flow occurs at speeds close to that of sound (i.e., of pressure disturbances). This greatly complicates the physical laws of transonic flow, and, consequently, its mathematics.

Before going into these problems, let us review the basic laws of aerodynamics as briefly as possible.

Although gases are highly compressible, as we know from everyday experience, slow-moving gases behave very much like liquids. With changing velocity, only their pressure changes; the density remains constant for all practical purposes. This kind of flow that resists changes in its volume is therefore called *incompressible*. However, when the velocity of a gas is increased, changes in its density, and with those its temperature, become more and more pronounced in addition to the change in pressure. Where the volume of the gas no longer stays constant, flow is said to be *compressible*.

Since transonic flow is compressible, it behooves us to begin by deriving the general equations of compressible fluid dynamics before going into the specific transonic problems. Moreover, the equations for incompressible gas flow may then be obtained directly by holding the density terms constant. Because the random motion of gas molecules is superimposed on their average or mean motion, defined as the gas speed, there is constantly an exchange of molecules, normal to the mean velocity direction, between neighboring gas layers. Therefore, momentum is transferred from one layer to the other. When the velocities of the layers are equal, this exchange has no effect on the mean velocities. However, if there exists a velocity gradient between the layers, then the faster layer pulls the slower one ahead, and the slower layer holds the faster one back. The gas behaves very similar to a viscous liquid and this situation is called *viscous* flow.

Important cases of viscous flow are the motion of a gas over a solid surface, and the exhausting of a gas into a space filled with a gas at rest or of a markedly different speed. In the former case, the gas is at rest directly at the wall,[1] but remains at the undisturbed free-stream velocity at a certain, usually small, distance from the wall. The velocities in between, which are, in first approximation, directed parallel to the wall, form a large gradient normal to the wall. Thus, a *boundary layer* is formed by the viscous forces between the braking wall and the pulling undisturbed outer flow. Of course, the flow theoretically continues to decelerate to the infinitely distant streamline, but the velocity differentials between adjacent layers soon become too small for a measurable effect, and a finite boundary layer thickness can be defined.

A completely analogous process forms a mixing layer in the second case mentioned. Of course, here both the central jet and the ambient flow form viscous layers, separated by a surface within which the mass flow is constant and that of the jet before mixing started.

A boundary layer formed in this manner is called a *laminar boundary layer* because it is the result of interactions between adjacent, but basically stable, layers (laminae). However, as the flow of a river near the bank shows, fluids, including gases, may also form eddies when they move along rough walls or layers of very different speeds. These eddies are of various sizes and move laterally across the boundaries of adjacent layers in a way similar to the individual molecules within a laminar layer. However, here the layers are no longer well defined because the rotating motion of the eddies is of the order of the mean speed of the flow. In their motion normal to the wall, the eddies also exchange their momentums, resulting in a velocity profile similar to that of the laminar boundary layer. The thickness of the *turbulent boundary layer* can be defined as in the laminar case: eddies are no longer visible in the river at a certain distance from the bank.

Flows in adjacent layers interact in such a way that a velocity gradient normal to the flow direction is created. Such a flow is called *shear flow*. It should be noted here, that viscous effects also appear within a stream tube that is suddenly accelerated or decelerated. Such effects fall under the heading of *longitudinal viscosity*.

Viscous effects are of great importance for the proper description of almost all practical aerodynamic problems. However, since viscous effects are almost always restricted to small ranges in an inviscid flow field, viscous flow is determined, in the first approximation, on the inviscid flow patterns.

The equations of inviscid, compressible flow will now be derived as the basis for all aerodynamic flow description.

First, we express the fact that no mass can be created or lost in the flow by considering a small cube (dx, dy, dz) of which we must require that as much mass enters it per second as leaves it, as long as the density in the cube remains constant (i.e., as long as the flow is steady). The mass entering per second through the area $(dy \cdot dz)$ is $\rho u (dy \cdot dz)^2$ and that leaving through the opposite side is

$$\left(\rho + \frac{\partial \rho}{\partial x} dx\right)\left(u + \frac{\partial u}{\partial x} dx\right) dy\, dz$$

$$= \left(\rho u + \rho \frac{\partial u}{\partial x} dx + u \frac{\partial \rho}{\partial x} dx + \text{higher order terms}\right) dy\, dz$$

Brief Review of the Basic Laws of Aerodynamics

Hence, the difference between inflow and outflow is

$$\left(\rho \frac{\partial u}{\partial x} + u \frac{\partial \rho}{\partial x}\right) dx\, dy\, dz = \frac{\partial(\rho u)}{\partial x} dx\, dy\, dz$$

Corresponding terms are obtained for the flow through the two other pairs of sides and, thus, the conservation of mass is expressed as

$$\frac{\partial(\rho u)}{\partial x} + \frac{\partial(\rho v)}{\partial y} + \frac{\partial(\rho w)}{\partial z} = 0 \tag{1.1a}$$

This is the so-called continuity law of steady flow, which, in vector notation, becomes

$$\operatorname{div}(\rho \mathbf{W}) = 0 \tag{1.1b}$$

In unsteady flow, the density in the cube varies with time. Then, inflow and outflow can no longer be equal, otherwise mass would be created or lost, and for increasing density in the cube the outflow must be smaller than the inflow. Hence, the continuity equation for unsteady flow becomes

$$\frac{\partial \rho}{\partial t} + \frac{\partial(\rho u)}{\partial x} + \frac{\partial(\rho v)}{\partial y} + \frac{\partial(\rho w)}{\partial z} = 0 \tag{1.2}$$

Now let us examine the consequences of Newton's second law. As in every dynamic system, a mass element of the gas is accelerated or decelerated under the influence of a force. Forces acting on a gas mass element are gravity forces, viscous forces, and the pressure differential across the volume (grad p) of the mass element. For the time being, since we are restricting ourselves to inviscid flow, the viscous force will be disregarded. Gravity forces in the atmosphere are compensated by the atmospheric pressure gradient and may also be disregarded for most flight problems. Consequently, we obtain

$$-\operatorname{grad} p = \rho \frac{D\mathbf{W}}{Dt} \tag{1.3}$$

This is Newton's second law for a volume element. Here the so-called substantial differential quotient $D\mathbf{W}/Dt$ which covers both the steady and the unsteady terms, was introduced. It is defined as

$$\begin{aligned}
\frac{D\mathbf{W}}{Dt} &= \mathbf{i}\left[\frac{\partial u}{\partial t} + \frac{\partial u}{\partial x}\frac{\partial x}{\partial t} + \frac{\partial u}{\partial y}\frac{\partial y}{\partial t} + \frac{\partial u}{\partial z}\frac{\partial z}{\partial t}\right] + \mathbf{j}\left[\frac{\partial v}{\partial t} + \frac{\partial v}{\partial x}\frac{\partial x}{\partial t} + \frac{\partial v}{\partial y}\frac{\partial y}{\partial t} + \frac{\partial v}{\partial z}\frac{\partial z}{\partial t}\right] \\
&\quad + \mathbf{k}\left[\frac{\partial w}{\partial t} + \frac{\partial w}{\partial x}\frac{\partial x}{\partial t} + \frac{\partial w}{\partial y}\frac{\partial y}{\partial t} + \frac{\partial w}{\partial z}\frac{\partial t}{\partial w}\right] \\
&= \mathbf{i}\left[\frac{\partial u}{\partial t} + u\frac{\partial u}{\partial x} + v\frac{\partial u}{\partial y} + w\frac{\partial u}{\partial z}\right] + \mathbf{j}\left[\frac{\partial v}{\partial t} + u\frac{\partial v}{\partial x} + v\frac{\partial v}{\partial y} + w\frac{\partial v}{\partial z}\right] \\
&\quad + \mathbf{k}\left[\frac{\partial u}{\partial t} + u\frac{\partial w}{\partial x} + v\frac{\partial w}{\partial y} + w\frac{\partial w}{\partial z}\right]
\end{aligned} \tag{1.4}$$

The first terms in the brackets give the acceleration at a fixed station (i.e., unsteady acceleration), while the other terms give the acceleration towards the adjacent point on the streamline (i.e., the steady acceleration).

By setting grad $p = \mathbf{i}(\partial p/\partial x) + \mathbf{j}(\partial p/\partial y) + \mathbf{k}(\partial p/\partial z)$ in Eq. 1.3 and introducing Eq. 1.4, this equation may be separated into its components, yielding

$$\rho\left(\frac{\partial u}{\partial t} + \frac{\partial u}{\partial x}u + \frac{\partial u}{\partial y}v + \frac{\partial u}{\partial z}w\right) + \frac{\partial p}{\partial x} = 0 \tag{1.5a}$$

$$\rho\left(\frac{\partial v}{\partial t} + \frac{\partial v}{\partial x}u + \frac{\partial v}{\partial y}v + \frac{\partial v}{\partial z}w\right) + \frac{\partial p}{\partial y} = 0 \tag{1.5b}$$

$$\rho\left(\frac{\partial w}{\partial t} + \frac{\partial w}{\partial x}u + \frac{\partial w}{\partial y}v + \frac{\partial w}{\partial z}w\right) + \frac{\partial p}{\partial z} = 0 \tag{1.5c}$$

These are the Euler equations of inviscid, unsteady flow, of which the equations for steady flow are obtained by dropping the first terms.

It should be noted that these equations have been derived for a system in which the coordinates are fixed in space, and the flow field is described through the velocity components and their derivatives at the individual points in this space. This kind of a system is named after Euler. There is another system that has been developed by Lagrange. Here the fluid elements are described in their motion through the space, something that explicitly is not obtained in the Euler system. However, the mathematical difficulties in the Lagrange system are so great that only a very few cases have ever been treated in this system. We shall use the Euler system throughout this book.

There is often a desire to know the changes in the flow variables (i.e., pressure, density, and the magnitude of the velocity vector) along a streamline. Such a relationship is obtained directly by integration of the Euler equations after introduction of the streamline equations. Because the velocity vector is tangent to the streamline by definition, its components are related to the coordinates through $u:v:w = dx:dz$, or

$$dy/dx = v/u; \quad dy/dz = v/w; \quad dz/dx = w/u \tag{1.6}$$

where the first equation is that of a streamline in plane flow.

We first multiply the Eqs. 1.5 with dx, dy, dz, respectively, and introduce Eqs. 1.6 such that v and w in Eq. 1.5a are replaced by the expressions containing u; u and w in Eq. 1.5b are replaced in 1.6 by those containing v; and u and v in Eq. 1.5c by those containing w. We then add the corresponding terms of the three equations so that the pressure terms become the total derivative

$$dp = \frac{\partial p}{\partial x}dx + \frac{\partial p}{\partial y}dy + \frac{\partial p}{\partial z}dz$$

Brief Review of the Basic Laws of Aerodynamics

and the steady velocity terms become the total derivative $d(W^2/2) = d(u^2/2) = d(v^2/2) + d(w^2/2)$. Hence, the steady terms of Eq. 1.5 can be integrated directly and we arrive at

$$\int \frac{dp}{\rho} + \frac{W^2}{2} = C \quad \text{Bernoulli equation for steady flow}[3] \tag{1.7}$$

The integral is taken on the streamline from the station $W(p, \rho) = 0$, where $p_w, \rho_w \neq 0$, to the station under consideration. The so-called Bernoulli constant C, therefore, gives the total energy in the stream tube, which is the potential energy at flow stagnation ($W = 0$).[4]

Let us now derive the comparable equation for unsteady flow. Here, however, no simple integral of the unsteady terms

$$\int \left(\frac{\partial u}{\partial t} dx + \frac{\partial v}{\partial t} dy + \frac{\partial w}{\partial t} dz \right) \tag{1.8}$$

can be found, because in unsteady flow the stream lines may change with time and no unique relationship of pressure and velocity can be established. However, when the flow comes from a reservoir of constant pressure and density, then the Bernoulli constant of all streamlines is the same, and we have so-called potential flow, as will be explained in greater detail later. The velocity potential ϕ is defined through

$$d\phi = \frac{\partial \phi}{\partial x} dx + \frac{\partial \phi}{\partial y} dy + \frac{\partial \phi}{\partial z} dz = u\, dx + v\, dy + w\, dz$$

Hence,

$$\frac{\partial \phi}{\partial t} = \int \left(\frac{\partial u}{\partial t} dx + \frac{\partial v}{\partial t} dy + \frac{\partial w}{\partial t} dz \right),$$

which is identical to Eq. 1.8. Thus, the Bernoulli equation for unsteady potential flow becomes

$$\frac{\partial \phi}{\partial t} + \int \frac{dp}{\rho} + \frac{W^2}{2} = C(t) \tag{1.9}$$

where the Bernoulli "constant" may now be a function of time.

This equation applies, for example, to a "blow-down" wind tunnel, where air flows from the atmosphere into a vacuum vessel. Without provisions for steady flow, the test section flow velocity would decrease while the vessel fills up, and the time-dependent first term of Eq. 1.9 describes the change of the flow conditions along the tunnel with time. However, since the flow originates at the time-independent atmospheric conditions, $C(t)$ is a constant (the normal Bernoulli constant). For the whole process of such a tunnel run; see Prob. 1.9. Now, if the vacuum in the vessel is held constant through pumping, both time-dependent terms become zero, and the Bernoulli equation for steady flow applies. Finally, for the flow from a pressure vessel to the atmosphere, both time-dependent terms must be retained because here the Bernoulli constant changes with the pressure drop in the vessel.

We indicated that the Bernoulli constant is a measure of the total energy of the flow, showing that fluid flow is also a thermodynamic problem. Specifically, the first (energy) and second (entropy) laws of the thermodynamics must be satisfied in the flow field.

The energy law says that the sum of all kinds of energy involved in a certain process must remain constant as long as no energy is added from outside of the system under study. Therefore, the heat energy, dq, added to a gas element of unit mass must be equal to the sum of the increase in the internal energy, e, of this gas element and the work done by the system. The latter may be the work done by displacing a volume dV^5 of the ambient gas at pressure p, or the work dL done by moving a mechanical system. Thus,

$$dq = de + p\,dV = de + dL \qquad \left(V = \frac{1}{\rho}\right) \tag{1.10}$$

From this equation the basic relationships between energy and entropy, as required in aerodynamics, may be derived. This can best be done by examining the processes that govern the cycles of an ideal piston engine. In that system heat is converted into mechanical work and vice versa. This can be made directly relevant to fluid flow by replacing dL by $d(W^2/2)$, the change in the kinetic energy of the fluid element of unit mass.

We now restrict the derivations of the thermodynamic relationships required in this book to "perfect" gases (see Note 7). Although the following description of the processes in a piston engine are valid for any gas, it must be kept in mind that the equations derived are those of perfect gases. The gas in the cylinder is heated, causing the piston to move from the starting position 1 to the end position 3. The piston is then pushed back to position 1, say, by the energy of a flywheel that was set in motion in the expansion phase. The original conditions of pressure and temperature must be regained because the whole engine operation would otherwise become erratic.

What kind of processes take place during such an engine cycle?

1. At any moment, the heat dq required to hold e and, in a perfect gas, the temperature T constant, is added. The work done in such an isothermal process ($de = 0$) is equal to the total heat energy added, $L_{13} = \int_1^3 dL = q_{1,3}$. However, the same work must be done by the flywheel to isothermally push the piston back to position 1 so that all the heat is recovered. Such an engine would serve no purpose because no net work is done.

2. No heat is added to the cylinder ($dq = 0$). The gas expands adiabatically, and both temperature and pressure decrease with the increasing cylinder volume. Here, $L_{13} = \int_1^3 dL = e_1 - e_3$, but again, the energy needed to push the piston back to position 1 is the same. No net work is done by this engine either.

However, by combining these two processes, a workable engine can be

Brief Review of the Basic Laws of Aerodynamics

designed, through which the meaning of the second law of thermodynamics, the entropy law, may be shown.

To this end, we need an expression for the total work potential, h, of the gas at any moment. This potential must be equal to the energy required to produce the state of the gas (i.e., its temperature T and pressure p in the volume V) so that, when the gas of potential h_1 does the work L_t, the final value of h_2 will be given as $h_2 = h_1 - L_t$.[6] This energy may be thought to be produced in a space of constant pressure, p, ($dp = 0$) by heating a very small volume V_0 at a correspondingly low temperature T_0 until the volume V is obtained at the temperature T, so that

$$h = \int_0^T [de(T) + p\, dV(T)] = e + pV \qquad (1.11a)^6$$

and the differential of h becomes

$$dh = de + p\, dV + V\, dp = dq + V\, dp \qquad (1.11b)^6$$

For obvious reasons, pV has been called *displacement work* (i.e., the work needed to produce the volume of the gas at the temperature T and the pressure p).

There seems to be a discrepancy between the result of case 2, in which the adiabatic compression (expansion) work is equal to $L_c = e_2 - e_1$, and the definition of h, given earlier, which requires that $L_t = h_2 - h_1$. However, L_c is strictly the adiabatic work of compression, whereas L_t is the technical work that must be done in a continuous process in which a new batch of working gas is provided for every cycle. Therefore, the work required to push the used-up gas out of the system and to fill the cylinder with the new gas must be added to the compression work. These terms are those that distinguish h from e, namely, pV.[7] Of course, when heat is added to or removed from the outside, as in a piston engine, additional terms are needed, as will be seen later.

Because it contains both a mechanical and a thermal energy term, there has been some difficulty in finding a proper name for h. From the preceding derivation, in which h is strictly the result of heat addition, it is understandable that the term *heat content* has been used, particularly in the German literature (Waermeinhalt). However, to avoid any confusion with the amount of heat q, it now is generally accepted to call h the "enthalpy," a word suggesting nothing else.

It is now obvious that not only e but also pV is proportional to T, and consequently h, as well, and we write

$$e \propto T, \quad h \propto T \quad \text{and} \quad pV \propto T \quad \text{(conditions for a perfect gas)}$$

The latter relationship goes back to the seventeenth-century physicists Boyle and Marionette. It is called the *Equation of State* of the perfect gas, written as

$$pV = RT^8 \qquad (1.12)$$

where R is a constant, characteristic of the gas.

Meaningful names for the coefficients of h and e are found as follows: For a process at constant volume, Eq. 1.10 yields $dq = de = d(c_v T)$, where c_v is the amount of heat required to heat the gas by a unit temperature, called the *specific heat at constant volume*. On the other hand, for a process at constant pressure, Eq. 1.11b yields $dh = dq = d(c_p T)$, with c_p correspondingly called *specific heat at constant pressure*, so that $R = c_p - c_v$. The expression $c_p/c_v = \gamma$ is an important magnitude in thermodynamics, in which γ obviously is again a material constant. For air its value is very close to 1.4, which value is sufficiently accurate for most aerodynamic problems.[9]

We now can design a piston engine cycle that does mechanical work. Instead of moving the piston isothermally or adiabatically to the end position 3, it is moved isothermally to an intermediate position 2, and then adiabatically to position 3. To complete the cycle, the piston is moved isothermally to a position 4, so that $V_4/V_3 = V_1/V_2$, and at last adiabatically back to position 1.

From cases 1 and 2, it can be seen that the work done by the adiabatic parts of the cycle cancel each other because $e_1 = e_2$ and $e_3 = e_4$ so that $L_{23} + L_{41} = e_3 - e_1 + (e_1 - e_3) = 0$. Adiabatically, no work is done. Conversely, the isothermal parts do not cancel because, with Eq. 1.12, $dq = dL = RT(dV/V)$, and integrating we have $q_{21}/T_{1,2} = R\ln(V_2/V_1)$ and $q_{43}/T_{3,4} = R\ln(V_4/V_3)$. Hence, with the preceding relationship between the volumes,

$$-\frac{q_{21}}{q_{43}} = \frac{T_{1,2}}{T_{3,4}} = -\frac{L_{21}}{L_{43}} \tag{1.13a}$$

(the work done is taken as positive that returned as negative). This relationship shows the important rule that the temperature difference between the compression and expansion phases of the engine should be as great as possible. Hence, the optimal thermal efficiency $\eta_{\max}$, becomes;

$$\eta_{\max} = \frac{|L_{21}| - |L_{43}|}{|L_{21}|} = \frac{T_{1,2} - T_{3,4}}{T_{1,2}} \tag{1.13b}$$

The efficiency of a thermodynamic engine has a natural limit that cannot be exceeded for a given temperature range. For a general proof of this rule see Problem 1.5. There it is assumed that a cycle is not sharply separated into isothermal and adiabatic parts, as is the case in all practical engines.

To generalize the results on thermodynamic processes, we have seen that the states of a gas are characterized by a number of "properties" that unequivocally describe them. The gas at rest is characterized by the properties of temperature T and pressure p, which determine the volume per unit mass V through the equation of state (Eq. 1.12). A moving gas or a gas exchanging work of any kind (e.g., mechanical work) is characterized through other properties. An adiabatic compression or expansion requires the work $L_c = e_1 - e_2$,[10] where the internal energy e is the property governing those processes. However, if the process is repeated continuously (i.e., if new mass elements are introduced after every cycle), a "technical" work L_t is done, with the enthalpy h being the governing property so that $L_t = h_1 - h_2$.[10]

The meaning of "property" becomes obvious in processes with heat addition or removal, which are governed by $dL = p\,dV = dq - de$, or $L = \int_1^2 p\,dV = q_{12} - (e_1 - e_2)$.[10] The value of this integral depends on the "path" from condition 1 to condition 2 in the p–V diagram (Fig. 1.1). Of the infinite number of possible paths, those marked I and II may be evaluated without difficulty. In case I, the integral becomes $p_1(V_1 - V_2)$ and $p_2(V_1 - V_2)$ in case II. Since $e_1 - e_2$ (depending on $T_1 - T_2$ only) has the same value in all our cases, the heat that must be added, and consequently the work done in going from condition 1 to condition 2, depends on the kind of processes involved and is not determined by the end conditions 1 and 2. However, a "property" must be an unequivocal function of the conditions at the beginning and the end of a process (e.g., e and h). Therefore, the heat q is not a gas property. Mathematically, a property is the integral of a total differential, as is shown for h by Eq. 1.11b and as may be verified from Fig. 1.1. Here $\Delta h = e_2 - e_1 + p_2 V_2 - p_1 V_1$, both along path I and along path II, and since any path can be thought to be produced by very small alternating steps of $p = \text{const}$ and $V = \text{const}$, Eq. 1.11b is generally true.[11]

As the discussion about the piston engine with heat addition has shown, there should be a property governing these processes, because, at the end of one cycle, the original state of the gas has been restored, in spite of the fact that the magnitude q, which is not a property, is involved. A clue to the establishment of such a property is given by the

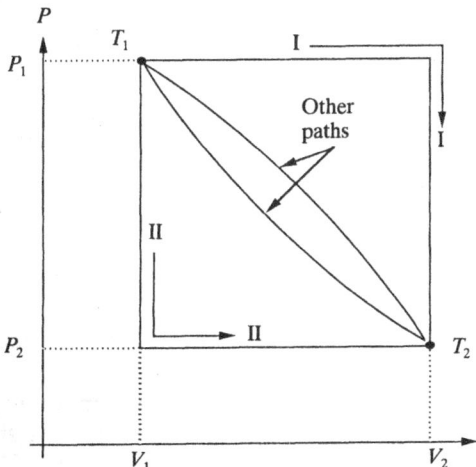

Fig. 1.1. The p–V diagram of a gas expanding from T_1 to T_2.

result of Eq. 1.13a, where the heat added in the isothermal expansion phase, divided by the temperature at which the heat is added, was equal to the same quotient of the heat removed in the compression cycle. Writing, therefore,

$$dS = \frac{dq}{T} + \frac{de + p\,dV}{T} = c_v \frac{dT}{T} + \frac{p}{T} dV \qquad (1.14a)$$

we arrive, with the help of Eq. 1.12, at the total differential

$$dS = c_v \frac{dT}{T} + R \frac{dV}{V} \qquad (1.14)$$

whose integral $\int_1^2 dS$ only depends on the end conditions of the process, independently of the intermediate conditions.

The property S is called the *entropy*. This property, in addition to e and h, describes processes involving heat exchange with the surroundings and "irreversible" processes in which heat is produced internally through dissipation of potential work (e.g., through turbulence). Therefore, from $dq = T\,dS$, the most general description of a single thermodynamic process is given as

$$T\,dS - de = p\,dV = dL_c \qquad (1.15a)$$

or, if a continuous process is considered, as

$$T\,dS - dh = dL_t \qquad (1.15b)$$

We have seen that the changes in entropy of a total engine cycle cancel each other, so that the entropy of the beginning of the process is restored, as are the enthalpy and the internal energy. However, and we now come to the most important physical meaning of the entropy: The simple relationship $dq = T\,dS$ only holds as long as the process is conducted in a "reversible" manner, and is therefore usually written as $dq = T\,dS_{\text{rev}}$. Here the whole system must be in equilibrium so that every infinitesimal step may be reversed completely. This condition is clearly met in the adiabatic portions of the engine cycle. But how about the isothermal portions? Here heat is added from a reservoir or removed to a reservoir to keep the gas temperatures constant. But only in the practically impossible case that the reservoir temperatures T_{res1} and T_{res2} are exactly equal to the gas cycle temperatures T_1 and T_2, respectively, could the condition of reversibility be met. When $T_{\text{res1}} > T_1$ and $T_{\text{res2}} < T_2$, the process cannot be reversed because no heat can be transferred from the lower to the higher temperature. In this case, the entropy changes in the reservoirs and in the gas are different, and the total entropy change of the process is given by the sum of the four entropy changes. In the reservoirs they are $-q_1/T_{\text{res1}}$ and $+q_2/T_{\text{res2}}$, whereas in the gas they are $+q_1/T_1$ and $-q_2/T_2$. Thus, the total entropy change of the process is given as

$$\Delta S = \frac{q_2}{T_{\text{res2}}} - \frac{q_1}{T_{\text{res1}}} \quad (1.16a)$$

because the entropy change of the gas cycle is zero (Eq. 1.13). Applying this relationship ($|q_1| = |q_2|\,(T_1/T_2)$) to the equation for ΔS, we finally arrive at

$$\Delta S = \frac{q_2}{T_{\text{res1}}}\left(\frac{T_{\text{res1}}}{T_{\text{res2}}} - \frac{T_1}{T_2}\right) > 0 \quad (1.16b)$$

From Eq. 1.16a we see that the entropy of the reservoirs (i.e., of the surroundings) increases when the entropy of the working cycle is held constant, as required for a stable process. From this fact we conclude that the entropy of any dynamic process increases and is therefore irreversible because no dynamic system in this world can operate without turbulence, friction, combustion, condensation, or any other process that partially converts the work potential into heat. However, this heat cannot be retransferred into the original level of the work potential without an entropy increase in the surroundings. All dynamic processes produce "debased" heat energy so that the work potential of the world continually decreases. According to classical thermodynamics, the world moves toward "heat death." The temperature gradients that are the source of all life in the world will eventually disappear.

We now return to aerodynamic flows and the importance of entropy in assessing their characteristics.

Aerodynamic flows are affected to varying degrees by friction, both with solid surfaces or between layers of markedly different velocities, and by turbulence. All these processes are irreversible because the heat created cannot restore the flow conditions that existed before. An important example is the boundary layer flow, in which, owing to inner gas friction or turbulence, the flow velocity increases from the solid wall to the free-stream condition. Mathematically, this behavior may be expressed by the relationship

$$\oint \mathbf{W} \cdot d\mathbf{s} \neq 0 \quad (1.17a)$$

This definition of a "rotational" flow may be seen directly by assuming a path s, formed by two stretches on two different streamlines, connected by two lines of zero velocity components (normal to the streamlines). Similarly, in a vortex, where the velocities increase with the distance from the center of rotation, the inequality Eq. 1.17a holds for any path of the same design. It is the necessary conditions for rotational flow as distinguished from potential flow.[12]

By Stokes' theorem, the integral of Eq. 1.17a is related to the curl vector as

$$\oint \mathbf{W} \cdot d\mathbf{s} = \iint \operatorname{curl} \mathbf{W} \cdot d\mathbf{A}^{13} \tag{1.17b}$$

and, consequently, the condition for viscous flow may also be written as $\operatorname{curl} \mathbf{W} \neq 0$, because A is always a finite magnitude.

The components of the curl vector are given as

$$\operatorname{curl} \mathbf{W} - \mathbf{i}\left(\frac{\partial w}{\partial y} - \frac{\partial v}{\partial z}\right) + \mathbf{j}\left(\frac{\partial u}{\partial z} - \frac{\partial w}{\partial x}\right) + \mathbf{k}\left(\frac{\partial v}{\partial x} - \frac{\partial u}{\partial y}\right)$$

where, for plane flow, only the last term applies, showing that the curl vector points in the direction of the axis of rotation.

By first adding and then subtracting the terms $v(\partial v/\partial x)$ and $w(\partial w/\partial x)$ in the first stationary Euler equation (Eq. 1.5a), the terms $w(\partial w/\partial y)$ and $u(\partial u/\partial y)$ in the second equation, and $u(\partial u/\partial z)$ and $v(\partial v/\partial z)$ in the third, all the terms obtained in this way may be rearranged to form the six components of the vectorial product of the velocity and the curl vectors, with the remaining terms being the components of the gradient of $W^2/2$. Hence we arrive at

$$\frac{1}{\rho}\operatorname{grad} p + \operatorname{grad}\frac{W^2}{2} = (\mathbf{W} \times \operatorname{curl} \mathbf{W}) \tag{1.18}$$

of which the **i**-component is given as

$$\frac{1}{\rho}\frac{\partial p}{\partial x} + \frac{\partial}{\partial x}\left(\frac{u^2}{2} + \frac{v^2}{2} + \frac{w^2}{2}\right) = \left[v\left(\frac{\partial v}{\partial x} - \frac{\partial u}{\partial y}\right) - w\left(\frac{\partial u}{\partial z} - \frac{\partial w}{\partial x}\right)\right]$$

and corresponding equations apply to the other components.

This new version of the Euler equations explicitly includes the case of rotational flow ($\operatorname{curl} \mathbf{W} \neq 0$) (i.e., flow with changes of entropy between the stream tubes). Consequently, the two terms on the left-hand side of these equations must implicitly contain the gradient of the entropy. This may be seen as follows: The equation defining entropy is obtained from Eq. 1.11b, with $dq = T\, dS$, as

$$T\, dS = dh - V\, dp \tag{1.19}$$

The change of the enthalpy, dh, is equal to the mechanical work done, as shown on page 17. In a streaming fluid this work is the change of the kinetic flow energy and we have $L_t = W_2^2/2 - W_1^2/2 = h_1 - h_2$, and for $h_1 = h_{W_1=0} = h_0$ we arrive at

$$h_0 = h + \frac{W_2^2}{2} \quad \text{and} \quad dh = dh_0 - d\frac{W^2}{2} \tag{1.20}$$

where h_0 is the stagnation enthalpy (i.e., the total enthalpy of a flow without heat addition from outside of the system). By introducing the expression for dh of Eq. 1.20 into Eq. 1.19 and applying vector notation, we obtain the the terms on the left-hand side of Eq. 1.18 as being equal to $-(\operatorname{grad} h_0 + T \operatorname{grad} S)$. Thus, finally we have

$$T \operatorname{grad} S = \operatorname{grad} h_0 - (\mathbf{W} \times \operatorname{curl} \mathbf{W}) \qquad (1.21)$$

This is the most general form of the stationary *Crocco equation,* stating that in an irrotational flow field of constant h_0 the entropy is constant. In a rotational flow field, however, the entropy changes normal to both the velocity vector and the curl vector. It does not change in the direction of $\mathbf{W}$ (i.e., in the direction of the stream tube). This latter statement is trivial, because all equations leading to the Crocco equation deal with the conditions of one and the same fluid element as it flows along a stream tube. The Crocco equation, therefore, describes the change in flow conditions when going from one stream tube of constant h_0 to the next.

The fact of constant entropy along the stream tube leads to the following conclusions:

1. When h_0 is constant in the whole field, a change in entropy according to Crocco's equation must occur in a zone of irreversible processes at constant total enthalpy, like flow through a grid of laterally varying mesh size, through a curved shock wave (the entropy increase depends on the shock angle!), etc.

2. When curl $\mathbf{W} = 0$ at the station under consideration, the velocities in adjacent stream tubes are equal. However, if the total enthalpies of these stream tubes are different, their velocities can be equal only if the flow has passed through a zone of irreversible processes as described earlier, which in this case may include processes with change in h_0 such as condensation or combustion. Obviously, it is very unlikely that those processes just produce equal velocities in adjacent stream tubes, and both grad h_0 and curl $\mathbf{W}$ must be expected to contribute to the change in entropy according to Crocco.

Since the Crocco equation is derived from inviscid flow equations, it does not apply to viscous flow in which momentum is exchanged between stream tubes, so that the condition of constant entropy in them no longer holds. The Crocco equation is only valid when the entropy differences between stream tubes are created through processes that occur upstream of the station under consideration in the manner discussed earlier. Then the momentum exchange between stream tubes of different flow velocities must be considered to be negligible, so that the flow can be called *quasi-inviscid.*

To conclude the discussion about the Crocco equation, we note that it allows for the definition of the validity range of the Bernoulli equation in a very simple way: by replacing the right-hand side of Eq. 1.18 with the corresponding terms of Eq. 1.21, we obtain the stationary Bernoulli equation by holding both h_0 and S constant. Thus, the Bernoulli equation is not only valid on the stream tube, the condition we imposed on the Euler equation when we originally derived the Bernoulli equation, but in the whole flow field if the flow is isotropic. In such a flow field a velocity potential exists. Consequently, only now does the result of the unsteady Bernoulli equation receive its full justification because, in assuming potential flow, we extended the validity of the Bernoulli equation over the whole flow field, without knowing whether that was permissible.

To complete this brief survey of aerodynamic principles, a few words must be said about viscous flow, which is much more complex than inviscid flow and requires more complicated mathematics. The classical viscous flow equations of Navier and Stokes are based on Stoke's coefficient of viscosity, which, as will be shown in Chapter 6, is not valid generally, and even with the much refined system of viscosity coefficients, not all cases may be covered satisfactorily.

The Navier–Stokes equations in a form suitable to the derivation of a viscous transonic equation will be given in Chapter 6. Here, only one importnat consequence of the form of these equations must be stated. In their simplest form, the Navier–Stokes equations are the Euler equations with one additional expression each of velocity component derivatives multiplied by a coefficient of viscosity μ, which is defined by $\tau = \mu(dv/dy)$, where τ is the shear force per unit area, and dv/dy is the velocity gradient normal to the flow direction. The latter, as we saw earlier, produces the interaction between neighboring flow layers, and μ is a material constant characteristic of the viscosity of a particular gas at a certain temperature. By writing the Navier–Stokes equations in dimensionless form (i.e., by relating the velocity components to a reference velocity v_0, the lengths to a reference length l, and the coefficient of viscosity to $\rho l v_0$, which is the dimension it has according to the preceding definition equation) these equations become identical for all flows in which the Reynolds number $\text{Re} = lv_0\rho/\mu$ is the same,[14] and the solutions to these equations are also identical. This is of great importance to aerodynamic work, because one computation, or, even more importantly, the results of an aerodynamic test under one flow condition, can be applied directly to a flight condition at the same Reynolds number. Thus, a wind tunnel test may be conducted in a special gas that may have certain advantages for the particular problem, and then, by way of the Reynolds number, give results for flight in air. Of course, the Reynolds number is exclusively valid only as long as the differential equations describing the flow conditions are those leading to the Re-relationship. For instance, for supersonic flow, which is governed by different equations, another dimensionless number must be matched for similarity considerations—namely, the Mach number $M = v_0/a$,[15] where a is the local speed of sound. Actually, for the whole range of inviscid, compressible flow ($m > 0.3$), M must be matched for similar flow.

Further modifications of the flow equations are necessary when additional physical processes are involved (e.g., when heat is transferred from streamline to streamline). But here again a dimensionless number exists that allows different cases to relate to one another. This is the Prandtl number $\text{Pr} = \rho\mu/\alpha$, where α is the coefficient of temperature conduction. More dimensionless numbers have been found for other special flow conditions that are not required within the framework of this book.

Notes

1. Under certain conditions, with which we are not concerned in this book, there is some motion of the gas even on a solid surface—so-called slip flow.
2. Here I am employing the standard notation, in which ρ is the density, and $\mathbf{W}$ the velocity vector and $\mathbf{W}$ has the components (u, v, w) in the directions (x, y, z).
3. See Eqs. 1.11 for the thermodynamic meaning of this integral.
4. Note that it is customary in thermodynamics to give the energy per unit mass, but to simply call it 'energy.' Also, the specific volume $V = 1/\rho$ is often used.
5. See Note 4 for the definition of V.
6. See Prob. 1.4 for a detailed derivation of this fact.
7. A *perfect gas* is a gas in which the attraction forces between the molecules are negligible (elastic collisions) and the molecules take up a negligible volume compared with the total gas volume. Both conditions are no longer valid when the gas pressure is high, so that the molecules are forced close together. The measured pressure is then modified by the forces of attraction between the molecules, and the volume of the molecules takes up a noticeable portion of the total volume. Such a gas is called a "real" gas.
8. In a real gas (see Note 7) the equation of state, and with it most thermodynamic relationships, must be modified through additional terms. However, atmospheric pressures do not fall into this range and for a basic theory those corrections are not required.
9. As the kinetic theory of gases shows (see, e.g., ref. 66), γ of a perfect gas may be written as $(f+2)/f = \gamma$, in which f stands for the "degrees of freedom" of the molecule, i.e., the number of energy-absorbing motion modes of the atoms in the molecule. In one-atom molecules, like helium, there are only three translational modes and $\gamma = 5/3$. For gases with two-atom molecules, rotation of the two atoms about the center of gravity and their vibrations against each other are additional degrees of freedom, and thus air, essentially composed of O_2 and N_2 molecules, has five active degrees of freedom, so that $\gamma = 7/5$.
10. The work done by the gas is taken as positive, that done on the gas (e.g., in a compressor) as negative. Heat added to the gas is positive, while that removed is negative.
11. Of course, this is mathematically obvious, because

$$dh = \frac{\partial h}{\partial e} de + \frac{\partial h}{\partial p} dp + \frac{\partial h}{\partial V} dV.$$

12. For the "potential" vortex, see Sec. 2.7.3.
13. $|A|$ is the area enclosed by s of the line integral. However, $\mathbf{A}$ must be described by a vector normal to the area elements because this area may have any shape (i.e., may be three-dimensional).
14. See Prob. 1.6.
15. The symbol M for the Mach number is the only, mainly British and American, deviation from a rule, established in the early days of modern aerodynamics and thermodynamics, namely, that the symbols for the dimensionless numbers should be the first two letters of the name of the person who first introduced this number (e.g., Re, Pr). Accordingly, in the

European literature, the Mach number usually is written as Ma. Recently, the McGraw-Hill Publishing Company has adopted the logical symbol Ma (e.g., in *Aerodynamics of the Airplane* by Schlichting and Truckenbrodt [1979]), see ref. 39).

Problems

1.1. Derive the expression for the speed of sound $a^2 = \partial p/\partial \rho$ from the adiabatic propagation of a small pressure wave in a pipe. Assume that the wave has a finite, but small, length between two steady-state flow conditions, with $p_1 = \rho_1 =$ const. upstream and $p_2 = \rho_2 =$ const. downstream of the wave. Realize that the upstream velocity $W_1 \neq 0$, because mass must be added to the downstream fluid at rest when the wave enters and compresses it, and that this mass addition to a pipe element of the length of the wave must be equal to the product of the speed of sound and the change in density across the wave.

1.2. Derive the relationship $(dp/d\rho)_{S=\text{const}} = a^2 = \gamma RT$ from Eq. 1.11b and the equation of state.

1.3. For adiabatic flow, derive
(a) $T/T_0 = f_1(M)$, $p/p_0 = f_2(M)$, $\rho/\rho_0 = f_3(M)$, and the corresponding relationships for M^*.
(b) the important relationship $p/\rho^\gamma =$ const., directly from Eq. 1.14.
Clue: Eqs. 1.11 and 1.12 lead to the expressions for $p/p_0 = f_4(T/T_0)$ and $\rho/\rho_0 = f_5(T/T_0)$. Then Eq. 1.19 gives the relationship $T/T_0 = f_6(W)$. At last, from Prob. 1.2, the sonic speed a is introduced for the establishment of M and M^* from W and $a(T)$ and $a^*(T^*)$, respectively.

1.4. Derive the relationship $L_t = h_1 - h_2$ for a compressor that draws air from the atmosphere and discharges it into a large vessel (constant pressure).

1.5. Derive q_{12} and ΔS for a polytropic process in which the temperature changes from T_1 to T_2 but the polytropic exponent n ($pV^n = p_1 V_1^n$) is constant. The heat is always added or removed at the instant gas temperature.
(a) Draw the p–V and the T–S diagrams of such a process
(b) Draw the conclusion about the value(s) of n required for a closed cycle in that work is done (i.e., $|q_{12}| > |q_{21}|$).

1.6. Show that the Navier–Stokes equation $\rho(uu_x + vu_y + wu_z) = p_x + \mu[u_{xx} + u_{yy} + u_{zz} + (u_x + v_y + w_z)_x]$ (see Sect. 7.3.2) becomes identical in all cases for which $\text{Re} = lv_0\rho/\mu =$ const., when the magnitudes u, v, w and x, y, z are made dimensionless with v_0 and l, respectively, and p with ρv_0^2.

1.7. From the definition equation of the shear stress $\tau = \mu(du/dy)$, where u is the velocity in streamline direction and y the direction normal to it, show that Re is a dimensionless magnitude.

1.8. Determine the expression for the maximum flow velocity of a given stagnation enthalpy h_0. Why is the velocity finite but the Mach number infinite?

1.9. Draw a sketch of a blow-down wind tunnel, and designate stations and cross-sectional areas of the tunnel inlet, of the test section and the entrance to the vacuum vessel of a chosen volume.

From Eq. 1.9, determine $p(x)$ and $W(x)$ at sufficient time intervals to draw a diagram $p(t)$ and $W(t)$ at each of these stations and in the vessel. The x coordinate is introduced through $\phi = \int_1^2 W(x)\, dx$.

2
THE THEORY OF INVISCID TRANSONIC FLOW

2.1 One-Dimensional Transonic Flow

Some of the important characteristics of transonic flow can readily be derived from inviscid one-dimensional gas dynamics. The shape of the Laval nozzle (Fig. 2.1) for the establishment of supersonic flow, for instance, is the result of the peculiar behavior of the flow at the Mach number of 1. In a Laval nozzle, the Mach number increases steadily, reaching the value $M = 1$ at the nozzle "throat," the station of minimum cross-sectional area A, and becomes supersonic in the diverging part of the nozzle. As the Mach number increases in the nozzle, the flow properties pressure p, density ρ, and temperature T decrease monotonically.

The peculiar flow conditions in the transonic range (i.e., when $M \approx 1$) become obvious by introducing the continuity equation for one-dimensional flow $v\rho A = v^*\rho^*A^*$, where the starred values are those at the nozzle throat, the so-called critical' values at $M = M^* = 1$.[1] This equation shows that the flow density ρv has its maximum when the cross-sectional area A is smallest at the throat. In Fig. 2.2, the dimensionless flow density is plotted against the velocity,[2] here made dimensionless by the sonic speed a^* at $M = 1$. The shape of this curve allows us to draw important conclusions about the relative difficulties in solving aerodynamic problems in the various Mach number regions. This becomes obvious from the fact that aerodynamic analyses may be simplified considerably if linearization is possible. To this end, a section of a curve or a nonlinear function is approximated by a straight line or a linear function, respectively.

Physically, linearization is justified in all cases in which the deviation from the flow properties of the undisturbed approach flow, as caused by the flight article, are small and monotonic. A necessary condition for such a behavior is, therefore, that the flight article be reasonably slender; it should also be reasonably slender to avoid excessive power requirements for its propulsion. Mathematically, linearization is accomplished by, for example, developing the flow equation into a Taylor series and retaining only the linear terms.[2] The range of the independent variable for which this can be done without introducing an unacceptable error (higher-order terms of same magnitude as linear term) depends on the shape of the curve. Obviously, at an inflection point linearization is very

The Theory of Inviscid Transonic Flow

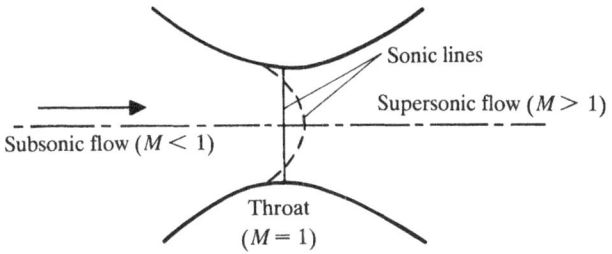

Fig. 2.1. Flow through a Laval nozzle. Sonic line in one dimensional flow (———) and in two- or three dimensional flow (- - -).

effective over a wide range; it is least suitable at a point of large curvature. Going back to Fig. 2.2, linearization of $\rho v/\rho^* v^*$ is effective at incompressible subsonic speeds and again around $M^{*2} = 3$ (inflection point for $\gamma = 1.4$).

Following Oswatitsch [2] we approximate $\rho v/\rho^* v^*$ in the transonic range as follows. First, develop $\rho v/\rho^* v^* = f(M^*)$ into a Taylor series at $M^* = M_1^*$. With the general form of the Taylor series

$$f(x) = f(x_1) + \left(\frac{df(x)}{dx}\right)_{x=x_1}(x-x_1) + \left(\frac{d^2f(x)}{dx^2}\right)_{x=x_1}(x-x_1)^2 \cdot \frac{1}{2!} + \cdots$$

and the general gas-dynamic equation for the density[3] in adiabatic flow

$$\frac{\rho}{\rho^*} = \left(\frac{\gamma+1}{2} - \frac{\gamma-1}{2}M^{*2}\right)^{1/(\gamma-1)}$$

we obtain

$$\frac{\rho}{\rho^*}M^* = \frac{\rho_1}{\rho^*}M_1^* + (M^* - M_1^*)\frac{\rho_1}{\rho^*}\left[1 - M_1^{*2}\left(\frac{\gamma+1}{2} - \frac{\gamma-1}{2}M_1^{*2}\right)^{-1}\right]$$

$$+ (M^* - M_1^*)^2 \frac{1}{2}\binom{\text{second}}{\text{derivative}}_{M^*=M_1^*} + \cdots$$

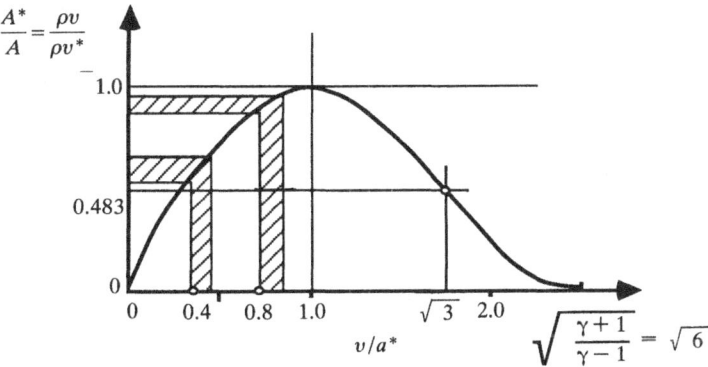

Fig. 2.2. Reduction of available ρv-variation ($\gamma = c_p/c_v = 1.4$) with increasing Mach number for the same perturbation range.

By dropping the second- and higher-order terms and dividing by $\rho_1 M_1^*/\rho^*$:

$$\frac{\rho}{\rho_1}\frac{v}{v_1} - 1 = \frac{M^* - M_1^*}{M_1^*}\left(1 - M_1^{*2}\left(\frac{\gamma+1}{2} - \frac{\gamma-1}{2}M_1^{*2}\right)^{-1}\right]$$

$$= \frac{M^* - M_1^*}{M_1^*}(1 - M_1^2) = \frac{v - v_1}{v_1}(1 - M_1^2) = \beta_1^2\left(\frac{v}{v_1} - 1\right) \quad (2.1a)$$

This expression is known as the Prandtl linearization. For $M_1 = 1$ we have $\rho v/\rho_1 v_1 = 1$, independent of $v - v_1$, obviously a wrong result. Moreover, even for $M_1 \approx 1$ (i.e., in the whole transonic range) the error is considerable, as seen from Table 2.1. Of course, this result is not surprising, because Eq. 2.1a represents the points on the tangent to the $\rho v^*/\rho^* v^*$ curve at the station M_1^* that for transonic flow strongly deviates from the exact curve, and, if used to describe the transonic flow over a profile, would lead to the impossible values $\rho v^*/\rho^* v^* > 1$ for the region in which $M^* > 1$. Therefore, a simplified expression for the transonic flow density can be obtained only if higher-order terms are introduced. Now, realizing that two- and three-dimensional flows are composed of one-dimensional stream tubes, we conclude that the transonic flow equations may not be linearized without severe restrictions in their applicability, a fact that should always be kept in mind.

For a better approximation we could add the second-order term of the Taylor series. Oswatitsch chose a different approach that has definite merits and shall be followed here. We write:

$$\frac{\rho v}{\rho_1 v_1} - 1 = \beta_1^2\left(\frac{v}{v_1} - 1\right) + A\left(\frac{v}{v_1} - 1\right)^2 \quad (2.1b)$$

and determine A such that $[(\rho v/\rho v_1) - 1]$ has its maximum for $v = a^*$. The advantage of this approach is obvious: We would have to introduce all the higher-order terms of the Taylor series (which means we would have to use the exact equation) to obtain a curve having its maximum at $M^* = 1$ for all $M_1^* \neq 1$ even when $M_1^* \approx 1$. It is important, however, that,

Table 2.1 Comparison of the Oswatitsch Approximation with the Prandtl Linearization

$M_1 = 0.8$; $\gamma = 1.4$			$\frac{\rho v}{\rho_1 v_1} - 1$	
M	M^*	Exact	Oswatitsch	Prandtl
0	0	−1.0	−1.209	−0.360
0.5	0.535	−0.225	−0.231	−0.126
0.7	0.732	−0.051	−0.051	−0.041
0.8	0.825	0	0	0
0.9	0.915	0.029	0.029	0.039
1.2	1.158	0.007	0.007	0.145
1.5	1.365	−0.117	−0.128	0.236

The Theory of Inviscid Transonic Flow

in approximating $\rho v/\rho_1 v_1$ near $M = 1$, the approximation has its maximum at $M = 1$. Thus, differentiating Eq. 2.1b with respect to v/v_1, and setting the result for $v = a^*$ equal to 0, we have

$$0 = \beta_1^2 + 2A\left(\frac{a^*}{v_1} - 1\right) \quad \text{and} \quad A = -\frac{\beta_1^2}{2\left(\frac{1}{M_1^*} - 1\right)} = -\frac{\gamma+1}{4} M_1^*(1 + M_1^*)$$

Introduction of this expression for A into Eq. 2.1b yields

$$\frac{\rho v}{\rho_1 v_1} - 1 = \beta_1^2\left(\frac{v}{v_1} - 1\right) - \frac{\gamma+1}{4} M_1^*(1 + M_1^*)\left(\frac{v}{v_1} - 1\right)^2. \quad (2.2a)$$

This is a parabola connecting $(\rho v/\rho^* v^*)_{M_1^*}$ and $(\rho v/\rho^* v^*)_{M^*=1}$. As an example, Table 2.1 shows that this approximation is very good for $M_1 = 0.8$, whereas Prandtl's linearization is only acceptable for very small deviations from v_1, confirming the earlier statement that in the subsonic range Prandtl's equation is a suitable linearization in the incompressible range only. In the case $v_1 = a^*$ or $M_1^* = 1$, Eq. 2.2a reduces to

$$\frac{\rho v}{\rho^* v^*} - 1 = -\frac{\gamma+1}{2}(M^* - 1)^2 \quad (2.2b)$$

The linear term has disappeared because now the parabola is symmetric to the $M^* = 1$ ordinate.

Although the relationship between the flow density and the flow field geometry as expressed by the continuity equation cannot be linearized at transonic speeds, the pressure function has an inflection point at $M = 1$[4] (see Fig. 2.3) and, therefore, is linear in the transonic range. Consequently, certain estimations of the flow on the body surface in transonic flight are easily made, because the value $\gamma \Delta v/v$ may be replaced by $-\Delta p/p$.[5] Also, since at $M = 1$, $\Delta A/A = 0$ (minimum of cross-sectional area), the continuity equation yields $\Delta v/v = -\Delta \rho/\rho$ (see also Prob. 2.1).

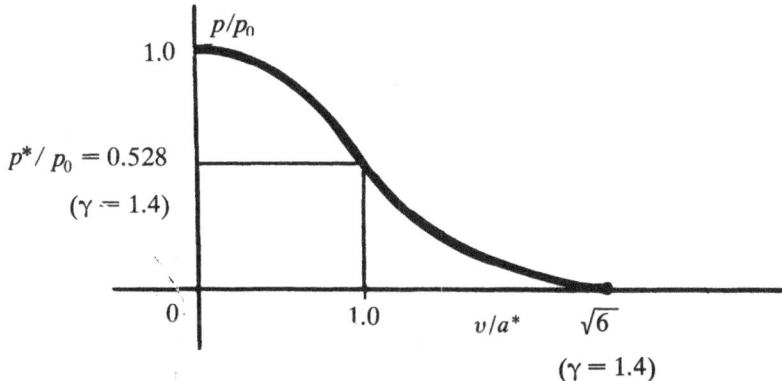

Fig. 2.3. Pressure ratio vs. dimensionless velocity. Inflection point at $v/a^* = 1$ ($M = 1$).

Hence, the following very simple relationships apply in slender body transonic flow:

$$\frac{\Delta p}{p} = -\gamma \frac{\Delta v}{v} = \gamma \frac{\Delta \rho}{\rho} \qquad (2.3)$$

Obviously, this approximation is very poor in the low subsonic and the high supersonic ranges.

What conclusions can we now draw from the results of one-dimensional analysis? Realizing that one-dimensional theory assumes that the flow conditions normal to a mean streamline are constant, it is limited to stream tubes whose cross-sectional areas change very gradually. It is quite obvious, therefore, that a Laval nozzle with a strong contraction and expansion cannot be treated by one-dimensional theory. Conversely, a stream tube of a flow about a slender body may very well satisfy the stated condition of slow change in cross-sectional area. Therefore, for such a stream tube the results of the one-dimensional theory should apply. Returning now to Fig. 2.2, it can be seen that the change in cross-sectional area with Mach number decreases to zero as M approaches 1. Assuming an approach velocity $v = 0.8a^*$ and a range of velocity variations $\Delta v = +0.1a^*$, the cross-sectional area varies by about -3.5%. At an approach velocity $v = 0.4a^*$, the same variation in Δv leads to an area variation of about -19%. We conclude that the stream tubes about a body can contract much more at low Mach numbers (and high supersonic Mach numbers) than at a Mach number near $M = 1$. The stream tubes are forced to follow the body contour more and more closely when the incident flow Mach number approaches unity, (see Fig. 2.4). Since the stream tube on the body cannot contract much, the next stream tube is forced away from the body, and so on.

We see that *in transonic flow the flow field is influenced by the body*

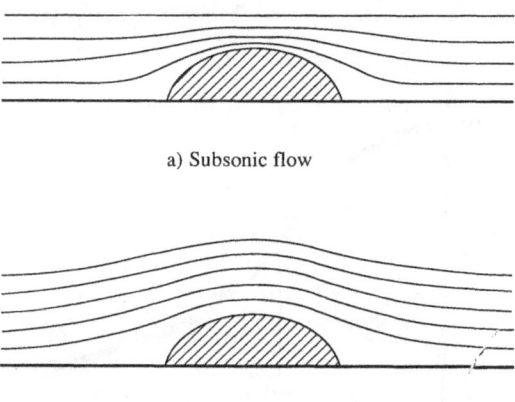

a) Subsonic flow

b) Transonic flow

Fig. 2.4. Schematic streamline pattern of the flow over a symmetric profile: (a) subsonic flow, (b) transonic flow.

The Theory of Inviscid Transonic Flow

much farther out than in subsonic or supersonic flow. This is a most important finding and *an essential part of the problems of transonic flight.*

Thus, because at an approach Mach number of exactly 1 no contraction of the stream tubes could occur, the distance of the streamlines at $M = 1$ over a very slender two-dimensional body would be constant to infinity. Of course, we know that this is not the case. A simple proof that this result of one-dimensional theory cannot be right will be given later with the help of the relationship between streamline curvature and pressure gradient normal to the streamlines.

2.2 The Basic Three-dimensional Theory

Although viscous effects play an important role in transonic flow, inviscid flow theory provides the basis for the study of transonic pecularities. Assuming frictionless, steady flow without heat conduction, the entropy of a fluid particle, and thus the entropy of a stream tube, remain constant. However, differences in entropy between stream tubes are not excluded. Thus, the governing equations are (see Chapter 1):

Continuity equation

$$\frac{\partial}{\partial x}(\rho u) + \frac{\partial}{\partial y}(\rho v) + \frac{\partial}{\partial z}(\rho w) = 0 \qquad (2.4)^6$$

Euler's equation

$$\frac{1}{\rho}\frac{\partial p}{\partial x} + u\frac{\partial u}{\partial x} + v\frac{\partial u}{\partial y} + w\frac{\partial u}{\partial z} = 0 \qquad (2.5a)$$

$$\frac{1}{\rho}\frac{\partial p}{\partial y} + u\frac{\partial v}{\partial x} + v\frac{\partial v}{\partial y} + w\frac{\partial v}{\partial z} = 0 \qquad (2.5b)$$

$$\frac{1}{\rho}\frac{\partial p}{\partial z} + u\frac{\partial w}{\partial x} + v\frac{\partial w}{\partial y} + w\frac{\partial w}{\partial z} = 0 \qquad (2.5c)$$

Condition of constant entropy

$$\frac{dS}{dt} = \frac{\partial S}{\partial x}u + \frac{\partial S}{\partial y}v + \frac{\partial S}{\partial z}w = 0 \qquad (2.6)$$

and with $\rho = f_1(p, T)$ and $T = f_2(p, S) = f_3(p, S)$:

Equation of state

$$\frac{\partial \rho}{\partial x} = \frac{\partial \rho}{\partial p}\frac{\partial p}{\partial x} + \frac{\partial \rho}{\partial S}\frac{\partial S}{\partial x} = \frac{1}{a^2}\frac{\partial p}{\partial x} + \frac{\partial \rho}{\partial S}\frac{\partial S}{\partial x} \qquad (2.7a)$$

$$\frac{\partial \rho}{\partial y} = \frac{\partial \rho}{\partial p}\frac{\partial p}{\partial y} + \frac{\partial \rho}{\partial S}\frac{\partial S}{\partial y} = \frac{1}{a^2}\frac{\partial p}{\partial y} + \frac{\partial \rho}{\partial S}\frac{\partial S}{\partial y} \qquad (2.7b)$$

$$\frac{\partial \rho}{\partial z} = \frac{\partial \rho}{\partial p}\frac{\partial p}{\partial z} + \frac{\partial \rho}{\partial S}\frac{\partial S}{\partial z} = \frac{1}{a^2}\frac{\partial p}{\partial z} + \frac{\partial \rho}{\partial S}\frac{\partial S}{\partial z} \qquad (2.7c)$$

Here we have set

$$\left(\frac{\partial \rho}{\partial p}\right)_s = \frac{1}{a^2}, \qquad (2.8)^7$$

where a is the propagation speed of small disturbances (speed of sound). Note that no assumption has been made yet about the specific form of the equation of state.

Systematic elimination of p, ρ, and S from these equations leads to a form of the continuity equation that depends on the velocity components and the speed of sound only, and holds for inviscid flow even if it is rotational:

$$\frac{\partial u}{\partial x}\left(1 - \frac{u^2}{a^2}\right) + \frac{\partial v}{\partial y}\left((1 - \frac{v^2}{a^2}\right) + \frac{\partial w}{\partial z}\left(1 - \frac{w^2}{a^2}\right)$$

$$-\left(\frac{\partial u}{\partial y} + \frac{\partial v}{\partial x}\right)\frac{uv}{a^2} - \left(\frac{\partial v}{\partial z} + \frac{\partial w}{\partial y}\right)\frac{vw}{a^2} - \left(\frac{\partial w}{\partial x} + \frac{\partial u}{\partial z}\right)\frac{wu}{a^2} = 0 \quad (2.9)$$

Here, it should be pointed out that for isoenergetic,[8] adiabatic flow (i.e., when all streamlines have the same stagnation enthalpy h_0 and no heat is exchanged through the flow boundaries, so that $dq = dh - V\,dp = 0$) Eq. 2.9 may be reduced to an equation of the three dependent variables u, v, w only, because the local sound speed a may be replaced by the following function of the critical sound speed a^* and the local velocity components (see Note 21, Eq. 1.20, and Prob. 1.2)

$$a^2 = \frac{\gamma + 1}{2}a^{*2} - \frac{\gamma - 1}{2}(u^2 + v^2 + w^2)$$

$$= a_0^2 - \frac{\gamma - 1}{2}(u^2 + v^2 + w^2) \qquad (2.10)$$

For an irrotational flow field a velocity potential Φ exists, defined as $\mathbf{W} = \operatorname{grad} \Phi$, and the continuity equation may be written as

$$\Phi_{xx}\left(1 - \frac{\Phi_x^2}{a^2}\right) + \Phi_{yy}\left(1 - \frac{\Phi_y^2}{a^2}\right) + \Phi_{zz}\left(1 - \frac{\Phi_z^2}{a^2}\right) - 2\Phi_{xy}\frac{\Phi_x \Phi_y}{a^2}$$

$$- 2\Phi_{yz}\frac{\Phi_y \Phi_z}{a^2} - 2\Phi_{zx}\frac{\Phi_z \Phi_x}{a^2} = 0, \quad \text{where } \Phi_x = \frac{\partial \Phi}{\partial x} = u, \text{ etc.} \quad (2.11)$$

Similarly, the axisymmetric equation becomes (see Prob. 2.19)

$$\Phi_{xx}\left(1 - \frac{\Phi_x^2}{a^2}\right) + \Phi_{rr}\left(1 - \frac{\Phi_r^2}{a^2}\right) - 2\Phi_{xr}\frac{\Phi_x \Phi_r}{a^2} + \frac{\Phi_r}{r} = 0 \qquad (2.12)$$

The continuity equation in polar coordinates is given as Eq. 2.13.

All equations derived so far are general; they are valid for the entire range of Mach numbers from 0 to ∞. However, as we have previously stated, there are always shockwaves present in the transonic region.

Therefore, these equations are perfectly valid downstream of straight (normal or oblique) shocks because the entropy jumps are equal on all streamlines through the shock. For curved shocks, as always present over transonic flight articles, viscous effects will play a role because of the velocity gradients between the downstream streamlines. As far as those effects are small, the flow might be called quasi-inviscid and may be treated with sufficient accuracy by the above equations.

2.2.1 An Application of the Basic Theory

A simple application of the basic theory to a curved flow element will now be given that leads to a result that is very useful in estimating flow patterns. In a flow field, we consider a section small enough for the streamlines to be approximated by concentric circles. The streamline under consideration may have the radius of curvature R (Fig. 2.5). Then the flow can be described in a polar coordinate system (r, ω). If ϕ is the potential function of the flow, we define

$$\phi_r = V \quad \text{and} \quad \phi_\omega = rw$$

For circular flow around the origin of the coordinate system we have $\phi_r = v = 0$. The general continuity equation in polar coordinates (see Prob. 2.19),

$$\left(1 - \left(\frac{\phi_r}{a}\right)^2\right)\phi_{rr} + \left(1 - \left(\frac{\phi_\omega}{ra}\right)^2\right)\frac{\phi_{\omega\omega}}{r^2} - 2\phi_{r\omega}\frac{\phi_r \phi_\omega}{r^2 a^2} + \frac{\phi_r}{r}\left(1 + \frac{\phi_\omega^2}{r^2 a^2}\right) = 0 \tag{2.13}$$

reduces under these assumptions to

$$\left(1 - \frac{\phi_\omega^2}{r^2 a^2}\right)\frac{\phi_{\omega\omega}}{r^2} = 0 \tag{2.14}$$

Since $1 - (\phi_\omega/ra)^2 \neq 0$, except in very special cases, the only general equation remaining is $\phi_{\omega\omega} = 0$.

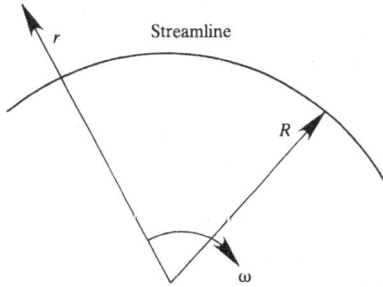

Fig. 2.5. Curved streamline in polar coordinates.

From Euler's equation,

$$\frac{dp}{\rho} = -d\left(\frac{W^2}{2}\right) \quad \text{or} \quad dp = -\frac{\rho}{2}d\left(\phi_r^2 + \left(\frac{\phi_\omega}{r}\right)^2\right)$$

we obtain

$$dp = -\frac{\rho}{2}d\left(\frac{\phi_\omega}{r}\right)^2 = -\frac{\rho}{2}\left(\frac{2\phi_\omega \phi_{\omega\omega}}{r^2}d\omega - \frac{2\phi_\omega^2}{r^3}dr\right) \quad (2.15)$$

and with $\phi_{\omega\omega} = 0$

$$dp = \frac{\rho}{r^3}\phi_\omega^2 \, dr$$

or, with $\phi_\omega = rw$ and $r = R =$ radius of curvature

$$\frac{dp}{dr} = \frac{w^2\rho}{R} \quad (2.16)$$

Now, by replacing the differentials dp and dr by differences Δp and Δr small enough to allow that the right-hand side of Eq. 2.16 may be considered to be a constant, and by multiplying both sides with a small area element ΔA normal to r, we obtain

$$\Delta p \, \Delta A = \frac{v^2\rho}{R}\Delta R \, \Delta A$$

The left-hand side is a force $F = \Delta p \, \Delta A$ acting upon the area ΔA and the right-hand side can be written as $w^2 m/R$ with $m = \rho \, \Delta R \, \Delta A$ being the mass of the volume element $\Delta R \, \Delta A$. The resulting equation,

$$F = \frac{w^2 m}{R}$$

is the equation of the centripetal force holding in a circular orbit of radius R a mass m moving at the velocity v. Consequently, Eq. 2.16 shows that a pressure gradient exists in a curved flow that is exactly determined by the centrifugal force of the flow element under consideration. Specifically, the flow over a convex surface produces a pressure gradient such that the pressure is lowest on the surface and increases with distance from it. From Bernoulli's equation we can furthermore conclude that, for a symmetric airfoil in infinite space, the stream velocity at the station of maximum thickness is higher than free-stream velocity. Conversely, it is smaller than free stream velocity near the stagnation points, because here the streamlines curve in the opposite direction and the pressure is higher than free stream pressure.

This result confirms the statement on page 33, namely, that linear theory does not give realistic answers at $M_\infty = 1$, because it would require that, in two-dimensional flow, all streamlines—up to infinity—were equally far apart and consequently had equal curvature. Thus, with Eq.

The Theory of Inviscid Transonic Flow

2.16, each streamline would contribute the same finite amount to the total static pressure difference between free stream pressure, and the pressure on the body surface, so that the pressure on the body surface would obtain the impossible value of $p_b = \pm\infty$, depending on the sense of the body curvature.

Now, as is better seen from the analysis on page 112, this is an oversimplification, even of linearized flow, because, first of all, even over a very slender body the Mach number varies slightly about $M = 1$, and certain streamtube contractions will always occur. However, the basic fact that linear theory cannot correctly describe transonic flow is obvious, and it appears that nonlinear effects must be considered for correct answers.

2.3 Simplified Transonic Theory Using Small Perturbations

The general continuity equations, Eqs. 2.11, 2.12, and 2.13, are nonlinear and new solutions cannot be found by simple superposition of known solutions.

In subsonic and supersonic flow (not including hypersonic flow), linear equations can be obtained through the application of small perturbations. Unfortunately, in transonic flow, this method again leads to nonlinear equations.

The first step in deriving small perturbation equations consists in composing the x-component of the flow vector $\mathbf{W}$ from the undisturbed approach velocity U and a perturbation component u ($W_x = U + u$), where u is of the order of the y- and z-components v and w, respectively, of the flow vector. Thus Eq. 2.9 becomes:

$$(a^2 - (U+u)^2)\frac{\partial u}{\partial x} - (U+u)v\left(\frac{\partial u}{\partial y} + \frac{\partial v}{\partial x}\right) + (a^2 - v^2)\frac{\partial v}{\partial y} = 0 \quad (2.17a)[9]$$

Setting

$$a^2 = a_\infty^2 - \frac{\gamma-1}{2}(2uU + u^2 + v^2)$$

(Eq. 2.10 with $a_\infty^2 = a_0^2 - (\gamma-1)U^2/2$) and $U/a_\infty = M_\infty$ (Mach number of the undisturbed flow), there follows:

$$(1 - M_\infty^2)\frac{\partial u}{\partial x} + \frac{\partial v}{\partial y} = M_\infty^2\left((\gamma+1)\frac{u}{U} + \frac{\gamma+1}{2}\frac{u^2}{U^2} + \frac{\gamma-1}{2}\frac{v^2}{U^2}\right)\frac{\partial u}{\partial x}$$

$$+ M_\infty^2\left((\gamma-1)\frac{u}{U} + \frac{\gamma+1}{2}\frac{v^2}{U^2} + \frac{\gamma-1}{2}\frac{u^2}{U^2}\right)\frac{\partial v}{\partial y} + M_\infty^2\frac{v}{U}\left(1 + \frac{u}{U}\right)\left(\frac{\partial u}{\partial y} + \frac{\partial v}{\partial x}\right)$$

By disregarding all terms including squares or products of the perturbation velocities, this equation reduces to

$$(1 - M_\infty^2)\frac{\partial u}{\partial x} + \frac{\partial v}{\partial y} = M_\infty^2(\gamma+1)\frac{u}{U}\frac{\partial u}{\partial x} + M_\infty^2\frac{v}{U}\left(\frac{\partial u}{\partial y} + \frac{\partial v}{\partial x}\right) \quad (2.17b)$$

where, in addition, the term $M_\infty^2(\gamma - 1)(u/U)(\partial v/\partial y)$ has been disregarded as small compared with $\partial v/\partial y$.

Now, the important consideration for transonic flow is as follows: All terms on the right-hand side contain perturbation velocities that in subsonic and supersonic aerodynamics are usually neglected in comparison with the terms on the left-hand side that do not contain the perturbation velocities (only their derivatives!). However, when M_∞ approaches unity and thus $(1 - M_\infty^2)$ becomes very small, the latter term may no longer be large compared with the coefficient of $\partial u/\partial x$ on the right-hand side. Therefore, the perturbation equation for transonic flow must retain all terms of Eq. 2.17b.

The relative importance of the terms $M_\infty^2(\gamma + 1)(u/U)$ and $(1 - M_\infty^2)$ depends on both u and M_∞. For slender bodies ($u \ll U$) these terms are comparable only at approach Mach numbers close to 1, but for thicker bodies they may be comparable even at rather low approach Mach numbers. However, because we have no way yet to estimate the magnitude of the last term of Eq. 2.17b, the above interpretation of this equation should be taken with caution. In other words, so far we must assume that the derivatives of the perturbation velocities may not be of equal order of magnitude.

A more direct approach to the transonic equation uses the critical sonic speed a^* as the reference velocity instead of U. Here, the small perturbation method yields [3]

$$-(\gamma + 1)u\frac{\partial u}{\partial x} - 2v\frac{\partial u}{\partial y} + a^*\frac{\partial v}{\partial y} = 0 \qquad (2.18)$$

As should have been expected, Eq. 2.17b reduces to Eq. 2.18 for $M_\infty = 1$, $U = a^*$ and $\partial u/\partial y = \partial v/\partial x$, assuming irrotational flow. Obviously, this equation is not suitable for a direct estimation of its validity range either.

An approach that clearly defines the relative magnitudes of the terms in the transonic equation is due to Guderley [4]. His derivation is closely connected with the transonic similarity rule. For a better physical understanding of this approach, we first derive the characteristic equations for transonic flow. Because the low supersonic range plays an important role in transonic flow, the equations governing low supersonic flow must also be satisfied by a transonic equation. Supersonic flow is described by a hyperbolic differential equation (Eq. 2.17b with the right-hand side set equal to zero, and, because $M_\infty > 1$, the coefficient of $\partial u/\partial x$ negative). The peculiarity of hyperbolic flow, namely, that flow disturbances (e.g., a deflection by a cone or a wedge) are felt only downstream of the disturbance and only in a well defined range, separated from the undisturbed approach flow by a discontinuity surface, has led to the development of the so-called method of characteristics. According to this method, the supersonic flow field may be computed through incremental steps, governed by two equations, the first one giving the direction of the discontinuity (or characteristic) as

$$\frac{dy}{dx} = \pm\left(\frac{a^2}{W^2 - a^2}\right)^{1/2} = \tan \mu \qquad (2.19)$$

where W is the magnitude of the approach flow vector in the x direction, a is the corresponding speed of sound, and μ is the so-called Mach angle. The second equation gives the relationship between the change in flow direction and the flow velocity at the characteristic as

$$d\theta = \pm\left(\frac{W^2 - a^2}{a^2}\right)^{1/2} \frac{dW}{W} \qquad (2.20)$$

where θ is the flow angle. This equation is sometimes called the compatibility equation.

These two equations have been derived in various ways, and the interested reader is referred to, refs. 3, 4, 6, for example.

Unfortunately, Eqs. 2.19 and 2.20 are very impractical in the transonic range, because they are quite inaccurate for small variations of $W/a = M$ near $M = 1$, where $(d\mu/dM)_{M=1} = (dW/d\theta)_{M=1} = \infty$. Therefore, small perturbation equations for $M \approx 1$ are introduced by setting $W = a^* + \Delta W$, where $(\Delta W)^2 \ll \Delta W \ll a^*$. Then with

$$a^2 = \frac{\gamma + 1}{2} a^{*2} - \frac{\gamma - 1}{2} W^2$$

(see Eq. 2.10), Eq. 2.19 becomes

$$\frac{dy}{dx} = \pm\left((\gamma + 1)\frac{\Delta W}{a^*}\right)^{-1/2} \qquad (2.19a)$$

and Eq. 2.20, after the small-perturbation transformation and integration, becomes

$$\frac{2}{3}(\gamma + 1)^{1/2}\left(\frac{\Delta W}{a^*}\right)^{3/2} \mp \theta = 0 \qquad (2.20a)$$

Remembering that Eqs. 2.19a and 2.20a have been derived for the purpose of establishing order-of-magnitude relationships between the perturbation velocities and their derivatives, it is expedient to introduce a small quantity τ that, raised to the proper power, is multiplied with the variables of these equations. Thus, all variables are of the order 1, but their magnitudes are expressed by the powers of τ. Now, the order of magnitude of the variables appearing in both equations certainly must be the same. Consequently, multiplying Eq. 2.19a by $\tau^{-1/2}$ and Eq. 2.20a by $\tau^{3/2}$ ($\tau < 1$), we obtain

$$\frac{d(y\tau^{-1/2})}{d(x\tau^0)} = \pm(\gamma + 1)^{-1/2}\left[\frac{(\Delta W\tau)}{a^*}\right]^{-1/2} \qquad (2.19b)$$

and

$$\frac{2}{3}(\gamma+1)^{1/2}\frac{(\Delta W\tau)^{3/2}}{a^{*3/2}} \mp (\theta\tau^{3/2}) = 0 \qquad (2.20b)$$

These equations for flow near $M_\infty = 1$ show that the solutions remain unchanged when, in Eqs. 2.19 and 2.20, the scales of θ, ΔW, and y are changed by $\tau^{3/2}$, τ, and $\tau^{-1/2}$, respectively. A similarity rule for the transonic method of characteristics has thus been established that must be satisfied by a generally valid transonic equation, and it will be seen now that a transonic potential $\bar{\phi}(\xi, \eta, \zeta)$ in a distorted coordinate system exists, so that

$$\phi = x_0 a^* \left[\frac{x}{x_0} + \tau\bar{\phi}(\xi, \eta, \zeta) \right] \qquad (2.21)[10]$$

where x_0 is an arbitrary reference length (e.g., the chord of a profile) and $\bar{\phi}$ is the dimensionless perturbation potential in the dimensionless coordinate system (ξ, η, ζ).

Since, in first approximation, ΔW is the perturbation velocity component u, and $a^*\theta$ is proportional to v ($W \sin \theta \approx a^*\theta$), the distortion rules of Eqs. 2.19b and 2.20b are satisfied by writing the velocity components in the (x, y, z) system, as derived from Eq. 2.21 as

$$\frac{\partial \phi}{\partial x} = a^* + u = a^* + x_0 a^* \frac{\partial \bar{\phi}}{\partial \xi}\frac{\partial \xi}{\partial x} = a^*\left(1 + \tau\frac{\partial \bar{\phi}}{\partial \xi}\right) = a^* + \tau\bar{u}(\xi, \eta, \zeta) \qquad (2.22a)$$

$$\frac{\partial \phi}{\partial y} = v = x_0 a^* \frac{\partial \bar{\phi}}{\partial \eta}\frac{\partial \eta}{\partial y} = a^*\tau^{3/2}\frac{\partial \bar{\phi}}{\partial \eta} = \tau^{3/2}\bar{v}(\xi, \eta, \zeta)$$

$$\frac{\partial \phi}{\partial z} = w = x_0 a^* \frac{\partial \bar{\phi}}{\partial \zeta}\frac{\partial \zeta}{\partial z} = a^*\tau^{3/2}\frac{\partial \bar{\phi}}{\partial \zeta} = \tau^{3/2}\bar{w}(\xi, \eta, \zeta) \qquad (2.22b)$$

where

$$\text{(a) } \xi = \frac{x}{x_0} \quad \text{(b) } \eta = \tau^{1/2}\frac{y}{x_0} \quad \text{(c) } \zeta = \tau^{1/2}\frac{z}{x_0} \qquad (2.23a,b,c)$$

Before drawing the final conclusion from Eqs. 2.22 and 2.23, the steps taken so far will be reviewed briefly. From the characteristic equations of supersonic flow (Eqs. 2.19 and 2.20), transonic characteristic equations (2.19a and 2.20a) are derived by introducing a small first-order perturbation quantity ΔW. The relative orders of magnitude of all the variables of these equations are then established by multiplying them by a small quantity τ^n, where n turns out to have a different value for each variable.[11] The variables themselves now become quantities of order 1. Finally it is shown that the potential equation Eq. 2.21 and the Eqs. 2.22 and 2.23 form a consistent system resulting from this procedure. It is only required of the quantity τ that it is small enough to be consistent with the small-perturbation assumption made earlier and no more can be said for the time being.

However, a physical meaning for τ can already be given: the geometry of a two-dimensional profile of chord c and maximum thickness h may be expressed as $y/c = hf(x)/c$, where $f(x)$ is a shape function ($0 \leq f(x) \leq 1$), and x, y are the coordinates of the profile contour. A streamline forming the contour is given as $dy/dx = v/(a^* + u) \approx v/a^*$. With Eq. 2.22b we finally have $h \sim \tau^{3/2}$ for profiles of the same $f(x)$ and c. The profile thickness, and consequently also the thickness ratio $t = h/c$, are of the order $\tau^{3/2}$. Thus, Eqs. 2.22 and 2.23 may be rewritten in terms of the thickness ratio t. The full significance of this result will be seen when the complete transonic similarity parameters are derived in Section 2.5.

We shall now complete the derivation of the transonic continuity equation of a flow in which τ is small enough to allow second-order terms to be neglected. For this purpose we introduce Eqs. 2.22 and 2.23 into the general continuity equation 2.11. The expressions $(a^2 - \phi_x^2)$, etc., are again evaluated using Eqs. 2.10 and 2.22, resulting in

$$a^2 - \phi_x^2 = -\tau(\gamma + 1)a^*\bar{u} + O(\tau^2) \quad (2.24a)$$

$$a^2 - \phi_y^2 = a^{*2} + O(\tau) \quad (2.24b)$$

$$a^2 - \phi_z^2 = a^{*2} + O(\tau) \quad (2.24c)$$

Further evaluating all required partial derivatives of Eq. 2.21, and again retaining only the lowest powers of τ, yields the transonic continuity equation for perturbations referred to a^*:

$$-(\gamma + 1)\frac{\partial \bar{\phi}}{\partial \xi}\frac{\partial^2 \bar{\phi}}{\partial \xi^2} + \frac{\partial^2 \bar{\phi}}{\partial \eta^2} + \frac{\partial^2 \bar{\phi}}{\partial \zeta^2} = 0 \quad (2.25a)$$

Comparing this equation with Eq. 2.18, the term $2v(\partial u/\partial y)$ is found to be negligible if the perturbation potential is expressed through Eqs. 2.21 to 2.23, where τ is a sufficiently small quantity. As was shown earlier, τ is directly related to the thickness ratio t of a flight article, and, therefore, Eq. 2.25 is valid for bodies sufficiently slender in the sense of the transonic similarity parameters to be discussed in Section 2.5.

The transonic potential equation may also be written as

$$-\phi_x\phi_{xx} + \phi_{yy} + \phi_{zz} = 0 \quad (2.25b)$$

here $x = \xi$, $y = (\gamma + 1)^{1/2}\eta$ and $z = (\gamma + 1)^{1/2}\zeta$.

Since they are based on perturbation velocities referred to a^*, Eqs. 2.25 are impractical for most applications where the approach Mach number is explicitly given. In these cases an equation that contains M_∞ is preferable. Such an equation may be derived from Eq. 2.17b by comparing the orders of magnitude of the terms $u(\partial u/\partial x)$ and $v(\partial u/\partial y + \partial v/\partial x)$. According to Eqs. 2.22 and 2.23, the former term is $\sim \tau^2$, whereas the latter two terms are $\sim \tau^3$ and may be dropped. Hence, the transonic equation assumes the form

$$(1 - M_\infty^2)\frac{\partial u}{\partial x} + \frac{\partial v}{\partial y} = M_\infty^2(\gamma + 1)\frac{u}{U}\frac{\partial u}{\partial x} \qquad (2.26)$$

The coefficient of $\partial u/\partial x$

$$1 - M_\infty^2\left(1 + (\gamma + 1)\frac{u}{U}\right)$$

will now be expressed by the local Mach number M. With $M_\infty = U/a_\infty$, $M = [(\bar{U}^2 + v^2)^{1/2}]/a$, where $\bar{U} = U + u$, $\varphi_x = u/U$, $\varphi_y = v/U$, the following equations are generally valid:

$$a^2 = \frac{\gamma + 1}{2}a^{*2} - \frac{\gamma - 1}{2}(\bar{U}^2 + v^2),$$

$$M^2 = \frac{U^2[(1 + \varphi_x)^2 + \varphi_y^2]}{\frac{\gamma + 1}{2}a^{*2} - \frac{\gamma - 1}{2}[U^2\{(1 + \varphi_x)^2 + \varphi_y^2\}]}$$

Dropping terms of order φ_x^2 and φ_y^2 in keeping with small-perturbation procedures results in

$$M^2 = \frac{U^2(1 + 2\varphi_x)}{\frac{\gamma + 1}{2}a^* - \frac{\gamma - 1}{2}U^2(1 + 2\varphi_x)} = \frac{U^2(1 + 2\varphi_x)}{\frac{\gamma + 1}{2}a^* - U^2\frac{\gamma - 1}{2} - U^2\left(\frac{\gamma - 1}{2}2\varphi_x\right)}$$

With the help of Eq. 2.10 in the form for the undisturbed flow field,

$$\frac{\gamma + 1}{2}a^* - \frac{\gamma - 1}{2}U^2 = a_\infty^2$$

we arrive at

$$M^2 = \frac{M_\infty^2(1 + 2\varphi_x)}{1 - M_\infty^2(\gamma - 1)\varphi_x}$$
$$= M_\infty^2(1 + 2\varphi_x)[1 + M_\infty^2(\gamma - 1)\varphi_x - \cdots]$$

and by dropping the terms φ_x^2 and rearranging, we have

$$M^2 \approx M_\infty^2[1 + (\gamma + 1)\varphi_x + (M_\infty^2 - 1)(\gamma - 1)\varphi_x]$$

For transonic flow, the last term is of order $(\varphi_x)^2$ because $M_1^2 - 1 \approx 2(M_\infty - 1)$, which is of the order of φ_x. Dropping this term, we finally arrive at

$$M^2 = M_\infty^2[1 + (\gamma + 1)\varphi_x] \qquad (2.27)$$

where we are justified in replacing the $\approx$ sign by the $=$ sign when the perturbation values are sufficiently small. Hence the transonic continuity equation may be written as

$$(1 - M^2)_{tr}\varphi_{xx} + \varphi_{yy} = 0 \tag{2.28a}$$

which, with Eq. 2.27 again gives Eq. 2.26:

$$[1 - M_\infty^2(1 + (\gamma + 1)\varphi_x)]\varphi_{xx} + \varphi_{yy} = 0 \tag{2.28b}$$

For $M_\infty = 1$ we have, in complete agreement with Eq. 2.25a,

$$-(\gamma + 1)\varphi_x\varphi_{xx} + \varphi_{yy} = 0$$

Equation 2.28a is occasionally found in the literature.

In concluding this section on transonic equations it must be emphasized that they are valid only within the validity range of the similarity parameter τ as established above, and the question is whether even within this basic validity range higher-order equations might improve the results. For this reason, second- and higher-order equations have been derived.

Before such derivations are given, the transonic oblique shock equations and the transonic similarity rules will be developed, to deepen our understanding of the small-perturbation concept and produce relationships that will be useful in the derivation of the higher-order theory.

2.4 Transonic Shock Relations

As has been pointed out previously, any transonic theory must describe the flow through a shock wave. We saw that Guderley based his derivation of the relative magnitudes of the perturbation velocities on the method of characteristics for flow near $M = 1$. Of course, the shock equation should be based on the same relative perturbation magnitudes. Following Guderley, the transonic shock equation is derived from the general shock relationship in an (x, y, z)-system:

$$W_{In} \cdot W_{IIn} = a^{*2} - \frac{\gamma - 1}{\gamma + 1}W_t^2 \tag{2.29}[12]$$

where the indices I and II designate the vectors before and behind the shock, and n and t the components normal and parallel to the shock. Without violating the generality of the derivation, we relate the perturbation velocities to the critical speed of sound:

$$W^2 = (a^* + u)^2 + v^2 + w^2$$

With Eq. 2.22 the transonic velocity vector becomes

$$\mathbf{W} = \mathbf{i}(a^* + \tau\bar{u}) + \mathbf{j}\tau^{3/2}\bar{v} + \mathbf{k}\tau^{3/2}\bar{w} \tag{2.30}$$

Let the equation of a general shock surface in the (ξ, η, ζ) system of Eqs. 2.22 and 2.23 be given as

$$f(\xi, \eta, z) = 0 \tag{2.31}$$

Then the unit vector normal to the shock in the undistorted (x, y, z) coordinates of Eqs. 2.29 and 2.30 becomes (with Eq. 2.23b)

$$\left(\mathbf{i}\frac{\partial f}{\partial \xi} + \mathbf{j}\tau^{1/2}\frac{\partial f}{\partial \eta} + \mathbf{k}\tau^{1/2}\frac{\partial f}{\partial \zeta}\right)\left\{\left(\frac{\partial f}{\partial \xi}\right)^2 + \tau\left[\left(\frac{\partial f}{\partial \eta}\right)^2 + \left(\frac{\partial f}{\partial \zeta}\right)^2\right]\right\}^{-1/2} \quad (2.32)$$

Since the component of the velocity vector **W** normal to the shock is given by the scalar product of the unit vector normal to the shock and the vector **W**, from Eqs. 2.30 and 2.32 we obtain

$$W_n = \frac{\left(\mathbf{i}\frac{\partial f}{\partial \xi} + \tau^{1/2}\mathbf{j}\frac{\partial f}{\partial \eta} + \tau^{1/2}\mathbf{k}\frac{\partial f}{\partial \zeta}\right)(\mathbf{i}(a^* + \tau\bar{u}) + \mathbf{j}\tau^{3/2}\bar{v} + \mathbf{k}\tau^{3/2}\bar{w})}{\frac{\partial f}{\partial \xi}\left|1 + \frac{\tau}{(\partial f/\partial \xi)^2}\left\{\left(\frac{\partial f}{\partial \eta}\right)^2 + \left(\frac{\partial f}{\partial \zeta}\right)^2\right\}\right|^{1/2}}$$

Expanding the denominator into a binominal series and retaining only the lowest-order terms yields

$$W_n = \tau\bar{u} + a^* \left|1 - \frac{\tau}{2}\frac{\left(\frac{\partial f}{\partial \eta}\right)^2 + \left(\frac{\partial f}{\partial \zeta}\right)^2}{\left(\frac{\partial f}{\partial \xi}\right)^2}\right| \quad (2.33)$$

This expression is valid before and behind the shock and corresponding indices may be attached to W_n and $\bar{u}$.

Following the same reasoning, the tangential component W_t is given by the magnitude of the *vector* product of Eqs. 2.30 and 2.32:[13] This vector product becomes:

$$\frac{\mathbf{i}\left[\tau^2\left(\frac{\partial f}{\partial \eta}\bar{w} - \frac{\partial f}{\partial \zeta}\bar{v}\right)\right] + \mathbf{j}\left[\tau^{1/2}(a^* + \tau\bar{u})\frac{\partial f}{\partial z} - \tau^{3/2}\bar{w}\frac{\partial f}{\partial \xi}\right] + \mathbf{k}\left[\tau^{3/2}\bar{v}\frac{\partial f}{\partial \xi} - \tau^{1/2}(a^* + \tau\bar{u})\frac{\partial f}{\partial \eta}\right]}{\frac{\partial f}{\partial \xi}\left[1 + \frac{\tau}{\left(\frac{\partial f}{\partial \xi}\right)^2}\left\{\left(\frac{\partial f}{\partial \eta}\right)^2 + \left(\frac{\partial f}{\partial \zeta}\right)^2\right\}\right]^{1/2}} \quad (2.34)$$

To form the magnitude of the vector we have to compute the square root of the sum of the squares of the three components. Again, expanding the denominator of Eq. 2.34 into a binomial series and retaining only the lowest-order terms, we obtain

$$W_t = \tau^{1/2}a^*\left[\frac{\left(\frac{\partial f}{\partial \eta}\right)^2 + \left(\frac{\partial f}{\partial \zeta}\right)^2}{\left(\frac{\partial f}{\partial \xi}\right)^2}\right]^{1/2} \quad (2.35)$$

The Theory of Inviscid Transonic Flow

Introducing Eqs. 2.33 and 2.35 into Eq. 2.29, and again retaining only lowest-order terms, a relation for the sum of the x-components of the velocity vectors before and behind the shock results:

$$\bar{u}_I + \bar{u}_{II} = \frac{2}{\gamma+1} a^* \frac{\left(\frac{\partial f}{\partial \eta}\right)^2 + \left(\frac{\partial f}{\partial \zeta}\right)^2}{\left(\frac{\partial f}{\partial \xi}\right)^2} \qquad (2.36)$$

Hence, the change of the x-component of the velocity vector across an oblique shock is given as

$$\Delta u = \tau(\bar{u}_{II} - \bar{u}_I) = \tau \left[-2\bar{u}_I + \frac{2}{\gamma+1} a^* \frac{\left(\frac{\partial f}{\partial \eta}\right)^2 + \left(\frac{\partial f}{\partial \zeta}\right)^2}{\left(\frac{\partial f}{\partial \xi}\right)^2} \right] \qquad (2.37)$$

To find the changes of the v- and w-components Δv and Δw, we should remember that the tangential component W_t remains unchanged across the shock ($W_{It} = W_{IIt}$). The Δv and Δw expressions can therefore be obtained from Δu by multiplying Δu with $-dx/dy$ and $-dx/dz$, respectively, as can be seen from Fig. 2.6. Also, between the components of the vectors $\mathbf{W}_I$ and $\mathbf{W}_{II}$ the following relationships are always true:

$$v_{II} \geq v_I \quad \text{and} \quad u_{II} \leq u_I$$

Applying the transformations Eqs. 2.22 and 2.23, the left-hand side of Eq. 2.37 yields

$$\Delta v = \tau^{3/2}(\bar{v}_{II} - \bar{v}_I) = \tau^{3/2}(\bar{u}_{II} - \bar{u}_I)\left(\frac{\partial f}{\partial \eta}\bigg/\frac{\partial f}{\partial \xi}\right) \qquad (2.38a)$$

$$\Delta w = \tau^{3/2}(\bar{w}_{II} - \bar{w}_I)\tau^{3/2}(\bar{u}_{II} - \bar{u}_I)\left(\frac{\partial f}{\partial \zeta}\bigg/\frac{\partial f}{\partial \xi}\right) \qquad (2.38b)$$

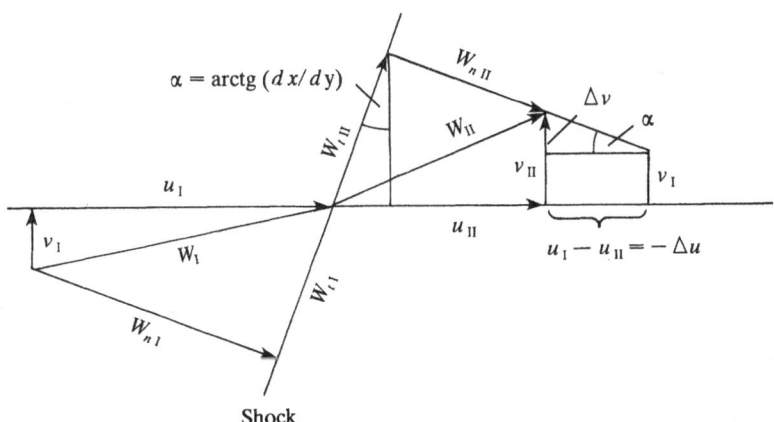

Fig. 2.6. Oblique shock relationships.

where the general chain rule for the three partial differentials of a function of two variables

$$\frac{\partial f}{\partial \xi}\frac{\partial \eta}{\partial f}\frac{\partial \xi}{\partial \eta} = -1$$

has been used.[14]

Finally, setting $\bar{v}_{II} - \bar{v}_I = \Delta \bar{v}$ and $\bar{w}_{II} - \bar{w}_I = \Delta \bar{w}$ and replacing the terms containing the partial differentials by means of Eq. 2.36 we obtain the equation of the *transonic shock polar*:

$$\frac{\sqrt{(\Delta \bar{v})^2 + (\Delta \bar{w})^2}}{a^*} = \sqrt{\frac{\gamma + 1}{2}} \sqrt{\frac{\bar{u}_I + \bar{u}_{II}}{a^*} \cdot \frac{\bar{u}_I - \bar{u}_{II}}{a^*}} \qquad (2.39)$$

It is important to realize that τ has dropped out of this equation (and most of the intermediate equations). This means that these equations are valid in the undistorted system and the bars over the u-, v-, w- components may be removed. The small number τ was used only to determine the relative magnitudes of the terms considered. Using the transonic shock polar however, requires that the basic assumptions of small perturbations of flow angularity and Mach number (deviation from $M = 1$) not be violated.

The important special case of the normal shock is obtained by setting $\Delta v = \Delta w = 0$. Since the flow direction remains unchanged across the shock, there is $v_I = v_{II}$ and $w_I = w_{II}$, confirming the assertion. Now, since the condition $u_I - u_{II} = 0$ can be true only for a flow without shock, the condition $\Delta v = \Delta w = 0$ is only satisfied for

$$(u_I + u_{II})_{\text{N.S.}} = 0 \qquad (2.40)$$

This is the transonic normal shock relation, which states that the flow velocity behind a transonic normal shock is as much lower than the critical speed of sound a^* as the flow before the shock is higher than a^*.

A few words must still be said about the above derivation of the transonic shock polar. It is based on the assumption that within the validity range of small perturbances the flow before the shock is at an arbitrary angle with the x direction, so that $W_I^2 = (a^* + u_I)^2 + v_I^2 + w_I^2$. In spite of this, both the correction term of Eq. 2.33 (second term in the brackets) and the expression for W_t (Eq. 2.35) do not depend on the incident flow velocity but only on the inclination of the shock wave. Referring to Fig. 2.8, it is seen that W_I may be turned and at the same time changed in magnitude without changing u_I, and thus the expressions Eqs. 2.33 and 2.35 for W_{In} and W_t remain unchanged. Thus, the shock polar Eq. 2.39 is unchanged, and it could have been derived from the general shock polar equation just by introducing the perturbation velocities and dropping terms of higher order. This result clearly shows the limitations of first-order perturbation equations, but it also shows the basic weakness of the above derivation in that no comparison is made between the magnitudes of the terms $\partial f/\partial \xi$, $\partial f/\partial \eta$, $\partial f/\partial \zeta$ and the parameter τ. For instance, if the flow is incident at an angle with the x direction, Eq. 2.36 does not give the result $u_I + u_{II} = 0$ for a normal shock, because it is not normal to the x direction and therefore the partial derivative $\partial f/\partial \xi$ is no longer infinite.

2.5 Similarity Rules

In Chapter 1 dimensionless numbers (Re, Pr, etc.) were introduced as a means for the application of results of one aerodynamic problem to others related by those numbers. For the same purpose, rules have been established that allow a similar coordination of problems solved by small-perturbation equations: These "similarity rules" are of particular importance for the treatment of nonlinear equations, because otherwise every problem would have to be computed individually, without recourse to known solutions. In this way the disadvantage of nonlinear equations in comparison to linear equations, for which new solutions are found through superposition of old solutions, is diminished.

In almost all aerodynamic problems the forces that act upon the surfaces of the article under consideration must be determined. Therefore, the pressure distribution on those surfaces must be found, that is, both the flow field and the boundary conditions are elements to be contained in similarity rules.

The application of similarity rules is indicated in all cases where a solution exists that can be translated into the solution of another problem, and particularly a more difficult problem. Thus, for a known pressure distribution on a given surface at a given approach Mach number (e.g., from wind tunnel measurements), the distribution on a different surface at a different Mach number may be obtained if the two surfaces are related in a definite way. Another important case might be the determination of a compressible flow field from the result of the computation of an incompressible flow field without the need for solving another more difficult equation.

We shall now derive the transonic similarity rule, step by step, applying three different methods. The rules for plane subsonic, supersonic, and transonic flow will be derived by the first method. Here, the individual steps are described in detail, and in particular, it will be shown that the geometric similarity and the similarity of the potential fields can be made compatible only by special means. Also, the requirements for the similarity of the body contours will be given in the most general form while introducing the very important source-sink method for the computation of flow fields about arbitrary bodies, which will be needed later in the book. The second method takes advantage of the findings of the first method and will be applied to the derivation of the similarity rules for axisymmetric subsonic and supersonic flow. A third method will be required to find a similarity rule for axisymmetric transonic flow, which cannot be obtained by the two other simpler methods.

2.5.1 Similarity Rules for Two-dimensional Subsonic and Supersonic Flows

By following Sauer [5], the first method will now be illustrated for the computation of a compressible flow field about two-dimensional profiles that are symmetric with respect to the x axis. Setting the right-hand side of Eq. 2.17b (the transonic correction) equal to zero, the linearized continuity equation for subsonic and supersonic (but not transonic) compressible flow is obtained as

$$\phi_{xx}(1 - M_\infty^2) + \phi_{yy} = 0 \tag{2.41}$$

where ϕ = the perturbation potential. For *incompressible* flow ($M_\infty \sim 0$) the Laplace equation

$$(\phi_i)_{x_i x_i} + (\phi_i)_{y_i y_i} = 0 \tag{2.42}$$

is obtained, for which standard solution methods are available.

By applying the so-called Prandtl–Glauert transformation of compressible flow,

$$x = x_i, \tag{2.43a}$$

$$y = y_i \frac{1}{\sqrt{1 - M_\infty^2}} = \frac{y_i}{\beta} \tag{2.43b}$$

we can transform Eq. 2.41 into the simpler Eq. 2.42. This transformation holds even for the additional assumption

$$\phi_i = \lambda \phi \tag{2.44}$$

resulting in the same Laplace equation. The need for the introduction of λ will become clear during further discussion.

With Eqs. 2.43 and 2.44, the relationships between the perturbation velocity components of an incompressible and a compressible flow, that can be evaluated through the Laplace equation become

$$u_i = \frac{\partial \phi_i}{\partial x_i} = \lambda \frac{\partial \phi}{\partial x} \frac{dx}{dx_i} = \lambda \frac{\partial \phi}{\partial x} = \lambda u$$

$$v_i = \frac{\partial \phi_i}{\partial y_i} = \lambda \frac{\partial \phi}{\partial y} \frac{dy}{dy_i} = \frac{\lambda}{\beta} \frac{\partial \phi}{\partial y} = \frac{\lambda}{\beta} v \tag{2.45a}$$

Consequently, the transformation of the flow angle ϑ is given as

$$\vartheta_i \approx \operatorname{tg} \vartheta_i = \frac{v_i}{U} = \frac{\lambda}{\beta} \frac{v}{U} = \frac{\lambda}{\beta} \operatorname{tg} \approx \frac{\lambda}{\beta} \vartheta \tag{2.45b}$$

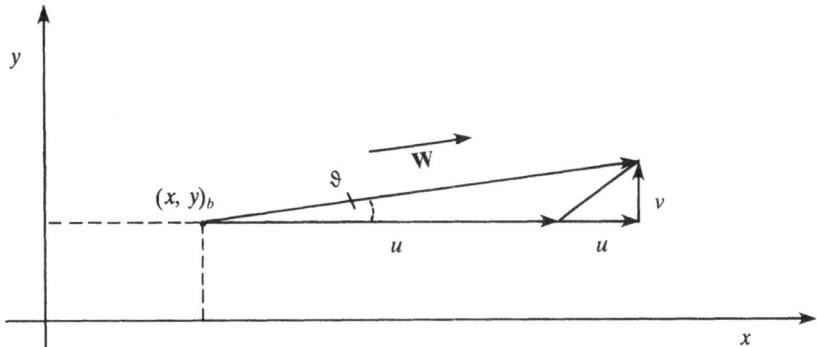

Fig. 2.7. Velocity vector **W** at station $(x, y)_b$ of the compressible flow field.

Here we have made the small-perturbation assumption $(U + u) \approx (U + u_i) \approx U$, where U is the approach velocity of the compressible flow that must be assumed for the incompressible flow to be equal, because U does not appear explicitly in Eqs. 2.41 and 2.42. Expressed differently, we deal with two different perturbation potentials in the same basic flow potential field, where $\partial \phi_\infty / \partial x = U = $ const.

What do the relationships Eqs. 2.42 through 2.45 tell us? Let us begin with a compressible flow field about a symmetric body. In Fig. 2.7, the flow vector **W**, its components, and the flow angle ϑ are shown at the body station $(x, y)_b$. With Eqs. 2.42 through 2.45 we obtain from this figure the corresponding Fig. 2.8, where β has been assumed to be 0.5 and λ to be 1. The transformed vector $\mathbf{W}_i$ is located at the point $(x_i, y_i)_{b?}$, which is the so-called "affine" point to the point $(x, y)_b$. The question mark behind the subscript b of the point $(x_i, y_i)_{b?}$ will be explained shortly.

Applying this procedure to every point of the equipotential lines of the compressible flow field, we obtain the transformed equipotential lines in the incompressible flow field. However, there remains the important

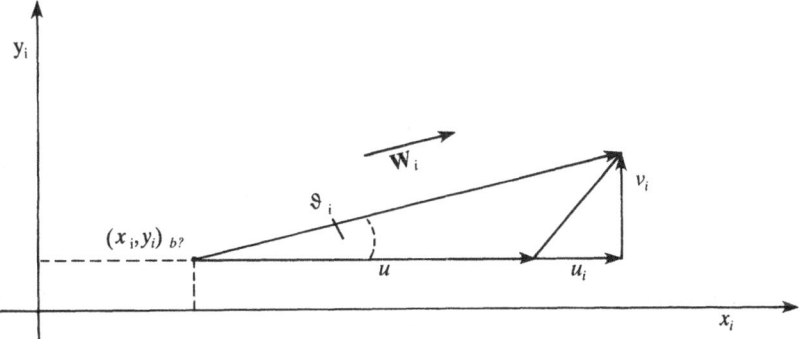

Fig. 2.8. Velocity vector **W** at the affine station $(x_i, y_i)_{b?}$ of the compressible flow field, transformed from the vector **W** of Fig. 2.7 ($\beta = 0.5$; $\lambda = 1$).

question: Are the *body surface stations* of Fig. 2.7 transformed into body surface stations in Fig. 2.8?

Since we assumed that the compressible flow vector **W** of Fig. 2.7 is tangent to the body surface at the station $(x, y)_b$, forming the flow components u and v and the flow angle ϑ, this question may be expressed in more detail as follows.

Are the flow vectors $\mathbf{W}_i$ of the incompressible flow field of Fig. 2.8 tangent to the affine contour of the body contour of the compressible flow field? In the case shown, with $\lambda = 1$ and $\beta = 0.5$, apparently not. If the points $(x_i, y_i)_{b?}$ formed a body contour, the flow angles ϑ_i of $\mathbf{W}_i$ would have to be smaller than ϑ, because transformation of the ordinates of the compressible body surface—which is a streamline—into the incompressible system according to Eq. 2.43 would result in a streamline forming a more slender body ($y_i < y$ and thus $\vartheta_i < \vartheta$). However, comparison of Figs. 2.7 and 2.8 shows that the opposite is true ($\vartheta_i > \vartheta$). Thus, this example with the special values of λ and β shows that all points of a given *equipotential line* of the compressible flow field are transformed into affine points lying on one and the same equipotential line in the incompressible flow field. The points of a *streamline* in the compressible flow field, however, may, as in this example, be transformed into points each of which is lying on a different streamline of the incompressible flow field. Therefore, the question arises whether there exist value pairs of λ and β for which both the equipotential and the streamlines are transformed from the compressible to the incompressible field. To answer this question, we shall express the perturbation potential ϕ as a function of the body shape and establish the desired values of λ and β, if they exist.

Such a computation may be done by applying the so-called source-sink method.[15] More will be said about this method in later chapters. Here it should suffice to explain its basic principle:

The potential of a source consists of concentric (two- or three-dimensional) equipotential lines (or surfaces). Superimposing this potential field on the potential field of an undisturbed parallel flow produces the potential field of the sought flow field about the body under consideration. Since the stream functions of the two flow fields are linear functions as well, they may also be superimposed, leading to a streamline pattern such as shown in Fig. 2.9, for example.

A stagnation point forms on the x axis at the station where the velocity of the source flow is equal in magnitude to, but reversed in sign from the approach velocity U. Downstream of this point a streamline pair symmetric to the flow axis develops, the value of their stream function being that of the approach flow on the x axis. In this way an inner and an outer flow field are formed. The streamlines separating these two flow fields can be assumed to be the surface of the body under consideration. The inner flow field has no physical meaning and is strictly a mathematical necessity to accomplish the goal of expressing the flow field about the

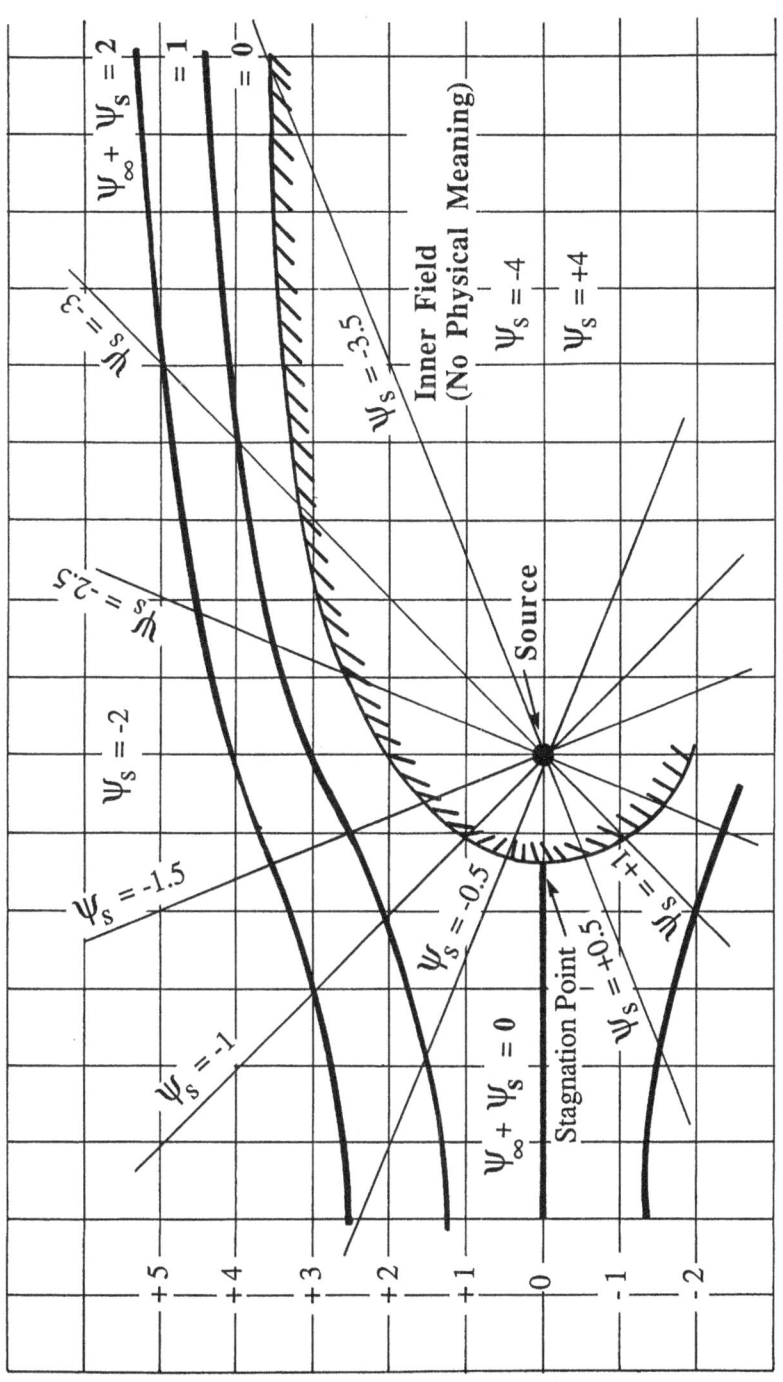

Fig. 2.9. Superposition of the stream functions (streamlines) of a parallel flow (ψ_∞) and an incompressible source flow (ψ_s). The resulting stream line $\psi_\infty + \psi_s = 0$ forms a stagnation point at which it separates into two branches, forming a blunt body contour. For the case of a compressible source, see Prob. 2.9.

body in a suitable way. It is easily seen that now that arranging a sink somewhat downstream of the source on the x axis, but of the same strength as the source, results in a closed body that is formed by the separating streamlines. Hence, any body shape may be generated by continuously distributing sources and skins on the centerline.

We now apply the source-sink method to the derivation of the conditions under which two flow fields about a given body are similar. Then the aerodynamic performance of the body in one flow field can be related directly to that of the other field through "similarity parameters." Since the evaluation of the incompressible (Laplace) equation (2.42) is simpler than that of the compressible equation (2.41), we derive the similarity parameters for these two cases, from which general parameters directly follow.

The potential of a source of two-dimensional incompressible flow must satisfy the Laplace equation. This is true for

$$\phi_i = \frac{1}{2\pi} Q \ln r \qquad (r^2 = x^2 + y^2) \qquad (2.46)[16]$$

where Q is the source strength and r is the distance from the source. Hence, a continuous source-sink distribution[17] between the stations a and b on the ξ_i-axis yields at the station x_i, y_i

$$\phi_i = \frac{1}{2\pi} \int_a^b q(\xi_i) \ln\sqrt{(x_i - \xi_i)^2 + y_i^2} \, d\xi_i \qquad (2.47)$$

where $q(\xi)$ is the source strength per unit length.

As Fig. 2.10 shows, the potential ϕ_i at the point (x_i, y_i) is the integral of all the infinitesimal contributions of the source function $q(\xi)$, where the value of r_i of Eq. 2.46 varies with ξ_i. By applying Eqs. 2.43 and 2.44 to Eq. 2.46, the corresponding equation for compressible flow becomes

$$\phi = \frac{1}{2\pi\lambda} \int_a^b q(\xi) \ln\sqrt{(x - \xi)^2 + \beta^2 y^2} \, d\xi \qquad (2.48)[18]$$

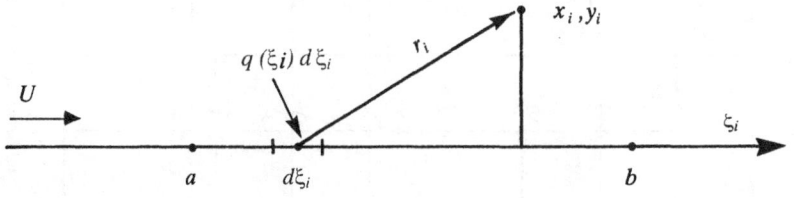

Fig. 2.10. The relationships of Eq. 2.54.

The Theory of Inviscid Transonic Flow

satisfying Eq. 2.41. Thus, the velocity components are

$$u = \frac{\partial \phi}{\partial x} = \frac{1}{2\pi\lambda} \int_a^b \frac{q(\xi)(x-\xi)}{(x-\xi)^2 + \beta^2 y^2} d\xi \tag{2.49a}$$

$$v = \frac{\partial \phi}{\partial y} = \frac{\beta^2 y}{2\pi\lambda} \int_a^b \frac{q(\xi)}{(x-\xi)^2 + \beta^2 y^2} d\xi \tag{2.49b}$$

We now make the usual approximation for the flow over two-dimensional slender bodies, namely, that the velocity components on the body surface may be assumed to be those on the centerline of the fictitious flow field within the body, as obtained by the superposition of the undisturbed flow field and the source-sink field. Hence, letting y go to zero in Eqs. 2.49 yields

$$u_b = u = \frac{1}{2\pi\lambda} \int_a^b \frac{q(\xi)}{x-\xi} d\xi, \qquad v_b = v_0 = \frac{1}{2\lambda} \beta q(x) \tag{2.50a,b}$$

Since limit operations of this kind are frequently required in the computations of source-sink problems, they will be given here in detail. The limit operation transforming Eq. 2.49a into Eq. 2.50a is straightforward. However, a word of caution is necessary. Since for $x = \xi$ the argument under the integral becomes infinite, the integral must be evaluated through its "principal value," given as

$$\int_a^b \frac{q(\xi) d\xi}{x - \xi} = \lim_{\varepsilon \to 0} \left[\int_a^{x-\varepsilon} \frac{q(\xi) d\xi}{x - \xi} - \int_{x+\varepsilon}^b \frac{q(\xi) d\xi}{\xi - x} \right] \tag{2.51}$$

The derivation of Eq. 2.50b from Eq. 2.49b is more involved. Here, because y stands in the numerator, it cannot be disregarded as being small with respect to $(x - \xi)$. The contributions to the value of v for $y \to 0$ become $\infty \times \int_a^b q(\xi) d\xi$ for $x = \xi$ and $0 \times \int_a^b [q(\xi)/(x-\xi)^2] d\xi$ for $x \neq \xi$ (i.e., indeterminate expressions) because the proper values of the integrals at these points are unknown. The way out of this dilemma is to replace ξ by a new variable η that does not create a singularity at $x = \xi$. This is accomplished by setting $\xi = x - \beta y \cot \eta$ ($\eta = \pi/2$ for $x = \xi$). Hence, $d\xi = (\beta y/\sin^2 \eta) d\eta$ and

$$(x - \xi)^2 + (\beta y)^2 = (\beta y)^2 (1 + \cot^2 \eta) = (\beta y)^2 (1/\sin^2 \eta) \tag{2.52}$$

This relationship between ξ and η is illustrated in Fig. 2.11. The introduction of the expressions of Eqs. 2.52 into Eq. 2.49b yields

$$v = \frac{\beta}{2\pi\lambda} \int_0^\pi q(\eta) d\eta \tag{2.53a}$$

Now, as Fig. 2.11 shows, for a fixed value of η, the $q(\eta)$-value approaches $q(\pi/2) = q(x)$ for $y \to 0$, and only $q(\xi \approx x)$-values contribute to the integral. Thus, $q(\eta)$ may be taken to have the constant value $q(x)$

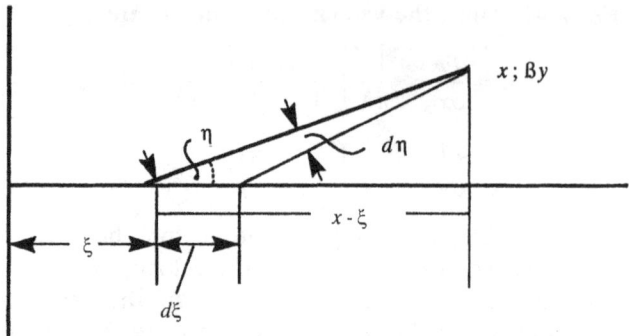

Fig. 2.11. The relationship between ξ and η of Eq. 2.59.

and may be set before the integral:[19]

$$v_0 = \frac{\beta}{\pi\lambda} \cdot q(\eta)_{\eta=\pi/2} \int_0^\pi d\eta = \frac{\beta}{2\lambda} q(n)_{\eta=\pi/2} = \frac{\beta}{2\lambda} q(x) \qquad (2.53b)$$

We are now in the position to determine the y-coordinate transformation of the body surface through which the surface becomes a streamline of the affine potential field obtained by the transformation of Eq. 2.43. To this end we introduce the body shape function $F_b(x) = y_b$. Since in the theory of slender, two-dimensional bodies the values of the velocity components on the body surface are assumed to be equal to those on the body centerline, it follows that

$$\frac{dy_b}{dx} = \frac{dF_b(x)}{dx} = \frac{v_0}{U+u} \approx \frac{v_0}{U} \qquad \text{(streamline equation)} \qquad (2.54)^{20}$$

By combining Eqs. 2.50b and 2.54 we obtain the source distribution in relation to the body shape function as

$$q(x) = \frac{2\lambda}{\beta} v_0 = \frac{2\lambda}{\beta} U \frac{dF_b(x)}{dx} \qquad (2.55)$$

Setting $\lambda = \beta$ in Eq. 2.55, the source distribution $q(x)$ no longer depends upon the approach Mach number. However, $q(x)$ is proportional to the approach Mach number and, consequently, the body shapes are equal and independent of the Mach number for equal $(q(x)/U)$-functions. Thus, we have found those values of λ through which an incompressible flow field is transformed into a compressible flow field about the same body. However, the pressure distributions are different on the two bodies, because, for $\lambda = \beta$, the small-perturbation pressure coefficient c_p is obtained from Eqs. 2.50 and 2.55 as

$$c_p = -\frac{2}{U} u_0 = -\frac{1}{\pi\beta} \int_a^b \frac{q(\xi)\,d\xi}{U(x-\xi)} = -\frac{2}{\pi\beta} \int_a^b \frac{dF_b(\xi)}{d\xi} \frac{d\xi}{(x-\xi)} \qquad (2.56a)^{21}$$

The Theory of Inviscid Transonic Flow

The pressure coefficients at the same bodies are proportional to $1/\beta$.

We now admit bodies of different thickness ratio t but the same shape function by setting $F_b(x) = tf_b(x)$. The shape function $f(x)$ is identical for the bodies under consideration, so that the integral in Eq. 2.56a becomes identical too when t is set before the integral. Thus we obtain c_p as a function of both β and t (where the invariant terms have been expressed through $f_1(x)$) as

$$c_p = \frac{t}{\beta}(f_1(x)) \tag{2.56b}$$

With this result we have obtained the first similarity rule: The pressure coefficients on the surfaces of two bodies (profiles) are equal for an equal quotient of the body thickness ratio and the function $(1 - M_\infty^2)^{1/2}$ of the approach Mach number.

Additional similarity rules can now be easily established. By introducing t into Eq. 2.55, setting $F_b(x) = tf_b(x)$. we obtain the most general expression for the source function $q(x)$:

$$q(x) = \frac{2\lambda t}{\beta} U \frac{df_b(x)}{dx} \tag{2.57}$$

Now $q(x)$ becomes independent of M_∞ for

$$\lambda t = \beta \quad \text{or} \quad \lambda = \frac{\beta}{t} \tag{2.58a,b}$$

Before we introduced the thickness ratio t into the equations, we based all our computations on the condition $\lambda = \beta$. This is now shown to be the condition $t = 1 = \text{const}$. Consequently, we had to deal with bodies of constant thickness ratio given as $F_b(x)$. On the other hand, in deriving Eq. 2.56b we obtained the rule for $\lambda = 1 = \text{const}$.

For $\lambda = 1$, the similarity of c_p in an incompressible and a compressible flow field requires that

$$\frac{t}{t_{inc}} = \frac{\sqrt{1 - M_\infty^2}}{1}$$

This relationship can be expressed in general form, in which the argument of the function f_p is to be held constant, as

$$c_p = f_p\left(\frac{t}{\sqrt{1 - M_\infty^2}}\right) \tag{2.59}$$

showing that for $t/\sqrt{1 - M_\infty^2} = \text{const.}$, c_p has the same value in a compressible flow field as in an incompressible field.

Finally, using the *general* expression Eq. 2.58b instead of setting $\lambda = 1$, we obtain, with Eq. 2.50a, the general form of the subsonic and supersonic similarity rule:

$$c_p = f_p\left(\frac{t^2\lambda^2}{1 - M_\infty^2}\right) \tag{2.60}$$

Here, the argument of the function f has been squared to eliminate the imaginary value of the square root at supersonic Mach numbers. Obviously this does not affect the equation, since if an expression is constant its square is also constant.

The generality of Eq. 2.60 can be shown immediately. Setting $\lambda^2 = 1 - M_\infty^2$, we obtain the rule Eq. 2.56, and by setting $\lambda^2 = 1$ the rule Eq. 2.59. Additional similarity rules may be established by replacing λ in Eq. 2.60 by any other combination of t and β.

So far, all derivations have been based on the comparison of compressible flow fields with an incompressible field, the potentials of which are related by $\lambda\phi = \phi_i$. For general similarity rules we must compare flow fields that are related by $\lambda_1\phi_1 = \lambda_2\phi_2$. There is no need for deriving the general similarity rule, Eq. 2.60, once more. It is obvious that Eq. 2.60 is valid in this case as well.

2.5.2 Similarity Rule for Two-dimensional Transonic Flow

So far, only the similarity rules for subsonic and supersonic flow have been established. These rules do not apply to transonic and hypersonic flow $(M_\infty > \sim 5)$. We are not concerned here with the latter case. However, it is necessary that we now try to establish similarity rules for transonic flow. We saw that in the subsonic and supersonic cases an arbitrary parameter λ is available, allowing the establishment of the most suitable rule for a given problem. But we shall see that this parameter must be given a specific value for the transonic rule.

Going back to Eq. 2.26 in the form

$$\frac{\partial^2 \phi_1}{\partial x_1^2} + \frac{\partial^2 \phi_1}{(1 - M_{\infty 1}^2)\partial y_1^2} = \frac{M_{\infty 1}^2}{U_1} \frac{(\gamma_1 + 1)}{(1 - M_{\infty 1}^2)} \frac{\partial \phi_1}{\partial x_1} \frac{\partial^2 \phi_1}{\partial x_1^2} \qquad (2.61)$$

we see that application of the transformations Eqs. 2.43a,b to this equation do not lead to the Laplace equation.

Before writing down the transformed equation, let us make a slight change in Eq. 2.44. As stated, similarity rules have to satisfy both the potential function and the boundary condition on the model, which requires that the body surface be formed by streamlines. In two-dimensional flow this condition is expressed by

$$\left(\frac{dy}{dx}\right)_b = \frac{v}{U+u} \approx \left(\frac{v}{U}\right)_b = \frac{(\partial\phi/\partial y)_b}{U}$$

This condition is a function of the approach velocity U. It seems, therefore, that in comparing two flow fields about a body the approach velocities have to be taken into account explicitly. This can be done by changing Eq. 2.44 into

$$\phi_1 \frac{\lambda_1}{U_1} = \phi_2 \frac{\lambda_2}{U_2} \qquad (2.62)$$

By applying Eqs. 2.43a,b and 2.62 to Eq. 2.61, we obtain

$$\frac{\partial^2 \phi_2}{\partial x_2^2} + \frac{1}{1-M_{\infty 2}^2}\frac{\partial^2 \phi_2}{\partial y_2^2} = \frac{\lambda_2}{\lambda_1}\frac{M_{\infty 1}^2}{1-M_{\infty 1}^2}\frac{U_1}{U_2}\frac{\gamma_1+1}{U_1}\frac{\partial^2 \phi_2}{\partial x_2^2}\frac{\partial \phi_2}{\partial x_2} \quad (2.63)$$

Comparison of Eq. 2.63 with Eq. 2.61 shows that these equations assume an identical form by setting

$$\frac{\lambda_2}{\lambda_1}\frac{(\gamma_1+1)M_{\infty 1}^2}{1-M_{\infty 1}^2} = \frac{(\gamma_2+1)M_{\infty 2}^2}{1-M_{\infty 2}^2} \quad (2.64a)$$

To bring this result again into the form of the similarity rules of Eqs. 2.59 and 2.60, we write Eq. 2.64a in the general form

$$\lambda = \frac{(\gamma+1)M_\infty^2}{1-M_\infty^2} \quad (2.64b)$$

We have obtained the important result that similarity of transonic flows can be established only by giving λ the specific value of Eq. 2.64b. The introduction of this equation into the general similarity rule, Eq. 2.60, yields

$$\frac{c_p(\gamma+1)M_\infty^2}{1-M_\infty^2} = f_p\left(\frac{t(\gamma+1)M_\infty^2}{(1-M_\infty^2)^{3/2}}\right) \quad (2.65a)^{22}$$

where the argument of the function f_p (Eq. 2.60) has been used in the unsquared form.

Equation 2.65a is the transonic similarity rule for two-dimensional flow. Accordingly, similarity is obtained for only one relationship between the thickness ratio t and the approach Mach number.

Because Eq. 2.61 is also valid for subsonic and supersonic flows, the rule Eq. 2.65a (and 2.65b) is valid over the whole Mach number range (except for hypersonic flow). However, because the right-hand side of Eq. 2.61 is only required in the transonic range, Eqs. 2.65a and b would be unnecessarily complicated, and the subsonic and supersonic rules should be used in the nontransonic cases (see also Prob. 2.6).

The form of the transonic similarity rule as given first by von Kármán may be obtained from Eq. 2.65a by considering that the argument of f_p is a constant, or $t(\gamma+1)M_\infty^2 = \text{const.} \times (1-M_\infty^2)^{3/2}$. Solving this expression for $1-M_\infty^2$ and substituting for the denominator of the left-hand side of Eq. 2.65a we obtain

$$\frac{c_p[(\gamma+1)M_\infty^2]^{1/3}}{t^{2/3}} = f_p\left[\frac{|1-M_\infty^2|}{[t(\gamma+1)M_\infty^2]^{2/3}}\right] = f_p(\chi) \quad (2.65b)$$

where the argument of f_p has been raised to the $-2/3$ power and the constant has been included in f_p.

2.5.3 Similarity Rules for Axisymmetric Subsonic and Supersonic Flows

In this section we shall show that in axisymmetric flow, *even when it is subsonic*, the parameter λ can no longer be chosen arbitrarily. Since, as we found in the previous chapter, the parameter λ has a specific value in transonic flow, we find ourselves in the dilemma of being short of one arbitrary parameter for the establishment of a similarity rule for axisymmetric transonic flow. A different approach is therefore required to solve this problem. But let us first derive the similarity rule for nontransonic flow.

In axisymmetric flow, the slender body assumption that the v-component on the body surface is equal to that at the body centerline is no longer possible, as explained in Fig. 2.12. This figure shows that the v-component of the source flow on the centerline is infinitely great and even the v-component of the flow over the surface of a slender body is strongly dependent upon the distance y from the centerline. Thus the points of the surface of the transformed body have to be both affine points of the surface points of the original body and points of a streamline whose v-components are no longer equal to the v-component at the centerline but are functions of the distance $y = tf(x)$.

We now follow a simplified method of establishing similarity rules through which the previously found rules could also have been derived. By this method (e.g., as applied by Liepmann and Roshko [6]), the equations of the streamlines in the two systems are compared and the potentials are multiplied with the yet unknown magnitudes λ.

The equation of the streamline through point y_1 in the first system is given as

$$\left(\frac{\partial \phi_1}{\partial y_1}\right)_{y_1 = t_1 f_1(x)} = U_1 t_1 \frac{df_1(x)}{dx} \tag{2.66a}$$

We also express the left-hand side of this equation in terms of the affine point y_2 with the help of Eq. 2.62, and of Eq. 2.43, which is valid for axisymmetric flow as well (see Prob. 2.20), arriving at

$$\left(\frac{\partial \phi_1}{\partial y_1}\right)_{y_1 = t_1 f_1(x)} = \frac{\lambda_2}{\lambda_1} \frac{U_1}{U_2} \sqrt{\frac{1 - M_{\infty 1}^2}{1 - M_{\infty 2}^2}} \left(\frac{\partial \phi_2}{\partial y_2}\right)_{y_2 = \sqrt{(1 - M_{\infty 1}^2/1 - M_{\infty 2}^2)} t_1 f_1(x)} \tag{2.66b}$$

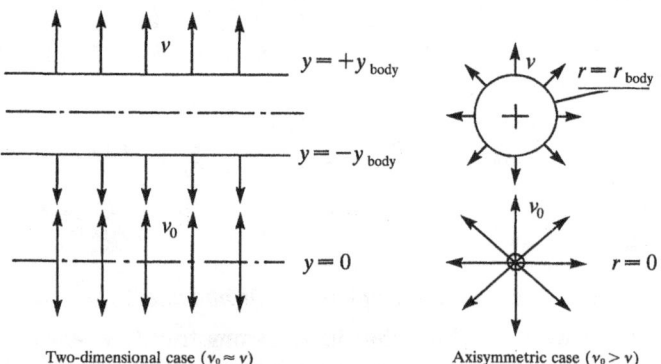

Fig. 2.12. Slender-body source flow, plane and axisymmetric cases.

The equation of the streamline through y_2 in the second system is given as

$$\left(\frac{\partial \phi_2}{\partial y_2}\right)_{y_2=t_2 f_2(x)} = U_2 t_2 \frac{df_2(x)}{dx} \tag{2.66c}$$

Now, to insure that the point y_2 in the second system is both affine to the point y_1 in the first system and lies on a streamline of the second system, we introduce Eq. 2.66b into Eq. 2.66a. With the previously established conditions $f_1(x) = f_2(x) = f(x)$ and $t_2/t_1 = \sqrt{(1-M_{\infty 1}^2)/(1-M_{\infty 2}^2)} = y_2/y_1$, because we compare affine points governed by Eq. 2.43, we obtain the following condition for λ with which the axisymmetric equations become similar:

$$t_1 f'(x) = \frac{\lambda_2}{\lambda_1} \sqrt{\frac{1-M_{\infty 1}^2}{1-M_{\infty 2}^2}} t_1 \sqrt{\frac{1-M_{\infty 1}^2}{1-M_{\infty 2}^2}} f'(x)$$

where $f'(x) = df(x)/dx$, and hence

$$\frac{\lambda_2}{\lambda_1} = \frac{1-M_{\infty 2}^2}{1-M_{\infty 1}^2}$$

or

$$\lambda = 1 - M_\infty^2 \tag{2.67}$$

By introducing Eq. 2.67 into the general similarity law Eq. 2.60, we obtain

$$c_p = \frac{1}{1-M_\infty^2} f_p(t\sqrt{1-M_\infty^2}) \tag{2.68}$$

This is the so-called Goethert rule, which is valid for both two-dimensional and axisymmetric flow. In words: By holding the product of body thickness ratio t and the function of Mach number $\sqrt{1-M_\infty^2}$ constant, the pressure coefficients on two similar bodies are inversely proportional to $1-M_\infty^2$.

2.5.4 Similarity Rules for Axisymmetric Transonic Flow

Since specific values of the parameter λ had to be given both to two-dimensional transonic flow and to axisymmetric compressible flow, a similarity rule for axisymmetric transonic flow cannot be established through the procedures discussed in the previous chapters. However, Oswatitsch and Berndt [7] succeeded in deriving a transonic similarity rule for axisymmetric slender bodies. In this method, first the contours (i.e., the *streamline* equations) of the similar bodies are established as

$$[y_1(\phi_1)_{y_1}(x, y_1)] = \frac{1}{2\pi} S_1'(x) \tag{2.69a}$$

$$[y_2(\phi_2)_{y_2}(x, y_2)] = \frac{1}{2\pi} S_2'(x) \tag{2.69b}$$

They are brought into compliance with the slender-body condition

$$\lim_{y \to 0} (y \cdot \phi_y) = \frac{S'}{2\pi} \tag{2.70}$$

Thus, the important assumption is made that the product of the distance y from the axis and the velocity component v is constant and proportional to the change with x of the body cross section for all points $x = $ const. within the slender-body validity range (see Eqs. 2.98b, 5.29 and 5.30).

Then, the original transonic differential equation

$$(1 - M_{\infty 1}^2)(\phi_1)_{xx} + (\phi_1)_{y_1 y_1} + \frac{1}{y_1}(\phi_1)_{y_1} = M_{\infty 1}^2 (\gamma_1 + 1)(\phi_1)_x (\phi_1)_{xx}$$

is transformed into an identical equation at a different Mach number by setting (see Eqs. 2.43)

$$y_1 = \frac{\beta_2}{\beta_1} \bar{y}_2 \qquad x_1 = x_2 = x \qquad \text{where } \beta = \sqrt{1 - M_\infty^2} \tag{2.71}^{23}$$

and in addition

$$\bar{\phi}_2(x, \bar{y}_2) = \frac{\beta_2^2}{\beta_1^2} \frac{\gamma_1 + 1}{\gamma_2 + 1} \frac{M_{\infty 1}^2}{M_{\infty 2}^2} \phi_1(x, y_1) \tag{2.72}$$

as can easily be verified.

These transformations are called *affine* because they transform one *potential* field into another, governed by the same differential equation, which leads to the same solution.

The slender-body condition, Eq. 2.70, now allows us to compute the relationship between $S_1'(x)$ and $S_2'(x)$. We first express the left-hand side of Eq. 2.69a in the *affine* system through Eqs. 2.71 and 2.72. Because of Eq. 2.70, the term $\bar{y}_2(\bar{\phi}_2)_{\bar{y}_2}$, included in the result, is equal to $y_2(\phi_2)_{y_2}$, and we can replace it by $S_2'(x)/2\pi$. Integration with respect to x results in the sought relationship between $S_1(x)$ and $S_2(x)$:

$$S_2(x) = \frac{\beta_2^2}{\beta_1^2} \frac{M_{\infty 1}^2 (\gamma_1 + 1)}{M_{\infty 2}^2 (\gamma_2 + 1)} S_1(x) \tag{2.73}$$

With $S(x) = \pi t^2 f(x)^2$, where the shape function $f(x)$ is the same for both contours, the radii of the two bodies are related as

$$r_2(x) = \frac{\beta_2}{\beta_1} \sqrt{\frac{M_{\infty 1}^2 (\gamma_1 + 1)}{M_{\infty 2}^2 (\gamma_2 + 1)}} r_1(x) = \frac{t_2}{t_1} r_1(x) \tag{2.74}$$

In analogy to the previously treated similarity cases, we have thus established the similarity parameter for axisymmetric transonic flow as

$$\frac{\beta}{t\sqrt{\gamma + 1} M_\infty} = \text{const.} \qquad \begin{pmatrix} \text{Similarity parameter} \\ \text{for axisymmetric} \\ \text{transonic flow} \end{pmatrix} \tag{2.75}$$

The Theory of Inviscid Transonic Flow

This result has been obtained through the equality of the product $y \cdot \phi_y$ of the similar and affine body. However, there may be a difference in the values of ϕ on the surfaces of the two bodies. This problem, which was overcome in establishing the previous similarity rules by finding a suitable potential field through the parameter λ, is solved here by determining the change in the potential in going on the line $x = \text{const.}$ from the affine contour to that given by the similarity rule.

Because the value of $(\phi)_x(x, r)$ is of particular interest as determining the pressure coefficient for slender, axisymmetric bodies

$$c_p(x, r) = -2(\phi)_x(x, r) - [r'(x)]^2, \tag{2.76}[24]$$

the transition from the affine $\bar{\phi}$ (Eq. 2.72) to ϕ of the similar body will now be derived for ϕ_x. This is done by differentiating Eq. 2.69b with respect to x and then integrating it from $\bar{r}_2$ to r_2 with respect to y, yielding

$$(\phi_2)_x(x, r_2) = (\phi_2)_x(x, \bar{r}_2) + \frac{1}{2\pi} S_2''(x) \ln \frac{r_2}{\bar{r}_2} \tag{2.77}$$

Hence, $(\phi_2)_x(x, r_2)$ is obtained in terms of the values of the original body from Eqs. 2.71 and 2.72 ($\bar{y}_2 = \bar{r}$), and from Eq. 2.74 as

$$(\phi_2)_x(x, r_2) = \frac{\beta_2^2}{\beta_1^2} \frac{M_{\infty 1}^2(\gamma_1 + 1)}{M_{\infty 2}^2(\gamma_2 + 1)}$$

$$\times \left[(\phi_1)_x(x, r_1) + \frac{1}{2\pi} S_1''(x) \ln\left(\frac{\beta_2^2}{\beta_1^2} \sqrt{\frac{M_{\infty 1}^2(\gamma_1 + 1)}{M_{\infty 2}^2(\gamma_2 + 1)}}\right) \right] \tag{2.78}$$

Finally, by expressing $c_{p_2}(x, r_r) = -2(\phi_2)_x(x, r_2) - (r_2'(x))^2$ in terms of the original potential and geometry through Eqs. 2.78 and 2.74, and then replacing $2(\phi_1)_x(x, r_1)$ by $(-c_{p1}(x, r_1) - [r_1'(x)]^2)$, the terms containing r cancel out and the pressure coefficient of the second body becomes

$$c_{p_2}(x, r_2) = \frac{t_2^2}{t_1^2} \left[c_{p_1}(x, r_1) + \frac{1}{\pi} S_1''(x) \ln\left(\frac{\beta_1 t_1}{\beta_2 t_2}\right) \right] \tag{2.79}$$

By expressing β_1/β_2 through the similarity parameter Eq. 2.75 and setting $(t_2^2/t_1^2) S_1''(x) = S_2''(x)$ from Eq. 2.74, we have

$$c_{p_2}(x, r_2) = \frac{t_2^2}{t_1^2} \left[c_{p_1}(x, r_1) + \frac{1}{\pi} S_1''(x) \ln\left(\frac{t_1^2}{t_2^2} \sqrt{\frac{M_{\infty 1}^2(\gamma_1 + 1)}{M_{\infty 2}^2(\gamma_2 + 1)}}\right) \right]$$

$$= \frac{t_2^2}{t_1^2} \left[c_{p_1}(x, r_1) + \frac{1}{\pi} S_1''(x) \ln(t_1^2 \sqrt{M_{\infty 1}^2(\gamma_1 + 1)}) \right]$$

$$- \frac{1}{\pi} S_2'' \ln(t_2^2 \sqrt{M_{\infty 2}^2(\gamma_2 + 1)}) \tag{2.80}$$

This equation was obtained through the introduction of the similarity parameter. It is completely symmetrical and may now be expressed like the previous similarity rules as

$$c_p + \frac{1}{\pi}S''(x)\ln(\beta t) = t^2 fp\left(\frac{\sqrt{|M_\infty^2 - 1|}}{t\sqrt{\gamma + 1}}\right). \tag{2.81}$$

In words: When $\sqrt{|M_\infty^2 - 1|}/t\sqrt{\gamma + 1}$ is kept constant, the expressions $c_p + (1/\pi)S''(x)\ln(\beta t)$ are related to each other as the squares of the thickness ratios of the models. For a *conical* model with the semiapex angle θ we set

$$t = \tan\theta = \theta \quad \text{and} \quad S(x) = \pi(x\tan\theta)^2$$

leading to

$$S''(x) = 2\pi\tan^2\theta \approx 2\pi\theta^2$$

Hence

$$\frac{c_p}{\theta^2} + 2\ln(\beta \cdot \theta) = fp\left[\frac{\sqrt{|M_\infty^2 - 1|}}{\theta\sqrt{\gamma + 1}}\right] \tag{2.82}$$

For $\gamma = \text{const.}$ the similarity parameter becomes $\beta/\theta = \text{const.}$ and, consequently, $\ln(\beta/\theta)$ is equal in both systems, so that

$$\frac{c_p}{\theta^2} + 4\ln\theta = fp\left(\frac{|1 - M_\infty^2|}{\theta^2}\right) \tag{2.83}$$

In words: For $|1 - M_\infty^2|/\theta^2 = \text{const.}$, the pressure coefficients of two models are related as:

$$\frac{c_{p1}}{\theta_1^2} + 4\ln\theta_1 = \frac{c_{p2}}{\theta_2^2} + 4\ln\theta_2 \tag{2.84}$$

2.6 Solutions Through Asymptotic Expansions

The method of asymptotic expansions has recently become an important tool in treating problems governed by small perturbations and must be discussed briefly. However, to maintain the continuity of this book, we first derive higher-order transonic equations without the formal definition of this method, because it will help to convey to the reader some insight into the basic thinking that has led to the asymptotic methods briefly described in Section 2.6.2.

2.6.1 Higher-order Transonic Equations

This derivation of higher-order equations is based on the paper of Cole and Messiter [8]. Guderley [4, section 2.3] established the first-order relationships between the perturbation velocities through the small magnitude τ that had to be raised to different powers for the x- and the y- and z-components to satisfy the characteristics equation and thus the shock equation near $M_\infty = 1$. Similarly, we now ask ourselves, what relationships have to be established between the first-order *and* higher-order perturbation velocities to satisfy the relationships essential in transonic flow.

We begin with the *general* continuity equation, which can be written in vector notation as

$$a^2 \operatorname{div} \mathbf{W} = \mathbf{W}\nabla \frac{W^2}{2} \tag{2.85}$$

where a = the sonic speed and

$$\mathbf{W} = \mathbf{i}\bar{U} + \mathbf{j}v' + \mathbf{k}w' \tag{2.86}$$

To conduct the following study for axisymmetric flow,[25] we introduce the radial perturbation velocity $v = \sqrt{v'^2 + w'^2}$ into Eq. 2.85 and obtain

$$a^2\left(\frac{\partial \bar{U}}{\partial x} + \frac{\partial v}{\partial y} + \frac{v}{y}\right) = \left(\bar{U}\frac{\partial}{\partial x} + v\frac{\partial}{\partial y}\right)\left(\frac{U^2}{2} + \frac{v^2}{2}\right) \tag{2.87}$$

First-order and higher-order perturbation velocities are now introduced, by setting

$$\frac{\bar{U}}{U} = 1 + \varepsilon_1(t)u_1 + \varepsilon_2(t)u_2 + \cdots$$

$$\frac{v}{U} = v_1(t)v_1 + v_2(t)v_2 + \cdots \tag{2.88}$$

where $\bar{U} = U + u$, and v are functions of x, $\tilde{y}$, M_∞, t; and $u_1, u_2 \ldots$ and $v_1, v_2, \ldots$ are functions of x, $\tilde{y}$, and an arbitrary parameter K that will be introduced later. The coordinate $\tilde{y}$ is defined through the thickness ratio t of the body as

$$\tilde{y} = t^\alpha y \tag{2.89}$$

where the exponent α makes the distortion function, to be specified later, as general as possible.

This Prandtl–Glauert distortion of y is required to assure that the perturbation components u_i and v_i are of the order 1, independent of compressibility effects. Usually, the Prandtl–Glauert distortion is expressed through the term $1 - M_\infty^2$. However, as we saw in the previous chapter on the similarity rules, $1 - M_\infty^2$ and the thickness ratio t are uniquely interrelated, and the form of Eq. 2.89 will prove to be more suitable for the following derivations. The expansion parameters ε_i and v_i are decreasing sequences, so that $\lim_{t \to 0}[\varepsilon_{n+1}(t)/\varepsilon_n(t)] \to 0$, and correspondingly for the vs (see note 34).

So far, all our considerations of this chapter have been completely general. We now take the first step in establishing relationships between ε, v, t, and α for transonic flow by determining the shock polar[26] for transonic flow, that is, for $M_\infty \approx 1$. The general shock relation is (see, e.g., ref. 5)

$$\frac{(v^{(II)} - v^{(I)})^2}{a^{*2}} = \frac{(\bar{U}^{(I)} - \bar{U}^{(II)})^2}{a^{*2}} \cdot \frac{\frac{\bar{U}^{(I)}\bar{U}^{(II)}}{a^{*2}} - 1}{\frac{2}{\gamma + 1}\left(\frac{\bar{U}^{(I)}}{a^{*2}}\right)^2 - \frac{\bar{U}^{(I)}\bar{U}^{(II)}}{a^{*2}} + 1}$$

where the superscripts (I) and (II) stand for the conditions before and behind the shock, respectively.

By introducing Eqs. 2.88, and with $U \approx a^*$ for $M_\infty \approx 1$, we obtain by retaining terms containing ε_1 and v_1 only:

$$v_1^2(v_1^{(II)} - v_1^{(I)})^2 + \cdots = \varepsilon_1^2(u_1^{(I)} - u_1^{(II)})^2 \frac{1 + \varepsilon_1(u_1^{(I)} + u_1^{(II)} + \cdots) - 1}{\frac{2}{\gamma + 1}(1 + \cdots) - 1 + \cdots + 1}$$

$$= \varepsilon_1^3(u_1^{(I)} - u_1^{(II)})^2(u_1^{(I)} + u_1^{(II)}) \frac{\gamma + 1}{2} \quad (2.90)$$

Because Eq. 2.90 would be reduced to an equation of one variable only if ε_1^3 and v_1^2 were of different orders, we must set

$$v_1^2 = \varepsilon_1^3 \quad (2.91)$$

In this way Eq. 2.90 becomes identical to Eq. 2.39, as we should expect since both Eq. 2.90 and Eq. 2.39 are first-order equations. Thus we have established a first relationshop between the expansion parameters.

By introducing Eq. 2.88 into Eq. 2.87, replacing v_1 by $\varepsilon_1^{3/2}$ according to Eq. 2.91, and setting

$$\frac{a^2}{U^2} = \frac{a_\infty^2}{U^2} + \frac{\gamma - 1}{2}\left(1 - \frac{\bar{U}^2 + v^2}{U^2}\right) \quad \text{(see Eq. 2.10)}$$

the axisymmetric transonic continuity equation in the general form of the small perturbation expansion becomes

$$\left[\frac{1}{M_\infty^2} - (\gamma - 1)(\varepsilon_1 u_1 + \varepsilon_2 u_2) - \frac{\gamma - 1}{2}\varepsilon_1^2 u_1^2 - \cdots\right]\left[\varepsilon_1 \frac{\partial u_1}{\partial x} + \varepsilon_2 \frac{\partial u_2}{\partial x} + \cdots\right.$$

$$\left. + \varepsilon_1^{3/2} t^\alpha\left(\frac{\partial v_1}{\partial \bar{y}} + \frac{1}{\bar{y}}v_1\right) + v_2 t^\alpha\left(\frac{\partial v_2}{\partial \bar{y}} + \frac{1}{\bar{y}}v_2\right) + \cdots\right]$$

$$= \left[(1 + \varepsilon_1 u_1 + \varepsilon_2 u_2 + \cdots)\frac{\partial}{\partial x} + \varepsilon_1^{3/2} t^\alpha v_1 \frac{\partial}{\partial \bar{y}}\right]\left[\frac{1}{2} + \varepsilon_1 u_1 + \varepsilon_2 u_2 + \varepsilon_1^2 \frac{u_1^2}{2}\right.$$

$$\left. + \varepsilon_1 \varepsilon_2 u_1 u_2 + \frac{\varepsilon_2^2}{2} u_2^2 + \cdots + \frac{\varepsilon_1^3 v_1^2}{2} + \varepsilon_1^{3/2} v_2 v_1 v_2 + \cdots\right] \quad (2.92)$$

Equation 2.92 contains all terms needed for first- and second-order approximations. Now, the relationships between v_1, v_2, ε_2, t and α must be established.

We first consider the special case of $M_\infty = 1$. Here the lowest-order terms, those containing only ε_1, cancel out, and the next higher-order terms are

$$\varepsilon_1^{3/2} t^\alpha \left(\frac{\partial v_1}{\partial \bar{y}} + \frac{v_1}{\bar{y}} \right) = \varepsilon_1^2 (\gamma + 1) u_1 \frac{\partial u_1}{\partial x}$$

Again, this equation would degenerate into an equation of only one variable if $\varepsilon_1^{3/2} t^\alpha$ and ε_1^2 were of different order. Thus, we have to assume a second relationship between the expansion parameters:

$$\varepsilon_1^{3/2} t^\alpha = \varepsilon_1^2 \quad \text{or} \quad \varepsilon_1^{1/2} = t^\alpha \tag{2.93}$$

By introducing Eq. 2.93 into the preceding equation we obtain

$$\left(\frac{\partial v_1'}{\partial \bar{y}} + \frac{v_1}{\bar{y}} \right) = (\gamma + 1) u_1 \frac{\partial u_1}{\partial x} \tag{2.94}$$

Note that the derivation of Eq. 2.94 has been independent of the particular coordinate system chosen. The same relationships between expansion parameters would have been obtained for the plane flow equations, since the y-component of div $\mathbf{W}$ remained unchanged during the derivation. Hence, the first-order equation for plane flow is obtained from Eq. 2.94 by dropping the second term on left-hand side, and we have

$$\frac{\partial v_1'}{\partial \bar{y}} = (\gamma + 1) u_1 \frac{\partial u_1}{\partial x}$$

This is exactly the plane-flow version of Eq. 2.24, and two different avenues of derivation have led to the same equation. In Guderley's approach, all three distortion parameters (for y, u, and v) are found from one mathematical procedure, namely, the method of characteristics for Mach numbers close to 1. In the present approach, the geometric (y) distortion parameter has been established by assuming the Prandtl–Glauert rule to be valid at $M = 1$, an assumption which is justified because Eqs. 2.89 and 2.23b are equivalent for $\tau^{3/2} = t$ (see page 41) and the plane flow value $\alpha = 1/3$ (see Eq. 2.101a). For the velocity components, the distortion parameters have been found from the transonic shock equation which does not contain geometric variables.

The reason that both approaches lead to the same first-order equation lies in the fact that in the limit $M = 1$ the characteristics become normal shocks of zero strength, and for $M \approx 1$ the characteristics and the oblique shocks are equal in the first approximation. This may be seen by expressing Eq. 2.90 in terms of the small-perturbation relationships $W = a^* + \Delta W \approx \bar{U}$ and $v \approx a^* \theta$ of Section 2.3. Then, with Eq. 2.88 (setting $U = a^*$), we have

$$\varepsilon_1 u_1 = \frac{\bar{U} - a^*}{a^*} = \frac{\Delta W}{a^*}, \quad v_1 v_1 \approx \frac{v}{a^*} = \theta$$

and thus

$$v_1(v_1^{(II)} - v_1^{(I)}) = d\theta$$
$$\varepsilon_1(u_1^{(I)} - u_1^{(II)}) = (\Delta W^{(I)} - \Delta W^{(II)})/a^* = d(\Delta W)/a^*$$
$$\varepsilon_1(u_1^{(I)} + u_1^{(II)}) = (\Delta W^{(I)} + W^{(II)})/a^* \approx 2\Delta W/a^*.$$

Hence, with Eq. 2.91, Eq. 2.90 becomes the compatibility equation in the differential form (Eq. 2.20b before integration).

Knowledge of the value of the exponent α was not required for the derivation of the first-order transonic equations. However this exponent must be specified for the transformation of the results of these equations from the $(x, \bar{y})$-system into the (x, y)-system. As in the derivations of the similarity rules of the previous chapter, we apply the condition of tangential flow on the body surface to the determination of this stretching parameter of the y-component.

The equation of the streamline forming the body surface is given as

$$\frac{dy}{dx} = tf'(x) = \frac{v(x, tf)}{\bar{U}(x, tf)} \tag{2.95a}$$

where $f(x)$ again is the universal body shape function.

With the expansions of Eqs. 2.88a and b, this equation becomes

$$\varepsilon_1^{3/2} v_1(x, t^{\alpha+1}f) + v_2 v_2(x; t^{\alpha+1}f) + \cdots$$
$$= [1 + \varepsilon_1 u_1(x, t^{\alpha+1}f) + \cdots] \cdot tf'(x) \tag{2.95b}$$

where

$$\bar{y}_{body} = tf \cdot t^\alpha = ft^{\alpha+1}. \tag{2.96}$$

At this point the plane flow and the axisymmetric cases must be treated differently. To satisfy Eq. 2.95b for $y \to 0$, the principles of slender-body theory may be applied, where it is assumed that the partial differentials $\partial u/\partial x$ on the body surface are small compared with the partial differentials $\partial v/\partial y$ and $\partial w/\partial z$.[27]

Of course, by this rule the transonic correction term of Eq. 2.26 disappears and the solutions for subsonic and transonic slender body flows become identical. Therefore, in reducing Eq. 2.25a to

$$\varphi_{\bar{y}\bar{y}} + \varphi_{\bar{z}\bar{z}} = 0 \tag{2.97}[28]$$

where η and ζ have been replaced by $\bar{y}$ and $\bar{z}$, respectively, only first-order terms are obtained for the following transonic analysis. However, this will prove sufficient for the determination of the magnitude of α, which means that the expansion coefficients ε_1, v_1, and α are valid for both subsonic and transonic flow.

In the plane flow case the integration of Eq. 2.97 with $\varphi_{\bar{z}} = 0$ yields $v_1 = \tilde{S}(x)$. The arbitrary function of integration must be a function of x because the differential equations are approximation of equations in x, $\bar{y}$ (and $\bar{z}$). This result is in agreement with the usual formulation of plane slender-body flow that the y-component of the flow vector on any body

The Theory of Inviscid Transonic Flow

surface station (x, y_b) is equal to the value at the station $(x, 0)$, and we write

$$v_1 = (v_1)_{y=0} = (v_1)_0(x) = \tilde{S}(x) \qquad (2.98a)$$

Now, in the axisymmetric case we set $u_1(\partial u_1/\partial x) = 0$ in Eq. 2.94. Integration of the resulting linear equation leads to

$$\ln v_1 = -\ln \tilde{y} + \ln \tilde{S}(x) \quad \text{or} \quad v_1 \tilde{y} = \tilde{S}(x) \qquad (2.98b)$$

Here, for $\tilde{y} \to 0$ it seems that we would have $\tilde{S}(x) = 0$, resulting in $v_1 = 0$ for $\tilde{y} \neq 0$. To obtain a meaningful result, we therefore must require that $\lim_{y \to 0} (v_1 \tilde{y}) = \tilde{S}(x)$, and Eq. 2.98b becomes the slender-body condition for axisymmetric flow.

From the derivation of the similarity rules of Sec. 2.5 we conclude that $\tilde{S}$ is directly related to the source distribution function which produces the profile contour as a streamline. A corresponding relationship is found for $\tilde{S}$ of an axisymmetric body. This relationship between $\tilde{S}(x)$, the source strength $q(x)$, and the body cross sectional area $S(x)$ is derived in Sec. 5.2.1.

Now we are ready to determine the value of α. By introducing Eqs. 2.98a and b, respectively, into Eq. 2.95b, and retaining the lowest-order terms only, the streamline equations become

$$\varepsilon_1^{3/2} \tilde{S}_1(x) \sim tf'(x) \qquad \text{(plane flow)} \qquad (2.99a)$$

and

$$\varepsilon_1^{3/2} \left(\frac{\tilde{S}_1(x)}{t^{\alpha+1} f} + \cdots \right) = tf'(x) \qquad \text{(axisymmetric flow)} \qquad (2.99b)$$

These equations are meaningful only if

$$\varepsilon_1^{3/2} = t \qquad \text{(plane flow)} \qquad (2.100a)$$

and

$$\varepsilon_1^{3/2} = t^{\alpha+2} \qquad \text{(axisymmetric flow)} \qquad (2.100b)$$

or, with Eq. 2.93, finally

$$\alpha = 1/3 \qquad \text{(plane flow)} \qquad (2.101a)$$

and

$$\alpha = 1 \qquad \text{(axisymmetric flow)} \qquad (2.101b)$$

These relationships confirm previously obtained results, and allow us to throw some more light on the meaning of the expansion parameter. From Eqs. 2.100a, 2.101a and 2.89 we obtain

$$\tilde{y} = \varepsilon_1^{1/2} y \qquad (2.102)$$

for both plane and axisymmetric flow.

This is in complete agreement with Eq. 2.23b, which was the result of the first-order analysis after Guderley. The magnitude of the expansion parameter ε_1 can now be estimated from the similarity rule for plane transonic flow, Eq. 2.65b. In this equation, the argument of f_p is invariant for similar flows, or $|1 - M_\infty^2| \sim t^{2/3}$. Thus, with Eq. 2.100a, we obtain

$$|1 - M_\infty^2| \sim \varepsilon_1 \quad \text{(plane flow)}^{29}$$

This result is in agreement with the requirement that the nonlinear term and the linear term of the transonic equation (Eq. 2.26) must be of the same order. Therefore, the expansion parameter ε_1 must be small enough to insure that $(1 - M_\infty^2)$ is of the same order of magnitude as u for all transonic values of M_∞.

The difference between the values of α in plane flow and in axisymmetric flow may be explained as follows. Obviously, the streamline displacement by a plane body is greater than that by an axisymmetric body of the same nose deflection angle. Consequently, the stretching of the y-component for compressibility effects has to be greater in plane flow than in axisymmetric flow. This is indeed the case because $t^{1/3} > t$ for $t < 1$.

It should be noted that the error made by the slender body assumptions ($v_b = v_{y=0}$ for plane flow and $(vy)_b = \lim_{y\to 0}(vy)$ for axisymmetric flow) is not reduced by adding second-order terms. Because some of the flow leaving the source made by assuming equality in these two expressions could be determined only by modifying the slender-body concept, but not by adding higher-order terms in the analysis. It should be realized, therefore, that the greater accuracy expected from the second-order analysis may in many cases not come about. The technique of establishing second- and higher-order equations should nevertheless be available and applied as deemed necessary.

Having derived the first-order transonic equations for the case of $M_\infty = 1$, we now remove this restriction and set $M_\infty \neq 1$. Then, the lowest-order term in Eq. 2.92 becomes

$$\varepsilon_1\left(\frac{1}{M_\infty^2} - 1\right)u_{1x}$$

Again, this is an expression in one variable only. Therefore, there is only one way to include M_∞ in the analysis, namely, to assume that this lowest-order term is a second-order term. Actually, it is a second-order term, as can be readily seen from the relationship between ε_1 and $1 - M_\infty^2$, established above on this page. Accordingly, by setting

$$\frac{1 - M_\infty^2}{M_\infty^2} = \varepsilon_1 K \qquad (2.103)$$

the preceding coefficient of u_{1x} becomes of the order ε_1^2. The parameter K is just a proportionality constant, independent of t. With $\varepsilon_1 = t^2$ (Eqs. 2.93 and 2.101b), Eq. 2.103 is the same as Eq. 2.83, except for the

The Theory of Inviscid Transonic Flow

γ-term, which may be assumed to be included in K. Thus, K is the similarity parameter for axisymmetric transonic problems.

There is no need to repeat the whole derivation of the continuity equation again. It can easily be seen that the relationships between the expansion parameters remain unchanged, and the equation containing M_∞ becomes

$$Ku_{1x} + v_{1\bar{y}} + \frac{v_1}{\bar{y}} = (\gamma + 1)u_1 u_{1x} \tag{2.104}$$

This is the perturbation equation of lowest possible order and will therefore be called the first-order equation. It has to be kept in mind, however, that Eq. 2.104 is only valid as long as K lies within the limits $0 \le K \le 0(1)$, which are imposed by the similarity rule. For $K \to 0$, Eq. 2.104 is reduced to Eq. 2.94. For $K > 1$, the right-hand-side term becomes negligible and the general equation of compressible flow should be used; the similarity parameter is no longer valid.

As was stated earlier, the transonic continuity equation must accurately describe the discontinuities across a shock wave, and the change of the velocity-vector components across a shock was exploited for the determination of the relationship between the first-order expansion parameters ε_1 and v_1. However, the question as to the magnitude of the change in entropy across the shock wave. To this end we have to introduce the expansion series, Eq. 2.88, into the expression for the entropy jump across an oblique shock and drop the higher-order terms:

Integration of the thermodynamic relationship for the entropy,

$$T\, dS = c_v\, dT + p\, d\left(\frac{1}{\rho}\right) \quad \text{(see Eq. 1.14a)}$$

results in

$$\frac{e^{(S_{II} - S_I)}}{c_v} = \frac{p_{II}/\rho_{II}^\gamma}{p_I \rho_I^\gamma} = \frac{k_{II}}{k_I}, \tag{2.105}$$

where S = entropy, c_v = specific heat at constant volume, and the indices I and II designate the stations at any point before and behind the shock. From Fig. 2.13 and remembering that the continuity and momentum laws apply to the *components* of the flow vector *normal to the shock wave*, the following relationships are easily derived:

$$\frac{\rho_I}{\rho_{II}} = \frac{\bar{U}_{II}}{U} - \frac{v_{II}}{U \tan \beta} \tag{2.106}$$

and

$$p_{II} = p_I + \rho_I U^2 \sin^2 \beta \left(1 - \frac{\rho_I}{\rho_{II}}\right), \tag{2.107}$$

where

$$\tan \beta = \frac{U - \bar{U}_{II}}{v_{II}} \qquad \sin^2 \beta = \frac{(U - \bar{U}_{II})^2}{(U - \bar{U}_{II})^2 + v_{II}^2}. \tag{2.108}$$

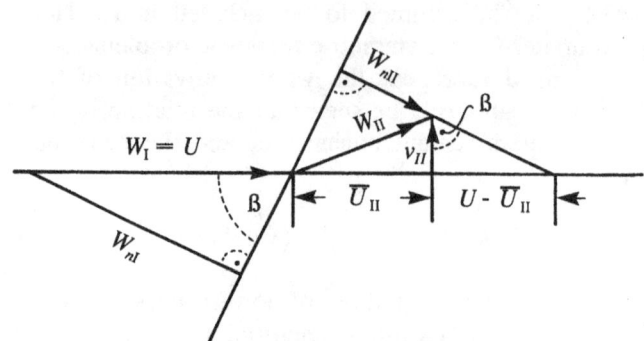

Fig. 2.13. Oblique shock relations.[32]

Introducing the expansions, Eq. 2.88, into the Eqs. 2.106 through 2.108 and observing Eqs. 2.100, 2.101 and 2.102, we finally arrive at the following relationships in which only the lowest-order terms have been retained:

$$\tan \beta = \frac{-Ut^2 u_1}{Ut^3 v_1} = -\frac{u_1}{tv_1} \tag{2.109a}$$

$$\sin^2 \beta = \frac{U^2 t^4 u_1^2}{U^2 t^4 u_1^2 + U^2 t^6 v_1^2} = 1 - t^2 \frac{v_1^2}{u_1^2} \tag{2.109b}$$

$$\frac{\rho_I}{\rho_{II}} = 1 + t^2 u_1 - \frac{t^4 v_1^2}{u_1} = 1 + t^2 u_1 + \ldots \tag{2.110}$$

And with $U^2 = M^2 \gamma p/\rho$ and Eq. 2.103:

$$\frac{p_{II}}{p_I} = 1 + \gamma(1 + Kt^2)^{-1}\left(1 - t^2 \frac{v_1^2}{u_1^2}\right)(-t^2 u_1 + \cdots) = 1 - \gamma t^2 u_1 + \ldots \tag{2.111}$$

The first-order entropy jump over a shock wave is now obtained by introducing the expressions Eqs. 2.110 and 2.111 into Eq. 2.105. Since this results in

$$\frac{k_{II}}{k_I} = 1 + o(t^2) \tag{2.112}[32]$$

we conclude that the change in entropy across a shock wave is of higher order, and there exists a perturbation potential φ_1, confirming our earlier assumption. Note that the change in the total pressure, like that of the entropy, is of higher order,[33] so that Eqs. 2.110 and 2.111 must satisfy the adiabatic (isentropic) relationship between p and τ; $p = \text{const} \times \rho^\gamma$.

We now have all the information needed for the second-order analysis. Going back to Eq. 2.92, we extract the second-order terms (the terms of u_2 and v_2, and the terms of u_1 and v_1 of higher order than $\varepsilon_1^2 = t^4$). Again starting with the case $M_\infty = 1$, the lowest-order terms become

$$v_2 t \left(v_{2\bar{y}} + \frac{v_2}{\bar{y}} \right) = (\gamma + 1) t^2 \varepsilon_2 (u_1 u_2)_x$$

$$+ t^6 \text{ (times terms of first-order variables only)} \quad (2.113)$$

Obviously, the term of order $v_2 t$ had to be retained to avoid the elimination of the variable v_2 from the relationship. Thus, Eq. 2.113 is only meaningful for

$$v_2 = \varepsilon_2 t \quad (2.114)$$

For the general case of $M_\infty \ne 1$, the terms of order ε_2 do not cancel out and M_∞ can be retained in the equation only if we again introduce the similarity relationship $(1 - M_\infty^2) = \varepsilon_1 K = t^2 K$. Hence, with Eq. 2.114, the general second-order equation becomes

$$\varepsilon_2 t^2 K u_{2x} + \varepsilon_2 t^2 \left(v_{2\bar{y}} + \frac{v_2}{\bar{y}} \right) = (\gamma + 1) \varepsilon_2 t^2 (u_1 u_2)_x$$

$$+ t^6 \text{ (times terms of first-order variables only)} \quad (2.115a)$$

Here the question arises whether or not the terms of the first-order variables should be retained. In the former case, it would be required that $\varepsilon_2 = t^4$, which also may be expressed as $t^4 = O(\varepsilon_2)$. In the latter case, however, it would be required that $t^4 = o(\varepsilon_2)$, so that t^6 will be of higher order than $\varepsilon_2 t^2$.[34] As will be determined from the following analysis, Eq. 2.115a will be compatible with our earlier choice of $v_1 \to \tilde{S}_1(x)/r$ as $r \to 0$ only if $t^4 = o(\varepsilon_2)$. Thus, the second-order continuity equation has been determined, without the knowledge of the relation between ε_2 and t, as

$$K \frac{\partial u_2}{\partial x} + \left(\frac{\partial v}{\partial \bar{y}} + \frac{v_2}{\bar{y}} \right) = (\gamma + 1) \frac{\partial (u_1 u_2)}{\partial x} \quad (2.115b)$$

Whereas the first-order Eq. 2.94 was nonlinear, this second-order equation is linear.

Although we could derive Eq. 2.115b without knowing the relation between ε_2 and t, $\varepsilon_2(t)$ must be determined for the establishment of the exact magnitude of the second-order terms of the Eqs. 2.88. Again we fall back on the condition for tangential flow on the body surface. With the help of Eqs. 2.96, 2.99b and 2.101b, Eq. 2.95b yields

$$t^3 \left[\frac{\tilde{S}_1(x)}{t^2 f(x)} + \text{higher-order terms} \right] + \varepsilon_2 t \left[\frac{\tilde{S}_2(x)}{t^2 f(x)} + \ldots \right]$$

$$= [1 + t^2 \tilde{S}_1^1(x) \ln(t^2 f) + \ldots] t f'(x) = (1 + 2 t^2 \tilde{S}_1^1(x) \ln t + \ldots) t f'(x),$$

$$(2.116)$$

because $\ln f \ll |\ln t^2|$.

Since $v_2 v_2$ is a correction term to the first-order term $v_1 v_1$, it is logical to introduce $\tilde{S}_2$ by the same reasoning as that applied for the introduction of $\tilde{S}_1$.

We now have to estimate the lowest order of t^3 times the "higher-order terms" in the first bracket on the left-hand side of Eq. 2.116, because it must be included in the determination of the relation between ε_2 and t if it is of the same order as $\varepsilon_2 t$ times the second bracket on the left-hand side of this equation. For this estimation we take advantage of the existence of the velocity potential for the first-order approximation, and we rewrite Eq. 2.104 as

$$\varphi_{1\tilde{y}\tilde{y}} + \frac{\varphi_{1\tilde{y}}}{\tilde{y}} = [(\gamma+1)\varphi_{1x} - K]\varphi_{1xx} \qquad (2.117)$$

A first approximation of φ_1 may be obtained from Eq. 2.104 by twice integrating this equation with respect to $\tilde{y}$ (i.e., by integrating Eq. 2.98b with respect to $\tilde{y}$), resulting in

$$\varphi_1 = \tilde{S}_1(x) \ln \tilde{y} + g_1(x) \qquad (2.118)^{35}$$

The first term on the right-hand side is the solution of Eq. 2.117 for $\varphi_{1xx} = 0$, where $\tilde{S}(x)$ represents the body shape (see Eq. 5.32). Obviously, $g_1(x)$ is completely arbitrary in this case. However, the pressure coefficient on the body, specified by $\tilde{S}(x)$, can assume any value by properly choosing $g_1(x)$, because c_p depends on $\partial \varphi_1 / \partial x = u_1$ (see Note 21). Therefore, considering that the right-hand side of Eq. 2.117 is a function of the variable u_1 only, it should be possible to choose g_1 so that φ_1 becomes the solution of the complete Eq. 2.117. Then, because the right-hand side of Eq. 2.117 is also a function of the parameter K, g_1 is properly written as $g_1(x; K)$.

Because it allows us to draw an interesting conclusion about the nonlinear term in Eq. 2.117, a few words should be said about the function g_1: The term $\varphi_{1x}\varphi_{1xx} = u_1 \partial u_1/\partial x = (dx/dt) \partial u_1/\partial x = \partial u_1/\partial t$ represents local flow accelerations and decelerations, strictly in the x-direction. This is obtained by a superposition of a potential $\bar{\varphi} = t^2 \cdot \int_a^x u_1 \, d\xi$ on the potential of the approach flow $\varphi_\infty = Ux$. Such a perturbation potential can be obtained through the introduction of a *spatial* source-sink distribution within the validity range of Eq. 2.117. The nonlinear term in the transonic equation is equivalent to a spatial source-sink distribution.

The order of $g_1(x; K)$ is obtained from the equation for $\bar{\varphi}$ as $O(t^2)$. The function $g_1(x; K)$ can be found only through integration of the transonic differential equation. This is shown in Sec. 5.2.1 in connection with results of Sec. 5.1.1.

After this side-glance on the meaning of $g_1(x; K)$, the "higher order terms" of Eq. 2.116 will now be determined. First, the higher-order terms of φ_1 must be found. This can be done through iteration of Eqs. 2.118 and 2.117, yielding

$$\varphi_1(x, \tilde{y}; K) = \tilde{S}_1(x) \ln \tilde{y} + g_1(x; K)$$
$$+ \tilde{y}^2 \ln^2 \tilde{y} \left[\frac{\gamma+1}{4} \tilde{S}_1'(x) \tilde{S}_1''(x) \right] + O(\tilde{y}^2 \ln \tilde{y}) \qquad (2.119)$$

The Theory of Inviscid Transonic Flow

as may be verified by forming the partial derivatives of $\varphi_1(x, \bar{y}; K)$ and substituting them into Eq. 2.117. The lower-order terms of $O(1/\bar{y}^2)$ and $O(\ln^2 \bar{y})$ cancel out and the third-order terms $O(\bar{y}^2 \ln y)$ remain. Hence

$$v_1 = \frac{\partial \varphi_1(x, \bar{y}; K)}{\partial \bar{y}} = \frac{\tilde{S}_1(x)}{\bar{y}} + O(\bar{y} \ln^2 \bar{y}) \tag{2.119b}$$

is the term sought in Eq. 2.116 and, consequently, the "higher-order terms" become of $O(\bar{y} \ln^2 \bar{y})$. By considering now only those terms of this equation that have not been employed for the first-order analysis, see Eq. 2.99b, we obtain with Eq. 2.97 the relationship whose lowest-order terms constitute the second-order equation of the streamline that forms the contour of the slender body:

$$t^3 \cdot O(t^2 \ln^2 t) + \varepsilon_2 t \left[\frac{S_2(x)}{t^2 f(x)} \right] = (2t^2 \tilde{S}_1'(x) \ln t) t f'(x) \tag{2.120}$$

Since the first term on the left-hand side is of higher order than the term on the right-hand side, it should be dropped and the two remaining terms must be of the same order for a meaningful result. Hence

$$\varepsilon_2 = t^4 \ln t \tag{2.121}$$

Consequently, the relationship $\varepsilon_2 = t^4$ that would have resulted from defining the last term of Eq. 2.115 as of $O(t^6)$, would be incompatible with the assumption that Eq. 2.98b should also be valid for the second-order variables. By choosing $\varepsilon_2 = t^4$, Eq. 2.116 would have remained meaningful only for $v_2 \sim \ln(\bar{y}/\bar{y}) = 2 \ln(t/t^2 f)$, in disagreement with $v_2 = S_2(x)/\bar{y} + \cdots$.

The requirement that Eq. 2.98b be valid for both first- and second-order equations was arbitrary, though practical, and we chose this assumption for our expansion procedure. With a different assumption a different expansion would have resulted.

Through an analysis identical to that for the first-order case, we find that the flow through a shock wave is isentropic even in second approximation:

$$\frac{k_{\mathrm{II}}}{k_{\mathrm{I}}} = 1 + o(t^4 \ln t) \qquad \text{and thus} \qquad (u_2)_y - (v_2)_x = 0$$

Therefore, a perturbation potential exists for the second-order velocity vector, too, and Eq. 2.115a may be written as

$$K\varphi_{2xx} + \varphi_{2\bar{y}\bar{y}} + \frac{\varphi_{2\bar{y}}}{\bar{y}} = (\gamma + 1)(\varphi_1 \varphi_2)_{xx} \tag{2.122}$$

Again a solution to this equation may be found through an iteration procedure, allowing the establishment of the third-order equation in the same way the second-order equation had been found. However, within the framework of this introductory book these further steps will not be given, and the interested reader is referred to ref. 8.

The highest-order terms of Eq. 2.119a were not used explicitly in finding the relationship between ε_2 and t. For completeness, they are given in the following expressions for the first- and second-order potentials:

$$\varphi_1 = \tilde{S}_1(x) \ln \tilde{y} + g_1(x; K) + \tilde{y}^2 (\ln^2 \tilde{y})\left(\frac{\gamma+1}{4} \tilde{S}_1'(x)\tilde{S}_1''(x)\right)$$

$$+ \frac{\tilde{y}^2 \ln \tilde{y}}{4}[(\gamma+1)(\tilde{S}_1'(x)g_1'(x; K))' - 2(\gamma+1)\tilde{S}_1'(x)\tilde{S}_1''(x) - K\tilde{S}_1''(x)]$$

$$+ \frac{\tilde{y}^2}{4}[\tfrac{3}{2}(\gamma+1)(\tilde{S}_1'(x)\tilde{S}_1''(x)) - (\gamma+1)(\tilde{S}_1'(x)g_1'(x; K))' + K\tilde{S}_1''(x)$$

$$+ (\gamma+1)(g_1'(x; K)g_1''(x; K)) - g_1''(x; K)] + O(\tilde{y} \ln^3 \tilde{y}) \qquad (2.123)$$

$$\varphi_2 = \tilde{S}_2(x) \ln \tilde{y} + g_2(x; K) + \frac{\gamma+1}{4}(\tilde{S}_1'\tilde{S}_2')\tilde{y}^2 \ln \tilde{y} + O(\tilde{y}^2 \ln \tilde{y}) \qquad (2.124)$$

As mentioned before, $\tilde{S}_1$ and $\tilde{S}_2$ are the source strength functions producing the body contour as a streamline and are related to the body shape function f as

$$\tilde{S}_1(x) = f(x)f'(x) \qquad (2.125)$$

and

$$\tilde{S}_2(x) = -2\tilde{S}_1\tilde{S}_1' = -2f(x)f'(x)[f(x)f'(x)]' \qquad (2.126)$$

as may be confirmed by inspecting Eqs. 2.120 and 2.12.[36]

The functions $g_1(x; K)$ and $g_2(x; K)$ remain unknowns and, as pointed out in ref. 8, can only be found by solving the differential equations Eqs. 2.104 and 2.122. They are important for the computation of the pressure distribution on a body. To illustrate this fact, the first-order pressure coefficient may be inspected. It is obtained as

$$\frac{C_p}{t^2} + 2\tilde{S}_1' \ln(t^2 f) + \frac{\tilde{S}_1^2}{f^2} = -2g_1'(x; K) + O(t^2 \ln t) \qquad (2.127)[37]$$

This equation shows that $g_1(x; K)$ is indeed important for the pressure distribution on a slender body in transonic flow. Also, this equation should be in agreement with the Oswatitsch–Berndt similarity rule for axisymmetric flow, Eq. 2.81. Because S in Eq. 2.81 is the body cross-sectional area, it may be written as $S = \pi t^2 f^2$, and with Eq. 2.125 the Oswatitsch–Berndt rule becomes

$$\frac{C_p}{t^2} + 2\tilde{S}'(x) \ln(\beta t) = f_p\left(\frac{\sqrt{|M_\infty^2 - 1|}}{t(\gamma+1)}\right) \qquad (2.128)$$

With the condition that the argument of the function f_p is a constant and, therefore, $\beta = \sqrt{|M_\infty^2 - 1|} = \sqrt{K}\, tM_\infty$, Eqs. 2.127 and 2.128 become equal by setting

$$f_p\left[\frac{\sqrt{|M_\infty^2 - 1|}}{t(\gamma + 1)}\right] = -\left(2g_1'(x; K) + \frac{\tilde{S}_1^2}{f^2} + 2\tilde{S}_1' \ln f\right)$$

where the term $2\tilde{S}'(x) \ln\sqrt{K} M_\infty$ has been included in $g_1'(x; K)$.

Thus we have been able to find an analytical expression for the function whose argument must be held constant in the Oswatitsch-Berndt rule.

With this result this section about the higher-order expansion method will be concluded. It should be pointed out once more, however, that a second- and higher-order treatment of a transonic problem may not lead to the hoped-for increase in accuracy, considering the many restricting assumptions that had to be made in the derivation and which very well may cause errors of the same magnitude as those made in the first-order analysis. Nevertheless, the higher-order analyses should always be kept in mind as a possible means for a better treatment of a problem. For that reason, this section was included to make the reader familiar with the technique of higher-order expansions.

2.6.2 Asymptotic Expansions

In Sec. 2.6.1 the dependent variables were expressed through "asymptotic" series of terms multiplied by increasing orders of small parameters (ε, ν), but such that the sum of all higher-order terms could be expressed by the order of magnitude of the last term employed for the computation. Thus, the error made by restricting the number of terms used may be determined, or, conversely, for a desired accuracy of the solution, the maximum magnitude of the parameter is given. For an expansion to be asymptotic, the terms must follow the condition

$$f(\varepsilon)_{n+1} = o[f(\varepsilon)_n]$$

where the o-symbol, as explained in ref. 9, signifies

$$\lim_{\varepsilon \to 0} (f_{n+1}/f_n) \to 0 \quad [38]$$

Thus, an asymptotic expansion might be

$$F(x, \varepsilon) = f_0(x) + \varepsilon f_1(x) + \varepsilon^2 f_2(x) + \varepsilon^3 f_3(x) + \cdots$$

but the coefficients could also be, for example,

$$\ln \varepsilon, \ 1, \ \varepsilon \ln \varepsilon, \ \varepsilon, \ \varepsilon^2 \ln^2 \varepsilon, \ \varepsilon^2 \ln \varepsilon, \ \varepsilon^2, \ldots$$

or any other terms satisfying the preceding limit procedure.

Asymptotic expansions are particularly useful for the solution of equations containing small parameters ε, like the small-perturbation equations. These equations cannot be solved in closed form when the value of ε varies with the initial and boundary conditions. However, through asymptotic expansions the solution of an equation $f(x_i, \varepsilon) = 0$, where the index i indicates the number of independent variables, is broken down into a series of solutions of simpler equations of increasing order of ε. The number of equations that must be considered for a certain accuracy of the result thus decreases with decreasing values of ε.

The derivation of higher-order transonic equations of Sec. 2.6.1 resulted in different types of equations for the different orders. The first-order equation was nonlinear but the second-order equation was linear. This derivation also showed that a power series of the parameter may not give the desired result, since, for instance, ε_1 and ε_2 turned out to be t^2 and $t^4 \ln t$, respectively.

The establishment of asymptotic expansions is by no means a simple task. Each case requires special considerations. For instance, in the case of the partial differential equations of Sec. 2.6.1 the relative magnitudes of the expansion coefficients of the two perturbation velocities were found through special flow properties, like flow through shock waves at $M \approx 1$ and flow over slender bodies. Only then could all parameters be expressed as functions of a single parameter t that became the coefficients of the asymptotic expansion.

The asymptotic methods that have received a wide range of applications go an important step further. They allow the treatment of cases in which initial and boundary conditions are not covered by the single expansion, because for $t \to t_0$ or $x \to x_0$ terms of the expansion become singular. Consequently, the boundary ranges $t_{-m} < t_0 < t_{+m}$ or $x_{-m} < x_0 < x_{+m}$ are poorly, or not at all, described by the "outer" expansion. However, these ranges may be represented by an equally correct expansion in terms of new variables, for instance $x' = (x - x_0)/\delta(\varepsilon)$ of an "inner" expansion that is regular in the considered boundary range, because $(x - x_0)$ and $\delta(\varepsilon)$ are of the same order. Beyond this range $\delta(\varepsilon)$ and $(x - x_0)$ are no longer of the same order and the inner expansion is invalid.

Because they are not valid over the whole range of the solutions of the original equation, the inner and outer expansions are called *nonuniform*. However, a uniform expansion may be obtained by matching the two expansions by making a certain number of their terms identical. This matching within an overlap range is an important part of the asymptotic process. It allows us to choose the width of the overlap and, consequently, higher-order boundary conditions may be satisfied. Actually, the overlap width decreases with the number of expansion terms used.

The many aspects of asymptotic expansions are documented in several extensive publications (e.g., refs 57, 58) to which the interested reader must be referred. A concise survey of applications of asymptotic expansions to transonic flow problems is given by Cole [59], including subjects as transonic small disturbance equations, transonic slender bodies, wind tunnel perturbations, perturbations of sonic flow, and shock-free flow. Also, the paper of Murman and Cole [60] on inviscid drag at transonic speeds is well suited for the study of asymptotic expansions. Their paper gives in addition details for a computer evaluation of the analytical result, thus supplementing the information of Chapter 7 on numerical methods.

2.7 The Hodograph Method

In the previous sections we have shown that, in the physical plane, transonic flow cannot be described by linear equations. Therefore, new solutions cannot be established by simply superimposing known solutions. However, because of the complexities of transonic flow such a simple procedure would be of particular benefit. Fortunately, this problem may be overcome, at least as far as the basic understanding of transonic flow is concerned, by working in the hodograph plane in which the transonic equations are linear. Undoubtedly, the studies of transonic flow in the hodograph plane have greatly promoted the understanding of transonic phenomena. In this respect, the works of Guderley [4] and Ferrari and Tricomi [10] deserve special attention.

2.7.1 Limitations of the Hodograph Approach

The use of the hodograph method is limited by two factors: first, it is available for two-dimensional flow only, and second, the independent variables are the components of the velocity vector, so that the geometry of a flow field can be determined only after the differential equation for the potential- or the stream-function has been solved. Therefore, geometric boundary conditions cannot be prescribed. Nevertheless, many aerodynamic problems can be treated in the hodograph plane as well as or even better than in the physical plane. Most important of these cases is the method of characteristics and its graphical representation. The streamlines of a supersonic flow field can be plotted in the characteristics chart, but only in terms of velocity and flow angle at any moment. A streamline in the characteristics chart connects endpoints of the velocity vectors of the physical streamlines, as drawn from a common origin, so that the geometric shape of the streamline cannot be determined from this chart. For instance, the Prandtl–Meyer expansion over a sharp corner and that over a curvilinear wall of the same total flow angle change have identical hodograph streamlines.

Because of the linearity of the differential equations, the hodograph method is ideally suited for problems in which the initial and boundary conditions can be given in terms of the velocity vectors. Therefore, for a general exploration of transonic flow characteristics, where exact geometric boundaries are not essential, the hodograph method is entirely adequate. And there are some practical cases in which the exact geometry of the flow need not be given, as in the case of computing the contour of a Laval nozzle. In its simplest form, this problem was solved by Th. Meyer back in 1908 [11]. He did not solve the hodograph equation, but his approach shows how geometric requirements can be approximated when the boundary conditions are given in terms of the velocity components. Meyer's "boundary" condition is the velocity distribution on the nozzle centerline. Using a two-dimensional Taylor expansion of the potential and observing the continuity law, he arrived at a set of streamlines, symmetric to the centerline, whose accuracy decreases with the distance from the centerline. A symmetrical pair of these streamlines, chosen sufficiently close to the centerline for accuracy, constitute the nozzle walls. Then, the degree of contraction and expansion of the nozzle may be changed in any desired way by changing the velocity distribution on the center line. In a very similar way, systematic studies in the hodograph plane may be evaluated for geometric requirements.

2.7.2 The Basic Hodograph Equations

Before we discuss a few more problems suited for the hodograph plane, for a better understanding of transonic flow the most important hodograph equations will be given without derivation. The reader interested in the derivations will find a particularly comprehensive treatment by R. Sauer [5].

There are two kinds of hodograph equations, those in terms of the potential- and stream-functions of the physical plane and those in terms of the so-called Legendre potential- and stream-functions. The most important differences in these two systems are seen from their partial derivatives, which lead directly to velocity vector components in the former case but to the flow coordinates in the latter through the following relationships.

(a) *For the velocity potential φ and the streamfunction ψ*

$$\frac{\partial \varphi}{\partial x} = u \quad \frac{\partial \varphi}{\partial y} = v; \quad \frac{\partial \psi}{\partial x} = -\frac{\rho}{\rho_0} v \equiv r, \quad \frac{\partial \psi}{\partial y} = \frac{\rho}{\rho_0} u \equiv q$$

but

$$\frac{\partial \varphi}{\partial u} \neq x \quad \frac{\partial \psi}{\partial u} \neq -y \quad \text{etc.}$$

(b) *For the Legendre functions Φ and Ψ*

$$\frac{\partial \Phi}{\partial u} = x \quad \frac{\partial \Phi}{\partial v} = y \quad \frac{\partial \Psi}{\partial \left(\frac{\rho}{\rho_0} u\right)} = -y \quad \frac{\partial \Psi}{\partial \left(\frac{\rho}{\rho_0} v\right)} = x$$

but

$$\frac{\partial \Phi}{\partial x} \neq u \quad \frac{\partial \Psi}{\partial x} \neq \frac{\rho}{\rho_0} v \quad \text{etc.}$$

The Theory of Inviscid Transonic Flow

where u and v are the components of the velocity vector, not the perturbation velocities.

The hodograph equations of the velocity potential and the streamfunction most likely to be found in the literature are

(1) $$\left(1-\frac{w^2}{a^2}\right)w^2\varphi_{ww} + w\left(1+\frac{w^4}{a^4}\right)\varphi_w + \left(1-\frac{w^2}{a^2}\right)\varphi_{\theta\theta} = 0 \qquad (2.129)$$

$$w^2\psi_{ww} + w\left(1+\frac{w^2}{a^2}\right)\psi_w + \left(1-\frac{w^2}{a^2}\right)\psi_{\theta\theta} = 0 \qquad (2.130)$$

with φ = velocity potential, ψ = stream function, $w = |\mathbf{W}|$ and θ the flow direction angle, and also

(2) $$\left(1-\frac{v^2}{a^2}\right)\Phi_{uu} + \left(1-\frac{u^2}{a^2}\right)\Phi_{vv} + \frac{2u\cdot v}{a^2}\Phi_{uv} = 0 \qquad (2.131)$$

$$\left(1-\frac{\rho_0^2}{\rho^2 a^2}q^2\right)\Psi_{qq} + \left(1-\frac{\rho_0^2}{\rho^2 a^2}r^2\right)\Psi_{rr} - 2\frac{\rho_0^2}{\rho^2 a^2}qr\Psi_{qr} = 0 \qquad (2.132)$$

with Φ = Legendre potential, Ψ = Legendre stream function, and $q = \psi_y$; $r = -\psi_x$; $x = -\Psi_r$; $y = \Psi_q$. Thus, in Eq. 2.132, the Legendre transformation (or Molenbroek transformation, see ref. 5) leads to the equation in the flow density plane, not the velocity plane.

We have seen that flow through transonic shock waves can be considered to be isentropic in first- and second-order approximations. This does not mean, however, that the flow through the shock wave is inviscid, only that the effect of viscosity is negligible in this particular case. Since there is an almost infinitely high deceleration in a shock wave, whose thickness is of the order of the mean free path of the gas molecules, there must exist a narrow zone of high viscosity, as manifested by the strong interactions of the molecules and the high turbulence resulting from extreme accelerations. Therefore, the limitations of inviscid flow computations should be indicated by the occurence of extremely high flow accelerations. Actually, in solving inviscid flow equations, such limitations may be found. This fact will now be shown for a few classical cases that will throw some more light on the peculiarities of transonic flow.

For practical applications, it is advantageous to substitute the stagnation speed of sound a_0 for the local speed of sound a in Eqs. 2.129 through 2.132. With the help of the integrated Bernoulli equation $a^2 = a_0^2 - (\gamma-1)w^2/2$, Eq. 2.130 becomes

$$w^2\left(1-\frac{\gamma-1}{2}\frac{w^2}{a_0^2}\right)\psi_{ww} + w\left(1-\frac{\gamma-3}{2}\frac{w^2}{a_0^2}\right)\psi_w + \left(1-\frac{\gamma+1}{2}\frac{w^2}{a_0^2}\right)\psi_{\theta\theta} = 0$$

$$(2.133)$$

2.7.3 Some Important Applications of the Hodograph Method

The hodograph method will now be applied to a few examples of inviscid flows that undergo very high accelerations, in order to show that viscous flow equations are required when flow accelerations exceed a certain value.

As the first example we reduce Eq. 2.130 to $d^2\psi/d\theta^2 = 0$ by the condition $\psi_w = \psi_{ww} = 0$, with the solution

$$\psi = K_1\theta + K_2 \tag{2.134a}$$

This results shows that θ is constant along streamlines ($\psi = $ const.), that is, the streamlines are straight lines and have the same origin, because they cannot intersect each other. Hence, Eq. 2.134a describes a two-dimensional source. The constant mass flow between two streamlines is related to the mass flow at sonic speed through the continuity law:

$$(r\,\Delta\theta)\rho w = (r^*\,\Delta\theta)\rho^* a^* \quad \text{or} \quad r/r^* = \frac{1}{M^*}\frac{\rho^*}{\rho} \tag{2.134b}$$

where r is the distance from the origin and the starred magnitudes are those at the speed of sound.

This relationship is plotted in Fig. 2.14, revealing the fact that there does not exist a solution for distances from the origin $r < r^*$.

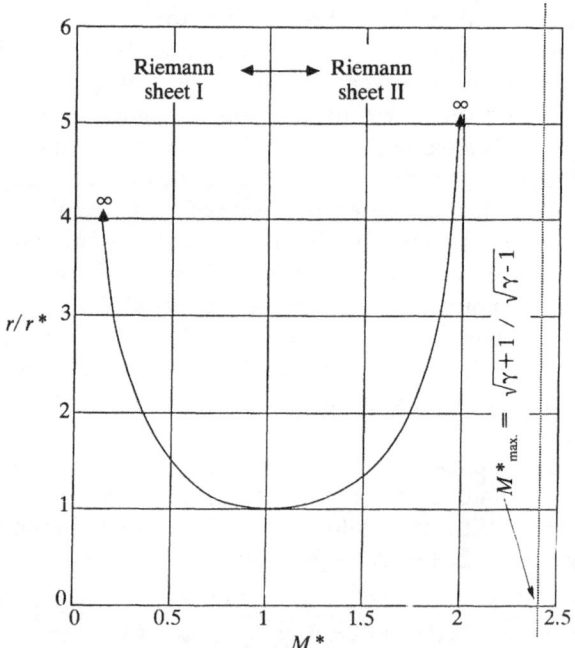

Fig. 2.14. Two-dimensional source flow. Dimensionless distance from the origin r/r^* vs. dimensionless flow velocity M^* (From [3]).

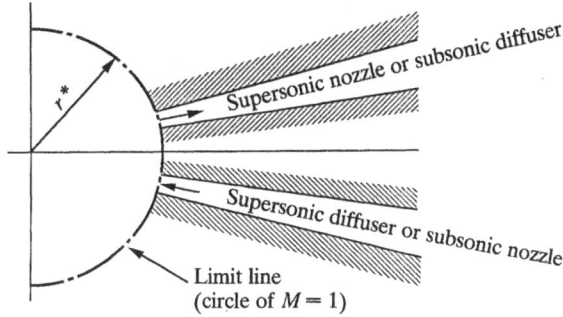

Fig. 2.15. Two-dimensional source flow in the physical plane; continuation of the flow beyond the limit line on a second Riemann sheet (From [3]).

We obtain a deeper insight in the meaning of Fig. 2.14 from Fig. 2.15 which discloses that the relationship of Fig. 2.14 consists of two so-called Riemann sheets connected at the circle of $M = 1$. The flow toward the origin and that away from it have been shown separately only for clarity. Actually, the two flows are on top of each other, something physically impossible.[39] Since the relationship of Eq. 2.134b cannot be extended beyond $M = 1$, whether it be a subsonic–supersonic or a supersonic–subsonic flow, this line is called the *limit line* or the *limiting line*. However, considering the complete solution of Eq. 2.134b, as shown in Fig. 2.14, at the limit line the flow turns by 180 degrees on the second Riemann sheet, which means a velocity change by $\Delta v = 2a$ and an infinitely high acceleration of the flow. As we pointed out earlier, such an acceleration should be accompanied by viscous effects,[40] and the pattern of flow approaching $M = 1$ attains a very different aspect. However, there is a very practical conclusion that can be drawn from this source flow study. Quite a number of papers have been written on the design of Laval nozzles whose supersonic portion was supposed to be laid out as a source flow. Our result clearly shows that such a design is impossible. In Fig. 2.16 the two sheets of Fig.. 2.15 have been joined at $M = 1$, forming a Laval nozzle. However, since in source flow the equipotential lines, and thus the lines of $M = 1$, are circular, the two source flows can be joined at the nozzle walls only. For a physically possible solution, the lense-shaped area between the two limit lines $M = 1$ would have to be at $M > 1$ for the flow coming from the subsonic side, but at $M < 1$ for the upstream

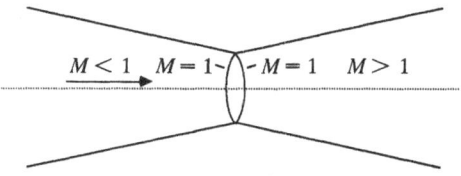

Fig. 2.16. Laval nozzle formed by joining two source flows at $M = 1$.

continuation of the supersonic flow on the right-hand side, thus requiring the elimination of one of the two limit lines. In either case, the straight source-flow walls can no longer be streamlines and viscous effects like flow separation and shock waves must be introduced for a solution. The considerable modifications made in the throat sections of the so-called source-flow nozzles confirms this fact. The necessity to introduce viscous effects to describe the flow near a limit line has been shown in this example.

In the following example of a flow leading to a limit line, we shall see that the limit line need not be a line of $M = 1$ but may be at any other supersonic Mach number as well.

We now seek a solution of the hodograph equation Eq. 2.133 for the case that the stream-function is independent of the flow direction,

$$\psi_\theta = \psi_{\theta\theta} = 0.$$

A vortex flow around the origin meets this condition. For the determination of the kind of vortex, the velocity change with distance from the origin, the ordinary differential equation consisting of the two terms of Eq. 2.133 must be solved. The result is given in Fig. 2.17. For the mathematics, reference is again made to ref. 3.[41] The result

$$\frac{r}{r^*} = \frac{a^*}{w} = \frac{1}{M^*} \tag{2.135}$$

is the equation for a potential vortex, characterized by $\oint \mathbf{v} \cdot d\mathbf{s} = 0$ for all integration paths not enclosing the origin.

As Fig. 2.17 shows, there again exists a range of r/r^* in which no solutions are possible. This time the limit line is the circle where $M^* = \sqrt{\gamma + 1}/\sqrt{\gamma - 1}$ or $M = \infty$. The physical flow pattern is given in Fig.

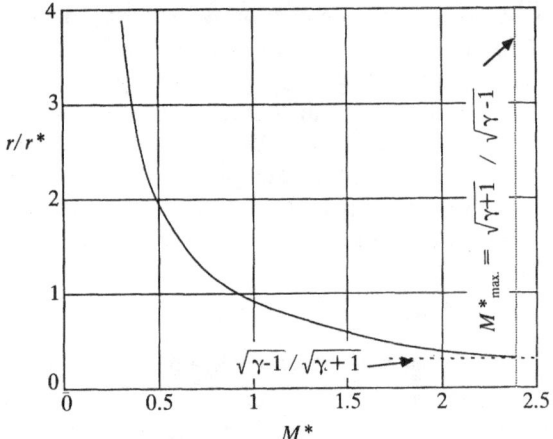

Fig. 2.17. Potential vortex flow; dimensionless distance from the origin vs. dimensionless flow velocity (From [3]).

The Theory of Inviscid Transonic Flow

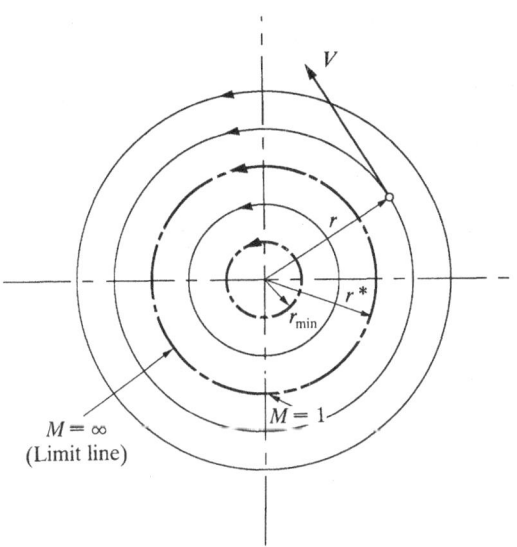

Fig. 2.18. Potential vortex flow in the physical plane; no solution for inviscid flow for $r < r^*$ (From [3]).

2.18, which shows that the flow has reached $M = \infty$ at a finite distance from the origin. Since there is no solution for the area within the $M = \infty$ streamline, connection with the vortex core is possible only through viscous effects.

Since Eqs. 2.134 and 2.135 are the solutions of the linear hodograph equation Eq. 2.133, a new solution of this equation may be found by superposition of these two solutions, which must be expressed in the form $\psi = f(r/r^*, M^*; Q)$ and $\psi = f(r/r^*, M^*; \Gamma)$, respectively. Addition of these two stream functions leads to the relationship shown in Fig. 2.19 (see ref. 3). Depending upon the ratio Q/Γ of source strength to vortex strength, the limit line may lie at any supersonic Mach number, in agreement with our earlier statement. For one Q/Γ-ratio, the flow pattern in the physical plane is shown in Fig. 2.20. It again shows that, on the limit line, the flow turns by 180 degrees onto a second Riemann sheet.

Whereas these first three examples of solutions of the hodograph equations may seem to be of academic interest only, the fourth and last example will answer an important question of transonic flow.

Since transonic flow is the flow of supersonic flow regions embedded into regions of subsonic flow, the transition from supersonic to subsonic flow is likely to occur in a shock wave. But does it have to be in shockwave? Are there solutions for a smooth transition from supersonic to subsonic flow? This question is of greatest importance in the design of airfoils, as we shall see in Chapter 8. In seeking another solution of the hodograph equation 2.133, F. Ringleb [61] gave a basic answer to this question.

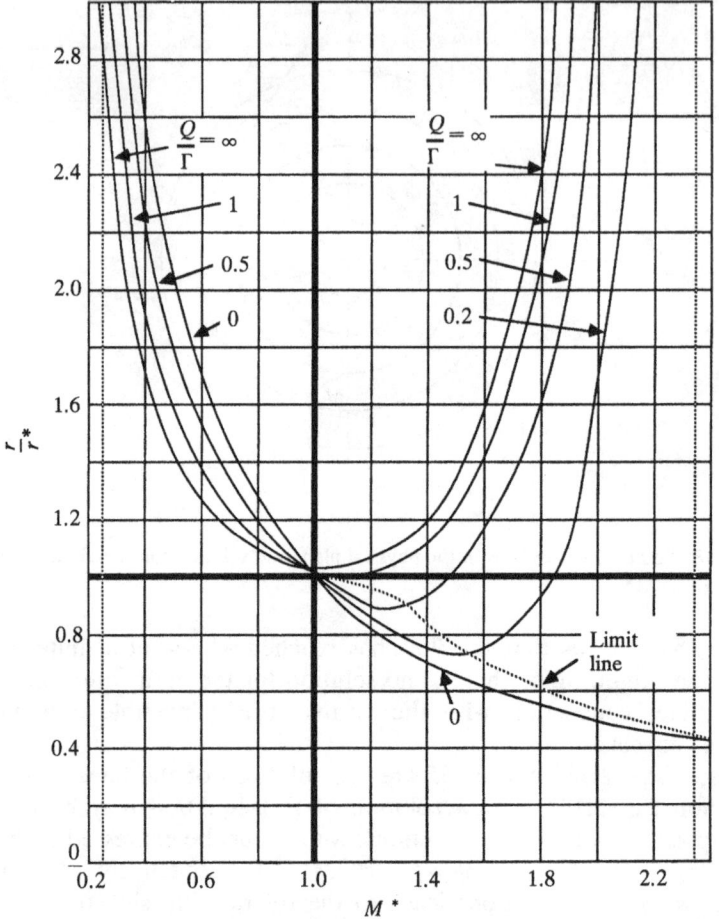

Fig. 2.19. Source-vortex flow. Dimensionless distance from the origin vs. dimensionless flow velocity, with the ratio of source strength to vortex strength as the parameter (From [3]).

By setting $\psi = P(w)Q(\theta)$, the simple solution of Eq. 2.133 becomes

$$P = \frac{1}{w} \quad \text{and} \quad Q = a_0^2 \cdot l \sin\theta$$

where $a_0^2 \cdot l$ has been introduced for dimensional reasons, with l being a characteristic length. Thus we arrive at

$$\psi = \frac{a_0^2 l}{w} \sin\theta$$

By backtracking the steps leading from the physical plane to the

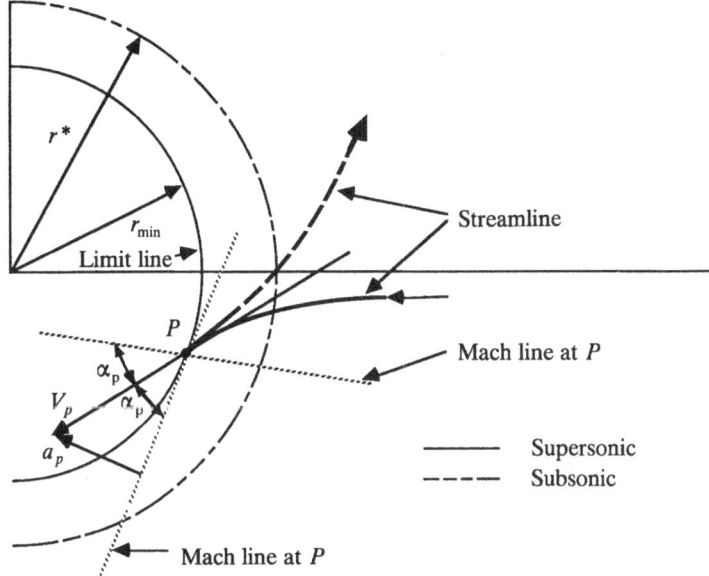

Fig. 2.20. Physical flow pattern of the source-vortex flow. No solution for $r < r_{min}$ [From [3]].

hodograph plane, (see, e.g., ref. 3), the final result becomes

(a) $$\frac{x}{l} = \frac{1}{2}\frac{\rho_0}{\rho}\left(\frac{a_0^2}{w^2} - 2\frac{\psi^2}{l^2 a_0^2}\right)$$

(b) $$\frac{y}{l} = \pm \frac{\rho_0 a_0}{\rho w} \frac{\psi}{a_0 l}\sqrt{1 - \frac{w^2}{a_0^2}\left(\frac{\psi}{l a_0}\right)^2}$$

(2.136)

which represents the coordinates of the streamlines $\psi/a_0 l = $ const. For incompressible flow, $\rho_0/\rho = $ const. $= 1$, the explicit streamline equation can be established, showing that the solution is the flow around a semiinfinite flat plate, the streamlines being confocal parabolas. Obviously the assumption of incompressible flow cannot be sustained because the streamlines close to the plate certainly are accelerated to very high velocities when rounding the plate edge. The solution of the unsimplified Eqs. 2.136, to be obtained graphically or by computer, is shown in Fig. 2.21. The striking feature of this picture is the limit line, which consists of a central circular section lying on the primary Riemann sheet (1) and two wings symmetric to the x-axis lying on the secondary Riemann sheet (2). Thus, some streamlines are reflected four times and finally reappear in the original plane. Nevertheless, only the streamlines that impinge on the limit line 1 have a physical meaning. In Fig. 2.21 they have the numbers $la_0/\psi < \sim 550$. These streamlines are not reflected from the limit line 2, which lies on the second Riemann sheet.

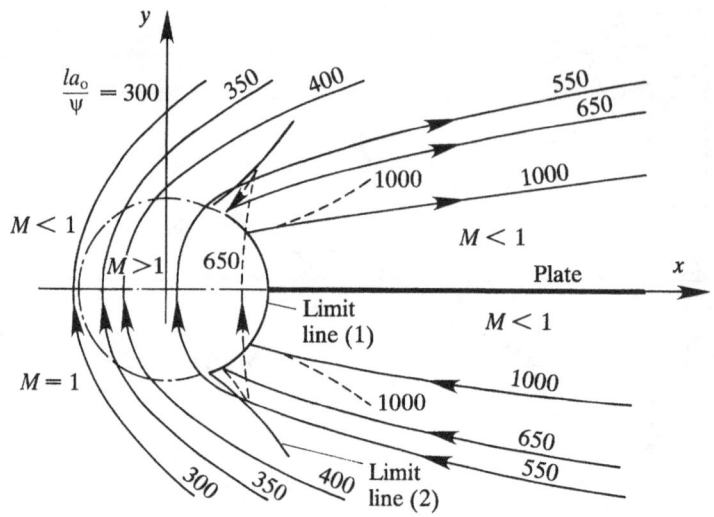

Fig. 2.21. Ringleb solution of the transonic flow around a semi-infinite plate [61].

Thus, the first streamline that does not impinge on the limit line 1 may be taken as a body surface in a transonic flow field whose streamlines from $la_0/\psi \approx 550$ to $la_0/\psi \approx 300$ enter an area of supersonic velocities but reenter the subsonic velocity range steadily without forming a shock wave. Thus it has been proven that there exist surface shapes that produce transonic flow fields without shock waves. However, it is obvious that such a surface is right for one specific approach Mach number only and therefore is of little or no practical value for airplane or rocket designs. Nevertheless, the fact that there are such surfaces has prompted several investigators to seek wing shapes that minimize the strength of shock waves over the operational range of an airplane. Those approaches and their success will be discussed in Chapter 8 on transonic airplane design.

2.7.4 The Transonic Shock Polar Curves

To conclude the discussions on the hodograph method, one more item should be mentioned, because it deals with a very useful method for the determination of the flow through curved shocks. Curved shock waves are always found in transonic flow fields about wing profiles. Forgoing the mathematics of this method (see ref. 4), its main features are shown in Fig. 2.22. Here the transonic shock polars are shown in the cartesian coordinates η and ϑ, where

$$\eta = (\gamma + 1)^{1/3} \frac{u' - a^*}{a^*} \quad \text{and} \quad \vartheta = \frac{v}{a^*}$$

The Theory of Inviscid Transonic Flow

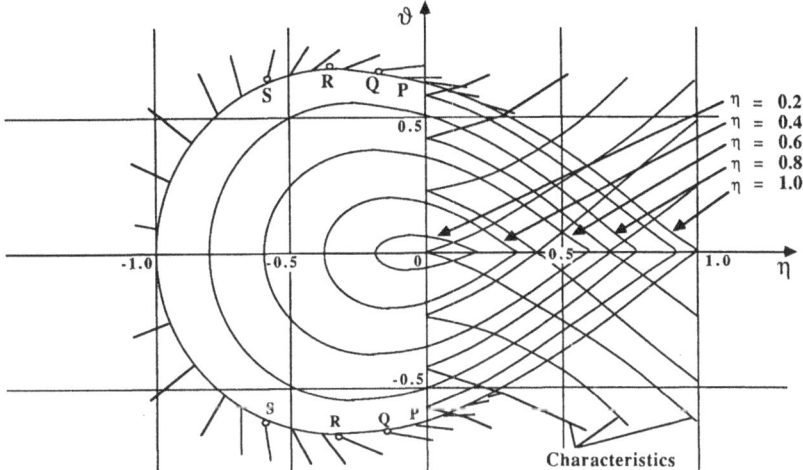

Fig. 2.22. Transonic shock polars and charatceristics in cartesian coordinates (From [4]).

With these substitutions Eq. 2.39 for two-dimensional flow becomes

$$\vartheta_{\mathrm{II}} - \vartheta_{\mathrm{I}} = \pm \sqrt{\frac{\eta_{\mathrm{I}} + \eta_{\mathrm{II}}}{2}} (\eta_{\mathrm{I}} - \eta_{\mathrm{II}}) \qquad (2.137)$$

where the transformations of Eqs. 2.22 have been taken into account.

As in the conventional shock polar diagrams, the apex of each of the polars (on the η axis) in Fig. 2.22 represents the approach velocity to the shock. Thus, for $M_\infty = 1$, $u' = a^*$ and $\eta_{\mathrm{I}} = \eta_{\mathrm{II}} = 0$; the shock polar is reduced to the point $\eta = 0$. The velocities before and behind a normal shock are given by the positive (η_{I}) and the negative (η_{II}) η-values, respectively, cut out by the polar curve on the η axis. As has been pointed out in connection with Eq. 2.39, $\eta_{\mathrm{I}} = -\eta_{\mathrm{II}}$ in the transonic range. For oblique shocks, the value of η_{II} is obtained from the intersection of the polar curve with the line for the flow deflection ϑ, which, in the cartesian system, is a line parallel to the η axis.

The important part of the transonic oblique shock diagram (Fig. 2.22) are the short lines drawn outward from the polar curve for $\eta_{\mathrm{I}} = 1$.[42] They indicate the streamline direction in the hodograph plane right downstream of a curved shock. This has to be understood as follows. The whole flow field behind a straight oblique shock is represented by a single point on the polar curve, the point ($\eta_{\mathrm{II}}, \vartheta_{\mathrm{II}}$), because velocity and flow angle are constant directly behind the shock. But when the shock is curved, velocity and flow angle change directly behind the shock in a way that is equivalent to moving along the polar curve in the hodograph plane. Now, if two adjacent streamlines were to continue behind the shock according to the η, ϑ value on the polar curve, they would diverge or converge, but certainly not satisfy the continuity law. They have to change their directions or their velocities or both, and it is interesting that there exists a unique solution for this streamline change.

Note that from the condition of the points S in Fig. 2.22, only the flow direction changes, whereas from the conditions of the points Q (Crocco point), the flow maintains its direction through the shock, but the velocity behind the shock is changed.

The benefit of Fig. 2.22 will now be demonstrated through the example of the flow from a supersonic nozzle against an ambient pressure higher than the static pressure of the jet at the nozzle exit. Here, one of three basic cases may occur.

(1) The ambient pressure is not much higher than the static jet pressure at the nozzle exit. Then the jet remains supersonic over a certain distance because the compression of the oblique shocks from the nozzle lip (Fig. 2.23) is insufficient to increase the static pressure to subsonic values. However, the pressure of the supersonic flow behind the "reflected" shocks 2 is now higher than the ambient pressure. To satisfy the boundary condition, flow expansion is necessary at the impingement points of the shocks 2 on the jet boundary. Because the flow is supersonic, the shocks are reflected from the free boundary as expansion waves. Behind these expansion fans ambient pressure is restored until the fans are "reflected" from the centerline, producing a pressure lower than the ambient value. To compensate for this deficiency, the fans are reflected from the boundary as shock waves, and so on, until friction forces reduce the flow to a subsonic jet of the ambient static pressure. This well-known "barrel flow" can be observed at rocket launchings.

(2) The ambient pressure is much higher than the static pressure at the nozzle exit, but of course lower than the jet stagnation pressure. Here a shock system does form in the nozzle, so that the sum of the pressure rise in the shocks to a subsonic value and the subsequent subsonic pressure rise in the expand- ing nozzle produces at the nozzle exit a subsonic jet of the ambient pressure.

(3) Between the extreme cases 1 and 2 we have conditions in which the pressure of the supersonic flow at the nozzle exit is lower than the

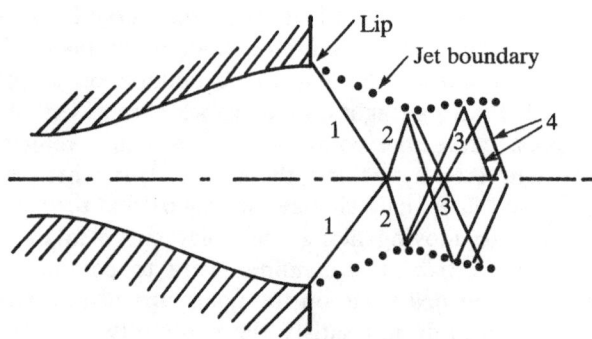

Fig. 2.23. Supersonic free jet (barrel flow).

The Theory of Inviscid Transonic Flow

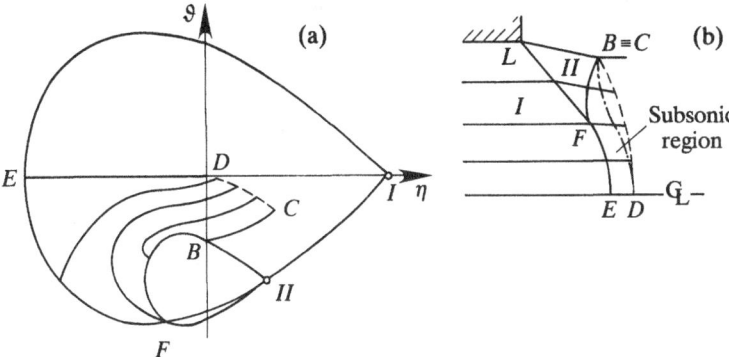

Fig. 2.24. Supersonic nozzle flow against a high ambient pressure. (a) Hodograph plane; (b) physical plane (from [4]); – · – · – · sonic line; – – – – – "terminating" characteristic.

ambient pressure so that oblique shocks from the nozzle lips must form to satisfy the boundary condition. The pressure behind these shocks is now so high that subsonic flow would result from the compression in the reflected shocks "2," however. The static pressure of this subsonic flow would be higher than the ambient pressure but no equivalent of the expansion fan of supersonic flow is available here to satisfy the boundary condition. Although shocks are needed at the nozzle exit, no "reflected" shocks are allowed to form. These two requirements can only be met by a curved shock from the lips that become normal at the centerline. Then the reflected shock has zero strength. Unfortunately, this is not yet the full answer. If the shocks were continuously curved from the lip to the centerline, they would produce a converging supersonic flow, resulting in a continuously increasing pressure in flow direction, and also at the boundary. Since the boundary condition would again be violated, a flow pattern of the kind shown in Fig. 2.24b seems to be the only solution. Here the shock from the lip is straight to a point F from which on it curves to the normal position at the centerline. The discontinuity at F requires a new curved shock from F to the boundary, compressing the flow in such a way that it is subsonic behind the shock but becomes sonic at the boundary, so that the boundary condition can be met through an expansion fan.

The great benefit of the hodograph presentation for a better understanding of this complex flow pattern will now be shown. In Fig. 2.24a the oblique shock formed at the nozzle lip L is represented in the hodograph plane by the large polar curve whose apex is determined by the nozzle flow condition I at the nozzle exit. The ambient-to-nozzle pressure ratio is such that the flow behind the oblique shock is still supersonic, and its velocity and direction are given by the point II on the large polar curve. Because the shock is straight, the whole range II in Fig. 2.24b is represented in Fig. 2.24a as a single point. This point, therefore, is the apex of a smaller polar curve, representing the possible flow conditions behind a shock approached by the parallel supersonic flow II.[43] This shock, starting at F and ending at B on the boundary, must be curved because it is approached by the parallel flow of region II but requires varying flow conditions behind it, namely, subsonic flow at F and at least sonic flow at B to allow for the flow expansion to the ambient pressure. This Prandtl–Meyer expansion appears in the hodograph plane as the characteristic curve from B to C and may be obtained from Fig. 2.22. The location of C is determined by the boundary condition of constant pressure, $\eta_C = \eta_{II}$, because $\eta \sim u/U \sim c_p$ (see Note 23). Downstream of the shock system B–F–E we have a converging subsonic flow field, so that the flow is again accelerated, reaching the sonic line B–D. For a more detailed description of this subsonic flow field, we now take advantage of Fig. 2.22, which gives the directions of the hodograph streamlines behind the shock. Between E and F, these stream lines originate at the polar curve I, at E from the normal shock value, but between F and B at the polar curve II. A second piece of information about the shape of the streamlines in the hodograph plane we obtain from the flow expansion to supersonic values from B to C. Such an expansion is represented in the hodograph plane as a characteristic, again obtained from Fig. 2.22. The streamlines between C and D are characteristics as well, because they represent the expansion fan at various distances from B. Because of the converging flow to the sonic line, they turn less and less, and become shorter and shorter in the hodograph plane to zero length at the centerline. Their end points are given by the characteristic C–D.[44] With this information, the qualitatively quite accurate hodograph streamlines may be drawn in the region E–F–B–C–D–E. With the help of a good version of Fig. 2.24b, the streamlines in the physical plane may then be deduced.

It must be realized that this is not the complete answer to the problem, because downstream of the characteristic C–B a converging supersonic flow is produced that again cannot satisfy the boundary condition. Something similar to another delta shock would be required to continue the flow. Nevertheless, this example should show the process of going back and forth between the physical and the hodograph planes for qualitative investigations of complex transonic flows.

It is hoped that these few examples of the hodograph approach to the solution of transonic flow problems have convinced the reader of the potential of this method. To get a comprehensive insight into this fascinating field, and particularly its mathematical foundation, the books of Guderley [4] and Ferrari and Tricomi [10] are highly recommended. However, it would be shortsighted to consider such a study as just an interesting but dispensable approach to transonic problems, particularly in light of the flood of published computer programs and solutions. The fact is that without an intimate knowledge of the physical phenomena of transonic flow no progress will be made in the accuracy of computer solutions. After more than a decade of transonic computer programming, the exact shape of even a single shock wave in the transonic flow field about a profile cannot yet be determined. Complex problems like the delta shock of our above example, followed by a subsonic region that is reaccelerated to supersonic flow would require too many mesh points to be handled by the computer in an acceptable length of time. And even if a perfect result could be obtained, it would take exactly the same time all over to solve a problem only slightly different from the first one, because no extrapolation of the results is possible in a nonlinear system of equations.

Notes

1. Not to be confused with the "critical Mach number" M_{cr}, introduced previously as the Mach number at which supersonic flow first occurs at the body surface.
2. There are other methods of linearization available that will be discussed in the chapters on solution procedures.
3. The interested reader may derive this equation (see Prob. 1.3). Also, he will obtain the equation for the curve of Fig. 2.2 by multiplying it by M^*.
4. The second derivative of the general gas-dynamic expression for the pressure is equal to zero at $M = 1$ (see also Prob. 1.3).
5. See Prob. 1.3.
6. In this chapter, u is used for the total x-component of the vector $\mathbf{W}$. In the following chapters it will usually be used for the perturbation component and will be designated accordingly.
7. See Probs. 1.1 and 1.2.
8. The assumption of isoenergetic flow is no significant restriction because, in most practical cases, differences in the Bernoulli constant (Eq. 1.18) from streamline to streamline occur only in the boundary layer that must be treated with viscous theory.
9. Since the z-components form terms identical to those of the y-components and are unchanged from Eq. 2.9, the w terms have been omitted and will be reintroduced as needed.
10. Here, the perturbation velocities have been related to the critical speed of sound a^*, which is no restriction in establishing the relative magnitudes only of the derivatives of the perturbation velocities. For practical applications, it may be preferable to relate them to the approach velocity U, as will be done in following chapters.
11. In this respect y and z, and v and w, are the same variables.
12. See, e.g., ref. 5.
13. Or by the scalar product of $\mathbf{W}$ and the tangential unit vector.
14. See Prob. 2.16.
15. It must be pointed out that a much simpler procedure, which will be applied to axisymmetric similarity rules later in the chapter, leads to the desired result. However, the source-sink method is one of the most important tools for the computation of aerodynamic flow fields and is therefore introduced here.
16. According to a sign convention, the flow is directed from the lower potential ($\phi = -\infty$ at $r = 0$) to the higher one ($\phi = +\infty$ at $r = \infty$).
17. Distributions of other singularities, like vortices and dipoles, produce bodies at an angle of attack, cambered profiles, and so on.
18. See Prob. 2.9 for the meaning of a "compressible source."

19. For the error made by this approximation, see Prob. 2.20.
20. Since the undisturbed flow field is given as $U = \text{const.}$, the source-sink potential constitutes the perturbations of the field.
21. The pressure coefficient is obtained from the definition $c_p = (p - p_\infty)/q_\infty = (2/\gamma M_\infty^2)[(p/p_\infty) - 1]$ by applying the general gas-dynamics equation (see Prob. 1.3)

$$p/p_0 = (T/T_0)^{\gamma/\gamma-1} = [1 + (\gamma - 1)M^2/2]^{-\gamma/(\gamma-1)}$$

To determine p/p_∞, the expression $[2 + (\gamma - 1)M_\infty^2]/[2 + (\gamma - 1)M^2]$ must be evaluated in terms of M_∞ and the velocity components. With $M_\infty = U/a_\infty$ and $M = W/a = \sqrt{(U + u)^2 + v^2 + w^2}/a$ and the energy law $W^2/2 + a^2/(\gamma - 1) = U^2/2 + a_\infty^2/(\gamma - 1)$, one arrives at the slender-body equation

$$c_p = \frac{2}{\gamma M_\infty^2}\left\{\left[1 + \frac{\gamma - 1}{2}M_\infty^2\left(1 - \frac{(U + u)^2 + v^2 + w^2}{U^2}\right)\right]^{\gamma/(\gamma-1)} - 1\right\}$$

Here, the second term in the square brackets is much smaller than 1 and applying the first two terms of the binominal expansion we have

$$c_p = -\frac{2u}{U} - (1 - M_\infty^2)\frac{u^2}{U^2} - \frac{v^2 + w^2}{U^2},$$

where the third- and higher-order terms are disregarded. In transonic flow, $M_\infty \approx 1$ and the second term is of higher order. Thus, we finally have

$$c_p = -\frac{2u}{U} - \frac{v^2 + w^2}{U^2} = -\frac{2u}{U} - \left(\frac{dy}{dx}\right)^2$$

In plane flow, the second term on the right-hand side is small compared with the first one and may be dropped. In axisymmetric flow, however, the second term must be retained, as will be explained later.
22. Note that the approach velocity has dropped out of the similarity rule, in agreement with the statement made on page 49: that the approach velocities may be assumed to be equal for similarity considerations.
23. Barred symbols designate *affine* points transforming *potential* fields.
24. See Note 21.
25. The two-dimensional plane flow case may be treated in an analogous fashion (see Prob. 2.14 for an example), and side-glances at the two-dimensional case will occasionally be made during the following derivation.
26. Since transonic flow practically always contains shock waves, the shock relations must be satisfied by a transonic equation.
27. This fact will be discussed in more detail in Sec. 5.2.1.
28. The existence of perturbation potentials, at least for the orders of expansion considered here, will be justified later (see, e.g., page 70).
29. The same result is obtained with the axisymmetric transonic similarity parameter Eq. 2.75. Here, with Eq. 2.100b, $\beta^2 \sim t^2 = \varepsilon_1$.
30. For this order-of-magnitude computation, no error is made by assuming that the velocity before the shock is the approach velocity U.
31. The index II has been dropped, because the changes across the shock are given unequivocally by the orders of the perturbation velocities behind the shock.
32. The symbol $o(t^2)$ means that the higher-order terms of k_{II}/k_I (H.O.T.) go to zero for $t^2 \to 0[\lim_{t^2 \to 0}(\text{H.O.T.}) = 0]$. For the definition of the symbols $O(\ )$ and $o(\ )$, see Note 34.

The Theory of Inviscid Transonic Flow 93

33. Entropy and total pressure are related as
$$\frac{S_2 - S_1}{R} = -\ln\frac{p_{02}}{p_{01}}$$
as integration from p_{01} to p_{02} of Eq. 1.14 yields for $T = T_0 = \text{const}$.
34. As explained in detail (e.g. in ref. 9), the order $O(\varepsilon)$ of a term $t(\varepsilon)$ means that $\lim_{\varepsilon \to 0}(t/\varepsilon) \leq k\varepsilon > 0$, that is, it is bounded, whereas $o(\varepsilon)$ stands for $\lim_{\varepsilon \to 0}(t/\varepsilon) \to 0$ (see also Note 32).
35. The corresponding equation for plane flow is $\varphi_1 = \bar{\bar{S}}_1(x)\bar{y} + \bar{\bar{g}}_1(x)$, as may be determined through integration of Eq. 2.98a.
36. Note that $\ln t$ is always negative, but ε_2 is a positive magnitude by definition. Thus the minus sign has to apply to $\bar{S}_2(x)$.
37. The derivation of Eq. 2.127 is left to the reader as Prob. 2.17.
38. Generally $\varepsilon \to \varepsilon_0$, where ε_0 is the limit point in the interval under consideration.
39. Considering the total source flow, not only the nozzle-type sectors shown in Fig. 2.15 for clarity, then it becomes obvious that we have to assume that the flow turns back into itself.
40. That is, when the flow approaches the limit line, only the viscous flow equations can give the right results, see Chapter 6.
41. See also Prob. 2.15.
42. The same $d\eta/d\vartheta$ lines apply to the affine points on any other polar curve.
43. The advantage of using cartesians instead of polar coordinates is obvious: the axes of all shock polars in cartesian coordinates are parallel, whereas in polar coordinates each axis would have a different slope, according to the approaching flow field direction, making the chart much more complicated.
44. For a more detailed information on the characteristics involved in this process, the reader must be referred to the literature—see, for example, refs. 4 and 5.

Problems

2.1. In Note 21 the pressure coefficient for small perturbations was derived from the general equations. Derive c_p for plane transonic flow from the relations of Eq. 2.3.

2.2. Derive the similarity rules Eqs. 2.59, 2.60 and 2.65a by the method applied in the derivation of the rule Eq. 2.68.

2.3. For slender bodies, the lift coefficient c_L and the drag coefficient c_D are related to the pressure coefficient in very simple ways. Establish these coefficients by expressing drag and lift forces through the pressure acting on a body surface element.

2.4. For three-dimensional plane flow in which the z-dimension (i.e., thickness) is much smaller than the x and y dimensions, the similarity law contains, in addition to the parameter for two-dimensional flow, a second parameter for the relationship between the lateral dimensions of the two bodies. Again, applying the method of Prob. 2.2, derive this similarity law:
$$c_p = \lambda f_p\left(\frac{t}{\lambda\beta}; b\beta\right)$$

where b is the lateral dimension that may be replaced by the aspect ratio $R = b^2/A_{wing} = b^2/cb \sim b$ (cord c_1 = cord c_2).

Clue: Starting from the potential equation

$$\beta_1^2 \phi_{1xx} + \phi_{1yy} + \phi_{1zz} = 0$$

both the y and the z coordinate must be stretched by the factor β_1/β_2 in order to arrive at an identical equation for the flow at the second Mach number. Then, the two streamline (body surface) equations must be established with this fact in mind. Since the body shape function is now a function of both x/c and y/b, but must be equal in both cases, one similarity parameter is obtained from $f_1 = f_2$, the other from $y_1/b_1 = y_2/b_2 = (y_1/b_2)(\beta_1/\beta_2)$, whereas $x_1/c = x_2/c$ by definition. Note that the result is valid for any value of λ, that is, also for the transonic value of $(\gamma + 1)M_\infty^2/(1 - M_\infty^2)$.

2.5. In a subsonic wind tunnel, the pressure coefficients c_p on a profile of thickness ratio t_{inc} are to be established for approach Mach numbers $0.5 \leq M_\infty \leq 1$ ($\gamma = 1.4$). Determine the thickness ratios t in relation to t_{inc} required to obtain the desired c_p values. Draw a diagram for t/t_{inc} vs. M_∞.

2.6. The so-called Prandtl–Glauert equation is obtained by setting the right-hand side of Eq. 2.26 equal to zero; that is, it is the small perturbation flow equation, excluding the transonic range. The PG equation is reduced to the Laplace equation by setting

$$x = \xi \quad \text{and} \quad y = \frac{\eta}{\sqrt{1 - M_\infty^2}}$$

where ξ and η are of the order 1.

The transonic correction term may be disregarded as long as it is small compared with the first term of the PG equation. A criterion for the validity range of the PG equation, therefore, is

$$(1 - M_\infty^2) \gg M_\infty^2 (\gamma + 1)(u/U)$$

or, conversely, the range in which the transonic equation must be applied is given as

$$\chi = \frac{|1 - M_\infty^2|}{M_\infty^2 (\gamma + 1)(u/U)} \leq a$$

where a is at least equal to 1, but may be chosen to be somewhat larger, depending on the accuracy required.

The magnitude of the perturbation velocity u is a function of the body thickness ratio t, so that the transonic flow range depends on a certain function between the approach Mach number and the thickness ratio of the model. Writing the perturbation potential as $\varphi = U\tau\bar{\varphi}(\xi, \eta)$, where $\bar{\varphi}$ is of the order 1:

(a) Develop the relationship between τ and t (both τ and t may be included in the streamline equation!).

(b) Show that by expressing u/U through t and a power of $(1 - M_\infty^2)$, the above condition for the range in which the transonic equations must be used becomes identical to the argument of the similarity function f_p in Eq. 2.65b. (Note that this result shows that the difference in the application of Eq. 2.65b to transonic and to subsonic and supersonic # The Theory of Inviscid Transonic Flow

problems lies in the magnitude of χ. In the former, $\chi \leq a \approx 1$, and in the latter $\chi \gg 1$).

(c) Explain why these two relationships should be equal.

2.7. To experimentally prove the validity of the transonic similarity rule, a two-dimensional model of thickness ratio t is tested in a wind tunnel equipped for operation with helium, air, and Freon. The He tests are done at $M_\infty = 0.7$, 0.8, and 0.9. According to the similarity rule Eq. 2.65a, by how much must M_∞ be changed to compare the values of c_p computed from the He tests with those of the tests with the other gases?

2.8. The pressure coefficients on the surface of a slender profile are given in an incompressible flow field as c_{pi}.
(a) Determine c_p for the same profile but the changed thickness ratio t according to the Goethert rule at the Mach numbers at which the subsonic and the transonic similarity parameters have the same value ($\gamma = $ const)
(b) Determine c_p and t at $M_\infty = 0.9$ according to the transonic similarity rule.

2.9. In the Eqs. 2.47 and 2.48, the sources per unit length, $q(\xi)$, are arbitrary functions in the particular solutions of the Laplace equation and the corresponding compressible flow equation. These small perturbation equations describe the deviations from a flow field of constant velocity in the x direction. Nevertheless, Eq. 2.38 could be interpreted as the flow from a point source in still air ($\beta = 1$ for $M_\infty = 0$). In all cases of $\beta \neq 1$, $q(\xi)$ is strictly a mathematical tool, because such sources cannot exist. However, in integrating Eq. 2.48, the perturbation potential lines that are superimposed in the integration process have a specific shape for each value of $q(\xi)$. The flow fields of these individual "sources" are of interest.

As particular solutions of the governing equations, determine the potential lines $\varphi = $ const. and the streamlines $\psi = $ const. of
(a) an incompressible flow source
(b) a subsonic compressible source
(c) a supersonic source ($\beta = -(M_\infty^2 - 1)^{1/2}$)
(d) a transonic source (neglecting the transonic correction term in Eq. 2.26 and, consequently, only receiving a first approximation)

Compare the results when approaching the transonic limit $\beta = 0$ from the subsonic and from the supersonic result. Note that the streamlines always intersect the equipotential lines at right angles.

2.10. From the results obtained for air in Prob. 2.7, determine, applying the same similarity rules, the change in c_p when the thickness ratio is (a) doubled, (b) decreased by one-half.

2.11. Show that the relationship Eq. 2.121 is in agreement with the condition $t^4 = o(\varepsilon_2)$ and that $t^4 = O(\varepsilon_2)$ when $\varepsilon_2 = t^4$.

2.12. Determine the relative importance of the second-order solution through the ratio $\varepsilon_2/\varepsilon_1$ for an axisymmetric body of thickness ratios $t = 0.05$, 0.1, 0.2, 0.5, and 1.0. Explain the reason for the apparent inconsistency of the results.

2.13. Conduct the iteration leading to Eq. 2.119a.

  Clue: By introducing Eq. 2.118 into Eq. 2.117, only the lowest-order terms that do not cancel in this process need to be considered for the next step.

2.14. Determine the relationship $\varepsilon_2 = \varepsilon_2(t)$, for two-dimensional plane flow, following the procedure for axisymmetric flow of Sec. 2.6, with the result of Eq. 2.121.

2.15. The solution of Eq. 2.133 for $\psi_\theta = \psi_{\theta\theta} = 0$ is $\psi = f(M)$. Thus, $M = $ const. along the streamlines ($\psi = $ const.), which must therefore be parallel to each other. Also, since $\psi_\theta = 0$ means that the streamlines cross the lines $\theta = $ const., it must be concluded that they are circles about the origin.
  (a) Derive the solution $\psi = f(M)$.
  (b) Since potential flow is assumed, the rotation of the flow must be zero. Show that this condition leads to Eq. 2.135.

2.16. Derive the chain rule

$$\frac{\partial x}{\partial y}\frac{\partial y}{\partial z}\frac{\partial z}{\partial x} = -1$$

2.17. Derive Eq. 2.127 from $c_p = (2/\gamma M_\infty^2)(p - p_\infty)/p_\infty$. As a transonic equation, it should cover the flow through weak shock waves. Is the adiabatic relationship $p/T^{(1/\gamma-1)} = $ const. applicable? Refer to the proper equation derived earlier. Express p/p_∞ as a function of M_∞, a, U, and γ.

2.18. In cylindrical coordinates, derive the continuity equation of incompressible flow ($\rho = $ cons.), that is, the divergence div $\mathbf{W}$ [coordinates $u(x)$, $v(r)$, $w(r\,d\omega)$] of the general flow through a volume element, limited by planes through the axis $\omega = $ const. and $\omega + d\omega = $ const., the planes $r = $ const. and $r + dr = $ const., and the planes $x = $ const. and $x + dx = $ const. Specialize the result for axisymmetric flow and flow in polar coordinates.

2.19. Derive Eqs. 2.12 and 2.13. Whereas Eq. 2.12 is readily obtained with div $\mathbf{W}$ for axisymmetric flow (Prob. 2.18) following the procedure indicated on page 34, the derivation of Eq. 2.13 requires the curl $\mathbf{W}$ operator for polar flow when, in the last step, the two terms multiplied with vw are compared with the condition of irrotationality. Contrary to the axisymmetric case, where the terms multiplied with uv are equal because the curl component $\partial v/\partial x - \partial u/\partial r = 0$ for irrotationality, the curl component in the polar coordinates includes a third term w/r that produces the last term of Eq. 2.13.

2.20. Compute $q(\xi)$ for a parabolic arc profile from Eq. 2.55. Determine the contributions $dv = Cq(\eta)\,d\eta$ to the integral of Eq. 2.53 for the stations (a) $x - \xi = \beta y(\cotg \eta = 1)$; (b) $x - \xi = 5\beta y$; and (c) $x - \xi = 10\beta y$ at (1) $y = y_{b\max}$, (2) $y = y_{b\max}/2$, and (3) $y = y_{b\max}/10$. Compare the contributions from the stations (a), (b) and (c) for the cases (1), (2) and (3).

3
NONSTEADY TRANSONIC FLOW

3.1 General Observations

Although the theory of a steady transonic flow, as given in Chapter 2, is well suited for computations of transonic flow fields, the reason for the much quoted "sound barrier"—that is, the strong increase in drag of a flying object at its approach to the velocity of sound—is not obvious from those theoretical studies. However, this important characteristic of transonic flight can be readily understood from nonsteady theory.

Since small disturbances of the atmosphere travel with the speed of sound,[1] the disturbances caused by a flying object are not immediately felt in the space around it. To get a clearer conception of this fact, let us assume that a very slender, frictionless body with a blunt nose[2] is instantly accelerated to a constant speed. At this moment, the stagnation pressure at the body nose is higher than the ambient static pressure, produces a spherical pressure wave that propagates outward at the speed of sound. An instant later, the body has moved by a very small amount, and a new spherical wave has moved in the meantime. This process continues as long as the body moves; of course, the time intervals to be considered are actually infinitesimally small.

Although the process just described of the generation of pressure waves is independent of the body's velocity, the resulting pressure distribution on the body varies greatly from one of the major speed ranges (subsonic, transonic, supersonic) to another: The pressure disturbances from a body moving at subsonic speed are felt in the entire space, with the sections of the spherical waves in front of the body lying closer together than those behind the body. For a body moving at supersonic speed, no part of the spherical waves can propagate ahead of the body nose. Their centers fall behind the body and their diameters increase with their distance from the body. The envelope of all these spherical waves forms the well-known Mach cone of supersonic flow. Outside of this cone, no disturbances are felt. Therefore, this zone is called the zone of silence; a missile approaching at supersonic speed cannot be detected acoustically.

Now, what happens when the body moves exactly at the speed of sound? Obviously, the front parts of the spherical waves stay exactly with the body; all waves are tangent to each other at the body. As the infinitesimal pressures pile up on the body, the stagnation pressure, and thus the drag, steadily increase. Assuming a linear law governing this process, pressure and drag would rise with time beyond any value. Since it is known that this cannot happen, nonlinear processes must take over at some point, limiting pressure and drag to a finite value. Actually, this mental experiment proves the need for nonlinear laws in the correct description of transonic flow. This physical requirement is another reason for the impossibility of linearizing the transonic continuity equation. In subsonic and supersonic (not hypersonic) flight linearization is possible because the disturbances generated by the body do not stay with the body, and thus the pressures stay finite.

3.2 Non-steady Transonic Theory

For a quantitative evaluation of the process just described, the simplification of a slender, frictionless body must be dropped. Pressure disturbances are created by all parts of a flying body, and these combine to produce different pressures at different stations of the body.

The mathematics of the processes just described is of interest, because it shows another way of solving flow problems. All our studies so far have been based on a coordinate system fixed in the body. Thus, the flow was assumed to approach the stationary body with the velocity U. This coordinate system could therefore be termed the test stand or wind tunnel system. For nonsteady computations it is advantageous to use the natural system, that is, a system corresponding to the actual aircraft flight in which the air far away from the body is at rest and the body is moving. Here the co-ordinate system is fixed in still air. In such a system only the perturbation velocities play a role. However, this means that the Mach number of the body velocity must be introduced into the computation through the boundary conditions, which are now functions of time as the body moves in the stationary coordinate system. The linearized potential equation of the flow becomes independent of the Mach number, as will be shown in the following brief derivation:

By expressing the partial derivatives of p through Eqs. 2.7 and 2.8 and introducing the velocity potential, the unsteady Euler equations, Eqs. 1.5, become

$$\frac{a^2}{\rho}\left(\frac{\partial \rho}{\partial x} - \frac{\partial \rho}{\partial S}\frac{\partial S}{\partial x}\right) = -(\Phi_{xt} + \Phi_x\Phi_{xx} + \Phi_y\Phi_{xy} + \Phi_z\Phi_{xz}) \quad (3.1a)$$

and two corresponding equations (3.1b) and (3.1c) for the y- and z-components, respectively. By integrating these three equations with respect to x, y, and z, respectively, and differentiating the equations thus obtained with respect to t, we obtain three equations that only differ by the integration functions $f_1(t; y, z)$, $f_2(t; z, x)$, and $f_3(t; x, y)$, resulting from the above integrations with respect to x, y, and z. However, because the three equations are identical otherwise, the integration functions cannot depend on x, y, or z, and must be the same function of

Nonsteady Transonic Flow

t. Thus we obtain

$$\frac{a^2}{\rho}\left(\frac{\partial \rho}{\partial t} - \frac{\partial \rho}{\partial S}\frac{\partial S}{\partial t}\right) = -(\Phi_{tt} + \Phi_x\Phi_{xt} + \Phi_y\Phi_{yt} + \Phi_z\Phi_{zt}) + f(t) \quad (3.2)$$

Solving Eqs. 3.1 and Eq. 3.2 for the partial derivatives of ρ, and introducing these expressions into the unsteady continuity equation (Eq. 1.2), we finally arrive at the unsteady potential equation:

$$\Phi_{xx}(a^2 - \Phi_x^2) + \Phi_{yy}(a^2 - \Phi_y^2) + \Phi_{zz}(a^2 - \Phi_z^2) - \Phi_{tt} + f(t) - 2\Phi_x\Phi_{xt}$$
$$- 2\Phi_y\Phi_{yt} - 2\Phi_z\Phi_{zt} - 2\Phi_x\Phi_y\Phi_{xy} - 2\Phi_y\Phi_z\Phi_{yz} - 2\Phi_z\Phi_x\Phi_{xz} = 0 \quad (3.3)$$

where the terms containing the entropy S cancel out because of Eq. 2.6. By defining a new potential function as $\Phi_{tt} + f(t) = \varphi_{tt}$, the function $f(t)$ may be eliminated, and, retaining the symbol Φ instead of φ, the unsteady equation differs from the steady (Eq. 2.12) just by the term

$$-(\Phi_{tt} + 2\Phi_x\Phi_{xt} + 2\Phi_y\Phi_{yt} + 2\Phi_z\Phi_{zt})$$

Finally, the linearized unsteady continuity equation is obtained from Eq. 3.3 without the eliminated term $f(t)$, by retaining the lowest-order terms only as

$$\Phi_{xx} + \Phi_{yy} + \Phi_{zz} - \frac{\Phi_{tt}}{a_\infty^2} = 0 \quad (3.4a)$$

Note that a has been replaced by a_∞. Since we are considering the propagation of disturbances in still air, the linearized sound speed is constant and equal to the ambient value, a_∞, as mathematically may be seen from the relationship between a and a_∞ given on page 37 by setting $U = 0$ in that equation and dropping the perturbation terms u^2, v^2 (w^2 had already been omitted in this equation for simplicity). As predicted, Eq. 3.4a does not contain the flight Mach number.

3.3 The Pressure Coefficient From Nonsteady Theory

We are now ready to compute the pressure build-up on a flying object from the superposition of infinitesimal pressure waves originating at every moment as a result of the body motion. By restricting the study to slender bodies we can, as in the case of steady theory, assume that the flow field about the body is produced by sources and sinks on the body centerline, the only difference being that now the source strength is a function of both time and the station in the space-fixed coordinate system. The integration of this source strength function leads to a perturbation velocity field that moves with the body and that is no longer added to an approach velocity, because the ambient air is at rest.

The spherical waves originating at the sources on the centerline are best expressed in spherical coordinates, in which Eq. 3.4a becomes

$$\Phi_{rr} + \frac{2}{r}\Phi_r - \frac{1}{a_\infty^2}\Phi_{tt} = 0 \quad (3.4b)$$

where $r^2 = x^2 + y^2 + z^2$. That the solution of this well-known equation is

$$\Phi = \frac{1}{r} f\left(t(\pm) \frac{r}{a_\infty}\right) \tag{3.5}$$

can easily be verified. Because we are interested in the waves propagating from the sources outward, only the negative sign must be considered.

The rate of flow from the source is given by the product of the surface area of a sphere with the source as its center and the flow velocity at this surface:

$$Q(t) = 4\pi r^2 \Phi_r$$

$$= 4\pi r^2 \left\{ -\frac{1}{r^2} f\left(t - \frac{r}{a_\infty}\right) - \frac{1}{ra_\infty} f'\left(t - \frac{r}{a_\infty}\right) \right\}$$

The source strength is obtained by letting $r \to 0$:

$$q(t) = -4\pi f(t) \tag{3.6}$$

Thus, combining Eq. 3.6 with Eq. 3.5, the potential of a source located at $x = x_1$, $y = 0$, $z = 0$, is obtained as

$$\Phi = -\frac{1}{4\pi R} q\left(x_1, t - \frac{R}{a_\infty}\right) \tag{3.7}$$

where $t - R/a_\infty$, which we will call t_1, is the time at which the source emits the disturbance, and, because we are interested in the conditions on the body surface, the distance r must be replaced by

$$R = \sqrt{(x - x_1)^2 + r_b^2} \tag{3.8}$$

where r_b is the body radius at the station x ($r_b^2 = y^2 + z^2$). The time difference for the disturbance to arrive at the station (x, r_b) and to leave the source at the station $(x_1, 0)$ thus becomes

$$t(x, r_b) - t_1(x_1, 0) = \frac{R}{a_\infty} \tag{3.9}$$

The total potential resulting from all centerline sources at the station x, r_b and at the time t is obtained as the integral

$$\Phi = -\frac{1}{4\pi} \int_{x_1=-\infty}^{x_1=+\infty} \frac{1}{R} q\left(x_1, t - \frac{R}{a_\infty}\right) dx_1 \tag{3.10}$$

Note that all perturbation contributions along the flight path must be included. At any time t, sources are located within the body only, but their disturbances may be felt by the flying body after it has left behind the station of the source. Therefore, in an (x, t) diagram, the range of sources to be considered lies between the two lines through the nose and the tail of the body, inclined at the angle $\alpha = \arctan(a_\infty t/x) = \arctan(1/M_\infty)$. Such diagrams are shown in Figs. 3.1. The sources that at any time affect the pressure at a certain station of the body surface (e.g.,

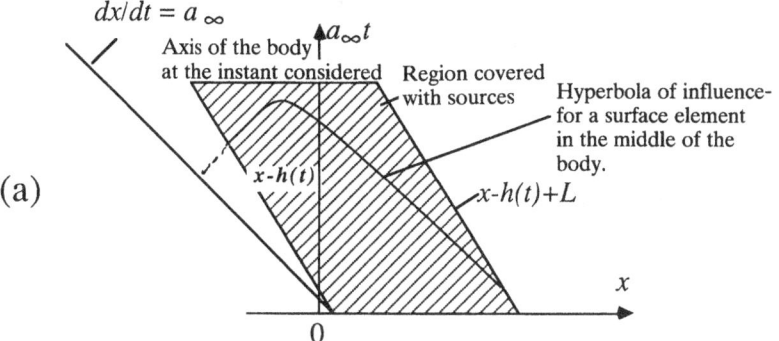

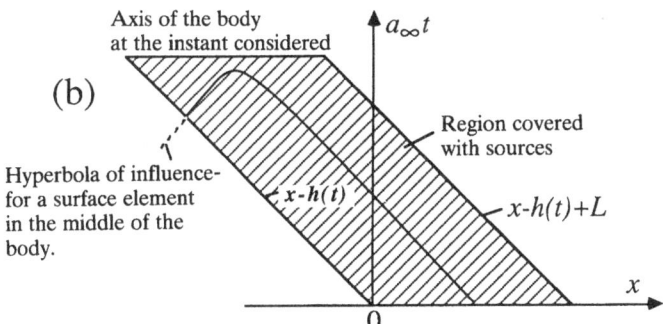

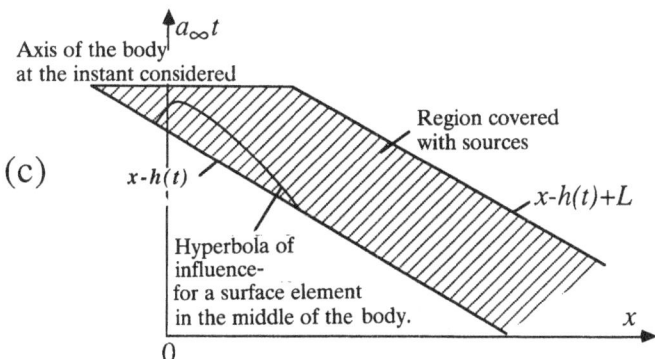

Fig. 3.1. The hyperbolas of influence for a body, starting abruptly from rest at (a) subsonic, (b) sonic, and (c) supersonic velocities. L = body length, a_∞ = sonic speed, t = time. (From Guderley [4]). In (a), the approach of the object is not felt to the left of the line $dx/dt = a_\infty$.

the station of maximum thickness) can be determined from Eqs. 3.8 and 3.9, which may be combined to give

$$t - t_1 = \frac{\sqrt{(x - x_1)^2 + r_b^2}}{a_\infty}$$

or (3.11)

$$\frac{(t - t_1)^2}{r_b^2/a_\infty^2} - \frac{(x - x_1)^2}{r_b^2} = 1$$

This equation shows that the stations (x_1, t_1) form a hyperbola on which all the sources lie that contribute to the disturbances at the station (x, t). These 'hyperbolas of influence'[4] are drawn in Figs. 3.1a, b, and c for subsonic, transonic (sonic), and supersonic flight, respectively. These figures show the important fact that in subsonic and supersonic flight both legs of the hyperbola are cut off by the boundary lines of the source range. However, in sonic flight, one leg of the hyperbola becomes infinitely long with time. The contributions of the sources to the pressure at a certain station of the body increase at every moment of the flight, whereas in subsonic and supersonic flight the contributions remain finite and constant. We must conclude, therefore, that in linear theory the pressures on a body flying at sonic speed become infinitely large with time. The so-called sound barrier thus finds its explanation. Of course, as has been pointed out before, the linear superposition of disturbances ceases at a certain point, nonlinear effects take over,[5] and the pressure build-up remains finite. Nevertheless, it exceeds anything possible in subsonic and supersonic flight, and the term *sound barrier* retains its significance. For the mathematical proof of the conclusion as drawn from

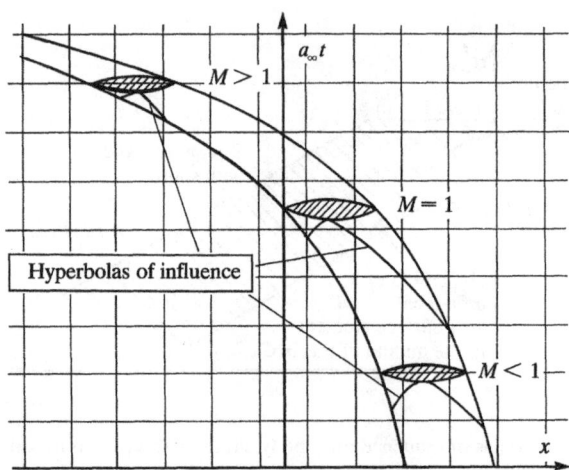

Fig. 3.2. Slender body accelerated from rest to supersonic velocity. linearized, unsteady theory. Space-fixed coordinate system. a_∞ = speed of sound sound in ambient, still air; t = flight time.

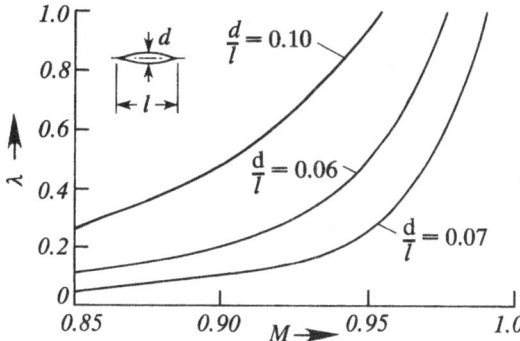

Fig. 3.3. The Mach number and thickness ratio range for which linear theory may still be applicable. (According to Gardner and Ludloff [12] and Cole [13].)

Fig. 3.1b, namely, that in transonic flight the pressure increases infinitely, the reader is referred to Guderley's derivation [4].

Now let us set aside the unrealistic assumption of instantaneous attainment of a constant velocity. In Fig. 3.2 the diagrams of Fig. 3.1 have been combined to the case of acceleration from $M = 0$ to supersonic velocity. The interesting conclusion is that, if the acceleration through the speed of sound is great enough, the time is too short for a sound barrier to form, that is, at $M = 1$, the hyperbola of influence[6] does not have an infinitely long leg, as shown in Fig. 3.2. Thus, high transonic drag could be avoided. Unfortunately, as several investigators have shown, little benefit can be derived from this fact [12, 13]. To put it differently, the minimum acceleration required to stay within the realm of linearized theory is too high for practical applications (see Cole [13]).

The variations of lift and drag with the rate of acceleration for Mach numbers between $M = 1$ and $M = 2$ were computed by Gardner and Ludloff [12]. Some of their results are reprinted in [4]. These studies led Gardner and Ludloff [12] and Cole [13] to establish criteria for the conditions under which linear theory is still sufficiently accurate. Some of their results are also found in [4] from which Fig. 3.3 is taken. In this figure, λ is a parameter characterizing the error made by using linear theory. Between $\lambda = 0$ and $\lambda = 1$ the error is sufficiently small in most cases. For $\lambda = 1$, a Mach number of 1 is just reached at one point of the body. As would be expected, the subsonic range that may be treated by linear theory approaches $M = 1$ only if the body is made thin enough.

Notes

1. Strong disturbances travel faster than the speed of sound, but in aeronautical applications the strength of an originally strong wave diminishes to a weak disturbance over a short distance. Thus, for the purpose of our study, it is admissible to assume that all waves propagate with the speed of sound throughout.

2. In this context even the finest machined point must be considered as being blunt, and for the time being it is assumed that disturbances are produced at the stagnation point only.
3. See Prob. 3.1.
4. This term was coined by Guderley [4].
5. For example, the propagation speed of strong disturbances is greater than the speed of sound.
6. Owing to the increasing speed, the line of influence is no longer a perfect hyperbola; nevertheless, it cannot become infinitely long.

Problems

3.1. Derive Eqs. 3.1, 3.2, 3.3, and 3.4a.

3.2. Derive Eq. 3.4b and verify its solution of Eq. 3.5.

3.3. From the nonsteady equations of this chapter, determine the increase with time of the pressure coefficient on the half-chord station of a parabolic-arc body of revolution for a sudden start to $M = 0.5$. Assume fineness ratios of the body of 0.1 and 0.2.

3.4. Following the derivation of Eq. 2.26, show that the small perturbation equation for three-dimensional nonsteady transonic flow is given as

$$[1 - M_\infty^2 - M_\infty^2(\gamma + 1)\varphi_x]\varphi_{xx} + \varphi_{yy} + \varphi_{zz} - M_\infty^2(2\varphi_{xt} + \varphi_{tt}) = 0$$

For an application of this equation, see ref. 63 where additional references on nonsteady transonic flow are given.

4
LIFT SLOPE AND DRAG RISE AT SONIC SPEED

Although, as has been shown in the preceding chapters, and will become even more obvious in the following chapters, the computation and the experimental determination of the aerodynamic coefficients at $M_\infty \approx 1$ are very difficult tasks, the slope of the c_p vs. M_∞ curve at $M_\infty = 1$, and thus the lift slope and the drag rise at this Mach number, can be computed approximately with amazing simplicity. This is of importance when experimental data up to high subsonic velocities and supersonic data from slightly supersonic Mach numbers upward are available. These two curves may be connected with good accuracy by giving the curve the slope at $M_\infty = 1$ that now will be derived.

The transonic normal shock equation $(u_I + u_{II})_{N.S.} = 0$ (Eq. 2.40), where u_I and u_{II} are the perturbation velocities before and behind the shock, respectively, may be written $M_I^* - 1 = 1 - M_{II}^*$, because $M^* = u'/a^* = (u + a^*)/a^*$. With $M^* \approx M$ at $M \approx 1$, the approximate relationship

$$M_I - 1 \approx 1 - M_{II} \tag{4.1}$$

results. This approximate slender-body relationship for $M_\infty \approx 1$ states that the Mach number behind the shock is as much smaller than unity as the Mach number before the shock is larger than unity. Now, increasing the body approach Mach number from high subsonic Mach numbers to $M_\infty = 1$, the Mach numbers on the body surface increase correspondingly. However, when the approach Mach number is further increased to values of $M_\infty > 1$, a far detached shock wave forms before the body and, according to Eq. 4.1, the Mach number to the body, decreases at the same rate it had increased when M_∞ approached unity. Therefore, the Mach numbers on the body have identical values for each pair of approach Mach numbers M_∞ that satisfy the relationship $M_{\infty I} = 2 - M_{\infty II}$, where $M_{\infty I} > 1$. Consequently, by increasing the approach Mach number from $M_\infty < 1$ to $M_\infty > 1$, where $M_\infty \approx 1$, the Mach numbers on the body first slightly increase up to $M_\infty = 1$, but then, when M_∞ increases further to supersonic values, they decrease again. In first approximation, this fact may be written as

$$\left(\frac{dM}{dM_\infty}\right)_{M_\infty \approx 1} = 0 \tag{4.2}$$

Here M stands for any Mach number on the body surface.

With the condition Eq. 4.2, the slope of the pressure coefficient c_p at $M_\infty = 1$ is obtained from the general gas-dynamic equation for c_p:

$$c_p = \frac{p - p_\infty}{\left(\rho \frac{v^2}{2}\right)_\infty} = \frac{2}{\gamma M_\infty^2}\left[\left(\frac{2 + (\gamma - 1)M_\infty^2}{2 + (\gamma - 1)M^2}\right)^{\gamma/(\gamma-1)} - 1\right] \qquad (4.3)$$

as

$$\left(\frac{dc_p}{dM_\infty}\right)_{M_\infty = 1} = \frac{4}{\gamma + 1}(1 - \tfrac{1}{2}(c_p)_{M_\infty = 1}) \qquad (4.4\text{a})$$

This equation shows the interesting fact that the change of c_p with M_∞ near $M_\infty = 1$ consists of a term that is independent of the body geometry and a term that is proportional to the pressure coefficient itself. Since c_p is proportional to the perturbation velocity, the latter term may be disregarded for sufficiently slender bodies ($u/U \ll 1$), and the simple relationship

$$\left(\frac{dc_p}{dM_\infty}\right)_{M_\infty = 1} = \frac{4}{\gamma + 1} \qquad \text{(slender bodies)} \qquad (4.4\text{b})$$

results.

From Eq. 4.4a, corresponding expressions for lift and drag may be derived: The drag coefficient c_d of a surface element whose pressure coefficient at an angle of incidence (between the element and the flight direction) α is c_p, may be written as

$$c_d = c_p \cdot \alpha \qquad (4.5)$$

Here, the index d is chosen for the drag coefficient of a surface element as distinguished from the coefficient c_D of a whole body. Also, the body is assumed to be slender enough that $\sin \alpha \approx \alpha$.

Consequently, from Eq. 4.4a we obtain

$$\left(\frac{dc_d}{dM_\infty}\right)_{M_\infty = 1} = \frac{2}{\gamma + 1}(2\alpha - (c_d)_{M_\infty = 1}) \qquad (4.6)$$

The drag coefficient of the whole body is obtained from the two-dimensional relationship

$$c_D = \frac{1}{h}\int_{-h/2}^{+h/2} c_d \, dy = \frac{1}{h}\int_{-h/2}^{+h/2} \alpha(y)c_p \, dy \qquad (4.7)$$

where h is the thickness of a body symmetric to the flight direction (zero lift). By applying these integrals to Eq. 4.4 and observing Eq. 4.5, the change of c_D with M_∞ becomes

$$(dc_D/dM_\infty)_{M_\infty = 1} = \frac{2}{\gamma + 1}(2\bar{\alpha} - (c_D)_{M_\infty = 1}) \qquad (4.8\text{a})$$

where $\bar{\alpha}$ stands for $(1/h)\int_{-h/2}^{+h/2} \alpha(y)\, dy$.

Lift Slope and Drag Rise at Sonic Speed

In contrast to the case of the pressure coefficient, where the slender-body expression (Eq. 4.4b) is independent of the body geometry, a distinction must be made in the case of the drag coefficient between half-bodies—those attached to infinitely long bodies of constant cross section, or blunt bodies of which the base drag has been subtracted—and closed bodies.

To this end, we first compute the drag rise $(dc_D/dM)_{M_\infty=1}$ of a slender wedge that is attached to an infinitely long plate of thickness h. In this case there is no contribution to the drag from the plate (friction drag is not considered), and the integral for $\bar{\alpha}$ becomes equal to α, the wedge half-angle, which is positive above and negative below the line of symmetry. Hence, Eq. 4.8a applies to the wedge-plate case by replacing $\bar{\alpha}$ with the wedge half-angle α. For the same reason as in the case of the pressure coefficient (Eq. 4.4a), the last term of Eq. 4.8a may be dropped for sufficiently slender bodies, and we obtain

$$\left(\frac{dc_D}{dM_\infty}\right)_{M_\infty=1} = \frac{4\bar{\alpha}}{\gamma+1} \quad \text{(slender \textit{half}-bodies)} \tag{4.8b}$$

where we have removed the restriction to a wedge, simply by reintroducing $\bar{\alpha}$ for a symmetric half-body.

Taking now a double wedge as an example of a closed body, it is immediately seen that the sign of $\bar{\alpha}$ on the rear portion is reversed from that at the front portion. Consequently, Eq. 4.8a must be split up in the expression for the front part of the body f and the rear part r:

$$\left(\frac{dc_{Df}}{dM_\infty}\right)_{M_\infty=1} = \frac{4}{\gamma+1}\bar{\alpha} - \frac{2}{\gamma+1}(c_{Df})_{M_\infty=1}$$

$$\left(\frac{dc_{Dr}}{dM_\infty}\right)_{M_\infty=1} = -\frac{4}{\gamma+1}\bar{\alpha} - \frac{2}{\gamma+1}(c_{Dr})_{M_\infty=1} \tag{4.9}$$

Since the total drag of the double wedge is the sum of the drag contributions of the front part and the rear part, the drag rise for the total wedge is the sum of the two equations 4.9. In forming this sum, the first terms on the right-hand side of these two equations cancel out and only the sum of the second terms remains. Hence, the drag rise of a body having finite length symmetric with respect to the x axis (the restriction to a double wedge may again be dropped) becomes

$$\left(\frac{dc_D}{dM_\infty}\right)_{M_\infty=1} = -\frac{2}{\gamma+1}(c_D)_{M_\infty=1} \quad \text{(\textit{closed} body)} \tag{4.10}$$

It is interesting to note that only the small perturbation terms remain in Eq. 4.10 and that, therefore, the drag rise at $M_\infty=1$ is much smaller than that of the half-bodies. Also, the slope now is negative, whereas it is positive for the half-bodies. Consequently, the drag coefficient has its maximum at $M_\infty > 1$ for the finite bodies, whereas the maximum lies at $M_\infty < 1$ for the half-bodies (see Fig. 4.3).

The value of Eqs. 4.8 through 4.10 may be seen from a comparison with results obtained at National Advisory Committee for Aerodynamics (NACA). By applying the transonic similarity law for plane flow (Eq. 2.65b). NACA established (c_D vs. M_∞) curves for wedges of three different wedge angles, allowing the determination of three curves that closely match the experimental data and can be computed for all Mach numbers except for $M_\infty \approx 1$. These curves are shown in Fig. 4.1. Their slopes at $M_\infty = 1$ are about 10% smaller than those computed from Eq. 4.8a. This agreement must be considered to be very good, since the test data of Fig. 4.1 include friction drag and do not, therefore, fully agree with the assumptions made in deriving Eq. 4.8. On the other hand, the good agreement suggests the combination of the method of this chapter with the similarity rules for quite an accurate estimation of the aerodynamic coefficients near $M_\infty = 1$ for a certain number of practical cases.

The good agreement of the drag rise as computed by the method of this chapter with that obtained from the similarity rule suggests that even simpler relationships may be obtained by expressing them through the transonic similarity parameter, $\chi = t(\gamma + 1)M_\infty^2/(1 - M_\infty^2)^{3/2}$, which was defined by Eq. 2.65b. By introducing the symbol C_p for the left-hand side of Eq. 2.65b and applying Eq. 4.4b, the slope of the pressure coefficient in similarity terms becomes

$$\left(\frac{dC_p}{d\chi}\right)_{\chi=0} = \left[\left(\frac{dC_p}{dc_p}\right)\left(\frac{dc_p}{dM_\infty}\right)\left(\frac{dM_\infty}{d\chi}\right)\right]_{M_\infty=1} = 2 \quad (4.11)$$

as may easily be verified.

The same value of 2 is obtained for $(dC_D/d\chi)_{\chi=0}$, because, from Eqs. 4.5, 4.7, and 4.8a, $c_D \approx \bar{\alpha}c_p$ and also $C_D \approx \bar{\alpha}C_p$, so that $\bar{\alpha}$ cancels out in Eq. 4.11 when the pressure coefficients are replaced by the drag coefficients. This result has been confirmed experimentally by Spreiter,

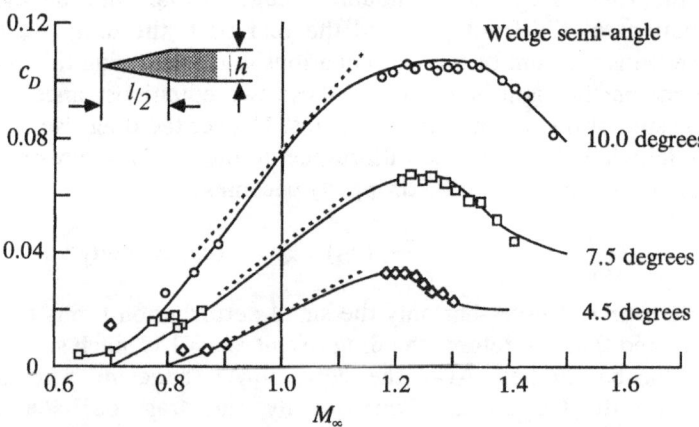

Fig. 4.1. Drag of wedge–semi-infinite plate systems of three different wedge angles from measurements and the transonic similarity rule (From [14]).

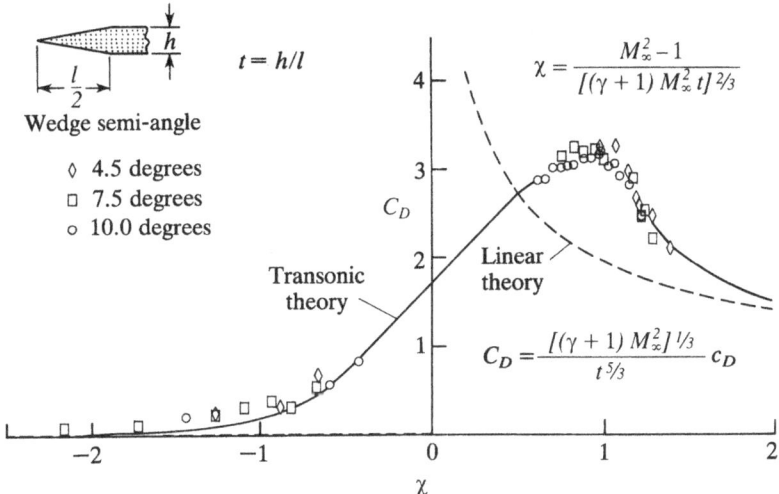

Fig. 4.2. Data of Fig. 4.1 in terms of the transonic similarity rule, verifying $(dC/d\chi)_{\chi=0} = 2$ (From [14]).

Bryson, and others [14]. One example is given in Fig. 4.2, where $(dC_D/d\chi)_{\chi=0} \approx 2$ for a wide range of wedge angles.

Finally, we compute the slope of the lift coefficient c_L of a profile at $M_\infty = 1$, which is given by the integral over the chord length c of the streamwise components of the pressure coefficient on the upper (u) and lower (l) profile surfaces. The contribution of a surface element is given as $c_l = c_p \cos \alpha \approx c_p$ for slender bodies. Hence the total lift coefficient becomes

$$c_L = \int_0^1 (c_{pl} - c_{pu}) \, d\left(\frac{x}{c}\right)$$

and with Eq. 4.4a,

$$\left(\frac{dc_L}{dM_\infty}\right)_{M_\infty=1} = \int_0^1 \left(\frac{dc_{pl}}{dM_\infty} - \frac{dc_{pu}}{dM_\infty}\right)_{M_\infty=1} d\left(\frac{x}{c}\right) = \frac{4}{\gamma+1} - \frac{2}{\gamma+1} (c_L)_{M_\infty=1}$$

In all practical cases c_L is smaller than 2 and, thus $(dc_L/dM_\infty)_{M_\infty=1}$ is positive. The maximum of c_L lies at supersonic speeds, for both closed and semiinfinite bodies, because α is not a factor in the final result, unlike the case of the drag coefficient (Eqs. 4.8 through 4.10).

In conclusion, the method described in this chapter is of considerable help in interpolating test data through the $M_\infty \approx 1$ range, where the reliability of test results is very low. Even in the cases in which the small-perturbation term of Eqs. 4.4a and 4.7 must be retained, a first approximate value may be obtained by setting this term equal to zero. The value thus obtained can then be used for a first iteration, which should result in values for the coefficients and their slopes at $M_\infty = 1$ that

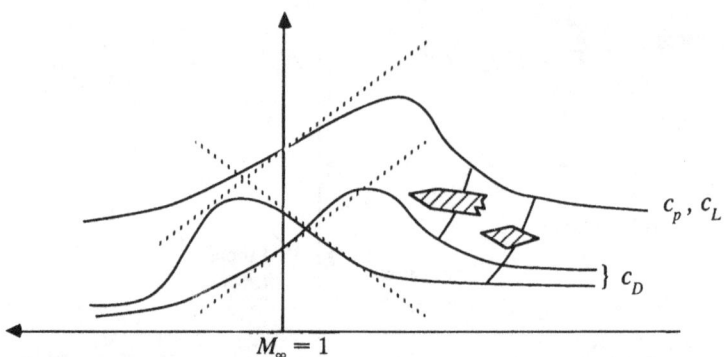

Fig. 4.3. The slopes of the coefficients of pressure, lift and drag for finite bodies (double wedges) and half-bodies (single wedges attached to semi-infinite plates) at $M_\infty = 1$. Schematic presentation.

are sufficiently accurate in most cases. More accurate values are obtainable by a second iteration.

In the case of the drag coefficient of the double wedge (Eq. 4.11), the iteration may be somewhat more cumbersome because the first estimate must be made from the trend of the experimental data at subsonic and supersonic Mach numbers. No theoretical approximate value is available. Nevertheless, a much more accurate value of $(c_D)_{M_\infty=1}$ will result from the application of Eq. 4.11 than that resulting from just a graphical interpolation, in which case, for example, the sign of the relatively small slope could easily be misjudged.

5
ANALYTICAL SOLUTIONS OF THE TRANSONIC CONTINUITY EQUATION

In the previous chapters the difficulty of solving the transonic equation because of its nonlinearity was pointed out. Several methods were given that bypass this difficulty and arrive at useful results. However, these methods are limited in their applicability. In this chapter, two major efforts will be discussed that have markedly extended the range of problems that may be solved analytically and have led to the "area rule," the indispensable tool of the aircraft designer. A third approach, the so-called similarity solutions,[1] has played an important role in the treatment of mainly basic problems. Because it was instrumental in clarifying certain aspects of viscous transonic flow, this method will be discussed in Chapter 6 on viscous transonic flow, although it also falls under the heading of this chapter.

5.1 Solutions of Transonic Equations by Linearization

As we have pointed out repeatedly in previous chapters, there is no way to obtain accurate results in the transonic range by linearization of the continuity equation. However, the accuracy obtained with linear equations obviously increases with a decreasing Mach number range for which a solution is sought. Thus, a flow field about a very slender body, producing very small perturbation velocities, may possibly be described reasonably well by the solution of a linear equation. There cannot be any doubt, however, that the cases in which this can be assumed are rare. To substantiate this fact, we shall now linearize the transonic equation and assess the results.

The axisymmetric transonic equation (for the corresponding plane flow equation, see Eq. 2.28b)

$$\varphi_{yy} + \frac{\varphi_y}{y} + \left[1 - M_\infty^2 - \frac{(\gamma+1)M_\infty^2}{U}\varphi_x\right]\varphi_{xx} = 0 \qquad (5.1a)$$

where $\varphi_x = u/U$ and $\varphi_y = v/U$, may be linearized in two ways:
1. By setting $\varphi_{xx} = \text{const.} = \alpha_p,^2$
2. By setting

$$1 - M_\infty^2 - \frac{(\gamma+1)M_\infty^2}{U}\varphi_x = \text{const.}$$

$$= \alpha \begin{cases} <0 & \text{for supersonic} \\ =0 & \text{for sonic} \\ >0 & \text{for subsonic} \end{cases} \text{approach flow} \quad (5.1b)$$

The variations of φ_x on the body surface must be small enough, so that the sign of α does not change because of a change in the sign of φ_x within the velocity range to be computed. In other words, for $M \approx 1$ the values of φ_x must be very small, and the body must be very slender. The sonic case of (2) therefore requires that $\varphi_x\varphi_{xx} \ll \varphi_{yy}$. This most drastic linearization reduces Eq. 5.1a to $\varphi_{yy} + \varphi_y/y = 0$, or, for plane flow, just to $\varphi_{yy} = 0$, with the solution

$$\varphi(x, y) = yf(x) + g(x) \tag{5.1c}$$

This result yields useful information on transonic flow fields. From the streamline equation $dy/dx = v/U = \varphi_y$ it follows that the slope of the streamlines $dy/dx = \vartheta(x) = f(x)$ is independent of y, and therefore all streamlines up to the infinite point have the same shape—the shape of the profile. This result is in agreement with the one-dimensional theory that showed that stream tubes cannot contract at $M_\infty = 1$. Because all streamlines have the same radii of curvature, each of them contributes the same increment to the total static pressure change in the y direction (see Eq. 2.16). Therefore, integration over all these increments from the profile surface to infinity would give a pressure infinitely higher or lower, depending on the sense of the surface curvature, than the "ambient" pressure at the infinitely distant point. Of course, there is not much sense in such an assumption. However, a somewhat different approach will throw some light on the peculiarity of the linearized solution.

We assume a plane transonic jet of finite width h, whose two boundary streamlines have the constant ambient pressure $-c_p/2 = 0 = u/U = \varphi_x$ (see Eq. 2.56a). However, these streamlines still follow the shape of the profile as do the intermediate streamlines. With $\varphi_x = 0$ at $y = h$, Eq. 5.1c yields $g'(x) = -h\vartheta'(x) = -h(d^2y/dx^2) = -h/R$, where R is the radius of curvature of the profile. Hence $\varphi_x = u/U = (y-h)/R$ and $c_p = -2(y-h)/R$. With $c_p = (p-p_h)/q$, where $q = (\rho W^2/2)_h$ is the dynamic pressure of the boundary streamline, the pressure rise from $y = 0$ to $y = h$ becomes $\Delta p = 2qh/R$. The same result is obtained by integrating the expression for the pressure gradient normal to a curved streamline, Eq. 2.16, by assuming that $\rho W^2 = 2q$ is constant, in the first approximation, between the streamlines $y = 0$ and $y = h$. Consequently, the linearized transonic equation 5.1c yields the right answer as long as the variation of the product of the flow density ρW and the velocity W (see Fig. 2.2) is of higher order, which certainly can be accomplished by holding the jet width h sufficiently small. This shows that linearized theory produces reasonable results in the near field of a body, but that the far field is described only by including the nonlinear terms of the transonic equation.

After this brief look at a basic problem of linearization, let us discuss the two linearization methods 1 and 2 of Eq. 5.1b in some detail. In case 1, the term φ_{xx} is held constant, that is, the acceleration of the x-constant, that is, the acceleration of the x-component of the perturbation velocity is assumed to be constant, but this velocity itself may have

Analytical Solutions of the Transonic Continuity Equation

any value. In this case, a parabolic equation is obtained, valid for both subsonic and supersonic flow, as long as the deviations from sonic speed are sufficiently small and the acceleration does not change its sign. The three choices of case 2 lead to three different differential equations, requiring a separate solution for each flow range. A more serious drawback of this method seems to lie in the fact that with φ_x constant, φ_{xx} becomes negligible. Thus, the computation is reduced to solving the equivalent of a compressible flow equation for a fictitious approach Mach number, determined by $1 - M_{f\infty}^2 = \alpha$, but satisfying the boundary conditions over a very small range only, a range that would be insufficient in any practical case.

5.1.1 Solution Through Local Linearization

Spreiter and his coworkers [14, 15] found a way out of this dilemma. They considered the term $1 - M_\infty^2 - (\gamma + 1)M_\infty^2 \varphi_x/U$ in Eq. 5.1a to be a constant α over a very small range in the x direction. Thus, the linearized equation is solved for arbitrary values of α. Into this general solution the expression for α from Eq. 5.1b is reintroduced as a variable. This leads to an ordinary differential equation for the perturbation velocity u over the total range of x considered. In our interpretation, the fictitious Mach number $M_{f\infty}$ has been made a function of x such that the boundary conditions are satisfied throughout the range considered. Obviously, this method is unacceptable from a purely mathematical viewpoint. Its justification can only be shown through comparisons with experimental data, which, as we shall see, are quite remarkably favorable in many cases. For this reason, and because local linearization contains a number of basic considerations for the solution of compressible flow problems, the mathematics of this approach will now be given in some detail.

The linearized equation

$$\alpha \varphi_{xx} + \frac{1}{y} \varphi_y + \varphi_{yy} = 0 \tag{5.2}$$

can be made formally identical to the linearized compressible flow equation if we set $\alpha = \beta^2 = 1 - M_\infty^2$. It may be solved by analogy with the two-dimensional equation of Sec. 2.5.1. Figures 2.10 and 2.11 are also valid for the axisymmetric case. Again, a source distribution is assumed on the axis of symmetry (ξ-axis) between the nose and the tail (points a and b) of the body whose flow field, superimposed on the constant approach flow field, produces the streamlines of the body contour. The potential of a single three-dimensional source Q at the distance R from the source may be written as

$$\varphi = -Q/4\pi R \tag{5.3}$$

For the computation of compressible flows the distance between a field point and the source, R, must be compressed in the y direction according to Eq. 2.43b. Thus, the solution of Eq. 5.2 for a continuous source distribution between the stations a and b becomes

$$\varphi = -\frac{1}{4\pi}\int_a^b \frac{q(\xi)\,d\xi}{\sqrt{(x-\xi)^2 + \alpha y^2}} \tag{5.4}^3$$

We now need the relationship between the source distribution $q(\xi)$ and the body geometry. To this end, we use the equation of a streamline

$$\frac{v}{U} = \frac{dy}{dx} \tag{5.5}$$

where v is the perturbation velocity in the radial y direction, and U, the approach velocity, has been substituted for $U+u$, the velocity in the x direction, according to the small-perturbation assumption. The slender-body assumption for axisymmetric bodies is introduced by setting $(vy)_o = v_b y_b$, where the index o indicates the conditions on the centerline and the index b those on the body surface (see Eq. 2.98b).

Thus, for the body surface, Eq. 5.5 becomes

$$(vy)_o = Uy_b \left(\frac{dy_b}{dx}\right) \tag{5.6}$$

With $v = \partial\varphi/\partial y$ and Eq. 5.4, the left-hand side of Eq. 5.6 becomes

$$\left(y\frac{\partial\varphi}{\partial y}\right)_{y\to 0} = \left[\frac{y}{4\pi}\int_a^b \frac{q(\xi)\alpha y\,d\xi}{\sqrt{(x-\xi)^2 + \alpha y^2}^{\,3}}\right]_{y\to 0} \tag{5.7}$$

As in Sec. 2.5.1, the argument of this integral becomes indeterminate for $(x-\xi) = y = 0$, that is, when approaching the station x at which the integral is to be evaluated. This difficulty can be overcome by again applying Sauer's substitutions (Eq. 2.52 and Fig. 2.11 in which β^2 must now be replaced by α). Then, by following the same reasoning about the magnitude of the contributions to the integral near $x = \xi$, which in the new coordinates is $\eta = \pi/2$, we arrive at

$$(vy)_o = \frac{q(\pi/2)}{4\pi}\int_0^\pi \sin\eta\,d\eta = \frac{2q(\pi/2)}{4\pi} = \frac{q(x)}{2\pi} \tag{5.8}$$

By introducing this result into Eq. 5.6 and setting

$$\frac{dy_b}{dx} = \frac{1}{2\pi y_b}\frac{dS}{dx}$$

where $S = S(x)$ is the cross-sectional area of the body, we obtain

$$\frac{q(x)}{2\pi y_b U} = \frac{dS}{dx}\cdot\frac{1}{2\pi y_b} \quad \text{or} \quad \frac{q(x)}{U} = \frac{dS}{dx} = S' \tag{5.9}$$

Hence, the solution of Eq. 5.2 in terms of the body geometry and the

Analytical Solutions of the Transonic Continuity Equation

approach velocity becomes

$$\varphi = -\frac{U}{4\pi} \int_0^l \frac{S'(\xi)\, d\xi}{\sqrt{(x-\xi)^2 + \alpha y^2}} \qquad (5.10)^4$$

where the integration limits a and b have been replaced by 0 and l.

Now, Eq. 5.10 must be solved for the perturbation velocity u, from which the pressure distribution on the body is obtained by letting $y \to 0$ in accordance with slender-body procedures.

Because we have constant integration limits, the differentiation can be done under the integral, resulting in

$$u = \frac{\partial \varphi}{\partial x} = +\frac{U}{4\pi} \int_0^l \frac{S'(\xi)(x-\xi)\, d\xi}{[(x-\xi)^2 + \alpha y^2]^{3/2}} \qquad (5.11)$$

This integral is solved through integration by parts:

$$\int_0^l \frac{S'(\xi)(x-\xi)\, d\xi}{[(x-\xi)^2 + \alpha y^2]^{3/2}} = \frac{S'(\xi)}{[(x-\xi)^2 + \alpha y^2]^{1/2}} \bigg|_0^l - \int_0^l \frac{S''(\xi)\, d\xi}{[(x-\xi)^2 + \alpha y^2]^{1/2}} \qquad (5.12)$$

The first term on the right-hand side is equal to zero for bodies with pointed nose and tail, or generally for bodies satisfying the condition $(dS/dx)_{x=0;l} = 0$.[5] To take advantage of this simplification the following computations will be restricted to pointed bodies.

For the solution of the integral (second term) on the right-hand side of Eq. 5.12, it must be kept in mind that αy^2 is larger than $|x-\xi|^2$ in the narrow range from $\xi = x - \Delta x$ to $\xi = x + \Delta x$, and that this contribution must not be suppressed. Outside of this range, the slender body routine may be applied. To this end, the integral is broken up into

$$\int_0^l \frac{S''(\xi)\, d\xi}{[(x-\xi)^2 + \alpha y^2]^{1/2}} = \int_0^l \frac{[S''(\xi) - S''(x)]\, d\xi}{[(x-\xi)^2 + \alpha y^2]^{1/2}} + \int_0^l \frac{S''(x)\, d\xi}{[(x-\xi)^2 + \alpha y^2]^{1/2}} = I_1 + I_2 \qquad (5.13)$$

where I_1 represents the contributions from $|x-\xi| > \alpha y$ and I_2 those from $|x-\xi| \approx \alpha y$. The Taylor series expansion of $S''(\xi)$ about $S''(x)$ yields

$$I_1 = \frac{\left[S'''(x)(r-\xi) + S^{IV}(x)\frac{(x-\xi)^2}{2!} + \ldots\right] d\xi}{[(x-\xi)^2 + \alpha y^2]^{1/2}} \qquad (5.14)$$

In this integral, the second and higher terms should be much smaller than the first one for all reasonably slender bodies and will be disregarded for this estimation. Thus we obtain $I_1 = S'''(x)l$ for $y = 0$.

The error thus made be estimated by computing the exact contributions made to the integral in the range where $|x-\xi| \approx \sqrt{\alpha}\, y$. This range is largest at the station of maximum thickness and we estimate the error for this condition. In this case $y_{\max} = h = lt/2$, where t is the body thickness ratio. Then, $|x - \xi| = al$, with a being the variable of the problem. Hence, the contributions to I_1 are

$$\frac{S'''(x)al\,d\xi}{[(al)^2 + \alpha(lt)^2/4]^{1/2}} = \frac{S'''(x)\,d\xi}{[1 + \alpha(t/a)^2/4]^{1/2}}$$

Although for $\xi = x$ ($a = 0$), the contribution is always zero, for $t/a = 1$ and $\alpha = 1$ (incompressible flow) the contribution has already reached $\sqrt{4/5}\,S'''(x)\,d\xi = 0.894\,S'''(x)\,d\xi$, and for transonic flow, with $\alpha \ll 1$ (see Eq. 5.1b), the contribution at this station is very nearly equal to $S'''(x)\,d\xi$ (see also Prob. 5.2). Thus, for $y = 0$, I_1 is only slightly larger than the exact value. Because, in addition, $S'''(x)$ will be much smaller than $S''(x)$ in most practical cases, $I_1 < I_2$, and with it the error will be even less noticeable. Hence it is justifiable to set $y = 0$ in the integral I_1, with the result

$$I_1 = \int_0^l \frac{[S''(\xi) - S''(x)]\,d\xi}{|x - \xi|} \tag{5.15}$$

Finally, it is obvious that the integrand of I_2 is not negligibly small for $\xi = x$, whereas $\alpha y^2 \ll (x - \xi)^2$ on the integration limits. Therefore the integral must be split so that the station $\xi = x$ is explicitly included, as

$$I_2 = \int_0^l \frac{S''(x)\,d\xi}{[(x-\xi)^2 + \alpha y^2]^{1/2}} = S''(x)\left\{\int_0^x \frac{d\xi}{[(x-\xi)^2 + \alpha y^2]^{1/2}}\right.$$

$$\left. + \int_0^l \frac{d\xi}{[(\xi-x)^2 + \alpha y^2]^{1/2}}\right\} \tag{5.16}$$

In evaluating these two integrals, the slender-body condition is applied by disregarding $\sqrt{\alpha}y$ relative to x and $(x - l)$, but retaining it otherwise. Thus, the solution of Eq. 5.11 on the body surface is obtained, after setting $\pi y^2 = S(x)$, as

$$u = \frac{S''(x)}{4\pi}U\ln\frac{\alpha S(x)}{4\pi x(l-x)} + \frac{U}{4\pi}\int_0^l \frac{[S'''(x) - S''(\xi)]\,d\xi}{|x - \xi|} \tag{5.17}$$

where the comments made in connection with Eq. 5.12 concerning the shape of the body have been incorporated.

The practical value of this equation becomes obvious when it is realized that it is also valid for the incompressible case for which $\alpha = 1$. Consequently, Eq. 5.17 may be written as

$$U = \frac{S''(x)}{4\pi}U\ln\alpha + u_{\text{inc}} \tag{5.18}$$

where u_{inc} is the solution of the linear incompressible equation.

Finally, to reintroduce the u-dependent value of α, first the change of u with x for a constant value of α is computed from Eq. 5.18.

Subsequently, the value of Eq. 5.1b is substituted for α, leading to an ordinary differential equation for u:

$$\frac{du}{dx} = \frac{S'''(x)}{4\pi} U \ln\left(1 - M_\infty^2 - u\frac{M_\infty^2(\gamma+1)}{U}\right) + \frac{du_{inc}}{dx} \quad (5.19)$$

Numerically, Eq. 5.19 is solved without difficulty.[6] In this way, the whole problem has been reduced to the solution of the simplest case of the partial differential equation of continuity, from which solutions for any compressible-flow Mach number can be obtained by way of an ordinary differential equation. Hence, taking the u resulting from Eq. 5.19 and making use of Eq. 5.5, the pressure coefficient can be obtained from

$$c_p = -\left[2\frac{u}{U} + \left(\frac{v}{U}\right)^2\right] = -\left[2\frac{u}{U} + \frac{(S'(x))^2}{4\pi S(x)}\right] \quad (5.20)[7]$$

Comparison of the values obtained from Eq. 5.20 with experiments, first- and second-order linear theory, and the application of similarity rules are shown in Figs. 5.1 through 5.4. It should be noted that all comparisons are limited to portions of the bodies between the nose and the station of maximum thickness. Downstream of this station, viscous effects and a corresponding boundary layer–wake interaction set in, greatly modifying the flow pattern, making strictly inviscid computations unrealistic. Nevertheless, the value of solutions in closed analytical form should not be underestimated, because, contrary to computer solutions of the exact systems of nonlinear equations, they allow determination of the trends resulting from variations in individual parameters. This fact cannot be overemphasized. Certainly, the computer is indispensable for the exact computation of a specific problem. However, the projection of solutions so obtained to cases that represent even the slightest modification is impossible, short of computing voluminous charts of solutions for all possible combinations of parameters—a monumental task even for today's finest computers.

For purely supersonic flow the pressure coefficients may be established in complete analogy to the above procedure for purely subsonic flow. The derivation will not be given here, and the reader is referred to the paper of Spreiter and Alkane [15]. The result is

$$\frac{d(u/U)}{dx} = \frac{S'''(x)}{4\pi}\ln\left(M_\infty^2 - 1 - u\frac{M_\infty^2(\gamma+1)}{U}\right) + \frac{df_H(x)}{dx} \quad (5.21)$$

where $f_H(x)$ replaces u_{inc} of the subsonic solution and is obtained from linear theory for $M_\infty = \sqrt{2}$.[8]

The result of Eq. 5.21 is again in very good agreement with step-by-step computations of the flow over a parabolic-arc body of revolution (Fig. 5.5).

Having examined the purely subsonic and supersonic cases, let us now take up the case of near-sonic approach Mach numbers, $M_\infty \approx 1$. Here,

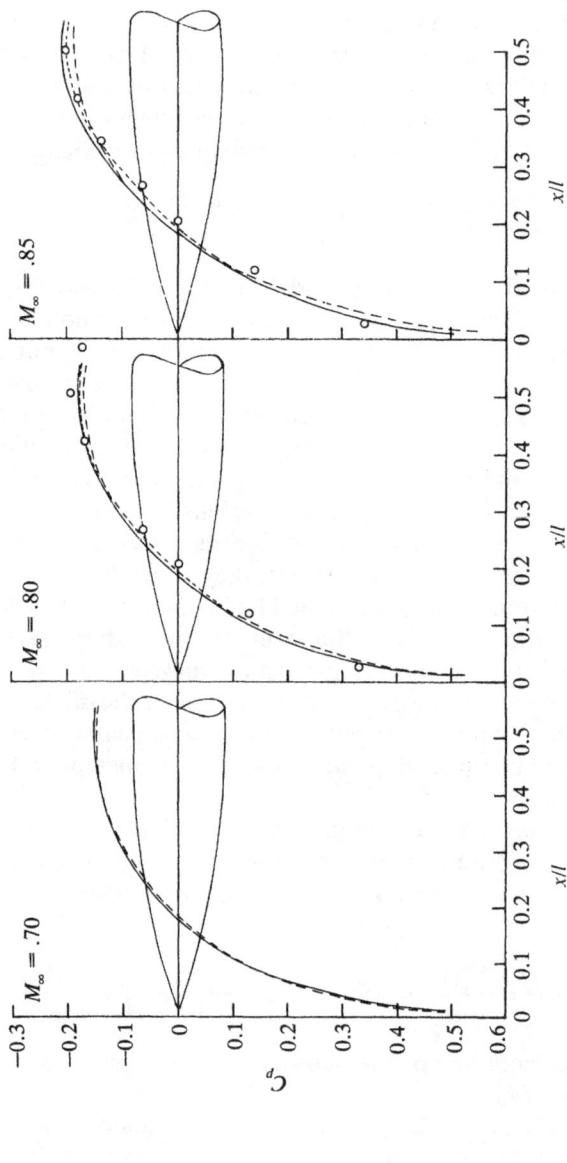

Fig. 5.1. Pressure coefficients of a parabolic-arc body of revolution at subcritical Mach numbers. Fineness ratio 6. (———) Eqs. 5.19 and 5.20, (– – –) first-order theory, (·····) second-order theory. (○) experiments (From [15]).

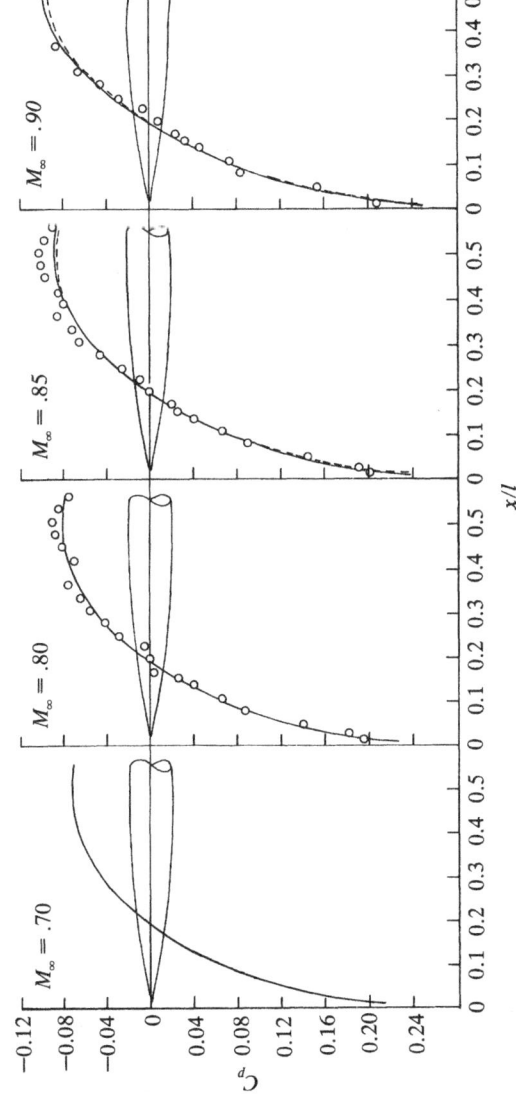

Fig. 5.2. Pressure coefficients of a parabolic-arc body of revolution at subcritical Mach numbers. Fineness ratio 10. (———) Eqs. 5.19 and 5.20, (– – –) first-order theory, (○) experiments (From [15]).

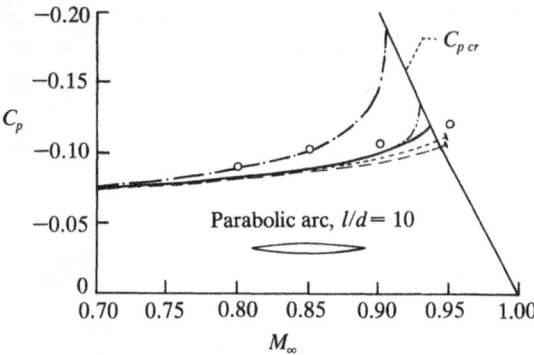

Fig. 5.3. Pressure coefficients at midpoint of axisymmetric body from Eqs. 5.19 and 5.20 (———), various first- and second-order approximations ($\cdots$; ---; -·-) and from experiments (o). (From [15]).

the assumption $\alpha = f(\varphi_x) = $ const. can no longer be made, because near $M_\infty = 1$ there is always a transition from subsonic to supersonic flow on the body surface and thus a station $u = \varphi_x = 0$ at which the sign of φ_x changes and with it the differential equation changes from the elliptic to the hyperbolic type. Consequently, linearization of one equation is possible only under the condition that φ_{xx}, the flow acceleration, is constant over sufficiently small increments of x. Thus, we must resort to

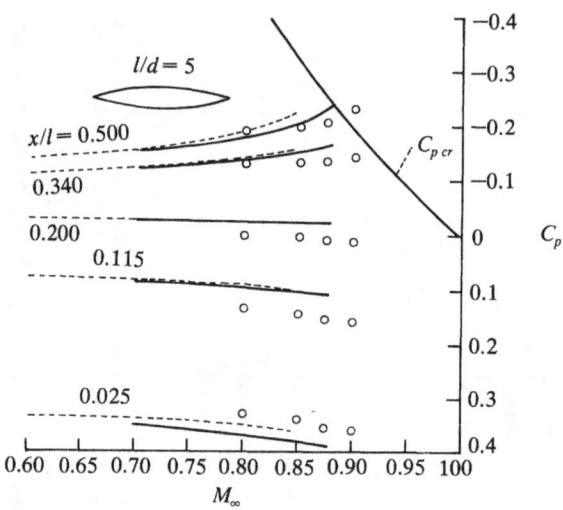

Fig. 5.4. Pressure coefficients at various stations of parabolic-arc body of fineness ratio 6 as obtained from Eqs. 5.19 and 5.20 (———), from computations for fineness ratio 10 through similarity rules (see Sec. 2.5) ($\cdots\cdots$), and from experiments (o). (From [15]).

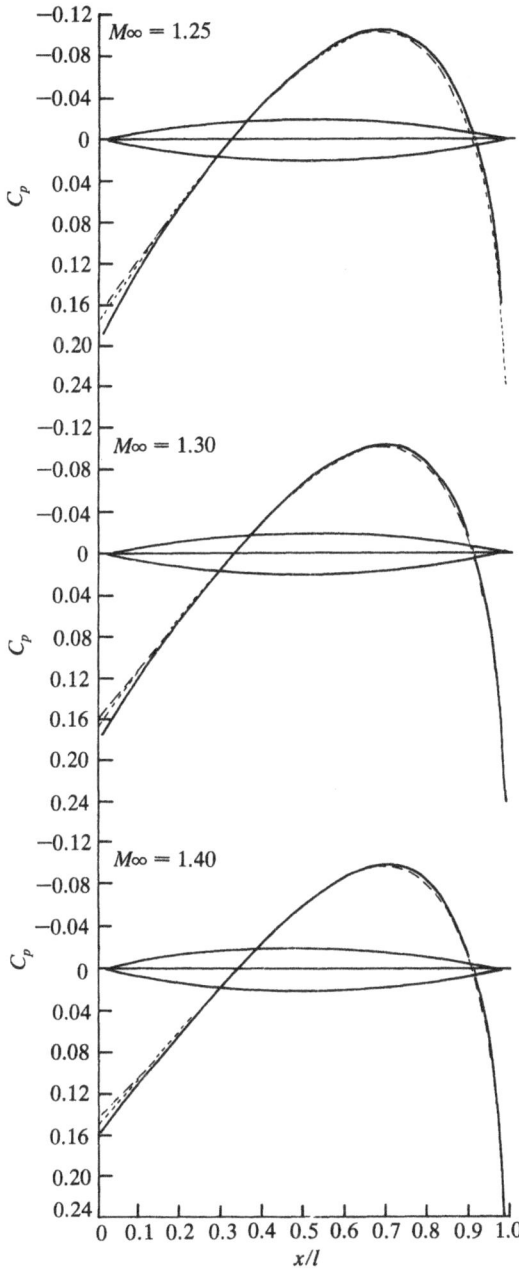

Fig. 5.5. Pressure distributions on parabolic-arc body of revolution of fineness ratio 10 at Mach numbers above the upper critical Mach number (no imbedded subsonic regions) as computed from Eq. 5.21 (– – –) and approximation methods (. . .; – – –) (From [15]).

the parabolic linearization, setting

$$\alpha = \alpha_p = M_\infty^2 \frac{\gamma+1}{U} \varphi_{xx} \tag{5.22}$$

Since the $(M_\infty^2 - 1)\varphi_{xx}$ term is very small compared with α_p for $M_\infty \approx 1$, Eq. 5.1a becomes[9]

$$\frac{1}{r}\varphi_r + \varphi_{rr} - \alpha_p \varphi_x = 0 \tag{5.23}$$

which can be solved by the methods used in the solution of the heat conduction equation. However, for the solution of the complete equation, that is, when $(M^2 - 1)\varphi_{xx} \equiv f_p$ is comparable to α_p (M_∞ markedly smaller than 1) and must therefore be retained, the following integral equation is obtained with the help of Green's theorem:

$$\varphi_p = -\frac{U}{4\pi}\int_0^x \frac{S'(\xi)}{x-\xi}\exp\left(\frac{-\alpha_p r^2}{4(x-\xi)}\right)d\xi - \frac{1}{\alpha_p}\int_0^{2\pi}d\Theta\int_0^\infty \rho\,d\rho\int_{-\infty}^x \sigma_p f_p\,d\xi \tag{5.24}[10]$$

where

$$\sigma_p = \frac{\alpha_p}{4\pi(x-\xi)}\exp\left\{-\frac{\alpha_p[r^2 + \rho^2 - 2r\rho\cos(\vartheta-\theta)]}{4(x-\xi)}\right\}$$

For the solution of this equation local linearization may again be applied according to Spreiter and Alksne [15] by setting

$$\varphi_{\xi\xi} = \frac{\partial u}{\partial \xi} = \alpha_p \bigg/ \frac{\gamma+1}{U}M_\infty^2 \tag{5.25}$$

and treating α_p as a constant. Then the integrals (Eq. 5.23) can be solved and the following equation is obtained

$$\frac{u_p}{U} = \frac{1-M_\infty^2}{M_\infty^2(\gamma+1)} + \frac{S''(x)}{4\pi}\ln\frac{\alpha_p S e^C}{4\pi x} + \frac{1}{4\pi}\int_0^r \frac{S''(x) - S''(\xi)}{x-\xi}d\xi \tag{5.26}$$

where C is Euler's constant $= 0.57721566\ldots$. Again substituting the right-hand side of Eq. 5.22 for α_p and expressing φ_{xx} through the relationship between the partial derivatives and the total differential at the body surface ($r = R$), we obtain

$$\frac{d}{dx}\left(\frac{u}{U}\right) = \left[\frac{\partial}{\partial x}\left(\frac{u}{U}\right)\right]_R + \left[\frac{\partial}{\partial r}\left(\frac{u}{U}\right)\right]_R \frac{dR}{dx}$$

Here, with $u/U = (S''/2\pi)\ln r$ (see Eq. 5.44), the last term becomes

$$\left[\frac{\partial(u/U)}{\partial r}\right]_R \left(\frac{dR}{dx}\right) = \frac{S'S''}{4\pi S}$$

and the ordinary differential equation for transonic flow about a slender body is obtained as

$$\frac{d}{dx}\left(\frac{u}{U}\right) = \frac{d}{dx}\left[\frac{u}{U} + \frac{M_\infty^2 - 1}{M_\infty^2(\gamma+1)}\right]$$

$$= \frac{S'S''}{4\pi S} + \exp\left\{\frac{4\pi}{S''(x)}\left[\frac{u}{U} + \frac{M_\infty^2-1}{M_\infty^2(\gamma+1)} - \frac{S''(x)}{4\pi}\ln\frac{M_\infty^2(\gamma+1)Se^C}{4\pi x}\right.\right.$$

$$\left.\left. - \frac{1}{4\pi}\int_0^x \frac{S''(x) - S''(\xi)}{x-\xi}d\xi\right]\right\} \quad (5.27)$$

As in the subsonic and supersonic cases, the integration constant must be chosen properly. In those cases Spreiter and Alksne chose them such that $u = u_{\text{inc}}$ or $u = f_H(x)$, respectively, at the station where $S''(x) = 0$, because there, as seen from Eqs. 5.18 and 5.21 the solutions are independent of α.

In the transonic case this method is again suggested for smooth forebodies. In the case of a break in the body contour, however, as at a cone–cylinder body, the integration constant must be chosen such that sonic velocity is obtained at the shoulder of the body, given by $(u/U)_{sh} = (1 - M_\infty^2)/[(\gamma+1)M_\infty^2]$.[11] In Fig. 5.6, results for a cone–cylinder model at $M = 1$ are given, showing that, at the station of maximum thickness or slightly downstream of this point, the theory disagrees with the experiments because here flow separation sets in.

With these examples of analytic solutions to the nonlinear transonic equation, the basis is laid for the derivation of a fundamental feature of transonic flow—the so-called equivalence rule—that leads directly to the extremely important area rule for the design of flight articles flying near the velocity of sound.

5.2 The Equivalence Rule

In simple terms, the equivalence rule states that the flow field about an "arbitrary" slender body flying at transonic velocity[12] can be computed by replacing the actual, irregular body by a body of revolution whose shape is determined through simple computations from the geometry of the actual body. The advantage of such an approach is obvious, since the computation is reduced to the solution of a nonlinear axisymmetric equation instead of that of a three-dimensional equation for a highly complex geometry, as in the case of an airplane, which, practically speaking, could never can be done analytically.

The transonic equivalence rule is a logical extension of slender-body theory that is based on the assumption that, near the surface of a slender body of small aspect ratio, the first term of the linearized compressible flow equation $(1 - M_\infty^2)\varphi_{xx} + \varphi_{yy} + \varphi_{zz} = 0$ may be disregarded in comparison with the two other terms. If this assumption holds,[13] the flow field near the body may be computed, in the first approximation, from the

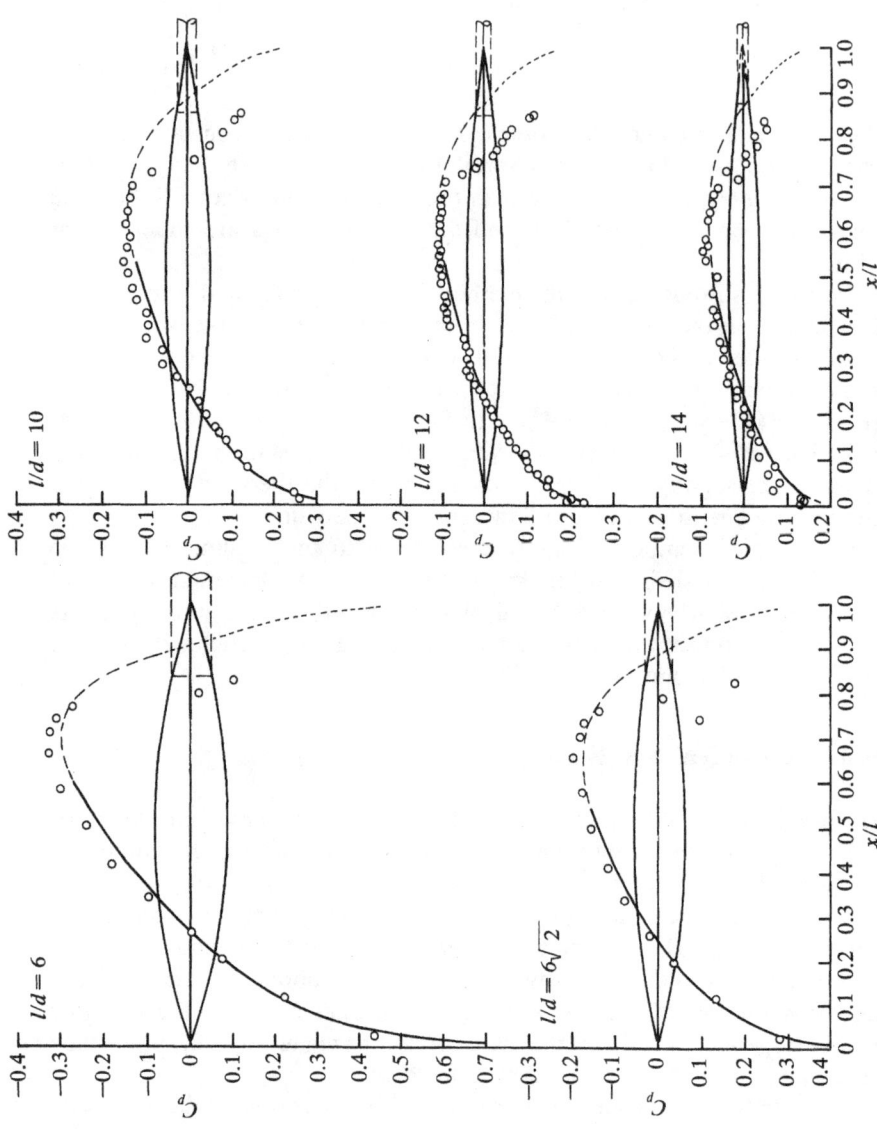

Fig. 5.6. Pressure distributions on parabolic-arc bodies of various fineness ratios at Mach number 1. (– – –) Eq. 5.27; (○) experiments by R. A. Taylor and J. B. McDevitt and G. Drougge (From [15]).

Laplace equation $\varphi_{yy} + \varphi_{zz} = 0$ at any station of the body axis. This assumption is by no means exactly valid in general, but it has led to useful results. For instance, Liepman and Roshko [6] show that in supersonic flow at small angles of attack the cross flow over a slender body is negligibly affected by the flow conditions away from the x,y plane under consideration, and can therefore be computed with the two-dimensional Laplace equation for this plane.

For a more specific evaluation of this assumption, the next section will discuss this matter in some detail. At the same time, this will give us an opportunity to throw some new light on certain results obtained in the previous chapters.

5.2.1 The Relative Magnitudes of $\partial u/\partial x$ and $\partial v/\partial y$ $(+\partial w/\partial z)$ in Slender-body Flow

In the following discussion, the correlations between the function $\tilde{S}(x)$ of Sec. 2.6, the source strength $q(x)$, and the body cross-sectional area $S(x)$ will be needed. A brief derivation of these expressions will first be given.

With the understanding that all symbols describe the conditions on the body surface, the body cross-sectional area is given as $S = \pi y^2$. With $dS/dx = S' = 2\pi y (dy/dx)$, the body contour streamline becomes

$$\frac{dy}{dx} = \frac{v}{U} = \frac{S'}{2\pi y} = \frac{q(x)}{2\pi y U} \quad \text{(see Eq. 5.9)} \tag{5.28}$$

$\tilde{S}(x)$ was defined by Eq. 2.98b as $\tilde{S} = v_1 \bar{y}$. From Eqs. 2.89, 2.101b and the definition of the body shape function $f(x) = y/t$, the relationship between $\bar{y}$ and y becomes $\bar{y} = ty = t^2 f$. The relationship between the first-order y-component of the perturbation velocity, v_1, and the y-component of the velocity vector, v, is obtained from Eqs. 2.88, 2.91, 2.100b, and 2.101b as $v_1 = v/t^3 U$. Hence we arrive at

$$\tilde{S} = \frac{vt^2 f}{t^3 U} = \frac{vf}{tU} \tag{5.29a}$$

On the other hand, with $dy/dx = tf'$ and Eq. 5.28 we have

$$S' = 2\pi y t f' = 2\pi t^2 f' f \tag{5.29b}$$

Thus, finally, with Eq. 5.28, we arrive at the complete relationship between $\tilde{S}(x)$, $q(x)$ and $S(x)$:

$$\tilde{S} = \frac{vf}{tU} = ff' = \frac{q(x)}{2\pi t^2 U} = \frac{S'}{2\pi t^2} \tag{5.30}$$

Note that this equation is in complete agreement with Eq. 2.125.

Now, to estimate the relative magnitudes of $\partial u/\partial x$ and $\partial v/\partial y + \partial w/\partial z$, it is sufficient to consider the axisymmetric case in which the radial component of the velocity and the radial coordinate are again designated as v and y, respectively. This estimate does not require sophisticated calculations; as a matter of fact, most of the information needed for a first-order result is contained in Chapter 2. Equation 2.118 gives the first-order perturbation potential for transonic slender-body flow, from which the values of $\partial u/\partial x$ and $\partial v/\partial y$ may be derived. Their relative magnitudes are best expressed in terms of the thickness ratio t, that is, the ratio of these expressions for $t \to 0$. To this end we form with Eqs. 2.88, 2.89, 2.110b, 2.101b, and with the definition $y = tf(x)$:

$$\frac{\partial u}{\partial x} = Ut^2 \left(\frac{\partial u_1}{\partial x} \right) = Ut^2 [\tilde{S}''(x) \ln \tilde{y} + g''(x)]$$

$$= Ut^2 [\tilde{S}''(x)(2\ln t + \ln f) + g''(x)] \quad (5.31a)$$

and

$$\frac{\partial v}{\partial y} = Ut^3 \left(\frac{\partial v_1}{\partial \tilde{y}} \right) \left(\frac{\partial \tilde{y}}{\partial y} \right) = -Ut^4 \left(\frac{\tilde{S}(x)}{\tilde{y}^2} \right) = -\frac{Ut^4 \tilde{S}(x)}{t^4(x)^2}. \quad (5.31b)$$

In these equations $\tilde{S}''(x)$ and $\tilde{S}(x)$ are functions of $f(x)$ only (see Eq. 5.29b), which is a dimensionless function whose values lie between 0 and 1. (Note that by dividing the above equations by U, the perturbation velocities become dimensionless and, therefore, the coordinates, and the functions depending on them, must be dimensionless, too.) Disregarding the term $g''(x)$ for the moment, we have

$$\frac{(\partial u/\partial x)}{(\partial v/\partial y)} = \frac{At^2 \ln t + Bt^2}{C}.$$

For $t \to 0$, this expression goes to 0. Thus, when $g''(x)$ is disregarded, $\partial u/\partial x$ is much smaller than $\partial v/\partial y$ for slender bodies. It could be larger only if $g''(x)$ were larger than order $1/t^2$.

The magnitude of $g''(x)$ may be obtained from Eq. 5.17. By forming the derivative of this equation:

$$\frac{\partial u}{\partial x} = \frac{U}{4\pi} \left\{ S''' \ln \frac{S}{4\pi x(l-x)} + S''' \ln \alpha + S'' \left(\frac{S'}{S} - \frac{l-2x}{x(l-x)} \right) + \frac{\partial}{\partial x} \int_0^l \cdots \right\}$$

the first term obtained becomes equivalent to the first term of Eq. 5.31a. This may be verified by applying the relationships Eqs. 5.29 and 5.30, and by taking the expression $4x(l-x)$ as the shape factor of the body. For a parabolic arc, it is exactly this factor and the first two terms of the two equations just differ by a factor of 2, but a perfect agreement cannot be expected, because the exact comparison should be made with Eq. 2.119a. Nevertheless, because of this qualitative agreement, the sum of the three remaining terms of Eq. 5.17 must be the equivalent of $t^2 g''(x, K)$ where K is related to α by Eqs. 2.103 and 5.14. Thus we obtain $g''(x, K) = O(1)$, because the two terms of Eq. 5.17 contain only derivatives of $S(x)$, which are proportional to t^2. Hence, $\partial u/\partial x$ is

Analytical Solutions of the Transonic Continuity Equation   127

definitely smaller than $\partial v/\partial y$. The magnitude of this ratio of the two partial derivatives depends largely on $f(x)$ as the above derivation shows.

Here, a warning is in order: the derivation of the ratio of the partial differentials was based on the slender body assumption $vy = \bar{S}(x)$, so that it only applies to the range immediately next to the body surface where this simplification makes sense. It does not mean that the velocity change in the x direction may be disregarded. Actually, this change must be included in the form of the boundary condition, and so the equation $\partial v/\partial y + \partial w/\partial z = 0^{14}$ is only valid together with the boundary condition on the body surface $v/(U+u) = dy/dx$. This system of equations contains all three velocity components, as must be the case.

5.2.2 The Basic Considerations Leading to the Equivalence Rule

The slender-body theory was conceived by M. M. Munk [16a] for the design of air ships traveling at low speeds and by Jones [16b] for pointed, low-aspect-ratio wings in the subsonic and supersonic velocity range in which the continuity equation can be successfully linearized. In all those cases, the very simple result, given basically by the Laplace equation of the cross-flow and the equation of the body-contour-forming streamlines, has proved to be quite useful. But these linear equations are not sufficient to describe the flow in the transonic range, which is governed by nonlinear effects. The question arises therefore whether there may be found another simplifying characteristic behavior in the transonic range that could be combined with the slender-body result to arrive at a method that, overall, would be simpler than the solution of the general nonlinear transonic equation.

As we saw in Chapter 3 on unsteady transonic flow, the nonlinear behavior of transonic flow may be explained by the fact that the pressure disturbances caused by the flight article cannot escape from the vicinity of the body, and thus the pressure about the body increases with time. Because this process would eventually cause a physically impossible infinitely high pressure, nonlinear effects set in that restrict the pressure rise and lead to a steady-state pressure field. Thus, two transonic flow peculiarities have been established: First, whereas in subsonic and supersonic flow the pressure disturbances are swept away from the body immediately, carrying an image of the body into the far-field and making the far-field aerodynamics a function of body shape (in addition to the body volume), in transonic flow, the pressure disturbances stay with the body and coalesce. Consequently, no image of the body is carried into the far-field and the far-field aerodynamics becomes independent of the body shape, dependent only on the body volume. The second important transonic flow feature, leading to the equivalence rule, is most clearly seen at exactly $M_\infty = 1$. Here the pressure waves from the body surface disturbances move out exactly in the plane normal to the flight direction. As has been shown in Chapter 3 (Fig. 3.1b), almost only the disturbances from surface points in this plane are superimposed and the contributions from points upstream of this plane are negligible. For Mach numbers slightly different from unity, more contributions come from the other planes. However, for Mach numbers sufficiently close to unity, the far-field pressures are, in the first approximation, only affected by the disturbances originating in the plane normal to the flight direction in which these pressures occur.

Combining these two transonic pecularities, we may conclude that the far field in transonic flow is, in the first approximation, determined by the shape of an "equivalent" body (e.g., a body of revolution whose cross-sectional areas are equal to those of the flight article under consideration). For instance, in the case of an airplane, the circular area of a cross section of the equivalent body must be equal to the area of the fuselage cross section plus the cross-sectional areas of the respective wing sections.[15]

5.2.3 The Formulation of the Equivalence Rule by Oswatitsch and Keune

In 1955, Oswatitsch and Keune [17] established the so-called 'equivalence rule', based on observations about transonic slender-body flow of the kind made in our previous sections. From what has been said there, the nonlinearity of transonic flow must be contained in any rule for the computation of transonic flow fields. However, much is gained if the nonlinear equation to be solved is reduced to the simplest possible form. Thus, the equivalence rule is the logical means for the simplification of the transonic flow problem, inherent in the problem itself.

With the discussions of the previous sections in mind, the following formulation of the equivalence rule should be obvious.

The potential of a slender body of any shape, but of small aspect ratio, may be composed from two parts: First, a potential satisfying the Laplace equation of the cross-flow in planes normal to the flight direction, with the equation of the streamlines forming the body surface as the boundary condition; and second, a "space influence potential" that depends on the body volume only, and therefore is equal for an arbitrary body and its axisymmetric equivalent body. Accordingly, any slender-body flight article of sufficiently small aspect ratio (delta wing airplane, etc.) can be computed taking the following steps.

1. Compute the potential φ_1 of the axisymmetric body that is equivalent to the actual body, from the general transonic equation

$$\varphi_{1rr} + \frac{\varphi_{1r}}{r} + \left[1 - M_\infty^2 - \frac{(\gamma+1)M_\infty^2}{U}\varphi_{1r}\right]\varphi_{1xx} = 0$$

where $r^2 = y^2 + z^2$

2. Compute, for the same equivalent body, the cross-flow potential φ_2 from the Laplace equation $\varphi_{2rr} + \varphi_{2r}/r = 0$, with the explained

boundary condition that takes the form $(\bar{v}/U)_b = (dr/dx)_b$, where $\bar{v}^2 = v^2 + w^2$.
3. Form the "space influence potential" $\varphi_3 = \varphi_1 - \varphi_2$.
4. Compute the cross-flow potential φ_4 from $\varphi_{4yy} + \varphi_{4zz} = 0$ for the actual body, again observing the boundary condition $(v/U)_b = (dy/dx)_b$.[16]
5. Form the potential of the actual body $\varphi_5 = \varphi_3 + \varphi_4$.

Thus, the difficult problem of computing the potential of an irregular slender body has been reduced to the much simpler problems of solving the two-dimensional Laplace equations, applying the body shape functions as the boundary conditions, and the solution of the transonic equation for an axisymmetric body (i.e., the equivalent body).

This method has been shown to be correct for increasing aspect ratios when approaching $M_\infty = 1$, showing that the equivalence law is particularly valuable in the transonic range. From the discussions of the previous sections, this fact should have been expected.

5.2.4 Comparison of the Equivalence Rule with the Parabolic Method of Flow Computations

To get a feeling for the relative simplicity of the equivalence rule for the computation of transonic flows, a brief account will now be given of a paper of Zierep [18] in which he computes the potential field about a simple three-dimensional body both by the linearized parabolic transonic equation and through the equivalence rule. The all-wing type of airplane body is shown in Fig. 5.7.

To slightly simplify the equations involved, the computations will be made for $M_\infty = 1$. Then the transonic equation may be written as

$$\varphi_{yy} + \varphi_{zz} = (\gamma + 1)\varphi_x \varphi_{xx} \tag{5.32}$$

corresponding to Eq. 2.24, that is, the potential is defined as in Eq. 2.22.

$$\frac{\partial \varphi}{\partial x} = \frac{u}{U} \quad \frac{\partial \varphi}{\partial y} = \frac{v}{U} \quad \frac{\partial \varphi}{\partial z} = \frac{w}{U} \quad (U = a^* \text{ at } M_\infty = 1) \tag{5.33}$$

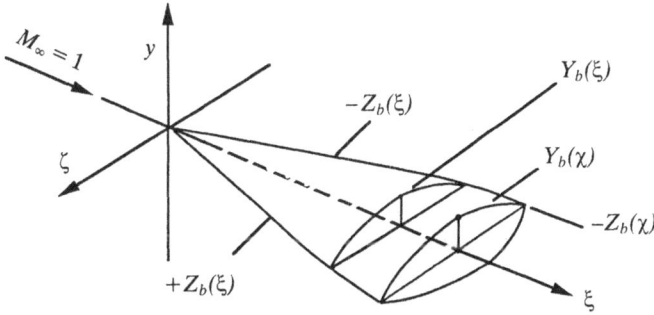

Fig. 5.7. Geometry of the slender body.

By setting $(\gamma + 1)\varphi_{xx} = \alpha_p$, we arrive at the linearized two-dimensional equivalent to Eq. 5.23

$$\varphi_{yy} + \varphi_{zz} - \alpha_p \varphi_x = 0 \tag{5.34}$$

As we stated in connection with Eq. 5.23, this is the only linearization method that covers both the subsonic and the supersonic ranges by a single integration. In analogy to Eq. 5.24 for $M_\infty \approx 1$, in which case the second term may be disregarded because $f_p \ll \alpha_p$, the solution of Eq. 5.33 becomes

$$\varphi(x, y, z) = \int_{\xi=0}^{x} \int_{\zeta=-z_b(\xi)}^{z_b(\xi)} \frac{q(\xi, \zeta)}{x - \xi} \exp\left(-\frac{\alpha_p(y^2 + (z - \zeta)^2)}{4(r - \xi)}\right) d\zeta\, d\xi \tag{5.35)[17]}$$

where the source distribution function $q(\xi, \zeta)$ now represents a two-dimensional source distribution and the body surface equation assumes the form

$$\varphi_y(x, 0, z) = \frac{\partial y_b(x, z)}{\partial x} \tag{5.36}$$

The limitation of the integration with respect to ξ is a mathematical necessity, because for $x < \xi$ the exponent of the e-function becomes positive and Eq. 5.35 no longer satisfies Eq. 5.34. This may seem to be a serious limitation of the method, but physically this limitation is justified. As may be seen from Fig. 5.8, in supersonic flow the region of influence lies within the Mach cone with its apex at the source. Sources at $\xi > x - y \cot \mu$ do not affect stations outside of the Mach cone with the Mach angle μ. Thus, the potential at a point on the Mach cone is obtained by restricting the integration to the range $\xi = 0$ to $x - y \cot \mu$. Now, for $M_\infty = 1$, $\cot \mu = 0$ and the upper integration limit becomes $\xi = x$. Of course, this result is in complete agreement with Fig. 3.1b, which showed that the hyperbola of influence in transonic flow ($M_\infty = 1$) lies entirely on and upstream of the body station under consideration. Obviously, for $M_\infty < 1$ or $M_\infty > 1$, the parabolic method becomes increasingly inaccurate with decreasing or increasing M_∞.

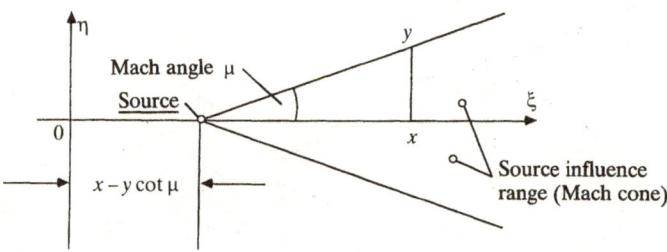

Fig. 5.8. The supersonic source influence range.

Analytical Solutions of the Transonic Continuity Equation

To determine $q(\xi, \zeta) = f(y_b)$, $\varphi_y(x, 0, z)$ must be computed from Eq. 5.35. However, the resulting equation has an indeterminate value for $\xi = x$. This difficulty can be overcome by a procedure very similar to that of Eq. 2.52, namely, to express the distances between the sources and the station x,y,z through y and functions that do not vanish for $\xi = x$ and $\zeta = z$:

$$\zeta - z = yZ \qquad d\zeta = y\, dZ \tag{5.37a}$$

$$x - \xi = y^2 X \qquad d\xi = -y^2\, dX \tag{5.37b}$$

Whereas Eq. 5.37a is equivalent to Eq. 2.52,[18] Eq. 5.37b has no simple trigonometric justification, but is chosen for the elimination of y. Because y is eliminated from the expression for $\partial\varphi/\partial y$ in this new coordinate system, the condition $y \to 0$ remains to be applied to Eqs. 5.37, resulting in $\xi = x$ and $\zeta = x$. Thus, $q(\xi, \zeta)$ becomes $q(x, z)$ and can be placed outside the integral. As in the case of the relationship between the source strength $q(x)$ and the body slope of Eq. 2.55, only contributions of sources very close to the source $q(x, z)$ play a role. Thus, the integral to be solved becomes

$$\varphi_y(x, 0, z) = -\frac{\alpha_p}{2} q(x, z) \int_{X=0}^{\infty} \int_{Z=-\infty}^{\infty} \frac{\exp\left(-\dfrac{\alpha_p(1+Z^2)}{4X}\right)}{X^2}\, dZ\, dX \tag{5.38}$$

where the new integration limits are found with Eq. 5.37.

The integration of Eq. 5.38 is straightforward, resulting in $\varphi_y(x, 0, z) = -2\pi q(x, z)$, and hence with Eq. 5.36 we finally arrive at

$$q(x, z) = -\frac{1}{2\pi}\left(\frac{\partial y_b(x, z)}{\partial x}\right)\text{[19]}$$

or generally

$$q(\xi, \zeta) = -\frac{1}{2\pi}\left(\frac{\partial y_b(\xi, \zeta)}{\partial \xi}\right)$$

Thus, because the pressure distribution over the body is the most important magnitude for the establishment of the aerodynamic characteristics of a flight article, and because $c_p = -2u/U - v_b^2/U^2$, we arrive at the following equation:

$$\varphi_x(x, 0, z) = -\frac{1}{2\pi}\frac{\partial}{\partial x}\int_0^x \int_{-z_b(\xi)}^{z_b(\xi)} \frac{y_{0\xi}(\xi, \zeta)}{x - \xi}\exp\left(-\frac{\alpha_p(z-\zeta)^2}{4(x-\xi)}\right) d\zeta\, d\xi \tag{5.40}$$

For the individual steps to be taken in solving Eq. 5.40, the reader is referred to the paper of Zierep [18], because it is strictly a mathematical exercise, however, a remark on the basic handling of such a problem is in order. For $\xi = x$, the integrand of Eq. 5.40 has an indeterminate value, possibly a singularity. Such a singularity, however, may be handled by setting $y_{b\xi} = y_{bx} - (y_{bx} - y_{b\xi})$, and Eq. 5.40 becomes

$$\varphi_x(x, 0, z) = -\frac{1}{2\pi}\frac{\partial}{\partial x}\int_0^x \int_{-z_b(\xi)}^{z_b/\xi} \left[\overbrace{\frac{y_{bx}(x,\zeta)}{x-\xi}\exp\left(-\frac{\alpha_p(z-\zeta)^2}{4(x-\xi)}\right)}^{I_1} \right.$$

$$\left. - \overbrace{\frac{y_{bx}(x,\zeta) - y_{b\xi}(\xi,\zeta)}{x-\xi}}^{I_2} \right] d\zeta\, d\xi \quad (5.41)$$

where the exponential term in I_2 has been set equal to unity, because a simple numerical check[21] shows that for small aspect ratios ($z_b(\xi) \ll \xi$) it deviates from unity only over the negligibly small portion $(x - \xi) \ll (z - \xi)$ of the integration range, so that the value of the integral is insignificably altered. Because this is the range containing the singularity, the exponential term must be left in I_1, which, however, can now be integrated in closed form to give the value of the singularity. In addition, I_1 gives the contributions at the stations $\xi \neq x$ from the constant source strength y_{bx}, where I_2 is the correction term, accounting for the varying source strength y_b along the ξ axis. It does not contain a singularity, because it has been taken care of by I_1. But it may also be shown by expanding $y_{b\xi_\bullet}$ in a Taylor series about y_{bx}, which eliminates the denominator $(x - \xi)$. With this simplification, the integration of Eq. 5.41 yields

$$\varphi_x(x, 0, z) = \frac{u}{U} = \frac{1}{\pi}\frac{\partial}{\partial x}\int_{-z_b(x)}^{z_b(x)} y_{bx}(x,\zeta) \ln|z-\xi|\, d\zeta$$

$$+ \frac{S''(x)}{4\pi}\ln\frac{\alpha_p e^C}{4x} + \frac{1}{4\pi}\int_0^x \frac{S''(x) - S''(\xi)}{x-\xi}d\xi \quad (5.42)$$

Now the same case will be computed using the equivalence rule. For this purpose we need the solutions of (1) the transonic equation for the equivalent axisymmetric body, (2) the cross-flow equation of this body, and (3) the cross-flow equation of the original body (the "wing").

For the solution of (1) we can fall back on Eq. 5.26 with $M_\infty = 1$:

$$\frac{u}{U} = \frac{S''(x)}{4\pi}\ln\frac{\alpha_p S e^C}{4\pi x} + \frac{1}{4\pi}\int_0^x \frac{S''(x) - S''(\xi)}{x-\xi}d\xi \quad (5.43)$$

To compute the u-component of the cross-flow perturbation velocity for the equivalent body, first the Laplace equation $\varphi_{rr} + \varphi_r/r = 0$ is integrated, giving $\varphi = q \ln r$. Now, with $\varphi_r = v/U$ and the slender-body condition for axisymmetric problems, $\lim_{r \to 0}(vr) = v_b r_b$, we arrive at $q = v_b r_b/U$. Eliminating v_b with the help of the boundary condition $v_b/U = dr_b/dx$ and introducing the expression thus obtained for q into

Analytical Solutions of the Transonic Continuity Equation 133

the solution of the Laplace equation, we have $\varphi = r_b(dr_b/dx) \ln r$. Finally, with $S(x) = \pi r_b^2$ we obtain $u/U = \partial\varphi/\partial x = (S''(x)/2\pi) \ln r$. On the body surface, $r^2 = r_b^2 = S/\pi$, so that the cross-flow perturbation of the equivalent body becomes

$$\frac{u}{U} = \frac{S''(x)}{4\pi} \ln \frac{S}{\pi} \tag{5.44}$$

Finally, the cross-flow perturbation in the x direction of the original body must be computed. Here the solution of the Laplace equation becomes

$$\varphi = \int_{-z_b(x)}^{z_b(x)} q(x, \zeta) \ln(y^2 + (\zeta - z)^2)^{1/2} \, d\zeta \tag{5.45}$$

Because we now have a basically plane problem, the condition for slender-body flow becomes $\lim_{y \to 0} \varphi_y = v_b/U = \partial y_b(x, \zeta)/\partial x$. Differentiating Eq. 5.45 yields

$$\varphi_y = y \int_{-z_b(x)}^{z_b(x)} \frac{q(x, \zeta)}{y^2 + (\zeta - z)^2} \, d\zeta \tag{5.46}$$

Here for $\zeta = z$ and $y = 0$, we have an indeterminate or singular value. Therefore, this case requires special consideration. Actually, realizing that y is exactly zero only at the edges of the wing-type body, the range requiring special attention comprises $(\varphi - z) \approx y$. But since y is very small compared with z, it is expedient to expand $q(x, \zeta)$ into a Taylor series in which the second and higher terms are much smaller than the first one:

$$\varphi_y = y \int_{-z_b(x)}^{z_b(x)} \frac{q(x, z)}{y^2 + (\zeta - z)^2} \, d\zeta + y \int_{-z_b(x)}^{z_b(x)} \frac{q'(x_1 z)(\zeta - z)}{y^2 + (\zeta - z)^2} \, d\zeta \tag{5.47}$$

The first integral has the solution

$$I_1 = yq(x, z) \frac{\arctan \frac{\zeta - z}{y}}{y} \Bigg|_{-z_b(x)}^{z_b(x)} = q(x, z)\pi \tag{5.48}$$

because at $\zeta = z_b(x)$ and $\zeta = -z_b(x)$, $y = 0$ and, therefore, $\arctan(\zeta - z)/y = \arctan \infty = \pi/2$.

The solution of the second integral becomes

$$I_2 = q'(x, z) \frac{y}{2} \ln(y^2 + (\zeta - z)^2) \Bigg|_{-z_b(x)}^{z_b(x)} \tag{5.49}$$

For $y \to 0$ we have $I_2 = 0$ and thus the contribution of $q'(x, z)(\zeta - z)$ to $q(x, \zeta)$ is negligible. Consequently,

$$q(x, \zeta) = q(x, z) = \frac{1}{\pi} \frac{\partial \zeta}{\partial y} = \frac{1}{\pi} \frac{v_b}{U} = \frac{1}{\pi} \frac{\partial y_b(x, \zeta)}{\partial x}$$

and the cross-flow perturbation velocity component in the x direction of the original body is given as

$$\frac{u}{U} = \frac{1}{\pi} \frac{\partial}{\partial x} \int_{-z_b(x)}^{z_b(x)} (y_b)_x \ln|\zeta - z| \, d\zeta \qquad (5.50)$$

Thus, we have the three results needed for applying the equivalence rule to our problem. By forming

$$\left(\frac{u}{U}\right)_{\text{Eq.5.43}} - \left(\frac{u}{U}\right)_{\text{Eq.5.44}} + \left(\frac{u}{U}\right)_{\text{Eq.5.20}}$$

we obtain the result of the direct computation from the parabolic flow equation (Eq. 5.42).

This agreement justifies the claim that the equivalence rule is a useful tool for the computation of the pressure coefficients of an arbitrary, low-aspect-ratio flight article at transonic speeds.[21]

In concluding this section, it remains to be shown that the far field in transonic flow is independent of the specific body shape if, according to the equivalence rule, the cross-sectional areas of the bodies are equal at corresponding stations in flow direction.

To this end we compare Eq. 5.24 (without the second term, which is zero for $M_\infty = 1$), which is an equation for axisymmetric flow, with Eq. 5.35, in which we substitute Eq. 5.39 for $q(\xi, \zeta)$. Because we want to compare the flow field far away from this wing-type body with that of the equivalent body, we set $z \gg z_b(\xi)$, that is, $z \gg \zeta$. Thus, the exponential function of Eq. 5.35 becomes independent of ζ, and with $y^2 + z^2 = r^2$ the exponential functions of Eqs. 5.24 and 5.35 are identical. It remains, therefore, to show that $(1/4\pi)S'(\xi)$ of Eq. 5.24 is equal to

$$\frac{1}{2\pi} \int_{-z_b(\xi)}^{z_b(\xi)} \frac{\partial y_b(\xi, \zeta)}{\partial x} \, \partial \zeta$$

of Eq. 5.35. This equality is obvious, however, because the integral in the second expression is equal to $S'(\xi)/2$, where $S(\xi)$ is now the cross-sectional area of the wing-type body at the station ξ.

5.2.5 The Area Rule as the Logical Extension of the Equivalence Rule

Historically, the area rule for the design of transonic flight articles was an important theoretical tool in the extension of the speed range toward the speed of sound by making a drag reduction possible in this speed range. As we have seen, the drag of a transonic flight article rises abruptly at a certain critical subsonic Mach number whose value depends on the body shape and, of course, strongly on the body thickness ratio. In Fig. 4.2, the drag rise of a wedge was shown in terms of the similarity parameter χ. In this figure, the critical drag rise occurs at about $\chi = -1$, a value obtained, for example, for $t/l = 0.2$ and an approach Mach number

$M_\infty \approx 0.8$. As Fig. 4.2 shows, the drag coefficient at $\chi = -1$ is $c_D \approx 0.2$, whereas $(c_D)_{M_\infty=1} \approx 1.7$, a drag rise of more than a factor 8 between $M_\infty = 0.8$ and $M_\infty = 1$. Here, it seems, the only way to shift $c_{D\,cr}$ to higher values of M_∞ would be to reduce the thickness ratio t/l. Unfortunately, there is a practical limit to the fineness of flight articles. Both structural and the payload requirements make it impossible to reduce their volume beyond a certain minimum value.

The wings of conventional high-speed aircraft have an even more detrimental influence on $c_{D\,cr}$. In the light of the discussion of the equivalence rule of the previous section, the detrimental effect of the wings can easily be understood: The equivalence rule states that the pressure coefficient c_p of a transonic flight article is that sum of the c_p values of two contributions. First, a contribution that only depends on the x-wise distribution of the body cross-sectional areas, which Oswatitsch has named the "space- or volume-contribution," as given by Eq. 5.43 minus Eq. 5.44. The second contribution depends on the actual body shape, but simply as the result of the two-dimensional Laplace equations of the cross-flows along the x-axis with the body contour (surface streamline) as the boundary condition (Eq. 5.50).

Now, in a conventional aircraft design in which the wings are attached to a fuselage section of constant or near-constant cross-sectional area, the cross-sectional area of the total aircraft abruptly increases at the upstream station of this fuselage section and abruptly decreases at its downstream station.[22] Compared with the fuselage alone, the space contribution, given by Eq. 5.43 minus Eq. 5.44 now has very high positive values at the limits of the range we have defined ($S'' \gg 0$); between these limits the space contribution is more negative than that of the fuselage in this range ($S'' < S''_{\text{fusel}} < 0$). Of course, the extreme values of $S''(x)$ at the limits of this range are bound to violate the basic requirements for the validity of the equivalence rule, particularly the slender-body requirement. Indeed, such a sudden rise in $S(x)$ caused by the wing most likely leads to the formation of shock waves, a major cause for the critical drag rise.

This conclusion leads to an important argument, namely, that if the equivalence rule is generally valid, that is, if the composition of the pressure coefficient from the space contribution and the cross-flow contribution is a valid assumption even for conventional fuselage–wing systems (as opposed to all-wing airplanes as used in the example of the previous section), then the detrimental effect of the wings, namely, the formation of shock waves, should be minimized by a design in which $S''(x)$ is again a monotone function or at least a function without any abrupt changes in its values.[23] Based on this concept, R. T. Whitcomb [20] proposed that transonic flight articles should have a restricted fuselage cross-sectional area over the wing range as defined earlier, such that no abrupt changes of the cross-sectional areas occur over the entire length of the airplane. This, of course, means that a compromise may be required between the strict area rule and the resulting fuselage shape, which must otherwise stay aerodynamically sound, so that it does not counteract the benefits of the area rule. In comprehensive wind tunnel tests the basic validity of this concept has been verified. Also, these tests have provided examples of the validity of the equivalence rule. For two kinds of airplane wings, Fig. 5.9 shows (1) the overall drag increase due to the addition of wings to the fuselage, (2) the shift of $M_{\infty cr}$ to smaller values as caused by the wings of the total airplane and by the hump of the equivalent body, and (3) the similarity of the drag rise of the total airplane with that of the equivalent body. These curves clearly suggest that the shock systems causing the drag rise, are mainly a function of the space contribution of the equivalence rule (see Sec. 5.2.3), whereas the difference between the curves is mainly given by the difference in the cross-flow contributions.

Inspection of Figs. 5.10 shows that the effect of the wings in the subsonic range ($M_\infty < 0.84$) is the same for the original body and for that modified according to the area rule. However, the drag rise and the shift in the critical Mach number $M_{\infty cr}$, the magnitudes of greatest effect on airplane cruising speed and stability, are very different in the expected sense. This result is another proof that it is the detrimental effect of the shock systems (not present in the subsonic range) that is markedly reduced by following the area rule.

As Whitcomb pointed out, certain irregularities of the curves must be attributed to measuring inaccuracies and to boundary layer effects, particularly shock-induced boundary layer separation, an effect of greatest importance to transonic flow over solid boundaries. This crucial feature of transonic flow will be discussed in some detail in Chapter 6.

The area rule has been successfully applied to a large number of production-line aircraft, mainly in the military realm. The best known example, however, is the conspicous hump on the fuselage of the Boeing 747 Transport upstream of the wings.

5.3 Transonic Flow with Heat Addition

Heat may be added to a transonic flow field in two basically different ways, namely, through combustion or condensation of fluid constituents and through heat transfer to the flow from a solid boundary. Both processes are governed by essentially the same aerodynamic equation, but in the former case additional equations describing the chemical and molecular changes are needed, and in the latter case viscous forces play a strong role because here the heat is added to a layer normal to the wall in which both the velocity and temperature of the fluid are changing.

The effect of heat addition or removal on the performance of an airplane may be considerable and must be investigated. This last example of inviscid transonic theory underscores the need for a so-called viscous transonic theory, which will be the subject of Chapter 6.

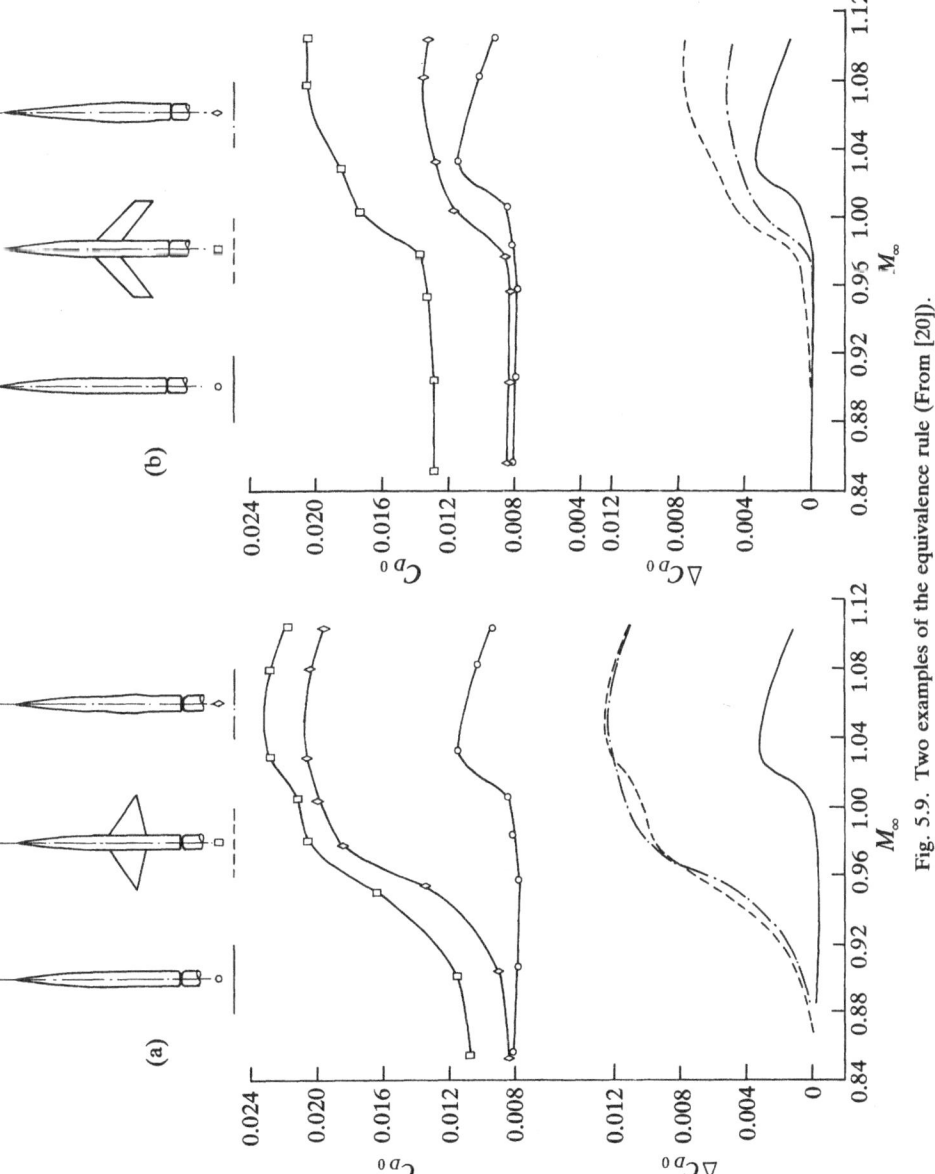

Fig. 5.9. Two examples of the equivalence rule (From [20]).

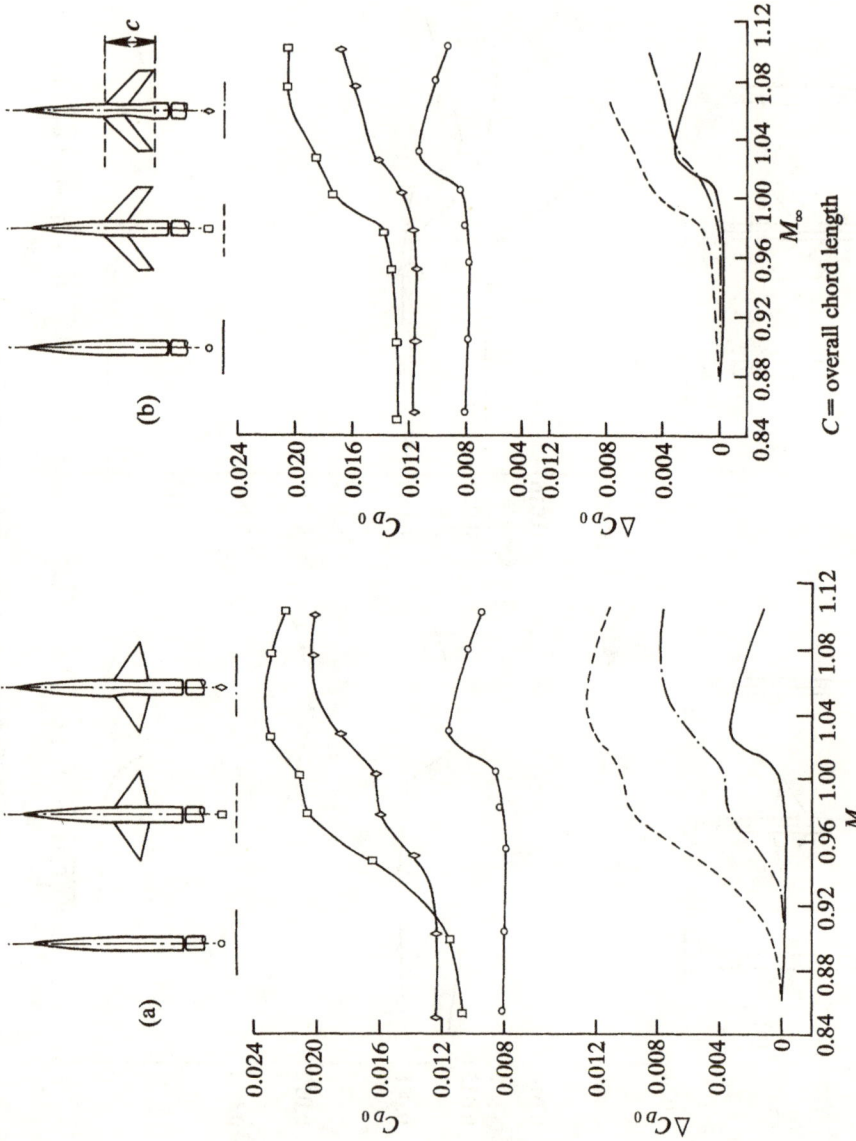

Fig. 5.10. The effect of the area rule on the drag of (a) a delta-wing–fuselage system, and (b) a swept-back-wing–fuselage system (From [20]).

5.3.1 The Equation for Inviscid Flow with Heat Addition

In deriving the equation for transonic flow with heat addition, the basic equations Eqs. 2.4 through 2.8 remain unchanged, with the exception of Eq. 2.6, where the addition of heat dQ at the temperature T causes the entropy increase $dS = dQ/T$, whereas $dS = 0$ in inviscid flow without heat addition. For two-dimensional flow, to which the following derivation will be restricted, Eq. 2.6 therefore must be replaced by

$$\frac{dS}{dt} = \frac{\partial S}{\partial x}u' + \frac{\partial S}{\partial y}v = \frac{1}{T}\frac{dQ}{dt} = \frac{1}{T}\left(\frac{\partial Q}{\partial x}u' + \frac{\partial Q}{\partial y}v\right)^{24}$$

and thus it follows that

$$\frac{\partial S}{\partial x} = \frac{1}{T}\frac{\partial Q}{\partial x} \qquad \frac{\partial S}{\partial y} = \frac{1}{T}\frac{\partial Q}{\partial y} \qquad (5.51)$$

The terms of Eq. 2.7 containing S no longer cancel out, and by eliminating p and S (the latter through Eq. 5.54), the basic equation for flow with heat addition becomes

$$(a^2 - u'^2)\frac{\partial u'}{\partial x} - u'v\left(\frac{\partial u'}{\partial y} + \frac{\partial v}{\partial x}\right) + (a^2 - v^2)\frac{\partial v}{\partial y}$$
$$= \frac{a^2}{c_p T}\left(u'\frac{\partial Q}{\partial x} + v\frac{\partial Q}{\partial y}\right) = \frac{a^{*2}}{c_p T^*}\left(u'\frac{\partial Q}{\partial x} + v\frac{\partial Q}{\partial y}\right) \qquad (5.52)$$

Hence, the only difference between the isentropic equation and that with the heat addition is in the term on the right-hand side of Eq. 5.52, replacing the zero of Eq. 2.9. Because the total enthalpy of flow with heat addition is given as

$$c_p T_0 + Q = c_p T + \frac{u'^2 + v^2}{2} \qquad (5.52a)$$

Eq. 2.10 must be replaced by

$$a^2 = \frac{\gamma+1}{2}a^{*2} - \frac{\gamma-1}{2}(u'^2 + v^2) + (\gamma - 1)Q \qquad (5.53)$$

where T_0 and a^* refer to the conditions before heat addition, while T, a, $u' = U + u$, and v refer to those after the addition of Q.

In following Guderley for the derivation of the small perturbation equation (see Eqs. 2.21 through 2.25), first the expressions for flow with heat addition equivalent to the Eqs. 2.24 must be computed. To this end, an estimation is needed of the order of magnitude of Q in relation to the changes of the perturbation velocity components caused by the addition of Q. As Eq. 5.53a shows, the addition of Q causes an increase of both T and $(u'^2 + v^2)/2$. The relative magnitudes of these two contributions depend on the specific flow conditions, for example, the change of the stream tube cross sections as the result of the heat addition.

The order-of-magnitude estimation for dQ may be made for the flow in a stream tube, that is, for one-dimensional flow. From

1. $dW/W + d\rho/\rho + dA/A = 0$ (continuity)
2. $W\,dW + dp/\rho = 0$ (Bernoulli, valid also for stream tube flow with entropy change)
3. $c_p\,dT + W\,dW = dQ$ (energy)
4. $dp = RT\,d\rho + \rho R\,dT$ (equation of state)
5. $a^2 = \gamma RT$ (speed of sound) (5.54)

we obtain

$$\frac{dW}{W} = -\frac{1}{1-M^2}\left(\frac{dA}{A} - \frac{dQ}{c_pT}\right) \quad (5.58)$$

by eliminating dT and dp in (4) with (5) and (2) respectively, then forming $d\rho/\rho$ from the thus-changed equation (4) and substituting for $d\rho/\rho$ in (1), observing (5).

By setting $dA/A = 0$ in Eq. 5.55, as being very small for $M_\infty \approx 1$ (exactly zero for $M = 1$), we finally arrive at

$$\frac{1}{1-M^2}\frac{dQ}{c_pT} = \frac{dW}{W} \approx \frac{u}{U} \approx \frac{a}{a^*} \quad (5.56)$$

where the two last terms on the right-hand side apply to slender-body flow near $M_\infty = 1$.

From this equation the magnitude of dQ is obtained by setting $M^2 \approx M^{*2} \approx [(a^* + u)/a^*]^2$, which certainly holds for $M_\infty \approx 1$, and introducing this expression for M into Eq. 5.56, resulting in

$$\frac{dQ}{c_pT} \approx \frac{2a^*u}{a^{*2}}\frac{u}{a^*}^{25}$$

and with $u = a^*\tau$ (see Eq. 2.22a), we finally have

$$dQ \sim \tau^2 \quad (5.57)$$

that is, near $M = 1$, dQ is very small for a velocity change of the order τ.

By replacing a^2 in Eq. 5.52 by Eq. 5.52b, observing Eq. 5.57 and expressing the velocity components and their derivatives in small-perturbation terms through Eqs. 2.21 and 2.23, and retaining the lowest orders only, we obtain the transonic potential equation for flow with heat addition. It differs, as might have been expected, from Eq. 2.25 only by the heat term $q(x,y)$:

$$\varphi_{yy} - (\gamma + 1)\varphi_x\varphi_{xx} = q(x,y) \quad (5.58)$$

where $\varphi_x = u/a^*$, $\varphi_y = v/a^*$, and $q(x,y) = (1/c_pT^*)(\partial Q/\partial x)$, and[26] x and y are dimensionless coordinates with a common reference length.

According to Zierep [21], a solution of Eq. 5.58 is found for the flow field near the surface of a slender body ($y \approx 0$) by the following procedure. First, setting

$$\varphi(x, y) = \varphi_h(x, y) + \varphi_i(x, y) \tag{5.59}$$

where φ_h is the complete solution of the homogeneous equation (i.e., the solution for the flow before heat addition) and φ_i is a particular solution of the inhomogeneous equation. By substituting Eq. 5.59 in Eq. 5.58, the following equation between φ_h and φ_i is obtained:

$$\varphi_i'(x)\varphi_{hxx}(x, 0) + \varphi_i''(x)\varphi_{hx}(x, 0) + \varphi_i'(x)\varphi_i''(x) = -\frac{1}{\gamma + 1} q(x) \tag{5.60}$$

where φ_i is the particular solution for $y = 0$, a good approximation for the flow near the surface of a slender body. Therefore, with the help of the homogeneous equation, all derivatives with respect to y have been eliminated from the equation. The integration of this ordinary differential equation yields the following quadratic equation for φ_i':

$$\varphi_i'^2(x) + 2\varphi_{hx}(x, 0)\varphi_i'(x) + \frac{2}{\gamma + 1} \frac{Q(x)}{c_p T^*} = 0 \tag{5.61a}$$

with the solutions

$$\varphi_i'(x) = -\varphi_{hx}(x, 0) \pm \sqrt{\varphi_{hx}^2(x, 0) - \frac{2}{\gamma + 1} \frac{Q(x)}{c_p T^*}} \tag{5.61b}$$

where the positive square root must be taken, because for $Q = 0$, $\varphi_i'(x)$ must also be zero. With increasing heat addition, the square root goes to zero, both for subsonic flow ($\varphi_{hx} < 0$) and for supersonic flow ($\varphi_{hx} > 0$), so that the perturbation velocity $\varphi'(x) = \varphi_i'(x) + \varphi_{hx}(x)$ decreases in either case toward zero, at which point the flow is choked ($W = a^*$). Hence, the maximum amount of heat that may be added to the flow in a stream tube of constant cross section is given by the condition for a real value of the square root

$$\varphi_{hx}^2(x, 0) \geq \frac{2}{\gamma + 1} \frac{Q(x)}{c_p T^*} \tag{5.62}$$

As could be expected, the amount of heat that may be added to the flow is determined by the flow conditions before heat addition, that is, the solution of the homogeneous equation.

It is noteworthy that the negative sign of Eq. 5.61b applies to a realistic process, too, namely, to the perturbation velocity behind a normal shock that is created by the heat addition in the supersonic flow where φ_{hx} is the perturbation velocity of the supersonic flow. With the plus sign applying to the supersonic flow (I) and the minus sign to the subsonic flow (II) behind the shock, the transonic shock relation $u_I + u_{II} = 0$ is satisfied.

Because of the relatively small change in cross-sectional area of the stream tubes in the transonic range, some qualitative conclusions may be drawn from the results of Eqs. 5.61 and 5.62 for heat addition to transonic flow in general. Since, according to Eq. 5.61, subsonic flow is accelerated by heat addition, choking in the subsonic portion of a transonic stream tube is promoted, whereas the deceleration through heat addition in the supersonic portion is delayed, because the flow acceleration in the diverging stream tube counteracts the deceleration due to the heat addition.

5.3.2 The Effect of Heat Addition on Aircraft Performance

Considering now the transonic flow over a symmetric profile where, even without heat addition, a station with $M = 1$ exists somewhere on the front parts of its surfaces, then the stream tubes near the surface have a throat at the sonic line, originating at the $M = 1$ station. Assuming that this station, as determined by the basic flow equations, does not, in first approximation, shift when heat is added to the surface stream tube, this fixed throat has the following consequence. Contrary to the case of constant-cross-sectional flow, in which a "throat" (i.e., a station of $M = 1$) is always formed, when a critical amount of heat is added that varies with the approach flow conditions (see Eq. 5.62), no heat can be added to the subsonic portion of the stream tube when a throat already exists, because any heat added is carried to the throat, at which, however, no heat can be added (Eq. 5.62 for $\varphi_{hx} = 0$). Conversely, in the supersonic portion of the stream tube, somewhat more heat may be added than according to Eq. 5.62, which is based on a stream tube of constant cross-section. Hence, as long as subcritical amounts of heat are added to the supersonic flow, a reduction in the flow velocity results (see Fig. 5.11), and when the critical amount according to Eq. 5.62 is added, the flow is slowed down to $M = 1$. Beyond this point the flow is reaccelerated due to the supersonic flow expansion over the convex surface of the profile until it is slowed down to the ambient flow conditions in the terminating shock wave and a final adiabatic expansion.

In contrast to this straightforward case, addition of a supercritical amount of heat in the supersonic region again leads to an impossible solution. As seen in Fig. 5.12, $M = 1$ is reached as soon as the critical amount of heat has been added, and an imaginary (i.e., physically impossible) solution governs the flow downstream of this choking station until the Mach number of the expanding flow has reached a value whose critical heat addition is equal to the amount that was originally intended to be added. Downstream of this point, the real solution for flow without heat addition is again valid.

Of course, nature does not follow this mathematical restrictions in heat transfer to both the subsonic and supersonic part of a transonic stream tube. Depending on the specific flow conditions, one or both of the following will occur: (1) the flow pattern about the profile will change to one that eliminates the choking conditions; (2) unsteady processes will take over in the form of pressure waves traveling upstream and

Analytical Solutions of the Transonic Continuity Equation 143

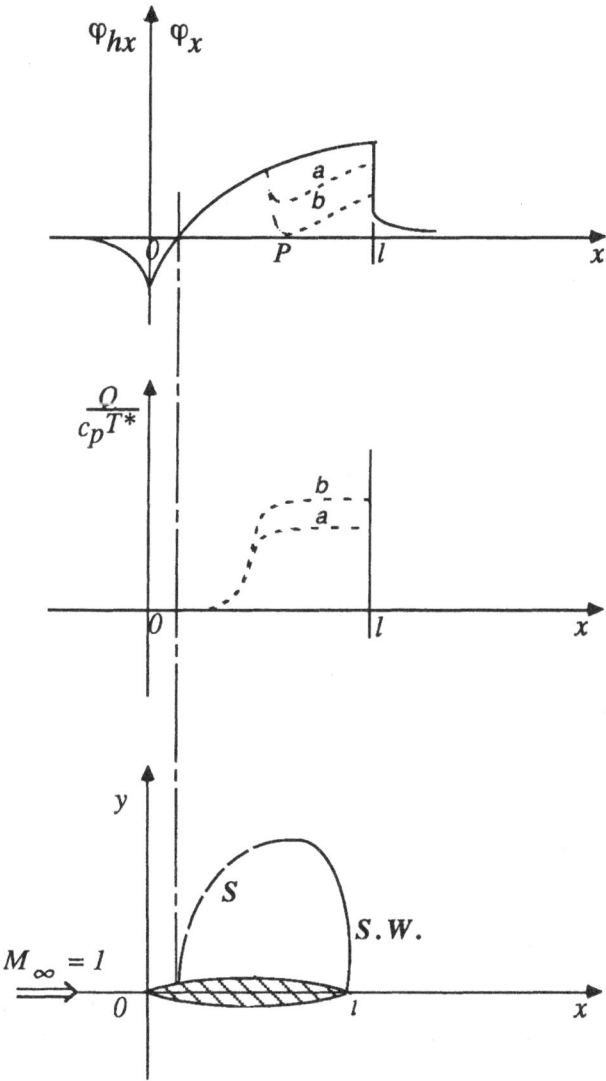

Fig. 5.11. Subcritical (a) and critical (b) heat addition to the transonic flow over a symmetrical profile. S = sonic line; $S.W.$ = terminating shock wave of the flow before heat addition (After Zierep [21]).

downstream from the station of heat addition, as was first discussed in detail by F. Bartlmä [22]. Actually, these two processes are interconnected, and Bartlmä's analysis gives closed solutions for a pipe flow.

Nevertheless, taking the physically possible case of heat addition of a subcritical amount in the supersonic range of a profile, a conclusion about the change of the drag coefficient of a flight article through heat addition may be drawn that warrants further studies. The expression for the drag

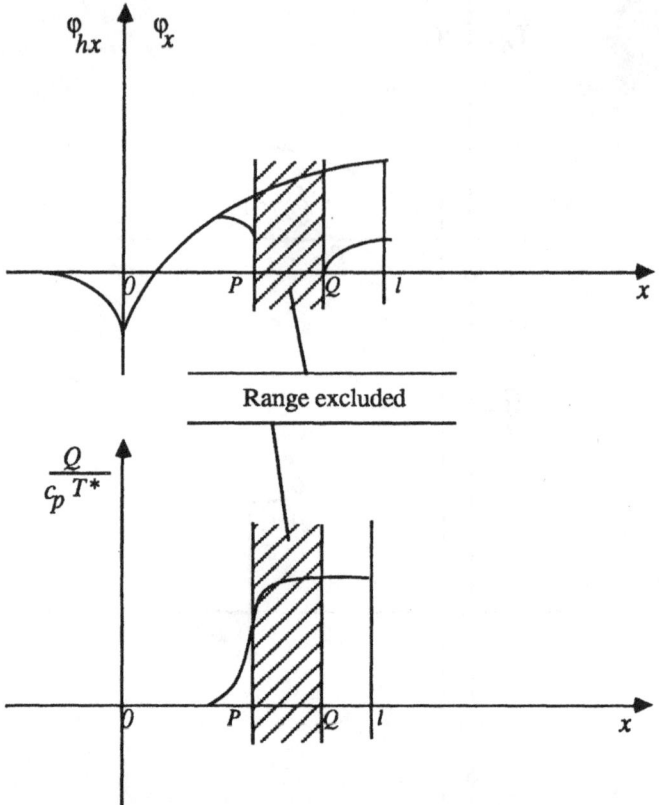

Fig. 5.12. The range of the supersonic part of a transonic stream tube over a profile that is mathematically excluded from supercritical heat addition (After Zierep [21]).

coefficient of a symmetric profile is directly obtained from Eq. 5.61. With the small-perturbation expression for the pressure coefficient $c_p = -2u/U$, and $U \approx a^*$, we have $c_p = -2\varphi_x$. The drag coefficient is obtained through integration of the components of the pressure coefficients in the flow direction on the two surfaces of a symmetric profile as

$$c_D = 2 \int_0^l c_p \left(\frac{dh}{dx} \right) dx$$

where dh/dx is the slope of the contour and, for a slender body, a sufficient approximation for the directional sine of the pressure force vectors, and l is the body length. Hence, with Eq. 5.61, the drag coefficient becomes

$$c_D = -\frac{4}{l} \int_0^l \sqrt{\varphi_{hx}^2 - \frac{2}{\gamma+1} \frac{Q(x)}{c_p T^*}} \frac{dh}{dx} dx \qquad (5.63)$$

This equation shows that the value of c_D is reduced for $Q(x) \neq 0$, so that

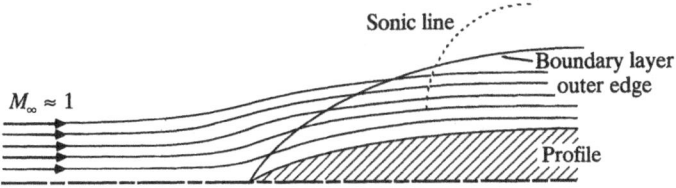

Fig. 5.13. Transonic flow in the boundary layer of a profile, demonstrating the complexity of heat transfer from the wall. Note that the sonic line does not reach the wall.

drag is reduced through heat addition, at least through a subcritical heat addition to the supersonic portion of the profile flow. If such an effect could be confirmed, it might be of considerable value as a means for the improvement of the performance of transonic flight articles.

Unfortunately, although the inviscid theory leads to this conclusive result, the fact that the heat would be transferred to a temperature boundary layer and not to a single stream tube satisfying the inviscid theory must not be overlooked. As shown in Fig. 5.13, with increasing distance in flow direction from the body nose, more and more of the approaching stream tubes become a part of the boundary layer and thus are slowed down in comparison with the velocities of the stream tubes farther away from the body that have not yet entered the boundary layer. Consequently, the stream tube directly on the body surface, which because of viscous forces can never become supersonic, is energized to higher velocities. This has an effect on the flow in the adjacent stream tube, and so forth. Thus, the exact pressure distribution on the body wall can only be found through the computation of a (viscous) boundary layer with heat addition, and its interaction with the solution of the inviscid outer flow, thus modifying the effective body shape. However, it should be safe to say that, qualitatively, the result of Eq. 5.63 is unlikely to change, that is, that the heat addition to the boundary layer in the range in which the outer flow is supersonic may cause a reduction in wave drag.

Specific cases of heat addition, as through combustion and condensation in wind tunnels, have been studied with quite accurate results (see, e.g., ref. 23). As to the unsteady processes created by heat addition, considerable work was done more recently by Sichel and Adamson [ref. 51, in this paper there is also given a comprehensive list of publications of this period]. These studies were conducted by applying the small-perturbation approach as given in Secs. 2.6 and 6.3, thus constituting another interesting application of this important tool of transonic analysis.

Notes

1. Not to be confused with similarity rules.
2. As shown in Eq. 5.22, it may be practical to include $(\gamma + 1)M_\infty^2/U$ in α_p.
3. For the definition of the perturbation sources, see Prob. 5.1.

4. Note that $\sqrt{(x-\xi)^2 + \alpha y^2} = R$, the equivalent distance between the source and the point (x, y), is a scalar magnitude and should be written as $R = \sqrt{(x-\xi)^2 + \alpha y^2}$ for $x > \xi$ and $R = \sqrt{(\xi-x)^2 + \alpha y^2}$ for $\xi > x$. In executing integrations, this fact must be kept in mind, and, if necessary, an integral from 0 to l must be broken down into the sum of the integrals from 0 to x and from x to l. As an example, the result of the first term on the right-hand side of Eq. 5.12 would be (for $(l-x)$ and $x \gg \sqrt{\alpha} y$)

$$\frac{S'(l)}{l-x} - \frac{S'(0)}{x}$$

5. The stations $x = 0$ and $x = l$, and consequently the adjacent nose and tail sections, must be excluded as being points of discontinuity of the body slope and, therefore, are not represented by Eq. 5.12. Moreover, at these stations, small perturbation is not applicable, because they are stagnation points where the velocity component $u \approx -U$, that is, not compatible with the condition $u \ll U$. This exclusion of small nose and tail sections of the body applies to all the results of this section (e.g., to Eq. 5.17). Also, the values at $x = 0$; l of Eq. 5.17 are misleading, because when $S(x)$ is given as a continuous function, the pointed ends are at the $S = 0$ stations of these functions that continue into the negative x coordinates, that is, that do not describe a discontinuity. The reader may obtain more insight into the need for excluding the body end stations from the computations through Prob. 5.2.
6. The integration constant is determined from $u = u_{\text{inc}}$ at the station $S''(x) = 0$, as seen from Eq. 5.18.
7. See Note 21 of Chapter 2.
8. As shown by Eq. 2.60, the supersonic similarity rule relates all cases to $M_\infty = \sqrt{2}$, for which $M_\infty^2 - 1 = 1$, whereas for subsonic flow $1 - M_\infty^2 = 1$ for $M_\infty = 0$.
9. y has been replaced by the radius r of the axisymmetric body.
10. For $M \approx 1$, the second term goes to 0 ($f \rightarrow 0$). This is shown, not using Green's theorem, by Zierep [18] (see page 130) for symmetric bodies of arbitrary cross section.
11. See Note 2.
12. The term "arbitrary" as applied to an aircraft flying near the velocity of sound implies that the aspect ratio is small (delta wing, swept-back wings, etc.).
13. See Sec. 5.2.1 for a detailed analysis.
14. Or the corresponding axisymmetric equation.
15. One could argue that it would be more appropriate to construct the axisymmetric "equivalent" body such that the length of the cross-section circumferences were equal to those of the actual body, because every length element of the contour is the source of a pressure disturbance. However, first of all, the slender-body concept requires small aspect ratios of the flight article for which the areas formed by the length of the circumferences are little different from the actual cross-sectional areas, and secondly, the pressure disturbances along the circumferences are not equal, that is, the contributions of the length elements of the wing may be very different from those of the fuselage. Since the whole concept of the "equivalent" body is a first approximation, it appears to be more logical that the equivalent body have the volume of the actual flight article, because here the overall air displacements of the two bodies are equal.
16. For rather irregular bodies, like a fuselage with wings much thinner than the fuselage height, a more complex boundary condition would be required, including the z-component of the perturbation velocity and the thickness change in the z direction.

Analytical Solutions of the Transonic Continuity Equation 147

17. As is easily verified by forming the derivatives of φ with respect to x, y and z and substituting into Eq. 5.34.
18. $Z = -\cotg \eta$ (η as defined in Fig. 2.11).
19. Note that $q(x, z)$ is a more general expression for the source strength than, for example, that in Eq. 5.4, where the factor $-1/4\pi$ was introduced as part of the physical definition of the potential, whereas in Eq. 5.35, φ is strictly the mathematical solution of Eq. 5.34 and the physically required factor now appears in the source strength term.
20. In analogy to the checking procedure following Eq. 5.14.
21. The simplification of the computation through the equivalence rule is even more obvious when all steps in the computation of Eq. 5.42 are taken.
22. That is, at an airplane with stwep-back wings, the cross-sectional areas here considered consist of three parts when they intersect the wing trailing edges (see, e.g, Fig. 5.10b).
23. It is impossible to entirely eliminate shock waves in transonic flight. However, the reduction of shock waves caused by discontinuities of the cross-sectional areas is of particular importance.
24. The small perturbation component $u = u' - U$.
25. As Eq. 5.56 shows, u is positive for $M < 1$ and negative for $M > 1$, which must be realized in interpreting the expressions for M^{*2} and $dQ/c_p T$.
26. Note that application of small perturbation procedures to Eq. 5.53 results in $a^2 \approx a_1^{*2} + (\gamma - 1)Q + O(\tau)$, where a_1^* is the critical sound speed before heat addition. However, by referring the perturbation velocity components to the critical velocity after heat addition a_2, the corresponding expression becomes $a^2 \approx a_2^{*2} + O(\tau)$. Because of $Q \sim \tau^2$, $a_1^* \approx a_2^*$ and no distinction is needed to be made between these two reference sound speeds.

Problems

5.1. Although Eq. 5.3, as a particular integral of the Laplace equation, represents a true source flow that can stand on its own, that is, without a superimposed flow field $\partial \varphi / \partial x = $ const., the corresponding solutions of the compressible flow equations, subsonic and supersonic, are meaningful only as perturbation flows, because these equations have been derived for a steady flow in the x direction onto which a three- (or two-) dimensional perturbation flow has been superimposed. Compute the potential- and streamlines of the two-dimensional perturbation sources, to show that the source ($\varphi = -\infty$) is a point source in subsonic flow, but a line source in supersonic and transonic flow. *Clues*: The potential of a two-dimensional source is readily obtained from Eq. 2.46, which is the potential of a source distribution. Note that in supersonic flow, the y coordinate as transformed according to Prandtl–Glauert is imaginary and $\beta^2 y^2$ is a negative magnitude. The streamlines are found by applying the mathematical rule for orthogonality to the equation for $\varphi = $ const.

5.2. (1) To apply the slender body concept to the nose and tail sections, the condition $y \ll (x - \xi)$ must hold. Find functions for $S(x)$ that satisfy this requirement.
(2) The elimination of the first term on the right-hand side of Eq. 5.12 is based on the assumption $(dS/dx)_{x=0;l} = 0$. (a) Are there pointed bodies that do not satisfy this condition? (b) How about blunt bodies?

(3) What thickness ratio of (a) a parabolic (pointed) body, (b) an elliptic (blunt) body must be chosen to hold the portion of the total body length not corresponding to the condition $y < 3(x - \xi)$ to 10%?

5.3. Through Spreiter's local linearization, compute the pressure coefficient c_p for the bodies you examined in Probs. 3.3 and 3.4 (i.e., for $M = 0$ to 1).

5.4. With the help of the equivalence rule, compute the pressure coefficient of a parabolic arc axisymmetric half-body with delta wings half as thick as the body diameter. Start the computation by finding a source distribution that produces such a device.

5.5. How much heat $Q(x)$ must be added in one of the cases computed in Prob. 5.3 to obtain $c_D = 0$?

6
VISCOUS TRANSONIC FLOW

6.1 Introduction

The effect of viscosity on the relative motion of a fluid and a solid body or of two fluids finds its manifestation in the fluid stress whose two components, the shear stress and the longitudinal stress can usually be treated separately. Actually, the shear stress is of much greater importance for the establishment of accurate aerodynamic relationships than the longitudinal stress.

The shear stress is caused by the transfer between adjacent streamlines of the momentum of the fluid molecules or the turbulence elements. This momentum transfer produces a gradual transition of the velocity of one streamline to that of another one, for example, from the stagnant air on the surface of a solid body to the velocity of the undisturbed fluid at a certain distance from the wall, or, in the case of a free jet, from the velocity of the undisturbed jet core to the velocity of the undisturbed ambient fluid. Outside of the boundary layer or mixing layer formed in this way, inviscid theory describes the flow field with sufficient accuracy. Therefore, viscous theory must only be applied to the flow in these "viscous layers." However, because the fluid velocities in these layers are smaller than that at their edges, as defined in Chapter 1, the cross sections of the inviscid stream tubes increase after entering the viscous boundary layer. Thus, the inviscid flow field is pushed outward and its effective boundary is altered. As the result, the boundary layer is altered, and so on. This interaction between the inviscid flow field and the viscous boundary layer is one of the main concerns of the computation of practical flow fields.

The second kind of viscous effect, the so-called longitudinal stress, is an interaction of the fluid elements in the flow direction beyond that of the Brownian motion of the molecules. Such interactions occur when the solution of the inviscid problem requires that the fluid have an infinitely high acceleration. This problem was already discussed in Sec. 2.1. there it was shown that in inviscid theory a so-called limit line is obtained that forms the locus of the points of infinite acceleration. Beyond the limit line, the inviscid solution lies on another "Riemann sheet" that has no physical meaning. Therefore, in reality, before the point of infinite acceleration is reached, viscous flow theory must be invoked. Viscous flow may manifest itself either as a shock wave, which falls outside of viscous flow theory, or in flows actually governed by the viscous equations, as in the case of "source flow" (see page 80).

In subsonic and supersonic aerodynamics, the effects of longitudinal viscosity can usually be approximated or replaced by exact equations describing the transition from one inviscid regime to the next one, as in the case of shock waves. In shock waves the viscous effects manifest themselves only through an increase of the flow entropy. The viscous processes as such occur over very short distance, of the order of the mean free path of the molecules, a length that must be considered only in highly rarified gases.

As we will see in the following section, in transonic flow certain phenomena may require solutions of the complete equation of viscous transonic flow before they can be thoroughly understood.

6.2 The Specific Problems of Transonic Flow Caused by Viscous Effects

6.2.1 Shock Wave–Boundary Layer Interaction

At least as far as the boundary layer is concerned, from the foregoing it seems that no difference exists in the viscous effects on subsonic and supersonic flow on the one hand and transonic flow on the other: All that seems to be necessary is to compute the viscous flow in the viscous layer and to match it to the inviscid flow surrounding it.

There is, however, one significant difference: Whereas in subsonic and supersonic flow the inviscid equations are derived by completely disregarding viscous terms, the transonic inviscid equation (Eq. 2.25a) is derived to satisfy the flow through shock waves, because transonic flow includes pockets of supersonic flow that are terminated by shock waves.[1] These shock waves change in position, strength, and extension with every change in flight condition, Mach number, and flight attitude. Hence, shock waves directly affect the "inviscid" solutions, whereas shock waves in entirely supersonic flow are fixed at geometric pecularities and can be treated independently of the purely inviscid flow fields they connect.

This significance of shock waves in transonic flow might be questioned, because we found in Sec. 2.6 that the entropy increase in transonic shock waves is of the order $t^4 \ln t$, where t is the body fineness ratio, so that the flow remains isentropic for all practical purposes. However, pressure and density undergo an increase of the second order (Eqs. 2.110 and 2.111) and cannot be disregarded. Also, shock waves have their foot points in the shear layer on the body surface, which must negotiate the sudden pressure rise of the shock. Depending on its history at the station under consideration, a shear layer shows a more or less strong tendency to separate from the body surface. The parameters that determine the station of separation are the Reynolds number of the flow, surface geometry and roughness and the distance from the shear layer origin. This tendency is greatly enhanced on a convex surface, because of the destabilizing pressure gradient in the flow away from the surface (see Sec.

2.2.1), whereas the opposite pressure gradient on a concave surface stabilizes the shear layer by compressing it. This is the normal situation in supersonic flows.

Thus, if the shear layer is "separation-prone," then even a very small pressure rise caused by the shock wave may suffice to separate it. As the low-energy stream tubes next to the body surface are no longer able to overcome this pressure differential, the flow in these stream tubes is stopped and eventually reversed (which is the criterion for separation). Thus, a separation "bubble" forms (Fig. 6.1) that may be local or may extend all the way to the trailing edge.[2] This causes two basic changes in the whole flow pattern. First, the effective geometry of the body is changed, resulting in a new "inviscid" solution with a new shock wave position, strength, and shape, producing new separation characteristics, and so forth. Consequently, a much more complex iteration procedure must be followed than in the supersonic case, where at most very minor shifts of the shock wave foot point occur. Second, because of the flow reversal with separation, the normal boundary layer assumption that the surface pressure is equal to that of the inviscid flow at the outer edge of the boundary layer is no longer justified. The surface pressure in the separation zone becomes greater than without separation and lift, drag, and the stability coefficients of the body change drastically and, as a rule, in an adverse sense. Changes in the flow pattern of that kind occur with every maneuver of an airplane flying at transonic speeds, aggravating the problem of flying beyond the critical Mach number. This Mach number, at which a marked supersonic region forms over the body, had earlier been characterized by a strong increase in drag. As we see now, an even more detrimental feature of flight beyond the critical Mach number is the

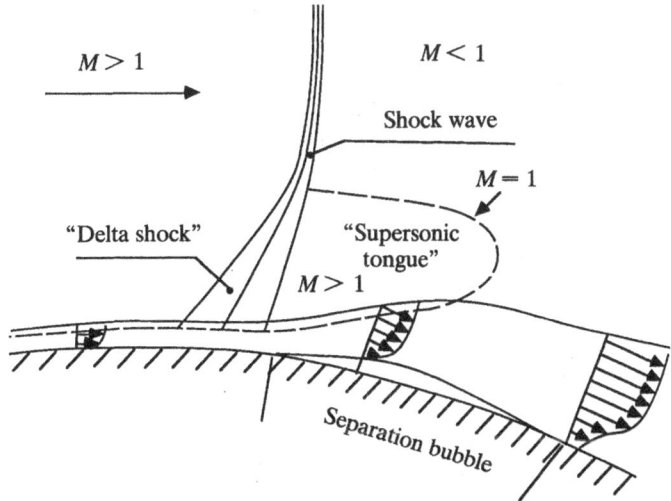

Fig. 6.1. Formation of a shock-induced separation bubble on a convex transonic profile.

change in flight stability with every flight maneuver as the result of the shift in the shock wave location and consequently of the separation point of the boundary layer.

6.2.2 The Shape of the Transonic Shock Wave

It was shown in the previous section that the transonic shock wave has its foot point somewhere in the boundary layer of the convex profile. The shock wave is the continuation of the sonic line (see Fig. 6.2) at the first streamline that remains entirely subsonic in passing by the profile. However, assuming for a moment that there is no boundary layer, the shock must be normal directly over the profile. Here, the streamlines are parallel to the surface and the flow direction behind the shock must remain parallel to the surface. Oblique shocks would change the flow direction, thus violating this condition.

The marked difference to the case of fully supersonic flow is noteworthy. Here normal shocks are never formed on solid surfaces. They occur only as an infinitesimal portion of a separated shock on the stagnation streamline before blunt noses or blunt leading edges. All shocks from solid surfaces are oblique.

To return now to the transonic case, the preceding argument that the shock wave must be normal at its foot point on a convex profile is incompatible with the Rankin–Hugoniot laws for normal shocks. As was shown in Sec. 2.2.1, a curved flow produces a pressure gradient normal to its direction. In the case of a convex surface, the pressure decreases toward the profile, both, before and behind the shock. However, according to the normal shock equations, this decrease of pressure before the shock, corresponding to a Mach number increase toward the profile, produces a Mach number decrease behind the shock and, consequently, a pressure increase toward the profile. Hence, the two physical requirements for the pressure gradients before and behind the normal shock wave are incompatible.

This result is quite unsatisfactory. After all, the physically realistic transonic flow over a convex surface must have a solution. There is one possible answer to this problem that comes to mind immediately, namely,

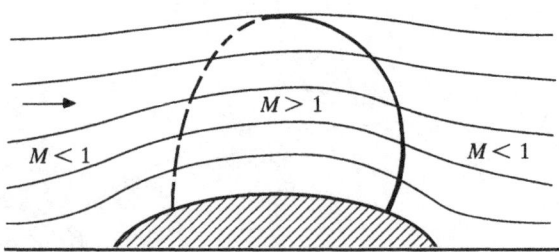

Fig. 6.2. Sonic line-shock wave system of transonic flow over a convex profile without boundary layer (schematic): (– – – –) sonic line; (———) shock wave.

that only viscous flow solutions exist. The viscous layer is subsonic on the body surface, and the shock wave can only exist outside of the $M = 1$ streamline at the shock location. Therefore, the shock wave intersects streamlines that no longer are parallel to the body surface, because the stream tube cross sections change as the result of both the entropy increase in the boundary layer and the inviscid solution of the outer flow. Consequently, the shock may not be normal and may assume a form like that shown in Fig. 6.1. Here, a fan of weak oblique shocks is formed by the curved streamlines of the supersonic portion of the boundary layer, which may even be followed by a "tongue" of adiabatic compression.

Although the validity of such viscous solutions has been confirmed experimentally, an inviscid solution may also exist. It could be a physically impossible solution, however, as in the case of the flow continuation beyond a limit line, described in Sec. 2.7.2. As it turns out, an inviscid solution was found by Zierep [24] and investigated further by Oswatitsch and Zierep [25], Gadd [26] and others. This solution is marked by a singularity in the form of an infinitely large curvature of the shock wave at its foot point on the body surface. As a consequence, the flow velocity right behind the shock undergoes an infinitely high acceleration, and the pressure behind the shock, accordingly, drops with an infinitely steep gradient from the value required by the normal shock equations (see Fig. 6.3). Thus, the discrepancy between the pressure gradients before and behind the shock disappears. Of course, a normal shock impinging on a curved profile is always curved at its foot point, even in inviscid flow, because the streamlines over the profile diverge or converge. However, the curvature of the shock alone does not solve the problem, rather the curvature at the foot point must be infinitely large.

Although the physical reality of singularities appearing in the solutions of theoretical studies should always be questioned, tests that preceded the theoretical studies by 12 years had shown the pressure drop directly behind the normal shock. As seen from Fig. 6.4, the agreement of these tests [27] with the Zierep theory is remarkably good.

Two interesting conclusions may be drawn from the experimental confirmation of the Zierep theory. First, because in the quoted tests at

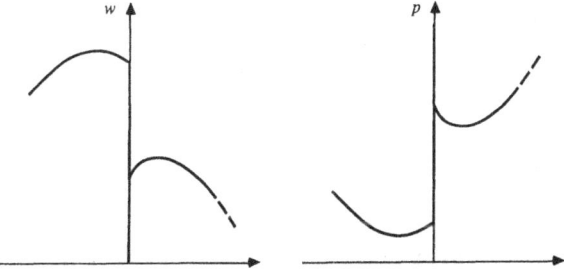

Fig. 6.3. Velocity and pressure of the flow across a shock wave on a convex profile. From Zierep [24].

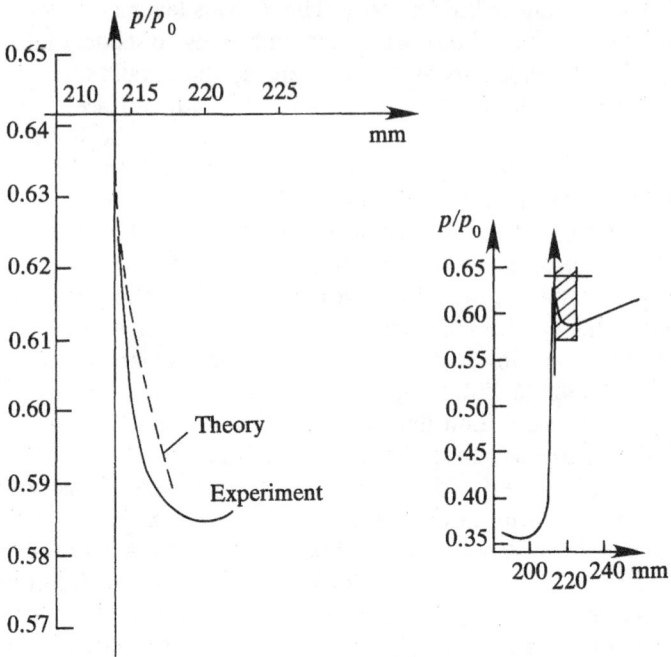

Fig. 6.4. Pressure rise across a shock wave on a convex profile. Comparison of the theory of Zierep [24] and the experiment of Ackeret, Feldman, and Rott [27].

least a thin boundary layer must certainly have existed, the viscous solution discussed earlier might have been more logical. However, the fact that the Zierep solution has been confirmed, at least qualitatively, shows its physical dominance under the particular test conditions. Consequently, a second conclusion can be drawn, namely, that in cases governed by the Zierep solution the effective pressure rise across the shock wave is reduced, and a shock-induced separation may not occur. Indeed, observations have been reported that boundary layers failed to separate behind shocks, contrary to expectations.

Before we discuss the steps that have been taken to reduce the adverse effects of the shear layer on the performance of transonic vehicles, a subject of major importance to the aircraft designer, the next section will cover the importance of the longitudinal, or compressive, viscosity on transonic flow. This will deepen our understanding of the shock wave–boundary layer interaction.

6.2.3 The Longitudinal (Compressive) Viscosity

In the previous sections it was shown that the viscous effects on transonic flow are most pronounced in the neighbourhood of the shock foot point. A theoretical inviscid solution was found for the discrepancy between the requirements of the shock conditions (the Rankine–Hugoniot relationships) and the surface curvature on the pressure gradient. Although these findings were seemingly confirmed by experiments, it could not be determined to what extent viscous effects might be involved. The considerable complexity of this problem obtains additional significance through the results on longitudinal viscosity in transonic flow, which are mainly due to A. Szaniawski and M. Sichel. Sichel's papers [28] contain a wealth of thorough analyses on this subject of which a few results will now be discussed.

So far we have always assumed that the shock waves in transonic flow were very thin, and that one and the same isentropic equation could cover the flow field both before and behind the shock because the entropy increases in the shocks were found to be of higher order. The shock wave itself could be introduced as a discontinuity in velocity, pressure, and temperature, as given by the Rankine–Hugoniot equations (e.g. see ref. 3). A marked change in our concept of shock wave–boundary layer interaction must be expected if treatment of the shock wave by viscous theory should indicate that the shock wave thickness is not negligible. Lighthill [52] determined that the shock wave thickness can be expressed as a function of the approach Mach number and the longitudinal viscosity by the relationship

$$h \approx \mu_l^*/\rho_l^*(M_1^* - 1)a^* \qquad (6.1)$$

where h = shock wave thickness; μ_l = longitudinal viscosity, and M_1^*, ρ_1^*, a^* = the critical values of Mach number, density, and sonic speed, respectively, ahead of the shock. As Eq. 6.1 indicates, the shock wave thickness may become comparable to that of the shear layer, depending on the longitudinal viscosity, the flow density and the approach Mach number. In such a case the shock foot point in the shear layer will require a completely different treatment, much more complex, but possibly eliminating the need for a singularity of flow parameters on convex surfaces.

As Eq. 6.1 shows, the extreme case $M_1 = 1$, for which h would become infinitely thick, is meaningless, because the shock strength for $M = 1$ is zero. But even for M_1 slightly larger than 1 the shock strength is too small to cause a marked disturbance of the boundary layer, and again the shock wave thickness would have little effect on the performance of aircraft. Consequently, the two other variables of Eq. 6.1, μ_l^* and ρ_1^*, should be of much greater importance to a possible influence on the flow behavior.

It seems, therefore, that the longitudinal viscosity has no special bearing on the transonic problems and should affect subsonic and supersonic flows equally much or little. However, looking at the issue from the definition of fluid stresses, the Mach number indirectly becomes a factor again. As we know, the shear stress in its simplest form, $\tau = \mu \, du/dy$, is proportional to the magnitude of the change in velocity normal to the flow direction. For this reason, the shear stress can be disregarded, except for the thin layer in which the flow velocity changes from that of one basically uniform body of fluids (or a solid wall) to another. In complete analogy, the longitudinal stress is given as $\tau_l = \mu_l \, du/dx$. Consequently, the longitudinal stress may not be negligible in areas of high flow acceleration. Shock waves are such areas, and because shock waves have a special significance in transonic flow the longitudinal stress requires special attention in transonic theory. However, shock waves are not the only phenomena that fall into this category. We pointed out in Chapter 2 that inviscid solutions of flow problems leading to limit lines could not have realistic values even in a certain range upstream of the limit line. This is a range in which the flow acceleration is too large for a solution of the inviscid equations. Consequently, when a limit line is obtained from the inviscid equation, then the viscous flow equations should produce a smooth transition to a physically realistic flow beyond the limit line.

Actually, several of those cases have been studied by Sichel in addition to his treatment of the shock wave problem, and a few of his results will be given. First, however, the basic steps in deriving the transonic viscous flow equation must be shown. These include the physical aspects of the longitudinal viscosity.

6.3 The Differential Equations of Viscous Transonic Flow

6.3.1 Formulation of the Longitudinal Viscosity

In Sec. 6.2.3, the term *longitudinal or compressive viscosity* was introduced without further clarification. A more formal description should be given for a better appreciation of the limitations of the viscous transonic equation, which will be introduced in the following section.

Because of its great importance to practical aerodynamics, the shear stress, causing the formation of boundary and mixing layers, has been investigated in depth, whereas the longitudinal stress between layers normal to the direction of propagation have been given less attention. These stresses, which are caused by strong changes of density, mainly in acoustic and shock waves, have often been expressed through the coefficient of shear stress μ. However, the elastic behavior of liquids suggests two independent coefficients of viscosity for its correct description, in analogy to the two moduli of elasticity of solids. This has led to the introduction of a so-called second coefficient of viscosity for a more general description of viscous effects in fluid dynamics.

Numerous publications on viscous flow (e.g., ref. 54), give the normal stresses of a compressible fluid element as

$$\sigma_x = -p + \mu_2 \left(\frac{\partial u}{\partial x} + \frac{\partial v}{\partial y} + \frac{\partial w}{\partial z} \right) + 2\mu \frac{\partial u}{\partial x}$$

$$\sigma_y = -p + \mu_2 \left(\frac{\partial u}{\partial x} + \frac{\partial v}{\partial y} + \frac{\partial w}{\partial z} \right) + 2\mu \frac{\partial v}{\partial y} \qquad (6.2)$$

$$\sigma_z = -p + \mu_2 \left(\frac{\partial u}{\partial x} + \frac{\partial v}{\partial y} + \frac{\partial w}{\partial z} \right) + 2\mu \frac{\partial w}{\partial z}$$

where p is the static pressure and μ_2 is the second coefficient of viscosity.[3]

Under the assumption that $\sigma_x + \sigma_y + \sigma_z = -3p$, μ_2 is no longer independent of μ and

$$\mu_2 = -\frac{2\mu}{3} \quad \text{(Stokes)} \tag{6.3}$$

This assumption due to Stokes has proved to be satisfactory in most shear flow computations. Also, in incompressible flow, the terms in brackets in Eq. 6.2 are zero and μ_2 is of no consequence. In compressible flow, however, these terms are a function of φ and its derivatives, and it becomes important to apply the correct value of μ_2.

As long as the dilatation term $(\partial u/\partial x + \partial v/\partial y + \partial w/\partial z)$ is small, as in most mixing layers, the error made by the Stokes relation is insignificant. However, when the dilatation is strong, as in shock or acoustic waves, the correct determination of μ_2 is mandatory. Considerable theoretical and experimental work on this problem has been done, mainly with respect to the propagation of plane acoustic waves [e.g., ref. 55]. It was found that μ_2 is a function of the relaxation effects of molecules with internal degrees of freedom (rotation, vibration). After the momentum transfer in the collisions of these multiatomic molecules, which constitutes the basic viscosity mechanism, it takes the relaxation time τ_r to reestablish equilibrium between the N degrees of freedom, so that $\sigma_x + \sigma_y + \sigma_z \neq -3p$ and consequently $\mu_2 \neq -2\mu/3$.[4] The exact values of μ_2 are still being investigated.

We now introduce the longitudinal or compressive stress in the x direction by setting $\partial v/\partial y = \partial w/\partial z = 0$ in Eq. 6.2, because the dilatation of the flow occurs only in this direction. Hence

$$\mu_l = 2\mu + \mu_2 \tag{6.4}$$

where, according to the preceding statements, μ_2 is a function of τ_r and N in such a way that for $N = 3$ the Stokes value is obtained.

This brief introduction to the longitudinal viscosity μ_l should suffice to warn the reader of the still existing uncertainties of the viscous transonic equations, although today the three viscosity coefficients[5] are known for a number of gases with sufficient accuracy.

6.3.2 The Small-perturbation Equation of Viscous Transonic Flow

In the previous section it was pointed out that two independent coefficients of viscosity are required for a general description of viscous flow. They are the coefficient of shear viscosity μ and a coefficient of viscosity μ_l that, in contrast to the other coefficient is a function of the molecular relaxation time. Consequently, the general Navier–Stokes equations must be applied to problems in which rapid variations of the

velocity in flow direction occur. These equations are:
Continuity:

$$(\rho u)_x + (\rho v)_y + (\rho w)_z = 0 \tag{6.5}$$

Momentum

$$\rho(uu_x + vu_y + wu_z) = \rho X - p_x + \mu[u_{xx} + u_{yy} + u_{zz}$$
$$+ (u_x + v_y + w_z)_x] + (\mu_l - 2\mu)(u_x + v_y + w_z)_x \tag{6.6a}$$

$$\rho(uv_x + vv_y + wv_z) = \rho Y - p_y + \mu[v_{xx} + v_{yy} + v_{zz}$$
$$+ (u_x + v_y + w_z)_y] + (\mu_l - 2\mu)(u_x + v_y + w_z)_y \tag{6.6b}$$

and a corresponding expression (6.6c) for the z momentum. Because viscosity causes an irreversible conversion of mechanical energy into heat energy, the energy equation in its general form is also required:

Energy

$$\rho T \left[u \left(\frac{\partial S}{\partial x} \right) + v \left(\frac{\partial S}{\partial y} \right) + w \left(\frac{\partial S}{\partial z} \right) \right]$$
$$= (kT_x)_x + (kT_y)_y + (kT_z)_z + \mu[2(u_x^2 + v_y^2 + w_z^2) + (u_y + v_x)^2$$
$$+ (v_z + w_y)^2 + (w_x + u_z)^2] + (\mu_l - 2\mu)(u_x + v_y + w_z)^2 \tag{6.7}$$

where, k is the coefficient of heat conduction.

As was pointed out, the second coefficient of viscosity $\mu_2 = \mu_l - 2\mu$ (see Eq. 6.2) plays no role in incompressible flow, because $u_x + v_y + w_z = 0$, so that the last term on the right-hand side of Eq. 6.7 becomes zero. The reason for the inclusion of the heat conduction terms in Eq. 6.7 is the interconnection of the molecular processes of heat conduction and viscosity. Both processes are momentum transfers between adjacent gas layers, so that in the first approximation, $k = c_v/\mu$. Thus, in boundary layer theory, one must distinguish between the fluid-dynamic and the thermal boundary layers.

The detailed derivation of the viscous transonic equation from Eqs. 6.5 through 6.7 may be found in ref. 30. However, a few words about the steps to be taken are in order. Basically, the procedure is very similar to that followed in Sec. 2.6 in deriving the higher-order inviscid equations. An important difference lies in the proper chosing of a reference length. In the derivation of the inviscid flow equations in Sec. 2.6, the reference length x_0 was arbitrarily chosen, and it turned out to be practical to make it the body length, which is not tied functionally to any other parameter in the equations. In viscous flow, the viscous effects are limited to generally narrow regions of high velocity gradients. In shear flow, this region is the boundary layer; in cases of longitudinal viscosity, it is the shock wave or the viscous layer near limit lines. Here the thicknesses of these usually quite thin layers are functions of other flow parameters, as seen from Eq. 6.1 in the case of shock waves. Therefore, it is logical to take the thickness of the viscous layers as the reference length in viscous

Viscous Transonic Flow

flow. In our present case of longitudinal viscosity, this reference length may be quite small, but should be larger than the parameter ε of the flow velocity expansions. As Eq. 2.103 shows, the term $(1 - M^*)$ in Eq. 6.1 is of the order of ε, and thus the shock wave thickness h is markedly larger than ε. Hence, limiting the derivation to the two-dimensional problem, the dimensionless coordinates in viscous flow become

$$x = \frac{x'}{h} = \frac{x'a^*\varepsilon}{v_l^*} = \frac{\varepsilon x'}{h'}$$

$$y = \frac{\varepsilon^{1/2}y}{h} = \frac{y'a^*\varepsilon^{3/2}}{v_l^*} = \frac{\varepsilon^{3/2}y'}{h'}$$

(6.18)

The expansions of the dimensionless velocity components, however, are simply

$$\frac{u'}{a^*} = 1 + \varepsilon u_1 + \varepsilon^2 u^2 + \cdots$$

$$\frac{v'}{a^*} = \varepsilon^{1/2}(\varepsilon v_1 + \varepsilon^2 v_2 + \cdots)$$

(6.9)

Contrary to Eqs. 2.88, where the expansion pameters had to be determined step by step from the special requirements of transonic flow over slender bodies, a simple power series in ε is sufficient in this case of undisturbed flow. Only the difference in the magnitudes of the small-perturbation velocity component u_i and v_i had to be retained.

Thus, the small-perturbation procedure for the derivation of viscous equations differs from that applied in Sec. 2.6 for inviscid flow, not only by the additional viscous and dissipation terms but also in its specific steps.

The present process is as follows. After the elimination of the entropy S from Eq. 6.5 by means of the basic thermodynamic equations, Eqs. 6.8 and 6.9, as well as expansions for T, μ, μ_l, c_p, and k of the same simple form as that of u'/a^*, are applied to Eqs. 6.5, 6.6 and 6.7. In retaining only the first-order terms, the viscous, heat conduction, and dissipation terms on the right-hand side of these equations are eliminated, whereas useful relationships between the first-order terms of ρ, p, u and T result. The second-order terms then are equated and the thermodynamic variables are eliminated by means of the relationships found in the first step. During this process the second-order terms and the thermodynamic variables cancel out and with the first-order relationship $u_1 - a_1 = u_1(\gamma + 1)/2$ we arrive at

$$[1 + \overbrace{(\gamma - 1)/Pr_l}^{A}]u_{xx} - \overbrace{(\gamma + 1)}^{B}uu_x + v_y = 0 \quad (6.10)$$

where $Pr_l = c_p u_l^*/k^*$ is the longitudinal Prandtl number, assumed to be constant, to which c_p, u_l^*, and k^* combine in deriving Eq. 6.10.

Thus, the viscous transonic equation (Eq. 6.10) differs from the inviscid equation (Eq. 2.25a, for instance) only by the first term. By setting $x = X$, $y = Y/A^{1/2}$, and by introducing a potential ϕ^6 with $\phi' = \phi(A/B)$, where u and v are partial derivatives of ϕ', Eq. 6.10 assumes the simple form

$$\phi_{XXX} - \varphi_X \phi_{XX} + \phi_{YY} = 0 \tag{6.11}$$

The solution of this third-order nonlinear differential equation poses considerable difficulties. Nevertheless, resorting to so-called similarity solutions, Sichel and Yin solved several problems that will be described briefly in the following section.

6.4 Applications of the Viscous Transonic Equation

6.4.1 Similarity Solutions of Partial Differential Equations

Frequently the difficulties of solving partial differential equations can be reduced by limiting the study to so-called similarity solutions. Those solutions may be sufficient when no specific boundary conditions must be met. A classical example is the flow through a Laval nozzle, where, after a transonic flow field has been computed, any streamline may be chosen as the nozzle contour. The flow field itself can be varied simply by changing the velocity distribution on the line of symmetry, and consequently a contour can be established that is sufficiently close to specific requirements.

As the term suggests, similarity solutions only apply to similar points whose coordinates are fixed by an analytical relationship between the independent variables, reducing the independent variables to just one. Consequently, the partial differential equation is reduced to an ordinary differential equation.

There is an infinite number of ways to accomplish such a transformation mathematically, and therefore the difficulty lies in the establishment of the proper relationship between the independent variables for a desired boundary condition. If, referring to one of the cases treated by Sichel [31], the viscous flow through a Laval nozzle is sought, a relationship must be used that leads to a flow symmetrical to the x axis. Hence, the new variable must have the form

$$S = x + b y^{2n}$$

where b is an arbitrary constant and n an integer greater than zero. Thus, the simplest relationship between the independent variables is given as

$$S = x + b y^2 \tag{6.12}$$

and the dependent variable in its simplest form becomes

$$U = Z(S) + f(y^2) \tag{6.13}$$

where $f(y^2)$ is an arbitrary integration function. Thus, Eq. 6.13 satisfies the conditions $U = Z(x)$ for $y = 0$ and $U = Z(a + by^2) + f(y^2)$ for any $x = a$, which is a function symmetrical to the x axis.

6.4.2 Viscous Flow Through a Laval Nozzle

The purpose of a Laval nozzle is the creation of supersonic flow at its exit. The computation of its flow field poses no problems. Taking into account the thickness of the wall shear layer, the effective wall geometry for a desired Mach number is obtained from inviscid theory. Transonic theory is not required, though the flow at the nozzle throat is transonic. Indeed, already in 1908 Th. Meyer [11] computed Laval nozzles from the general equation of inviscid flow by applying two-dimensional Taylor expansions to pregiven velocity distributions on the nozzle centerline. But such a simple approach only succeeds when the total pressure ratio across the nozzle exceeds a certain minimum value. For smaller ratios, the shock wave of the nozzle exit Mach number would, in the eventual reconversion to subsonic flow, produce an entropy jump too large for the given total pressure ratio.[7] This forces the shock to move upstream to a nozzle station of a smaller cross-sectional area, where the Mach number is lower and the increase in entropy smaller. The position of the shock wave in the Laval nozzle is determined by the total pressure ratio that produces the flow through the nozzle.

When the total pressure is further reduced to a certain value, an entirely subsonic "venturi" flow is obtained in which the maximum velocity occurs at the nozzle throat. This leads to the question of the flow pattern in the Laval nozzle at total pressure ratios between the venturi and the fully established supersonic "Meyer flow," a problem that has been treated by several investigators.

Historically, the results of Emmons [32] should be given first. He applied the so-called relaxation method to the computation of the nozzle flow field and concluded that the transition from the pure venturi flow to the shock-free subsonic–supersonic "Meyer"-flow begins with supersonic pockets forming on the walls at the throat (see Fig. 6.5),[8] which, when the total pressure ratio has reached a certain value, are each terminated by a shock wave.[9] With further increase in the pressure ratio, the two pockets and their shock waves grow to the centerline (see Fig. 6.5). At this point the two sonic lines and the shock waves meet. At last, a single shock wave moves downstream and a single sonic line spans the throat area. If a parallel-wall test section is attached to the nozzle, the shock jumps to the downstream end of the test section, the station at which the cross-sectional area is usually contracted to a second throat. This occurs at the total pressure ratio required for the desired test section Mach

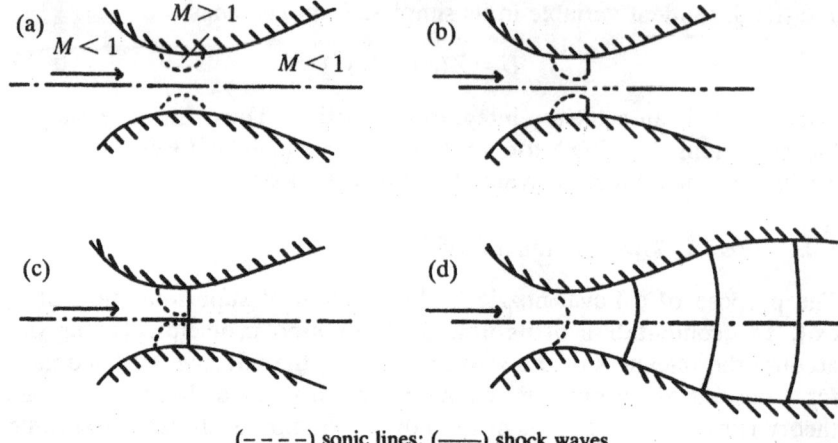

(- - - -) sonic lines; (———) shock waves

Fig. 6.5. Transition from venturi to Meyer-type nozzle flow according to Emmons. The total pressure ration required increases from a) (Taylor flow) to d), and in d) for the shock positions from left to right.

number. As logical as Emmons' results seem to be, unanswered questions remain.

The next step in the clarification of this problem was taken by Tomotika and Tamada [33], who analyzed a similarity solution of the inviscid transonic equation (Eq. 2.25b):

$$\varphi_{yy} - \varphi_x \varphi_{xx} = 0 \tag{6.14}$$

This equation may be converted into an equation for the first-order x-component of the perturbation velocity U by applying the condition of irrotationality $\varphi_{xy} = \varphi_{yx}$ after differentiation with respect to x. The equation, equivalent to Eq. 6.14, becomes

$$U_{YY} - (U^2)_{XX} = 0 \quad \text{with } Y = y \text{ and } X = x/2 \tag{6.15}$$

Here, x and y are given by Eq. 6.8 and U is given by u_1 of Eq. 6.9.

By applying the conditions Eqs. 6.12 and 6.13 (with $f(Y^2) = 2b^2 Y^2$) to Eq. 6.15, the ordinary differential equation

$$ZZ'' + (Z' - 2b)(Z' + b) = 0 \tag{6.16}$$

is obtained. As Fig. 6.6 shows, the solutions of this equation correspond

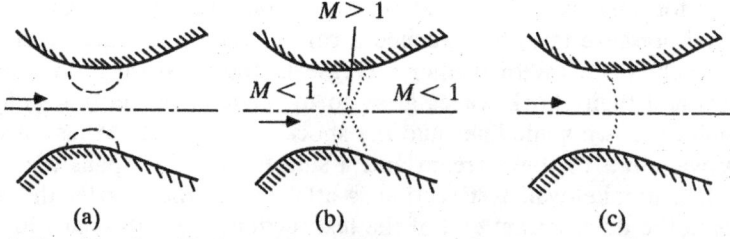

Fig. 6.6. Transition from Taylor to Meyer nozzle flow according to Tomotika and Tamada [33].

to the cases (a) and (d) of Fig. 6.5. However, the transition from the Taylor flow to the Meyer flow is quite different from Emmons' solution. The limiting Taylor flow in which the two supersonic pockets meet at the centerline now consists of two sonic lines. The transition from these lines to pure Meyer flow is not covered by Eq. 6.16. This fact is discussed in detail by Sichel [31] and led him to the question of whether the introduction of viscosity into the flow equation might overcome this problem.

To transform the partial differential equation of viscous transonic flow (Eq. 6.11) into an ordinary equation, the same steps may be taken as in the case of the inviscid equation. Applying the condition of irrotationality, Eq. 6.11 becomes

$$U_{XXX} - (U^2)_{XX} + U_{YY} - 0$$

and the same transformations, Eqs. 6.12 and 6.13, result in the ordinary differential equation for transonic viscous nozzle flow

$$Z''' - 2ZZ'' - 2(Z' - 2b)(Z' + b) = 0 \qquad (6.17)$$

In this viscous equation, singularity of the inviscid equation (Eq. 6.16) at the sonic point on the axis of symmetry has been eliminated through the term Z'''. In the inviscid case, for $Z = 0$, $X = Y = 0$, the only solutions are $Z' = 2b$ and $Z' = -b$, whereas in the viscous case a steady transition of the flow variables through the sonic line is obtained.

Although Eq. 6.17 is an ordinary differential equation, its solution poses considerable difficulties, as may be seen from Sichel's paper [31]. His results are shown in Fig. 6.7, where the cases (a) through (c) are obviously very similar to the inviscid cases of Fig. 6.6. However, Fig. 6.7d shows a steady transition from the limiting Taylor flow (Fig. 6.7c) to supersonic flow, terminated by a rapid deceleration that has the appearance of a finite-thickness shock wave. It should be noted, however, that the four cases of Fig. 6.7 do not represent the flow patterns for various pressure ratios in a nozzle of a given shape, because the geometric boundary conditions cannot be pregiven for similarity solutions. Consequently, the streamlines in Fig. 6.7, which are taken as the wall contour, have somewhat different shapes in the four cases. Nevertheless, the addition of the viscous terms to the transonic equation has obviously led to a quite consistent pattern of the nozzle flow development with total pressure changes. Moreover, the greatest deviation from a uniform boundary contour for all stages of the flow development occurs at the station of the shock-wave-type deceleration in Fig. 6.7d. This station moves farther and farther downstream with an increase in the flow pressure ratio, so that in the end the contour near the throat should become very similar to those of the other stages of Fig. 6.7.

The existence of a finite-thickness shock wave is even more obvious in the result of the flow through an axisymmetric Laval nozzle. To derive the corresponding similarity equation, we transform the axisymmetric

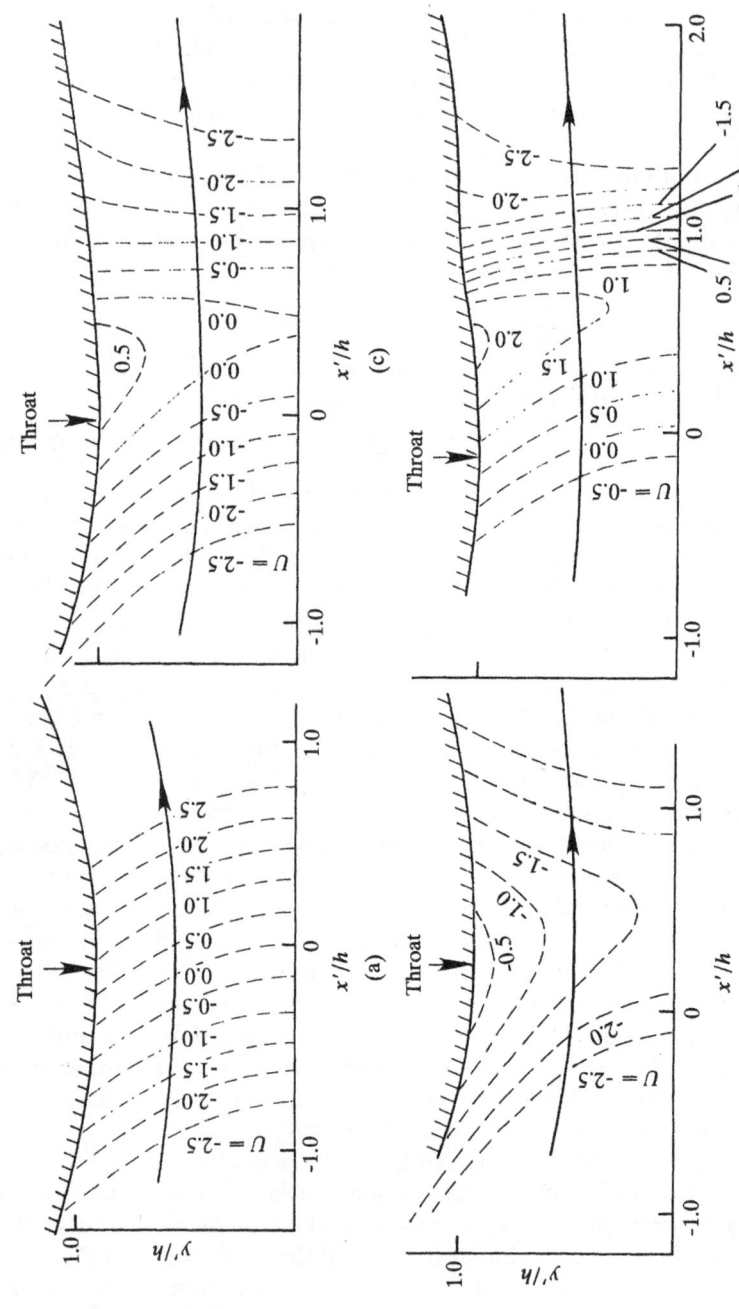

Fig. 6.7. Viscous flow through a Laval nozzle, according to Sichel [31]. (a) Meyer flow; (b) Transition from pure subsonic flow to Taylor flow; (c) Limiting Taylor flow, supersonic pockets extend to the centerline (equivalent to Fig. 6.6(b); (d) Transition from Taylor to Meyer flow, redeceleration similar to finite-thickness shock wave.

viscous transonic equation for the dimensionless perturbation velocity U,

$$U_{XXX} - (U^2)_{XX} + (U_R/R) + U_{RR} = 0$$

into the ordinary equation by again using the Eqs. 6.12 and 6.13, resulting in

$$Z''' - 2ZZ'' - 2(Z' - \omega_1 b)(Z' + \omega_2 b) = 0 \tag{6.18}$$

where $\omega_1 = \sqrt{5} + 1$; $\omega_2 = \sqrt{5} - 1$. As one should expect, the solution of this equation is very similar to that of the plane problem. However, as seen from Fig. 6.8, the redeceleration is much stronger, and therefore definitely has the appearance of a shock wave. For a detailed analysis of this case, the reader must be referred to the paper of Sichel and Yin [34].

6.4.3 Viscous Radial and Spiral Flow

As a last example of the cases in which viscous equations are required for physically realistic solutions of special problems of otherwise inviscid flow fields, a brief account of the analysis of Sichel and Yin [35] on radial and spiral will be given.

It was shown in Sec. 2.7.3 that source flow and flow of a potential vortex canot be extended beyond limit lines in inviscid theory. For source flow, the limit line lies exactly at the $M = 1$ circle. Consequently, only a purely supersonic flow issuing from a sonic source, or a purely subsonic flow into a sonic sink are the results of the inviscid continuity equation (see Fig. 2.15). For a potential vortex (Fig. 2.18), the limit line is the finite circle of $M = \infty$, which does not pose a transonic problem. However, by superimposing a source flow and a vortex flow, a spiral "source-vortex" flow is obtained (Fig. 2.20) with the limit line occurring

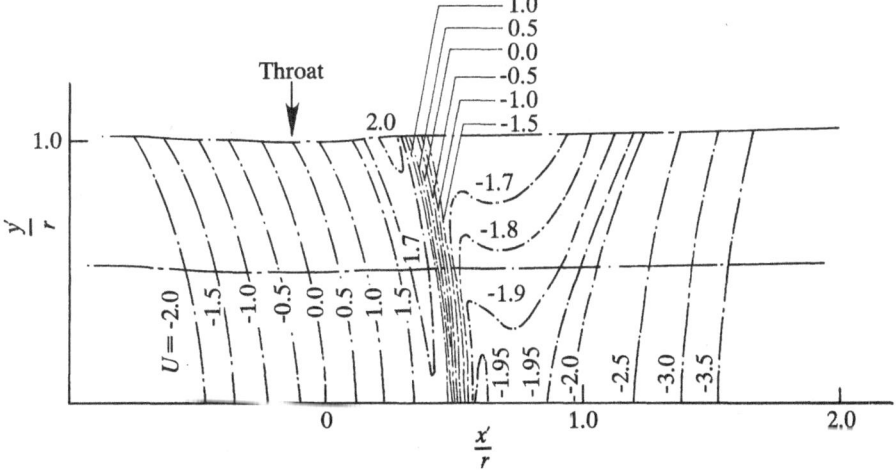

Fig. 6.8. Viscous transonic flow through an axisymmetric Laval nozzle with redeceleration in a finite-thickness shock wave (From Sichel and Yin [34]).

at any Mach number between 1 and ∞. Depending on the ratio of the source strength to the vortex strength, a certain range of cases falls into the transonic realm (see Fig. 2.19). It is this range that Sichel and Yin treat with the viscous equation.

Because this problem is of little general interest, no details of the analysis will be given here. However, the method chosen by Sichel and Yin for the derivation of the similarity equation is an example of mathematical methods that take advantage of small-perturbation procedures and may be applicable to more important problems. We shall therefore concentrate on that part of their paper.

As in the preceding section, the coordinates are made dimensionless with the thickness of a weak shock wave, which, according to Eq. 6.1, is a measure of the effect of μ_l near $M = 1$. Therefore, Eq. 6.10 should apply to the present problem, too.

By setting,

$$u = U\left[= \frac{u' - a^*}{a^* \varepsilon} \right]; \quad v\left(\frac{\gamma+1}{2}\right)^{1/2} = v\left[= \frac{v'}{a^* \varepsilon^{3/2}} \right];$$

$$x = X\left[2\left(1 + \frac{\gamma-1}{Pr_l}\right)\right] \Big/ (\gamma+1)\left[= \frac{x'}{h} = \frac{x'\varepsilon}{h} \right], \quad \text{with } h \text{ from Eq. 6.1}$$

and

$$M^* - 1 \approx \varepsilon, \quad y = Y\left[1 + \frac{\gamma-1}{Pr_l}\right] \Big/ [(\gamma+1)/2]^{3/2}\left[= \varepsilon^{1/2}\frac{y'}{h} = \varepsilon^{3/2}\frac{y'}{h} \right]$$

(6.19)

where the primed symbols stand for the dimensional variables, Eq. 6.10 is reduced to the simple equation

$$U_{XX} - 2UU_X + V_Y = 0 \tag{6.20}$$

Differentiating Eq. 6.20 with respect to X and applying the irrotationality condition $U_Y = V_X$, an equation of one dependent variable,

$$U_{XXX} - (U^2)_{XX} + U_{YY} = 0 \tag{6.21}$$

is obtained, in complete analogy to Eq. 6.11.

Here we deviate from our previous procedure of establishing an ordinary (similarity) equation. It turns out that it is advantageous in this case to reverse the independent and the dependent variables. The reason for this procedure will become obvious when the small-perturbation relationships between the coordinates X and Y and the dimensionless potential and stream functions are established.

To this end, dimensionless potential and stream functions are introduced. By defining the dimensionless potential function as $\phi = \phi' X / a^* x'$, where again the primed symbols denote dimensional magnitudes, we have

$$\phi = X + O(\varepsilon) \tag{6.22}$$

because $\phi' = \int u'\,dx' + \int v'\,dy'$, which by expressing u' and v' with the help of Eqs. 6.9 yields $\phi' = a^*x' + \varepsilon a^* \int u_1\,dx' + \cdots + \varepsilon^{3/2} a^* \int v_1\,dy'$. The definition of a dimensionless stream function as $\psi = \psi' Y/\rho^* a^* y'$ leads to

$$\psi = Y + O(\varepsilon^2) \tag{6.23}$$

Here the proof is a little more involved, and an exact derivation may be found in [4]. However, a sufficiently good approximation is found as follows. Again, the stream function is expressed in its basic form $\psi' = \int \rho u'\,dy' - \int \rho v'\,dx'$. As in the case of the potential function, the second integral is certainly of higher order than the first one, because v' is equal to the small-perturbation velocity component, whereas u^* is the total velocity component. As to the first integral, we can with sufficient accuracy replace u' by $w' = \sqrt{u'^2 + v'^2}$, that is, we may assume one-dimensional flow. Going back to Eq. 2.2b, we have exactly the expression we need to break down the first integral and arrive at

$$\psi' = \rho^* a^* y' - \varepsilon^2 \rho^* a^* (\gamma + 1)\frac{y'}{2}$$

because $|M^* - 1| \approx \varepsilon$ (see page 68). Introducing this expression into the definition equation for the dimensionless stream function results in Eq. 6.23.

The Eqs. 6.22 and 6.23 show that the dimensionless potential and stream functions ϕ and ψ are, in the first approximation, equal to the coordinates X and Y, made dimensionless with the weak shock wave thickness (see Eq. 6.19), and thus, it is clearly justified to make ϕ and ψ the independent variables. Logically, then, the total flow velocity (i.e., not its components) and the flow angle are chosen as the dependent variables. Indeed, the flow angle is proportional to the velocity component V as defined in Eq. 6.19, because

$$\theta = \arctan\frac{v'}{u'} \approx \frac{v'}{a^*} \approx \varepsilon^{3/2}\left(\frac{\gamma+1}{2}\right)^{1/2} V \tag{6.24}$$

This equation shows that within the validity range of our equations, the flow angle varies very little, being of the order $\varepsilon^{3/2}$. Therefore, $\cos\theta \approx 1$ and $u' = w'\cos\theta \approx w'$, and the dimensionless flow velocity becomes

$$\frac{w'}{a^*} = 1 + \varepsilon W = 1 + \varepsilon U \quad \text{or} \quad W = U \tag{6.25}$$

Hence, replacing U, X, and Y by W, ϕ, and ψ from Eqs. 6.22, 6.23, and 6.25, Eq. 6.21 takes the form

$$W_{\phi\phi\phi} - (W^2)_{\phi\phi} + W_{\psi\psi} = 0 \tag{6.26}$$

To establish a similarity equation, the independent variables ϕ and ψ must be combined in such a way that the characteristic behavior of spiral flow (with its special case of radial flow) is properly expressed. Clearly, such flows have one basic characteristic in common, namely, that velocity and direction relative to the radial direction are constant on circles around the origin, that is, the flow conditions are only functions of the distance from the origin R. This condition is satisfied by setting

$$W = f(S) \qquad S = \phi + \lambda\psi = g(R) \tag{6.27}$$

It is easily seen that the independent similarity variable S is a function only of the distance R from the origin if we realize that spiral flow is the superposition of the potentials and the stream functions of a pure source flow and a pure potential vortex flow.[10] Then the potential of the source flow and the stream function of the potential vortex are constant on circles about the origin, and therefore functions only of the distance R from the origin, independent of the polar angle ϑ. On the other hand, the stream function of the source flow and the potential of the vortex flow are constant on the radial lines from the origin and directly proportional to the angle, but independent of R. Furthermore, they are proportional to the source strength Q and the vortex strength Γ, respectively, so that by multiplying the stream function ψ of the source-vortex flow with $\lambda \sim \Gamma/Q$, the ϑ-dependent terms of S cancel out. Consequently, S is actually a function of the distance from the origin only if the parameter λ is chosen properly. For $\lambda = 0$, S depends on φ only and thus becomes the condition for pure source flow. This shows that the parameter λ is a direct measure of the vortex strength of the spiral flow.

The similarity equation for viscous spiral flow follows directly from the Eqs. 6.26 and 6.27 as

$$W''' - (W^2)'' + \lambda^2 W'' = 0 \tag{6.28}$$

As the step-by-step derivation of Eq. 6.28 from Eq. 6.21 has shown, the physical meaning of the individual terms has not been changed, so that Eq. 6.28 differs from the inviscid equation by W''' in the same manner as the viscous equation, Eq. 6.21 differs from the inviscid equation 6.15 by the term U_{xxx}. By twice integrating Eq. 6.28, we reduce it to

$$W' - W^2 + \lambda^2 W = c_1 S + c_2 \tag{6.29}$$

Here, W' represents the viscous term, so that the algebraic inviscid equation has the simple solution

$$S + \frac{\lambda^4}{4c_1} = \frac{(W - \lambda^2/2)^2}{c_1} \tag{6.30}$$

This relationship is shown in Fig. 6.9. Because $S = g(R) = f(r/r^* - 1)$ (Eq. 6.27) and $W = (M^* - 1)/\varepsilon$ (Eq. 6.25), Fig. 6.9 agrees quantitatively quite well with Fig. 2.19. Because it is a measure of the vortex strength relative to the source strength ($\lambda \sim \Gamma/Q$), λ determines the displacement of the apex of the $W-S$ parabola from the sonic point where it lies for source flow. It should be noted that Fig. 6.9 is valid only for a very small

Viscous Transonic Flow

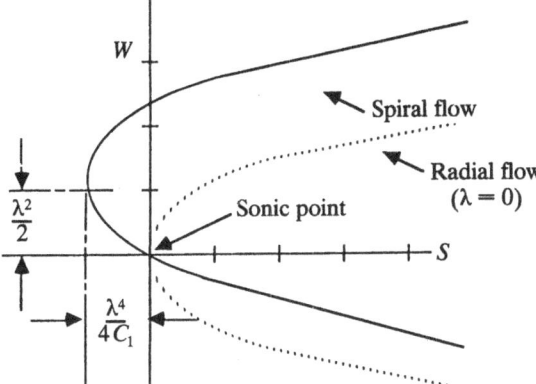

Fig. 6.9. Perturbation velocity W vs. dimensionless radial distance from the sonic point S for the transonic range of inviscid spiral flow. (From [35]).

portion of the cases shown in Fig. 2.19—say, the range from $Q/\Gamma = \infty$ to $Q/\Gamma = 1$. Beyond this range the transonic equations are no longer valid.

For the solution of the viscous equation, it is expedient to normalize the variables of the inviscid equation so that all inviscid solutions become the same parabola with its apex at the coordinates origin, with the new variables being $\hat{W}$ and $\hat{S}$. The resulting equation $(d\hat{W}/d\hat{S}) - \hat{W}^2 = -c_1\hat{S}$ can be solved through another substitution for $\hat{W}$, leading to a second-order linear equation whose solutions are expressed through the Airy functions. This result is shown in Fig. 6.10. Obviously, the limit line has disappeared, otherwise the curves would not continue into the half-space of negative values of $c_1^{1/3}\hat{S}$ (remember that through the normalization the apexes of the W–S parabolas that lie on the limit line fall on the origin of the coordinates). Also, instead of staying on either the supersonic or the subsonic branch of the curves with increasing distance from the source, as found in the inviscid case, in viscous flow the supersonic branch returns to the subsonic branch through a shock wave type recompression that becomes increasingly steep with increasing supersonic Mach number. Thus, it has been proved that viscous theory results in a flow field that extends steadily beyond the limit line of the inviscid flow field.

As Sichel and Yin [35] show, their theory eliminates the limit line singularity, but instead singularities appear for more negative values of $c_1^{1/3}\hat{S}$, so that the validity range of the theory is quite limited. A further problem in the interpretation of the results is seen in the determination of the reference length h. In the case of the nozzle flow it seemed logical to choose the Lighthill expression, Eq. 6.1, which is based on the balance between convection and dissipation. With the mechanism of the spiral flow near the limit line being less obvious, a different reference length may have to be chosen. Actually, Sichel and Yin point out a discrepancy in their analysis that suggests such a need.

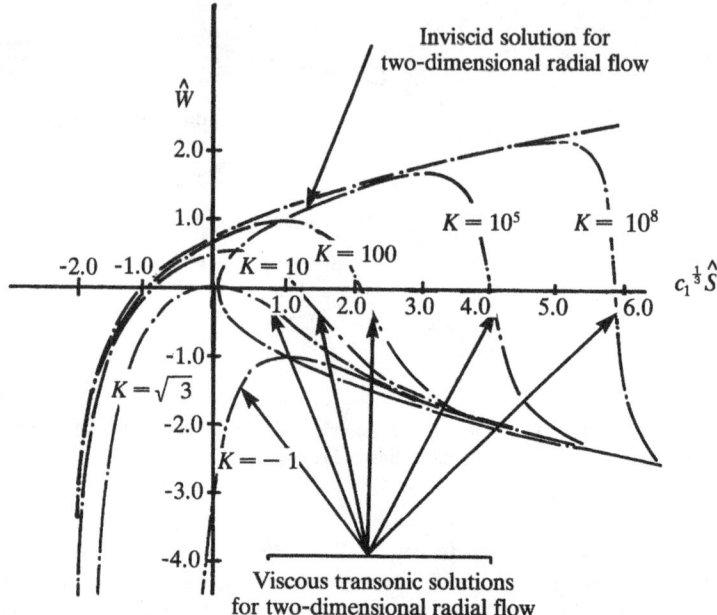

Fig. 6.10. Normalized perturbation velocity $\hat{W}$ vs. normalized radial distance from the sonic point, $c_1^{1/3}\hat{S}$ in the transonic range of viscous spiral flow. The diagram for spiral flow is obtained by shifting the coordinate origin according to Fig. 6.9. K = integration constant. (From [35]).

But even in the case of the nozzle flow, the viscous result is very difficult to be proven experimentally. As we pointed out on page 155, the thickness of a shock wave of measurable strength (i.e., for approach Mach numbers $M_\infty > 1.1$) is mainly a function of the critical density, so that it becomes appreciable only for rarified flow. But then the shear flow on the nozzle walls is also strongly affecting the flow, so that a clear separation of longitudinal and shear viscosity effects may be impossible. Because of the thin shock wave in flows of normal density, viscous theory does not apply to the nozzle flow problems, rather the flow is governed by shear flow adjustments to the nozzle wall shape and shock wave systems that form an effective wall shape that can support an inviscid core flow, possibly including weak shock waves (quasi-isentropic) or even unsteady pulsating flow.

With these remarks, this chapter must be closed, and the interested reader is referred to the literature on viscous transonic flow (e.g., refs 30, 31, 34, 35, 56) for a deeper insight into this still little-explored area of transonic flow.

Notes

1. Presently, shock-free solutions, such as that of Ringleb for inviscid flow, and those for viscous flow of this chapter, have at best a very limited value.

2. A recent study on the formation of the separation bubble by Doerffer and Zierep is described in ref. 65, where a comprehensive list of references on boundary layer-shock wave interaction is given.
3. In the literature, μ_2 is sometimes called the *coefficient of bulk viscosity*. However, more logically, this term is applied to the deviation from the Stokes value (see Note 4).
4. This inequality becomes an equality through the bulk viscosity (see Note 3) so that $\mu_{\text{bulk}} = \mu_2 + 2\mu/3$.
5. Coefficient of shear, longitudinal, and bulk viscosity.
6. The existence of a potential function that was proved for the equations of lower order in Sec. 2.6, remains valid here.
7. $\Delta S = R \ln(V_{02}/V_{01}) = R \ln(p_{01}/p_{02})$ as obtained by integrating Eq. 1.14 for $T_{01} = T_{02}$.
8. Note that these pockets are the direct result of the pressure gradient over curved walls discussed in Sec. 2.2.1.
9. The relaxation procedure could only be continued by introducing a Rankine–Hugoniot-type discontinuity (see Prob. 6.2).
10. Compare Sec. 2.7.3.

Problems

6.1. Compare the results of the viscous radial and spiral flows with the inviscid results of Sec. 2.7.3. Determine the Mach number at which the deviation of the inviscid and the viscous solutions becomes more than 10%.

6.2. Using a computer, compute the inviscid flow through a Laval nozzle for the boundary and initial conditions that led Emmons to the two supersonic pockets at the throat. Does the computation converge? Determine the nozzle entrance Mach number up to which the computation does converge. How does this Mach number vary with the nozzle shape?

6.3. Develop the exact equations of the velocity potential and the stream function for source-vortex flow. Start from the hodograph equations with the flow angle and the flow velocity as the independent variables. Show that the flow is a function only of the distance R from the center of rotation, not a function of the polar angle ϑ. Introduce the source strength Q and the vortex strength Γ for the final results.

7
NUMERICAL METHODS OF TRANSONIC FLOW COMPUTATION

7.1 Introduction

However much value analytical methods like the local linearization may have for the solution of certain transonic flow problems (see Sec. 5.1.1), their limitations become obvious when it is realized that they cannot describe the flow through a shock wave where the velocity is discontinuous and the acceleration is singular. This is because the requirements of such linearizations, namely, that either velocity or acceleration be constant, are at variance with these shock characteristics. Therefore, if the boundary conditions of a problem require that the flow pass through a shock wave, a requirement present in practically all transonic problems, linearization cannot lead to an answer. One should not be deceived by the fact that in Sec. 2.6 the transonic equation was derived to include the flow through a shock wave, because that is just one means to feed the peculiar flow behavior at $M \approx 1$ into the equation. Another approach for accomplishing this objective was chosen in Sec. 2.3, where the characteristic equations for $M \approx 1$ led to the same first-order transonic equation as in Sec. 2.6. (see also page 66, where it is shown that the transonic shock equation and the transonic characteristics equation are identical). Nothing is said, however, about the way the transition through a somewhat stronger shock wave takes place: Whether it is continuous or discontinuous and even, whether the flow behind the shock is irrotational.

Of course, as long as the approach Mach number to the shock is sufficiently close to unity, the entropy increase at all streamlines is of higher order, independent of the shock angle at the streamline, and the irrotational transonic equation is still valid behind the shock. The flow angles behind the shock, however, must be found by other means: They are not given by the transonic equation.

To account properly for the shock waves, computational procedures are required. Several approaches have been taken with more or less success. The two obvious ways to compute the flow through a shock wave are:

1. Through iterations, determine the exact position, shape and strength distribution of the shock wave, so that the velocity- and flow-angle distributions on the shock are the boundary conditions for the inviscid flow fields upstream and downstream.

2. Approximate the shock wave by a transition layer of finite thickness, so that discontinuities and singularities are excluded and inviscid or viscous flow equations can be applied.

Although the latter approach seems to be less accurate, the former, because of its complexity, has not been developed into a practical method and is at variance with the current computational systems. Of course, the latter method produces unqualified answers when the shock wave is sufficiently thick[1] owing to the flow conditions (e.g., low density) to allow it to be computed from the viscous equations (see Sec. 6.2.3).

7.2 The Relaxation Method

In both of the cases just stated, the big problem lies in the determination of the shock location, which depends on the inviscid flow fields upstream and downstream, which, in turn, depend on the shock wave properties. Thus it becomes obvious that the problem can be solved only by iteration processes. However, it is equally obvious that iterations of the analytical solutions of the inviscid equations would be a hopeless undertaking. Consequently, the computations must follow a totally different procedure, namely, the point-by-point matching of the flow equations, which may be the potential equations but can even be the two- or three-dimensional Euler equations or the viscous Navier–Stokes equations for transitions at the interface of viscous and inviscid areas. It should be noted, however, that the required computational effort greatly increases from the potential equations to the Navier–Stokes equations. The consequence of this fact will be discussed in Sec. 7.4. For the point-by-point computations, the flow field is overlaid by a suitable grid and the compliance with the flow equation of adjacent mesh point values is checked. Unfortunately, a price must be paid in this procedure, because the differential equations must be transformed into finite-difference equations that can, at best, be very good approximations. Nevertheless, those errors can be minimized to the point where the results are sufficient for the particular problems if the grid is chosen accordingly. Figure 7.1 is an example of a grid system that was once used. It gives an idea of possibilities for optimizing the accuracy of the computation according to the local flow variations. More recently, the curvilinear mesh arrangement, as shown in Fig. 7.1b for just the nose region of the model, is preferably used over the whole body and continued in either direction. Examples of presently used grids, also for three-dimensional cases, are shown, for example, in ref. 62.

The relationships between the mesh point values and the partial differentials of the original differential equation can be obtained in various ways so as to give the best results for a particular problem.

The whole procedure, then, starts out by assuming a certain flow pattern. This may be arbitrary, but it is preferably an educated guess.

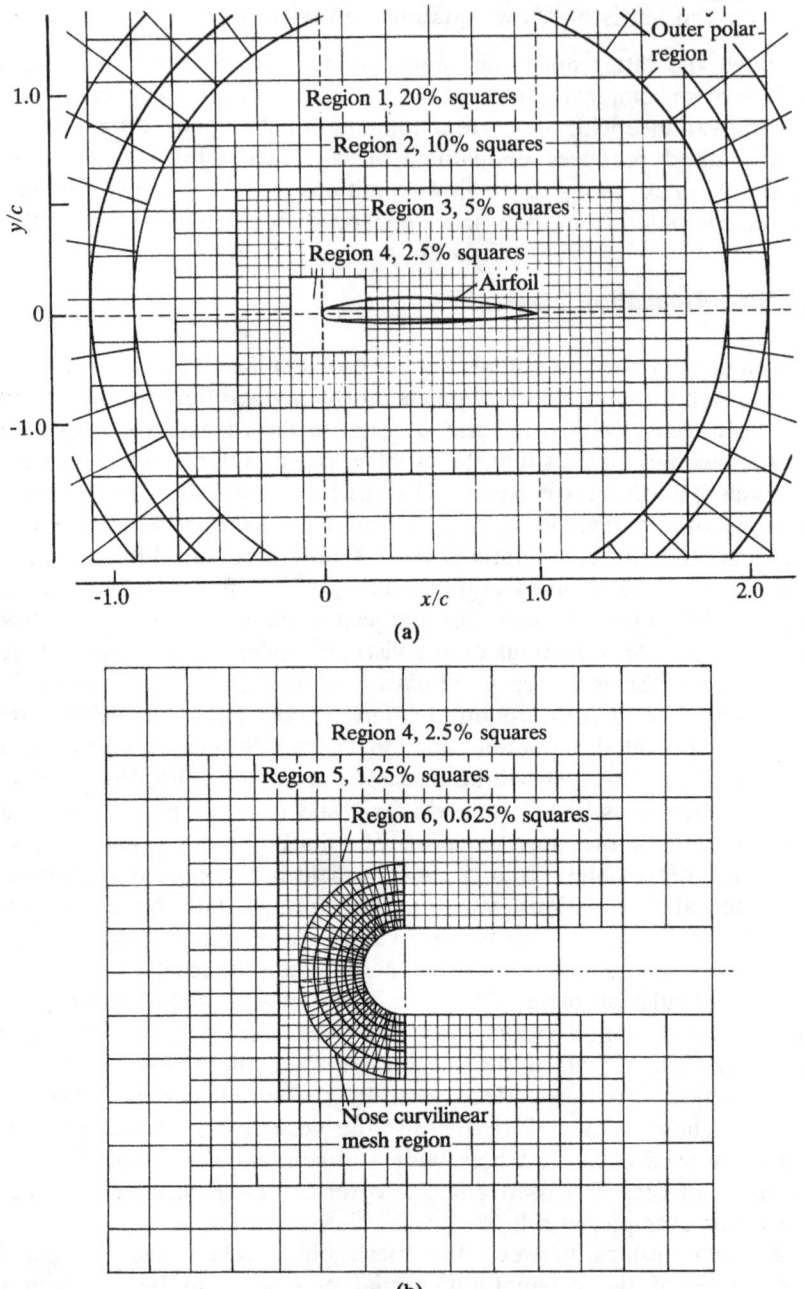

Fig. 7.1. Mesh system for the computation of the flow over an airfoil; (a) overall arrangement; (b) details of Regions 4 and 5. (From H. Yoshihara, AGARD LS-64, pp. 6.1–6.35).

Now, according to the finite-difference routine, the value at each mesh point is compared with the values obtained a certain number of neighboring mesh points, a relationship obtained from the original differential equation in the finite difference form. The originally assumed value at this mesh point is now "relaxed" toward the value computed in this way. In the simplest procedure it is given this new value. Thus a new set of values at the mesh points is obtained that now is relaxed again, and so until the iteration produces sufficiently small changes from the previous values. The fixed values in this procedure are the boundary values from where the relaxation scheme spreads over the entire flow field. The determination of the boundary conditions poses little difficulty for flow about a body in infinite space. However, flow in limited space, like a wind tunnel, does not have completely fixed boundary values of the flow upstream (in subsonic flow) and downstream (in both subsonic and supersonic flow) because, as the computation progresses, the strength of the disturbances changes which the body produces. In those cases, special provisions are needed to account for the current changes in those boundary conditions. For details of this technique, the reader must be referred to the extensive literature (e.g., ref. 1). A very good account of the practical aspects of the relaxation method is found in the classic papers of Emmons [32], who was instrumental in developing a workable—though, before the advent of the computer, quite cumbersome—scheme for flow field computations. Also, he found that in computing the flow fields through a Laval nozzle at the transition from subsonic–subsonic to subsonic–supersonic flow (increasing pressure ratio), the relaxation method would not converge unless discontinuities in the form of shock waves were introduced at certain locations of the flow. Complexities of that kind were almost impossible to handle economically without computers, through which the relaxation method has become one of the leading methods of numerical solutions of partial differential equations.

The relaxation method has shifted the emphasis of the computation from analytical refinements to the most suitable and accurate transformation of the differential equations into finite-difference equations. Consequently, it is most important to choose the best scheme for the determination of the relationship between the finite differences between a mesh point and its neighboring mesh points and the partial differentials (the first and second orders are usually needed) of the original differential equation. Again, no details can be given in this introductory book; however, with the help of Fig. 7.2, a few basic points will be offered.

At any step of the relaxation process, a certain value of the dependent variable, say w, is given to each mesh point $(i+m, j+n)$, where m and n are positive and negative integers. By means of the one-dimensional and the two-dimensional Taylor series, the values at the points adjacent to point (i, j) are related to the value $w(i, j)$-through the

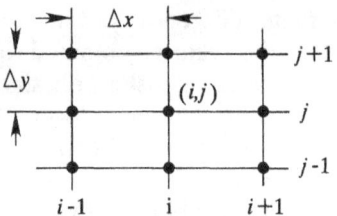

Fig. 7.2. Rectangular mesh element.

partial derivatives of the differential equation. As an example, we have

$$w_{i+1,j} = w_{i,j} + \frac{\partial w}{\partial x}\bigg|_{i,j}(x_{i+1,j} - x_{i,j})$$

$$+ \frac{\partial^2 w}{\partial x^2}\bigg|_{i,j}\frac{(x_{i+1,j} - x_{i,j})^2}{2} + \cdots$$

$$= w_{i,j} + \frac{\partial w}{\partial x}\bigg|_{i,j}\Delta x + \frac{\partial^2 w}{\partial x^2}\bigg|_{i,j}\frac{\Delta x^2}{2} + \text{higher-order terms} \quad (7.1)$$

Hence

$$\frac{\partial w}{\partial x}\bigg|_{i,j} = \frac{w_{i+1,j} - w_{i,j}}{\Delta x} - \frac{\partial^2 w}{\partial w^2}\bigg|_{i,j}\frac{\Delta x}{2} + \text{H.O.T.}$$

$$= \frac{w_{i+1,j} - w_{i,j}}{\Delta x} + O(\Delta x) \quad (7.2)$$

The important finding is the error of order Δx caused by the suppression of the higher-order terms of the Taylor series. Therefore, applying this simple transformation, extremely small steps Δx and Δy would have to be chosen in areas with steep gradients of the dependent variable to insure an acceptable accuracy of the computation. This "truncation error," resulting from the transition from differentials to finite differences, can be reduced by relating the value at the mesh point under consideration to more than the one neighboring mesh point used in the example above. Since the changes of w to neighboring points usually will not be equal, it is obvious that the so-called centered difference approximation, in which the "backward" and the "forward" Taylor expansions are combined, should produce a smaller truncation error. As the reader can ascertain himself, in this case the error is of order Δx^2 (see Prob. 7.1). Also, the second-order partial differentials cannot be obtained from the values at only two points. Therefore, the simplest expression for the second-order differentials is found from three points of a centered difference (see Prob. 7.2). However, more sophisticated systems are required, for instance, in transonic flow computations, where upwind differencing is used for the supersonic zones and central differencing in the subsonic zones.

7.3 The Time-dependent Method

The relaxation method discussed so far is applicable to steady-state computations only. However, unsteady problems need solutions too, and time-dependent equations must be treated. Basically, the point-by-point method works in those cases equally well. The main difference lies in the establishment of the finite-difference scheme, because here steps both in time, Δt, and in space, Δr, must be properly coordinated. Again, the reader must be referred to the literature for details.

Obviously, the time-dependent equations (e.g. Eqs. 1.5 and Chapter 3) are also applicable to steady-state problems in following the physical change of the flow pattern with time from an assumed original pattern to the steady-state pattern in accordance with the boundary conditions. As an example, the steady-state flow in the test section of a blow-down wind tunnel would be computed by starting from the air at rest before the valve to the downstream vacuum chamber is opened. At time zero, the valve is opened and the change with time of the flow upstream of the valve is computed until some consecutive iterations remain equal. Actually, computing-steady state problems from the unsteady equations has the marked advantage that the unsteady equations are of the hyperbolic type over the whole Mach number range (see Prob. 7.3). Consequently, the great difficulty of matching elliptic and hyperbolic equations is eliminated in computing transonic problems of the subsonic and supersonic areas.

7.4 Artificial Viscosity

These very basic examples of the means needed for a point-by-point computation of partial differential equations must suffice within the framework of this book, and the reader will have to explore the many approaches to this very important tool of applied mathematics from the extensive literature (see e.g., ref. 1). However, one very important by-product of the method sketched earlier must still be mentioned.

The correct computation of the flow through shock waves is one of the main concerns of transonic flow computations. Except for very weak shocks, the viscous effects in the shock, resulting in the dissipation of flow energy as heat (entropy increase), must be considered. This is accomplished, for example, when the change in the flow properties by the shock, as given by the oblique shock equations that describe the entropy increase correctly, is applied at the right location of the flow field. But as we have already seen, this results in very cumbersome and computer-time-consuming procedures.

The aim, therefore, should be to develop a single equation that describes both the inviscid flow away from the shock and the viscous flow through the shock. This happens to be accomplished automatically, to a certain degree, by the finite-difference transformation of the inviscid flow equations.

As will be shown now, the truncation error of the first-order finite-difference approximations has the mathematical form of the viscous terms of the Navier–Stokes equations. These terms, by which these equations differ from the (inviscid) Euler equations (compare Eqs. 1.5 and 6.6^2), are characterized by the second partial derivatives of the velocity components with respect to the space coordinates. Those truncation terms have similar forms to the viscous terms in the Navier–Stokes equations, but are of different magnitudes.

For $\operatorname{grad} p = 0$, an assumption that does not affect the following argument, the Navier–Stokes equation in vector notation,

$$\frac{D\mathbf{W}}{Dt} = -\frac{\operatorname{grad} p}{\rho} + \nu \Delta \mathbf{W}$$

where $D\mathbf{W} = Dt$ is the substantive derivative (see Eq. 1.4), becomes an equation of the form of the equation of heat conduction, which is known to describe an irreversible process, that is, a process in which the original state cannot be restored without heat addition to the system. Mathematically, this irreversibility is seen from the fact that reversal of the signs of the independent variables produces a different differential equation (the time-dependent term becomes negative, whereas the space term remains unchanged).

For the same reasons, the thermodynamic processes governed by the Navier–Stokes equations are irreversible—processes that are accompanied by an increase in entropy. Conversely, processes governed by the Euler equations, which remain unchanged when the independent variables are reversed, are reversible.

These discussion has shown that any thermodynamic equation of the form of the heat conduction equation has the property of energy dissipation and, consequently, the finite-difference equations with upwind differencing have such a property through the truncation error term. However, the truncation error becomes large enough to affect the result only when the spatial change in velocity is considerable, as in shock waves, so that the truncation error term will affect the result only where a shock wave is indicated in the inviscid flow computation. Thus, we have actually found an inviscid equation that detects the location of a shock wave and computes the flow through the wave in first approximation. It still remains impossible to obtain the correct shock thickness, which would require an infinitesimally fine mesh. Furthermore, the implied coefficient of viscosity is way off. The latter problem has been overcome to some extent by introducing parameters into the difference scheme that effect the better simulation of the physical viscosity. Through such measures, quite satisfactory results of the inviscid compressible transonic flow through shock waves have been obtained (see, for example, ref. 53).

For second-order difference approximations, as obtained from centered three-point computations, the truncation term no longer has the form of the Navier–Stokes equation, as seen from the result of Prob. 7.1. However, even there dissipative (viscous) terms can be obtained through certain explicit procedures.

It must be pointed out that for every scheme of finite-difference approximation and, consequently, for every kind of differential equation to be solved, the truncation term must be checked for the effect on the results, and certain correction terms must be introduced to suppress deleterious effects and to promote desirable features. In our case of transonic flow, the potential, Euler, and Navier–Stokes equations can be made to overlap to a certain extent through the truncation term modifications. Thus, the simple potential equation, with only one dependent variable, can produce reasonably good results in restricted rotational or viscous areas, eliminating the need of applying Euler or Navier–Stokes equations, respectively. This is very important, because the complexity of programming the potential equation is relatively low, so that even geometrically quite complex bodies, like airplanes, have been computed with good accuracy. The more complex Euler equations, with two or three dependent variables, are used when the potential equations no longer give acceptable results. However, the geometric complexity of the bodies treated must be lower. The Navier–Stokes equations, with their high complexity through the viscous terms, have, so far, only been successfully applied to quite simple geometries. A very good account of this trade-off between computational and geometric complexities is given by A. Jameson [62].

The difficulty of programming is further increased by the fact that the truncation term has, in addition, an important bearing on the stability of the computation. The difference scheme must be established such that, in the first place, the computation cycles do not produce erratic results. Stability analyses are an essential part of the computer programming.

7.5 Convergence and Concluding Remarks

This very brief account of the computational methods of aerodynamics would be incomplete without emphasizing that the convergence of the relaxation and time-dependent solutions poses a major problem. Without maintaining the proper relationship between the time and space steps and coefficients of the original equation, the iterations may never approach a final value; they may continue to fluctuate or even diverge. Therefore, these problems account for a considerable portion of the literature on computational aerodynamics.

The numeric methods for the solution of transonic problems as sketched in this chapter are basically mathematical. Therefore, within the framework of this book, no details can be given. However, the reader trying to acquaint himself with transonic flow should be aware of the fact that digital computers have opened a completely new realm of problems that can be solved. It must be emphasized again, however, that only through a thorough knowledge of the physical relationships of transonic flow and their analytic description can meaningful results be obtained. An excellent example of the complete solution of a transonic problem, from its statement through the analytic treatment to the discussion and establishment of the proper finite-difference equations, is the paper by Murman and Cole [60]. Here the paper of A. Jameson [62] must again be mentioned.

Notes

1. The shock thickness is of the order of the mean free path of the molecules.
2. Equations 6.6 are the compressible flow equations; the incompressible equations consist of the first lines only.

Problems

7.1. Compute the order of the error made using a "centered" difference by logically modifying Eq. 7.1.

7.2. Add the missing higher-order terms in Eq. 7.1 to obtain an expression for the second-order differentials corresponding to Eq. 7.2.

7.3. From the definition of elliptic and hyperbolic equations, confirm the hyperbolic character of the unsteady equation (Eq. 3.3) over the whole Mach range.

8
STEPS TOWARD THE OPTIMUM TRANSONIC AIRCRAFT

This chapter can only give a few outstanding problems in transonic aircraft design. The reader is encouraged to acquaint himself with this important discipline from the extensive literature. For a general study of aircraft performance and the special problems in the transonic speed range, see, for example, ref. 39.

8.1 The Basic Problems

The realization that the shock wave–boundary layer interaction has an outstanding effect on the performance of transonic flight articles was found to lead to studies trying to accomplish two major tasks: (1) to develop a computational method for the accurate determination of the shock wave–boundary interaction in terms of the pressure coefficient distribution on the body surface; and (2) to find body geometries for which the shock strength or the location of the shock wave would discourage separation and minimize the shifting of the shock wave during aircraft maneuvers.

The former task poses great difficulties, particularly in light of the fact that the very complex computations required consist of systems of nonlinear equations, excluding the establishment of general trends in performance with variations in flight parameters such as Mach number, flight attitude, and so on. This problem would exist even if the physics of a turbulent boundary layer were known in detail and documented in unequivocal mathematics, and even this is by no means the case. The interaction of a turbulent boundary layer with the ambient inviscid flow is still far from established in reasonably general terms. Even the basic Prandtl assumption that the pressure gradient normal to the flow direction is zero within an attached boundary layer has been shown to be invalid on the rear section of certain profiles.

Considering those difficulties, it is understandable that a considerable effort has been put into the latter task, the reduction of the shock wave–boundary layer interaction to a negligible magnitude. The first significant step in this direction was made in the late 1960s by Pearcey [36] and Nieuwland [37]. Their respective experimental and theoretical investigations resulted in a profile geometry that produces a weak shock wave, located sufficiently close to the profile nose so that the boundary layer is still thin enough, and consequently healthy enough, to prevent a shock-induced separation, or at least to reduce the separation to a small so-called separation bubble. Thus, the boundary layer remains attached—with the exception of this insignificant stretch of the separation bubble that has a negligible influence on the pressure distribution over the profile. Most importantly, the probability of the separation bubble combining with the trailing edge separation—the most dangerous process, which causes airfoil stall with absolute certainty—is avoided.

The Pearcey–Nieuwland body is characterized by so-called peaky flow, obtained by a quite blunt profile nose that produces a steep pressure rise directly on the nose followed by a rapid expansion into a short stretch of supersonic flow that, in turn, is terminated by a weak shock, or, ideally, by a shock-free transition to subsonic flow. This behavior of the flow over a blunt profile nose may not be surprising when we remember the Ringleb solution of flow around a semi-infinite thin plate (see page 86). There a shock-free supersonic region was obtained by assuming that the first streamline that does not end on a limit line represents a solid surface of a semi-infinite blunt body. Therefore, the peaky flow profile could be interpreted as one of the shock-free profiles whose existence has been proven by Ringleb. However, as in the case of the Ringleb profile, the peaky profile is ideal only for one Mach number and one profile attitude, and therefore loses some of its attraction for the design of aircraft that must operate over a considerable range of Mach numbers and flight attitudes. Nevertheless, the well-known studies of Pearcey and his co-workers have been of considerable benefit to the design of transonic aircraft. In addition to the aerodynamic benefits, the blunt nose of the peaky flow profile is quite favorable structurally and in terms of the wing volume is an important feature for the accommodation of the fuel tanks.

A completely different approach to the mitigation of the adverse effects of the shock wave–boundary layer interaction and the resulting boundary layer separation was taken by Whitcomb, also in the 1960s [38]. With his "supercritical profiles," in essence, the opposite to Pearcey's idea was tried: Instead of a short supersonic region near the profile nose followed by a weak shock wave unable to separate the still very healthy thin boundary layer, the supercritical profile keeps the flow supersonic over the major portion of the profile, except for a short section at the tail where separation is unavoidable anyway. The shock strength is thus of minor importance. As shown in Fig. 8.1, this feature is accomplished by making the upper surface of the profile almost straight over the major part. Consequently, a shift of the separation point with Mach number or angle of attack can be expected only on the short convex tail section. Thus, the vital stabilization of the aircraft performance has been accomplished. Because of the importance of the supercritical profile for the optimization of transonic aircraft performance, this profile will be discussed in more detail in the following section.

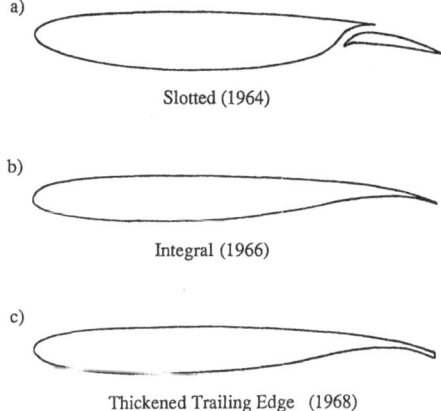

Fig. 8.1. The early evolution of the NASA supercritical profile.[1] (From [38]).

8.2 The Supercritical Airfoil

As its name indicates, the supercritical airfoil is characterized by flow velocities greater than the sound speed over a major portion of its upper surface, thus clearly distinguishing it from any airfoil that had been devised before, particularly the peaky airfoil that, as has been pointed out in the previous section, is characterized by a very short supercritical section. Nevertheless, both types of airfoils have common features, so that this section will deal with the criteria for shock-induced boundary layer separation, or, for that matter, any well designed transonic airfoil.

First of all, the pressure distributions on the upper and lower surface are of equal importance, and a change of the upper surface geometry calls for a corresponding change of the lower surface. This is readily seen in the case of the supercritical airfoil. Here, the almost straight upper surface (Fig. 8.1) requires an almost straight lower surface, because the conventional lower surface camber would produce an airfoil with a minimum thickness near the midchord point. On the other hand, in order to insure a smooth flow-off from the trailing edge, required by the so-called Kutta-condition (see, e.g., ref. 39), the angle between the two surfaces at the trailing edge of any airfoil must be as small as the structural requirements allow.[2] Consequently, a strong camber must be provided on the lower surface near the trailing edge.

The striking difference in the supersonic flow areas and in the pressure distributions on the upper and lower surfaces of a conventional (C.P.) and a supercritical profile (Sc.P) is shown in Fig. 8.2. The most important differences are as follows. (1) The Mach number on the upper surface of the C.P. increases steadily in flow direction up to the strong shock wave at, or slightly downstream of, the midchord point, whereas that on the Sc.P remains almost constant and is terminated in a much weaker shock

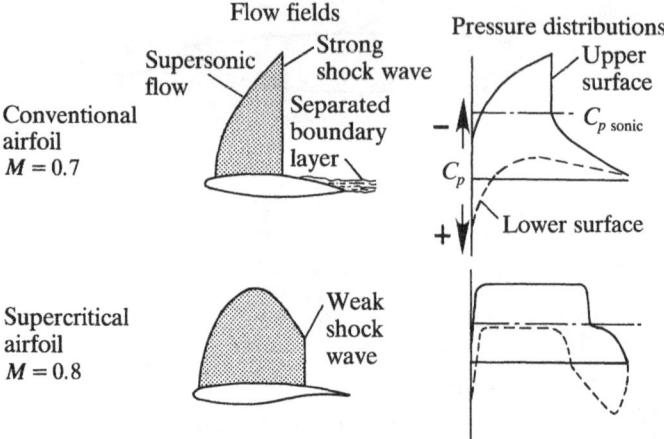

Fig. 8.2. Comparison of the extent of the supersonic regions and the pressure distributions of a conventional and a supercritical profile (From [38]).

wave at about the 2/3-chord station. (2) Whereas the shock of the C.P. is directly followed by a further, adiabatic compression, the Sc.P shock wave is followed by a pressure plateau with a strong pressure rise to about the ambient conditions occurring only over the last quarter-chord or less. (3) The pressure distribution on the lower surface of the C.P. remains rather constant, so that the lift distribution, that is, the difference between the pressure distributions on the upper and lower surface, is strongly concentrated on the front half of the profile, whereas the lift distribution of the Sc.P is almost constant over the whole chord, actually even producing a somewhat greater lift toward the trailing edge.

These three facts have important implications. As we know, the probability of boundary layer separation increases with the magnitude of the pressure rise in flow direction (unfavorable pressure gradient). In particular, pressure jumps, such as shock waves, promote separation, and the higher the Mach number the greater the pressure jump and the greater the danger of separation. This fact alone shows the reduced danger of separation of the Sc.P. However, an additional factor affects the tendency for separation, namely, the pressure gradient downstream of the shock wave. And here again, the Sc.P. with its pressure plateau downstream of the shock is greatly superior to the C.P. as far as the avoidance of separation is concerned because the growing-together of the trailing edge separation with a separation bubble behind the shock is disrupted through the pressure plateau in which the boundary layer is reenergized by mixing with the outer inviscid flow.

In Fig. 8.3, two measured pressure distributions are shown, one at about the design point, the other at a somewhat lower Mach number. These figures show that the shock Mach numbers are quite low as expected. But could they lead to flow separation? An answer is offered by Pearcey [40]. He found that flow separation must be expected when

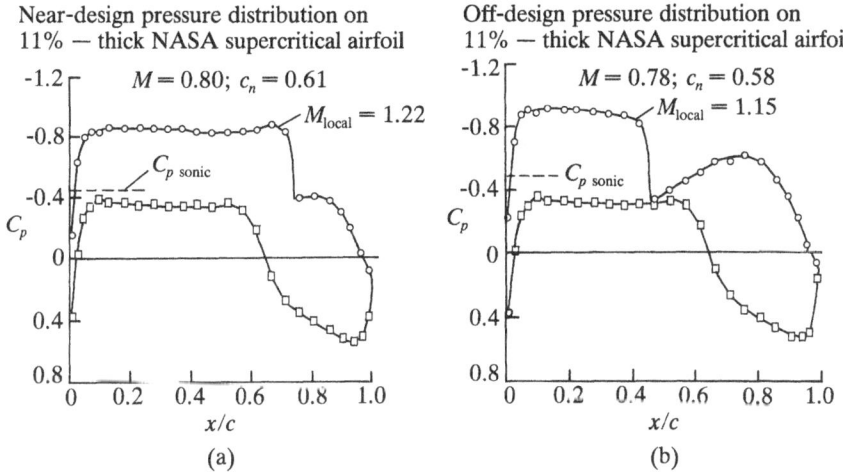

Fig. 8.3. Pressure distributions on a supercritical profile at and below the design Mach number (From [38]).

the shock wave is unable to raise the pressure to a subcritical value. The reason for this criterion lies in the streamline deflection away from the surface when separation sets in. Consequently, the normal shock near the surface splits up into a series of oblique shocks (delta shock) whose sum results in a smaller total pressure loss than that of a normal shock, so that the shock recompression ends with a slightly supersonic flow, and the recompression is completed through an adiabatic "supersonic tongue" (see Fig. 6.1). In the studies quoted, separation occurred, in accordance with this criterion, at $M_{shock} \approx 1.3$. The data of Fig. 8.3 confirm this Mach number, for, in Fig. 8.3b, $M_{shock} = 1.15$ and the shock pressure rises well above $c_{p\,sonic}$, whereas in Fig. 8.3a, with $M_{shock} = 1.22$, the shock pressure rises only slightly above $c_{p\,sonic}$.

Moreover, contrary to the very general statements made in the introduction to this chapter, in off-design cases the shock wave of supercritical profiles moves upstream, in the case of Fig. 8.3b to about the midchord station. However, this shock wave is not followed only by a plateau; the flow is even reaccelerated to supersonic Mach numbers before an adiabatic recompression to ambient conditions occurs near the trailing edge. This shows that in spite of the upstream movement of the shock, the flow remains attached, another proof of the remarkable stability of flow over supercritical profiles. For a comprehensive study of the pressure distributions on supercritical profiles, the reader is referred to Bauer et al. [41], in which an additional benefit of the supercritical concept is seen, namely, that the strong pressure rise on the lower surface, near the tail, increases the circulation in such a way that a certain lift may be realized at smaller (even slightly negative) angles of attack than possible with conventional profiles, thus improving the profile drag.

8.3 The Longitudinal Viscosity as a Possible Factor in the Correct Description of Transonic Flight

The previous sections of this chapter have demonstrated the outstanding role the shock wave–boundary layer interaction plays in the performance of transonic flight articles. On the other hand, the effect of the longitudinal viscosity seemed to be negligible in the cases discussed. This would be in agreement with the statements made in Chapter 6, namely, that the longitudinal viscous flow replaces Rankine–Hugoniot discontinuities only in rarified gases. However, as was shown in Sec. 6.4.3, the assumption that the Lighthill shock thickness (Eq. 6.1) is the proper reference length for cases other than shock waves in essentially parallel flow leads to inconsistencies in cases like spiral flow.

Moreover, it has become a strong possibility that longitudinal viscous flow may play a noticeable role even at normal densities. In 1959 Sternberg [42] found a serious disagreement with experiments when he computed the reflection of a weak shock wave from a straight solid wall with inviscid theory and Rankine–Hugoniot discontinuities. In particular, the inviscid theory required an infinitely large shock curvature at the triple point (see Fig. 8.4), the same kind of a problem found for the flow through a normal shock on a convex surface (Sec. 6.2.2).

Both Sternberg and Emmons (in his analysis of the shock foot point problem) [42, 32] suggested that the correct description of their cases required the introduction of viscous flow equations in order to eliminate the singularities, which cannot be physical realities. As Sichel and Yin's papers show, only small parts of the flow field are affected by the viscosity; however, because the viscous solution of these small regions may be quite different from the inviscid solution, an appreciable portion of the inviscid flow field may have to be modified.

Now a correction must be made to a statement following Eq. 6.1, in

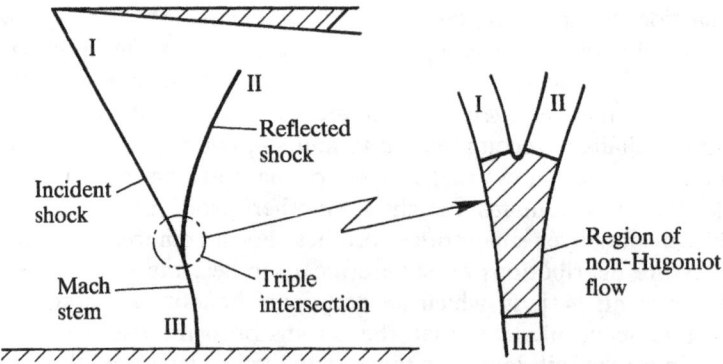

Fig. 8.4. Reflection of a weak shock wave from a solid wall, forming a non-Hugoniot region at the triple point (From [30]).

which it was asserted that the Mach number should have a negligible effect on the validity range of viscous theory. Of course, this is only true as far as the shock-induced boundary layer separation is concerned, for which the conclusion was drawn on page 155. However, in the two cases discussed in this section, the triple point in shock reflection and the shock foot point on a curved surface, the viscous effect as such determines the solutions in that it produces non-Rankin–Hugoniot flow conditions with reference lengths that increase with $1/(M^* - 1)$. Therefore, it would be very important to find a viscous solution to the shock foot point problem, because the experimental data of Ackeret, Feldmann, and Rott (see page 154) seem to confirm the singularity in the inviscid solution. However, it may well be that the singularity as such disappears in a viscous solution, but the basic trend of the flow downstream of the shock wave remains similar to that of the inviscid case.

The conclusion to the observations of this chapter therefore seems to be that the longitudinal viscosity should always be considered a possible factor in certain cases of otherwise unexplainable transonic flow behavior.

Notes

1. The advantages of a thickened trailing edge, beyond the structural reasons, are discussed by Holder et al. [29].
2. This requirement does not exclude a thin but blunt trailing edge.

9
TRANSONIC WIND TUNNEL TESTING

From the preceding chapters it has become obvious that a purely theoretical treatment of most transonic problems is not possible, at least today. For a reasonable assurance of the accuracy of the theoretical results, comparisons with test data are still a necessity. Data for this purpose may be obtained from free-flight tests or from wind tunnel tests. Both kinds of tests have their limitations.

Free-flight tests may be quite accurate; however, their cost precludes the taking of large series of data. On the other hand, wind tunnel data may be obtained in large numbers at a reasonably low cost. However, they have two major sources of errors. First, it is impossible to create a transonic flow field matching exactly that of a free-flying object. Second, the scaled-down wind tunnel models—and even the largest wind tunnels at best can accommodate full-scale models of a very few actual transonic vehicles—do not simulate the viscous effects like boundary-layer transition points, and so on, in the prototype.

As to the question of the wind tunnel flow field accuracy, the theoretical results discussed in the preceding chapters clearly show the problem: The streamlines about a transonic vehicle are distorted much farther out from the vehicle surface than those of the subsonic or supersonic flow fields. Consequently, solid wind tunnel walls markedly compress the stream tubes over the model, unless its height is extremely small compared with the tunnel height. In this case, however, the accuracy of the model geometry is reduced to the point where the aerodynamic forces to be measured are no longer in agreement with those on the prototype, even under the unrealistic assumption that the very small forces on a small model could be measured with great accuracy. Thus, the velocity on the surface of a model of practical size is higher, and consequently the pressure is lower, than in free flight at the same approach (flight) Mach number. Of course, this is true, to a lesser degree, for all subsonic Mach numbers. But whereas in the subsonic range very accurate correction procedures exist, in the transonic range such simple mathematical means are no longer available. This is understandable when considering the complexity of a flow field consisting of a subsonic flow field with an embedded supersonic range and at least one shock wave that, in free flight, might extend itself to the distance of the tunnel walls. And this immediately indicates another major problem of solid wall tunnel transonic testing, namely, that the shock waves, which are not far from normal at the transonic Mach numbers, are most likely reflected from the tunnel wall back onto the model, thus completely changing the flow pattern over the tail section of the model.

Because of these difficulties with transonic testing in closed-jet wind tunnels, the possible advantage of testing in "open-jet" tunnels has been investigated. In these tunnels the flow from the nozzle issues into a quasi-infinite space whose static pressure is equal to that of the jet. Unfortunately, this parallel-flow jet produces the opposite effect, namely, that the streamlines over a model are farther apart than in free flight. This can be seen from Eq. 2.16 for the flow over a curved surface: Integrating Eq. 2.16 from the body surface to the streamline of the undisturbed flow (subscript ∞) yields

$$p_\infty - p_{\text{body}} = \int_{\text{body}}^{\infty} \frac{v^2 \rho}{R} dy$$

Since the integration path in free flight is much longer than in the open-jet tunnel, whereas the density and velocity ranges of the approach flow are identical and, over a slender body, cannot be very different in the two cases, the pressure differences $p_\infty - p_{\text{body}}$ can only be equal if the streamline curvatures in the tunnel are larger than those in free flight. However, this means that the streamlines in the tunnel are farther apart than in free flight and the flow velocities are lower over the body than in the free flight case, as can be seen from Fig. 2.2. Finally, the Bernoulli equation shows that the surface pressure on the body is higher in the tunnel than in free flight. An iteration of this analysis with the new surface pressure leads to small changes in the streamline curvatures, but the basic difference between these two cases remains unchanged.

The problem that closed tunnels produce too high a velocity on the body surface (which may even lead to choking at approach Mach numbers exceeding a certain value), while open tunnels produce too low a velocity, has found a partial solution in two basic tunnel designs: those having two or four slotted walls, and those with porous or perforated walls. The longitudinal slots of the former, and the normal holes or holes tilted in the flow direction of the latter connect the test section with the so-called plenum chamber that encloses the test section.

In both concepts the underlying principle is the creation of a pressure drop through the walls that compensates for the incorrect pressure difference between the solid wall and the body surface as the result of the incorrect streamline curvatures in the solid wall tunnel. In this way, the correct streamline slopes at the wall are formed through the proper amounts of outflow and inflow through the wall. The required pressure drop across the wall is obtained by properly choosing the wall thickness, the plenum chamber pressure, and the percentage open wall area. Further, in the case of the slotted wall, the slot width and the shape of the slot edges must be chosen properly; in the case of the porous walls, the additional parameters are the hole diameters and the inclination of the holes from the normal direction.

To appreciate the difficulty of finding the proper wall parameter values for a given problem, it must be realized that the streamline slope at the tunnel walls is by no means a steady function of the tunnel station if shock and expansion waves are present. In those cases, the walls must serve the additional function of producing the streamline slopes corresponding to the flow downstream of the waves. This is equivalent to canceling the reflected waves. In this respect porous walls have proven to be very superior to slotted walls, in which the higher pressure behind the shock wave tends to extend upstream in the viscous slot flow, thus distorting the tunnel flow upstream of the shocks. However, the slotted walls have been found to have more favorable characteristics than the porous walls in the high subsonic flow range.

The complexity of the flow processes at the transonic walls is further increased by the tunnel-wall boundary layer, whose growth is affected by the wall irregularities. However, this growth can be varied by slightly tilting the tunnel walls, so that the boundary layer stays thinner for a converging wall pair than for a parallel or a diverging pair. Consequently, the wall inclination must be added to the parameters already mentioned that influence the flow angles at the tunnel walls.

Obviously, the interactions of these parameters are very complex, and a detailed account of transonic wind tunnel wall characteristics and test data corrections exceeds the scope of this book. The reader must be referred to the extensive literature on this subject. The most comprehensive account of the work in this field in the 1950s, when the first acceptable design of transonic walls was achieved, is given in the classical Agardograph of Goethert [43].

Unfortunately, in the 1960s more and more transonic test results proved to be of insufficient accuracy, and means were sought to further improve transonic tunnels. Two major elements of the problem were identified: First, it was found to be impossible to establish a schedule for the tunnel wall settings simply from the model specifications and the required test conditions, such as Mach number, model attitudes, and so on. Consequently, it was impossible to insure that the tests would be conducted under correct flow conditions or even under the optimum tunnel conditions. Second, considerable tunnel flow turbulence was found to modify the model boundary layer in an unpredictable way.

To remove the first problem, ways were sought to adjust the tunnel walls during the test. The results were the variable-porosity wall (see Fig.

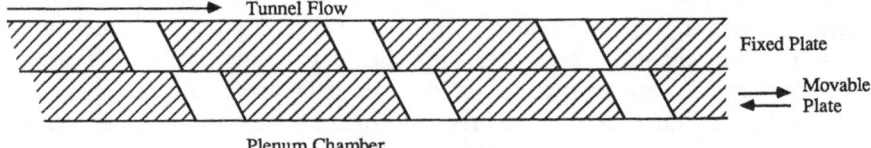

Fig. 9.1. Transonic wind tunnel wall with adjustable porosity.

9.1) and the flexible wall. The latter was obviously a complicated piece of equipment because it was intended to match exactly the shape of a streamline.

Meanwhile, it became clear that a new assessment of the transonic wall problem was needed if any decisive improvement in the tunnel test data could be expected. Thus, large studies were initiated in the early 1970s, most notably at the CALSPAN Laboratory in Buffalo, N.Y. [44]. These studies consisted of comparisons of test data for tunnels featuring various sizes and wall characteristics (see, e.g., ref. 50) and of theoretical procedures for tunnel-wall corrections. These theoretical studies exploited the new possibilities given by the capability of electronic computers to compute flow fields of specific boundary conditions within minutes. Thus, the flow field in the tunnel could now be scanned with suitable probes and the data obtained fed immediately into the computer, which produced a new set of tunnel wall parameter data from the discrepancy between the test data and the computed flow field. After a sufficient number of iterations of this kind, the wall interference was reduced to a magnitude small enough to insure a pressure distribution on the model of the desired accuracy. This procedure is described in detail by Ferri and Baronti [45] and applied, for example, by Weeks [46].

The second problem of transonic tunnel performance, the problem of the incorrect model boundary layers, was traced to tunnel turbulence produced by acoustic disturbances from the slots and holes. Intensive studies were initiated, mainly at the Arnold Center at Tullahoma, Tennessee, in close cooperation with NASA, in the course of which means were found for the suppression of the edge tones from the slots and holes that excited resonance fluctuations of the tunnel flow of discrete frequencies. In the case of the porous walls, the mechanism of the edge tone production is easily understood by inspecting Fig. 9.1. The turbulent boundary layer on the wall produces an ejector effect on the air in the holes such that a turbulent flow impinges on the trailing edge of the holes, splitting this jet into two parts, the lower of which periodically increases and then decreases the pressure in the holes, and these pressure fluctuations propagate into the tunnel test section. These edge tones can be avoided by taking the edge out of the mixing jet, that is, either by lowering the edge or by carrying the boundary layer over the hole without interference with the hole air. Both approaches were studied in the tests mentioned, but only the latter one showed an appreciable effect in the desired direction. Amazingly, simple splitter plates in flow direction, dividing the holes in two and to a depth of half the plate thickness, accomplished the effect. A similar benefit was gained in the case of slotted walls by covering the slots with a wire mesh.

Considering the decisive effect of boundary layer separation and therefore of boundary layer characteristics on the performance of transonic vehicles, as pointed out in Chapter 7, the accomplishment of these studies must not be underestimated. Details of these studies on perforated walls may be found in the papers of Dougherty [47] and Dougherty, Anderson and Parker [48]; the studies on slotted walls appear in a paper by Dougherty [49].

Concluding Remarks

This chapter has touched on the experimental problems in studying transonic flow. However, experimental verification of theoretical results is absolutely necessary, and the vast literature on experimental transonic research is proof of this fact. Conversely, experimental results are stimulating new theoretical approaches.

As the purpose of this book has been to relieve the reader from cumbersome literature searches for the acquisition of a basic knowledge of transonic theory, a similarly condensed account of the experimental results in this field should be of great benefit. Here the "Symposium Transsonicum III" [64] must be mentioned as an up-to-date survey on the state of the art of transonic flow research. With its numerous references, this book should give the reader an excellent opportunity to become competent in this difficult branch of aerodynamics.

REFERENCES

A considerable number of additional references are found in the following publications:

1. Roache, P. J., *Computational Fluid Dynamics*, Albuquerque, N.M., Hermosa Publishers, (1972); also, Roache, P. J., *Computational Mechanics*, pp. 195–256, Berlin, Springer-Verlag (1975)
2. Oswatitsch, K., *Gas Dynamics*, New York, Academic Press (1956)
3. Shapiro, A. H., *Compressible Fluid Flow*, New York, The Ronald Press Co. (1953)
4. Guderley, K. G., *The Theory of Transonic Flow*, Reading, MA, Addison-Wesley (1962)
5. Sauer, R., *Introduction to Theoretical Gas Dynamics*, Ann Arbor, J. W. Edwards (1947)
6. Liepmann, H. W., and Roshko, A., *Elements of Gas Dynamics*, New York, Wiley (1957)
7. Oswatitsch, K., and Berndt, S. B., KTH-Aero TN 15 (Sweden 1950)
8. Cole, J. D., and Messiter, A. F., *Z. Angew. Math. Phys.* **8**, 1–25 (1957)
9. Van Dyke, M., *Perturbation Methods in Fluid Mechanics*, Stanford, CA, The Parabolic Press (1975)
10. Ferrari, C., and Tricomi, F., *Transonic Aerodynamics*, New York, Academic Press (1968)
11. Meyer, Th., *Forschung a.d. Geb. d. Ing.* **62** (1908)
12. Gardner, C. S., and Ludloff, H. F., *J. Aeron. Sci.* **17**, 47 (1950)
13. Cole, J. D., "Transonic Limits on Linearized Theory", Guggenmeim Aeron. Lab., Cal. Inst. of Tech., Office of Scientific Research TN 228 (1954).
14. Spreiter, J. R., NACA TN 2726 (1952); also, Bryson, A. E., NACA TN 2560 (1951)
15. Spreiter, J. R., and Alksne, A. Y., NACA TR R-2 (1959)
16. (a) Munk, M. M., NACA Rep. 184 (1924); (b) Jones, R. T., NACA Rep. 835 (1946).
17. Oswatitsch, K., and Keune, F., *Z. Flugwiss.* **3**, H.2, 29 (1955).
18. Zierep, J., *Z. Angew. Math. Mech.* **45**, H.1, 19 (1965).
19. Keune, F., *KTH Aero TN* **21** (1952) and *DVL Bericht Nr.* **50** (1958)
20. Whitcomb, T. R., NACA Report 1273 (1952); also, *Aviation Week*, Sept. 19, 1955 and IAS paper 601 (1956)
21. Zierep, J., *Acta Mechanica* **8**, 126 (1969). This also contains references of previous publications on the subject.
22. Bartlmä, F., *Z. Flugwiss.* **11**, H.4, 160 (1963)
23. Jungclaus, G., and Van Ray, O., *Ing. Archiv.* **36**, 226 (1967)
24. Zierep, J., *Z. Angew. Math. Phys.* **9b**, 764 (1958)
25. Oswatitsch, K., and Zierep, J., *Z. Angew. Math. Mech.* **40**, T143 (1960)
26. Gadd, G. E., *Z. Angew. Math. Phys.* **11**, 51 (1960)
27. Ackeret, J., Feldmann, F., and Rott, N., *Mitteilungen a.d. Institut f. Aerodynamik der ETH, Zürich*, no. 10 (1946)

28. Sichel, M., *Phys. Fluids* **6**, 653 (1963) and *J. Fluid Mech.* **25**, part 4, 769 (1966). Additional references under 30, 31, 34, and 35
29. Holder, D. W., Pearcey, H. H., and Nash, J. F. "Some Aerodynamic Advantages of Using Wings with Thick Trailing Edges for Highspeed Aircraft," Lecture to R. Ae. S., Feb. 1962.
30. Sichel, M., *Phys. Fluids* **6**, 653 (1963); also, Szaniawski, A., *Acta Mechanica* **5**, 189 (1968)
31. Sichel, M., *J. Fluid Mech.* **25**, part 4, 769 (1966). This also contains references to similar studies by others
32. Emmons, H. W., NACA TN 1003 (1946) and NACA TN 1746 (1948)
33. Tomotika, S., and Tamada, K., *J. Appl. Math.* **7**, 381 (1950)
34. Sichel, M., and Yin, Y. K., *J. Fluid Mech.* **28**, part 3, 512 (1967)
35. Sichel, M., and Yin, Y. K., *Appl. Sci. Res.* **20**, 356 (1969)
36 Pearcey, H. H., and Osborne, J., ICAS paper 70-14 (1970), This reference contains a listing of Pearcey's publications on the peaky flow.
37. Nieuwland, G. Y., 5th Congress of the ICAS, London (1966)
38. Whitcomb, R. T., ICAS paper 74-10 (1974)
39. Schlichting, H., and Truckenbrodt, E., *Aerodynamics of the Airplane*, New York, McGraw-Hill (1979)
40. Pearcy, H. H., "Some effects of shock-induced separation of turbulent boundary layers in transonic flow past aerofoils," Aeronautical Research Council. Reports and Memoranda No 3108, June 1955, HMSO, London (1959)
41. Bauer, F., Garabedian, P., Korn, D., and Jameson, A., *Lecture Notes in Economics and Mathematical Systems*, Vol. 108, Control Theory, Berlin, Springer-Verlag (1975)
42. Sternberg, J., *Phys. Fluids* **2**, 179 (1959)
43. Goethert, B. H., *Transonic Wind Tunnel Testing*, AGARDograph No. 49, New York, Pergamon Press (1961)
44. CALSPAN Report No. AE-3059-A-1 "Wall Interference Effects in Transonic Flow." (1976)
45. Ferri, A., and Baronti, P., *AIAA J.* **11**, 63 (1973)
46. Weeks, T. M., AFFDL-TR-74-39 (1975)
47. Dougherty, N. S., AEDC-TR-77-67 (1977)
48. Dougherty, N. S., Anderson, C. F., and Parker, R. L., Jr., AIAA paper No. 76-50 (1976) and AEDC-TR-75-88, (1975)
49. Dougherty, N. S., AEDC-TR-79-16 (1979)
50. Dougherty, N. S., and Steinle, F. W., Jr., AIAA paper no. 74-627 (1974)
51. Sichel, M., *AIAA J.* **19**, No. 2, 165 (1981)
52. Lighthill, M. C., "Viscosity in Waves of Finite amplitude," in *Surveys in Mechanics*, ed. G. K. Batchelor and R. M. Davis, New York, Cambridge University Press (1956)
53. Rajan, S., AIAA Paper No. 73-131 (1973)
54. Ward-Smith, A. J., *Internal Fluid Flow*, Oxford, Clarendon Press, (1980)
55. Morse, M. M., and Ingard, K. U., *Theoretical Acoustics*, New York, McGraw-Hill (1968)
56. Sichel, M., "Two-dimensional shock structures in transonic and hypersonic flows," *Advances in Applied Mechanics*, Vol. 11, pp 131–207, New York, Academic Press (1971)
57. Kevorkian, J., and Cole, J. D., *Perturbation Methods in Applied Mathematics*, New York, Springer-Verlag (1961)
58. De Bruijn, N. G., *Asymptotic Methods in Analysis*, New York, Dover Publications, Inc. (1981)
59 Cole, J. D., Review of Transonic Flow Theory (Invited), AIAA 28th Aerospace Science Meeting, AIAA Paper 82-0104, (1982)

References

60. Murman, E. M., and Cole, J. D., "Inviscid Drag at Transonic speeds," AIAA Paper No. 74-540 (1974)
61. Ringleb, F., *Z. Angew. Math. Mech.* **20,** No 4, 185 (1940)
62. Jameson, A., "The Evolution of Computational Methods in Aerodynamics" *J. Appl. Mechanics, Trans. ASME,* **50,** Number 4b, 1052–1070 (Dec. 1983)
63. Turbatu, S. and Zierep, J. "Aperiodische instationäre schallnahe Strömungen", *Acta Mechanica* **21,** 165–169 (1975)
64. Symposium Transsonicum, IUTAM Congress Goettingen May 24–27, 1988, Berlin, Springer Verlag (1989)
65. Doerffer, P., and Zierep, J., "An Experimental Investigation of the Reynolds Number Effect on a Normal Shock Wave-Turbulent Boundary Layer Interaction on a Curved Wall." *Acta Mechanica* **73,** 77–93 (1988)
66. Lee, j. F., Sears, F. W., and Turcotte, D. L., *Statistical Thermodynamics,* Reading, MA, Addison-Wesley, 1963
67. Lachmann, C. V., *Boundary Layer and Flow Control,* Vol. 2, p. 1275, New York, Pergamon Press (1961)

INDEX

Affine (equipotential) lines 49, 50, 60, 92
Aircraft performance
  general 181–187
  effect of heat addition 142
Airfoil
  flow patterns 4, 6, 7
  off-design performance 185
  with thickened trailing edge 187
  supercritical 182–185
Area rule
  general 134, 136
  effect on drag 137
  restriction of fuselage cross-sectional area 135
Arrow stability 3
Aspect ratio 128
Asymptotic expansion
  general 62, 76
  expansion series 77

Bernoulli equation
  integrated 79
  one-dimensional flow 140
  steady flow 15, 23, 24
  unsteady potential flow 15
Boundary layer
  entropy increase 153
  in wind tunnel 190
  laminar 12
  separation-prone 151
  thermal layer 158
  turbulent 12
  with separation bubble 151, 171, 182
Body-shape function 66, 125
Boundary values (computer programming) 175
Boundary layer–shock wave interaction 150, 171, 181

Characteristics (method of)
  compatibility equation 39
  characteristics equation 39, 66
  small perturbation version 39
Continuity equation
  axisymmetric (velocity potential) 34, 64
  in polar coordinates 35
  in vector notation 63
  one-dimensional 28, 140
  second order 71
  small perturbations 37
  three-dimensional 33, 34
  transonic simplification 38
  unsteady 99
  viscous flow 158
Critical quantities
  velocity, density, area, Mach number, sound speed 28
  pressure 31
Crocco equation 23
Crocco point 88
Curl vector 22, 23

Differential equations (ordinary)
  solutions of local linearization 117, 123
  similarity solutions 160–170
Displacement work 17
Drag rise (transonic)
  general 105
  closed body 107, 110
  slender half-body 107, 108, 110
  in terms of transonic similarity rule 109

Efficiency (thermal) 18
Energy
  heat 16
  internal 16
Energy equation
  one-dimensional 140
  viscous flow 158
Enthalpy
  definition 17, 22
  stagnation 22
Entropy
  definition 16, 17, 20, 21
  condition of constant e. 33
  increase across shock waves
    general 69, 70, 150
    normal shock (Rankin–Hugoniot) 152, 154, 155, 171, 186
  of a fluid particle (stream tube) 33
  second law of thermodynamics 16, 17, 20, 21
Equation of state
  general 33
  one-dimensional
  perfect gas 17

Index

Equipotential lines 49, 50
Equivalent body 129
Expansion parameters 65–68, 159
Equivalence rule
  application 134
  effect on drag 138
  Oswatitsch–Keune formulation 128
  space (volume) contribution 135
Euler equation
  rotational flow 22
  steady flow 33
  unsteady (nonsteady) flow 14, 98, 179

Far field 128
Finite difference routine (computer) 175
Flight stability 3–8
Flow density 28
Forces
  gravity 13
  shear 24
  viscous 13
Fuselage cross-sectional area (restriction by area rule) 135
Flow
  adiabatic 26
  compressible 11, 12, 48
  frictionless 33
  incompressible 11, 48
  inviscid 12
  isoenergetic 34, 91
  peaky 182
  potential 21
  quasi-inviscid 35
  radial 80, 84
  rotational 21
  separation 150
  shear 12
  slender body 66
  spiral 83–85
  transonic (see under this heading)
  viscous 11, 22, 149 (see also "Viscous transonic flow")
  vortex 21
  with combustion 136
  with condensation 136
  with heat addition (see "Heat addition")

Gas
  perfect 16, 17, 25
  p–V diagram 19
  real 25
Goethert rule 59

Heat
  energy 16–20
  specific, at constant volume 18
  specific, at constant pressure 18
  ratio of specific h's 18, 25

Heat addition, flow with
  general 136
  basic theory 139–141
  choking condition 142–144
  critical amount 141, 142
  effect on aircraft performance 142
  effect of boundary layer 145
  energy equation 140
  unsteady processes 143, 145
Higher-order transonic equations 62–75
Hodograph equations 78, 79
Hodograph applications
  Ringleb flow (semi-infinite plate) 83, 86
  source flow 80, 81
  source-vertex flow 84, 85
  vortex flow 82, 83
Hodograph plane
  nozzle flow 88–90
  transonic shock polars 86, 87
Hyperbola of influence 101–103

Irreversible processes 20, 21

Kinetic theory of gases 25
Kutta condition 183

Lagrange system 14
Laplace equation 52, 125, 133
Laval nozzle 28, 29, 32 (see also under "Nozzle")
Legendre (Molenbroek) transformation 79
Lift slope 105, 109, 110
Limit (limiting) line 81, 82, 84, 85, 149
Linearization
  general 28
  local 113–123
  Oswatitsch 30
  over-simplified 36
  Prandtl 30
Longitudinal (compressive) stress 149, 156

Mach number 5
  critical (at sonic speed) 91, 151
  critical (onset of supersonic pockets) 10
Meyer flow (laval nozzle) 161
Mixing layer 12
Momentum
  equation of viscous flow 158
  transfer (viscosity) 11

Navier–Stokes equations 24, 26, 178, 179
Newton's second law 13
Nozzle flow, inviscid (see also "Hodograph plane")
  one-dimensional 29
  Meyer 161, 162

Taylor 161–163
Tomotika & Tamada 162
venturi 161, 162
Nozzle flow, viscous
  general 160–163
  axisymmetric 163, 165
Numerical methods
  general 172
  boundary values 175
  finite-difference routine 175
  mesh point grids 173–175
  relaxation method 161, 175, 176
  time-dependent method 177
  truncation error 176
  artificial viscosity 177

Order-of magnitude of flow variables (parameter τ) 39

Parabolic method of computation 129
Peaky flow 182, 183
Perforated (porous) wind tunnel walls 189, 190
Perturbation (see "Small perturbation")
Perturbation velocities
  Cole & Messiter 63
  Guderley 40
Piston engine 16
Potential (see "Velocity potential")
Plenum chamber (transonic wind tunnel) 189
Prandtl number
  inviscid 24
  viscous 160
Prandtl–Glauert transformation 48, 63, 94
Prandtl–Meyer expansion (convex turn) 77
Pressure coefficient
  general 92
  in similarity terms 108
  nonsteady theory 99
  small perturbance 54, 92
  space (volume) contribution 13
  subsonic flow 117, 118, 120
  supersonic flow 117, 118
  transonic flow 117, 118, 124
Pressure gradient
  in curved flow 36
  in boundary layer (destabilization) 150
Profile
  conventional 184
  supercritical 182–185

Quasi-inviscid flow 35

Radial flow
  inviscid 169
  viscous 165, 170

Rankin–Hugoniot relation 152, 154, 155, 171, 186
Rarified gas 150
Real gas 25
Relaxation method (see "Numerical methods")
Relaxation time (see "Longitudinal viscosity")
Reversible processes 20, 21
Reynolds number
  definition 24
  effect on flow separation 150
  reference quantities, 24, 158
Riemann sheet 80, 85, 149
Ringleb solution (shock-free flow) 83, 86, 182
Rotational flow 21

Schlieren optics 4
Shear flow 12, 151, 155
Shock wave
  curved 35
  in viscous flow 155
  normal 35, 152
  oblique 35, 70, 149, 152
  thickness (Lighthill) 155, 159, 180, 186
Shock on curved surface
  reflected shock (non-Hugoniot region) 186
  delta shock 151
  singularity 153, 154
Shock relations
  general 43
  normal shock 46, 141
  shock polar 46, 63, 86, 87
Shock-free solutions 83, 86, 170, 182
Shock–boundary layer interaction 150, 181
  induced separation 136
  separation bubble 151, 171
Similarity solution (partial differential equation) 160
Slender body
  definition 38
  condition for axisymmetric flow 60, 67
  condition for plane (two-dimensional) flow 53
  condition for three-dimensional flow 129
Similarity rule
  axisymmetric sub- and supersonic flow 57
  axisymmetric transonic flow 59–62, 74
  compressible flow (general) 55
  subsonic plane and axisymmetric flow (Goethert rule) 59
  transonic flow (Karman rule) 56
  three-dimensional flow 93, 94
  two-dimensional transonic flow 56
Small perturbations
  introduction 37, 63
  in viscous flow 159
  velocity potential 40

Sonar speed (speed of sound) 26, 34, 140
Sound barrier 102
Source (inviscid)
  unsteady flow 100
  slender body (plane and axisymmeric flow) 58
  subsonic, transonic, supersonic flow 95
  strength 52
Source distribution function
  general 55, 114
  influence range (supersonic) 130
Source-sink method 50, 52, 113
Source-vortex flow 84, 85
Space influence potential (equivalence rule) 128
Specific heats 18
Spiral flow
  inviscid 82, 83, 169
  viscous 165
Spiral-source flow
  inviscid 84, 85
  viscous 165
Stagnation flow 15
Stokes theorem 21
Streamline—equipotential (affine) line relationship 50
Stream function
  in hodograph plane 78–86
  in source flow 51
Streamline equation
  general 14
  in small perturbation terms 54, 58, 59, 66
  of body contour 125
Streamline patterns
  in boundary layer 145, 151
  in subsonic flow 32
  in transonic flow 32
Stress, normal in compressible fluid 156

Taylor flow (Laval nozzle) 161
Taylor series 28, 29
Tests
  free flight 188
  wind tunnel 24, 47, 188
Thermal efficiency 18
Thermodynamic laws 16, 17
Thermodynamic properties 18, 19
Thickness ratio 55
Time-dependent method (computer) 177
Transonic equations
  axisymmetric flow 111
  continuity 41–43
  first order plane flow 65, 69
  potential equation 40, 41, 60
  solution through linearization 111
  velocity components 40

velocity vector 43
viscous flow 156–160
Transonic theory
  Guderley method 38
  higher order 62–75
  simplified (small perturbations) 37–43
  viscous 149 (see also "Viscous transonic flow")
Truncation error (computer) 176
Turbulence 21

Unsteady (nonsteady) flow (see "Flow")

Velocity potential 15, 34, 40
  of cross flow 128
  first order approximation 72, 74
  second order approximation 73, 74
Viscosity
  general 12, 150
  artificial (computer) 177
Viscosity coefficients
  bulk 171
  second 157, 158
  shear 24
  Stokes 157
Viscosity, longitudinal (compressive)
  general 150–155, 186
  formulation 156
  reference length 159
  relaxation time 157
Viscous transonic equations 156–160
Viscous layer 12, 153
Viscous transonic flow (see also under "Flow" and "Transonic")
  general 149
  in Laval nozzle 161–165
  spiral flow 165–170
  radial flow 165–170
Volume (space) contribution 135 (see also "Equivalence rule")
Vortex
  potential 25, 165
  flow 82

Wind tunnel (transonic)
  blow-down 15, 27, 177
  closed jet 189
  open jet 189
  testing 24, 27, 188
Wind tunnel walls (transonic)
  adjustable 190
  porous (perforated) 189, 190
  slotted 189, 190
  correction methods 191
Work, technical 19

CPSIA information can be obtained
at www.ICGtesting.com
Printed in the USA
LVHW112227060520
655145LV00010B/200